D1011783

New York Times and *USA TODAY* bestselling author **Heather Graham** has written more than a hundred novels. She has won the Romance Writers of America Lifetime Achievement Award, a Thriller Writers' Silver Bullet and, in 2016, the Thriller Master Award from International Thriller Writers. She is an active member of International Thriller Writers and Mystery Writers of America and the founder of The Slush Pile Players, an author band and theatrical group. An avid scuba diver, ballroom dancer and mother of five, she still enjoys her South Florida home, but also loves to travel.

For more information, check out her website, theoriginalheathergraham.com, or find Heather on Facebook.

Delores Fossen, a *USA TODAY* bestselling author, has sold over seventy-five novels, with millions of copies of her books in print worldwide. She's received a Booksellers' Best Award and an RT Reviewers' Choice Best Book Award. She was also a finalist for a prestigious RITA® Award. You can contact the author through her website at www.deloresfossen.com.

New York Times Bestselling Author

HEATHER GRAHAM

SINISTER INTENTIONS

Previously published as *King of the Castle*

HARLEQUIN
BESTSELLING
AUTHOR
COLLECTION

**HARLEQUIN®
BESTSELLING
AUTHOR
COLLECTION**

Recycling programs
for this product may
not exist in your area.

ISBN-13: 978-1-335-14663-2

Sinister Intentions

First published as King of the Castle in 1987. This edition published in 2020.

Copyright © 1987 by Heather Graham Pozzessere

Confiscated Conception
First published in 2003. This edition published in 2020.
Copyright © 2003 by Delores Fossen

This edition published by arrangement with Harlequin Books S.A.

For questions and comments about the quality of this book, please contact us at CustomerService@Harlequin.com.

Harlequin Enterprises ULC
22 Adelaide St. West, 40th Floor
Toronto, Ontario M5H 4E3, Canada
www.Harlequin.com

Printed in U.S.A.

CONTENTS

Books by Heather Graham

Harlequin Intrigue

Undercover Connection
Out of the Darkness
Shadows in the Night
Law and Disorder
Tangled Threat

MIRA

The Seekers
The Summoning
A Lethal Legacy

Krewe of Hunters

Echoes of Evil
Pale as Death
Fade to Black
Dark Rites
Dying Breath
Darkest Journey
Deadly Fate
Haunted Destiny
The Hidden
The Forgotten
The Silenced

New York Confidential

A Dangerous Game
A Perfect Obsession
Flawless

For a complete list of titles by Heather Graham, visit the Author Profile page at www.Harlequin.com.

SINISTER INTENTIONS

Heather Graham

Prologue

It was a cold day. Miserable, wet, frigid. The wind tore around the jagged cliffs with such fury that its sound seemed to be a cry, high and forlorn. A banshee's wail, desolate and anguished. Kit was restless, though, and despite the wind and the mist and the forbidding gray sky, she was determined to walk along the cliffs. She didn't feel that she was being at all morbid, as Justin had accused her of being. She felt closer to Michael.

But it was another of those days when she felt as if she was being watched. She often felt that way.

She walked behind the cottage to the highest point, beyond the tufts of grass lying low to the wind. Vegetation disappeared, and the rock rose, high and naked and deadly. Down below, far, far below, the surf crashed against the stones known as the Devil's Teeth. Kit looked down. The wind picked up the heavy length of her chestnut hair and sent it flying wildly around her. She felt close to the elements here. Close to Michael. She could remember the laughing and the teasing that first day together. Her one day with him…as his wife. The accent he had feigned, the warnings he had given her about leprechauns and banshees and gods older than time, older than the elements.

The feeling came again: that she was being watched. She turned and looked back. To the right and left of the cottage, there was only forest, lush and rich and green. Darkly green, secretive. The trees seemed to have eyes. They seemed to call to her, to beckon, to rustle and whistle and moan out a warning along with the wind.

The poor murdered girl had died around here, she thought. Just like Michael…

He hadn't fallen. She knew he hadn't fallen. In her arms, before he died, he had painfully formed a single word: Kayla.

The wind whistled even more ferociously, the shrieking of the banshees, ghosts whose cries signaled the coming of death. Kit swallowed fiercely and curled her fingers around the medallion that lay between her breasts: the Celtic cross. Michael's last gift to her.

Kit trudged wearily back to the cottage. Justin was coming. He had said that he would take her to dinner, and he hadn't waited for an answer. He was Justin O'Niall. The O'Niall. He didn't wait for people to say yes or no; he spoke, then assumed that everyone would jump to do his bidding.

Justin was far more than a hereditary lord, she thought resentfully; they called him the King of the High Hill, and his family's supremacy went back beyond the days of Christianity. Justin had been brought up believing in his own importance, and it seemed that everyone had neglected to tell him that he was living in the twentieth century. Nor were they likely to do so in the future, she reflected. The villagers were content to look to him for leadership.

Superstitious fools, she told herself, and then she was contrite, for Justin had taken charge the night that Michael had died, and he had been unfailingly kind to her—though even his kindness came with a nearly unbearable arrogance.

Justin O'Niall. His power here was godlike, and he himself was as pagan and elemental as the chilled, windswept granite cliffs and the ruthless wind. He even looked like some ancient god, with his towering height and unwavering teal-blue eyes. The idea amused her, but then she remembered Michael reading to her about the druids who had once reigned here, believers in Bal, their horned goat-god, the creature who gave them bountiful harvests and demanded sacrifices in return. Kit shivered.

Justin wanted her gone. Because of that, she couldn't show him how utterly desolate she felt. He would press his case that she should leave, but she couldn't, not when Michael lay buried in Shallywae earth. He had been dead three months now. She still couldn't believe it, but because of it, she couldn't leave.

Walking quickly, she returned to the cottage. She hesitated, her hand on the doorknob, before entering. It was open. She could have sworn that she had locked it.

Kit went in, entering the kitchen first and grabbing the broom. Not much of a weapon, but still… But after she had nervously searched the parlor, the bedroom and the bathroom, she set the broom down with a little sigh of relief. She had obviously forgotten to lock the door. She went back downstairs to lock it—securely.

She was cold, so she put the kettle on for tea, lit the heater in the bathroom and drew a tub of hot water, filling it liberally with bubbles. Downstairs, she fixed her tea, then brought it back upstairs to sip while she luxuriated in her bath.

When she had finished the tea, she lay back in her bubbles, a smile curving her lips. For the first time since the accident, she felt no pain. She felt deliciously drowsy, the warmth of the water and the bubbles teasing her flesh. She could hear the wind outside the cottage, and it sounded like a melody, pleasant to her ears.

She felt...wonderful.

"Really wonderful," she said aloud. And she laughed. Drugged. That was it. She felt as if she had been drugged. Shot up with one of Doctor Conar's sweet wonder drugs. The kind of stuff he had given her after Michael's death to ease her worry and pain.

But no, this was different. It was as if someone had put something in her tea. Then she started to fall asleep. She was drowsy, but she didn't want to go to sleep. She wanted to keep feeling the bubbles against her skin. She could feel the water, too, and it was delicious against her flesh, gentle and sleek and erotic. The storm was really rising, she knew. And she could feel that, too. Feel the passion of the wind, the charged energy of the waves. She even imagined that she could hear them, thundering and crashing against the granite walls of the cliffs.

She heard her name called, as if from far away. She wanted to answer, and yet she couldn't be bothered. Her eyelids felt so heavy. Her lips continued to curl into a sweet smile.

"Kit!" She heard her name called again, more urgently, and closer. She forced her eyelids to open.

Justin was standing in the bathroom doorway. He wore a heavy wool coat, but beneath it she could see his suit. A black suit, stunning with his dark hair and teal eyes.

He was frowning at her—must he always frown? She wasn't a child....

"Kit, what's the matter with you? I've been calling and calling—I finally broke the damn door down."

She didn't answer him. She was ready to laugh, he looked so angry and exasperated. His bronze features were drawn as tightly as a thundercloud.

He pulled off his coat and approached her in the bath, kneeling down beside the tub and placing his hands on her shoulders to shake her. "Kit, have you been drinking?"

"Don't be absurd," she managed to say airily.

"Then what's the matter with you?"

She looked at him, amused that he should be so alarmed. But as she stared at him, a tight coil of heat seemed to form within her. Her breath caught in her throat, and she stared at his face. At his magnetic blue eyes. His dark, thick brows, the high planes of his cheekbones, the slight hollows beneath them. And his mouth, tight and compressed.

She touched his cheek with her dripping knuckles. She felt the rough velvet quality of his flesh.

"Justin…" she murmured. She started to slip in the tub, and she stopped herself, laughing.

"I've got to get you out of there," he muttered. "Don't drown!" he snapped, stepping out of the bathroom. He came back a second later—minus the coat, shirt and jacket. Then he stooped down, scooped her from the bubbles into his arms.

She felt the coarse hair on his chest rasp against her breasts. Beneath her fingers, she felt his muscles, contracting and rippling as he held her and walked with her. She threw her head back and smiled. "Justin…"

He glanced into her eyes; his seemed to be exceptionally hard, and she laughed again.

"Kit, lass, you must be drunk."

"I'm not!"

He started to deposit her on the bed and stand, but he couldn't because her hair had tangled around his hands, and she cried out sharply when he moved. He leaned closer to her, trying to disentangle himself.

"Justin!" she cried out, and he stopped to meet her eyes.

"Please, Justin…"

Her lips were trembling, her eyes liquid. Her arms curled around him, and she arched against him, crushing herself to his naked chest.

"Kit," he muttered. "Damn it, I'm no saint! Nor made of stone. Stop this. You would hate me for this—"

"Hate you?" She knew that she wasn't Kit anymore; she was some other woman, one who could tease and taunt a man and do with him what she would. Kit was a misty figure who belonged to another world. "Hate you? How could I hate the King of the High Hill? The O'Niall. The grand O'Niall. Ah, Justin! It's comical, you know, to an American. The way you had to take the poor little lass under your wing because her catastrophe happened on the King's high hill!" She broke into a gale of laughter.

He started to scowl. She had made him angry, but she didn't care.

He extricated himself from her embrace, firmly casting her arms aside. "I'll make tea," he muttered.

He left, but Kit didn't really care. She could say anything; she could do anything. She felt all-powerful. It was magnificent, as if the wind were part of her, as if she had its strength. A tempest was brewing, and she was part of it.

"Here, lass, drink this."

He was back beside her, lifting her by the shoulders. He made her sip the tea, and she heard him gulp some of it himself. She could feel him again. Her hair was splayed out all over his chest, and he was hot and taut, living steel, and resting against him was incredibly erotic. Of course, because she was naked and he was with her, she couldn't really be Kit. She was the wind; she was the earth. She was fire, all elemental. She was part of the mystical land.

She heard him murmur something unintelligible, and she felt him tremble. She turned, burying her face against his chest, teasing his flesh with her tongue.

"Kit, stop it. Kit…"

His voice faded into a ragged gasp, and she heard the teacup fall. She wound her arms around his neck and together they rolled over, until he braced himself above her, staring down at her in a confused fury.

She tangled her fingers into his hair, pulling his head to hers, and she pressed her lips to his. She heard him groan softly, and then his arms were around her. It was wonderful to lie within them. His lips covered hers, his tongue delving hungrily into her mouth.

She felt it all acutely, and it was so good that she almost wept. His hands moved to her breasts, and she arched and twisted, crying out as his thumb teased a nipple, gasping as his mouth burned a trail of hot whispered kisses down her throat, then tugged with sweet fire at her breasts. His hand moved lower to her hip, caressed her belly, then traveled again before resting between her thighs.

His hands were so warm. Where he touched her, she felt as if she were melting; where he didn't, she longed that he might. He knew where she wanted to be touched, and his every touch was bold and sure and confident. She whimpered his name; she writhed, aching for him. She showered his shoulders with kisses, and all the while she heard the winter wind raging around them, urging her into a more volatile passion.

She was the wind, she thought, as he was fire, searing her, igniting her. He was as hard and rugged as the cliffs, and she had never known such intimate ecstasy as the feel of him against her. Her cries rose with the storm to a raging crescendo, again and again, until exhaustion blanketed the magic and she drifted into a nether realm of sleep.

She began to dream, the same haunting, recurring nightmare. Phrases slashed through her mind—spoken in Michael's voice.

"The druid priest arrived… He was the one to take the virgin… The next year would be her sacrifice. When the harvest was in. They slit her throat first…blood, you know…"

He had laughed and teased her. Michael, the great scholar of ancient Irish history.

But he wasn't laughing now.

She saw Michael on the rock. His eyes were open, accusing, and he spoke in a rasp like a saw against wood. "Kayla!"

He was walking toward her, smiling. Then, suddenly,

the man coming for her wasn't Michael anymore. It was Justin. Muscled and sleek. Naked. Stalking her. Then she saw that he wasn't naked at all; he was wearing a black cloak, and he was putting on a mask.

The mask of the horned goat.

Kit awoke with a pounding headache—and the dawning of horror.

She could remember, but the memory was foggy, confused and distorted. She had been in the bathtub, and then she had been in Justin's arms, and then…

She swallowed. She could still feel him. His hand was cast negligently over her breast.

She opened her eyes. His dark head was near her shoulder, and he was sprawled beside her, still holding her. Naked and muscled and sprawled across her bed— touching her.

He was sleeping soundly and easily.

She choked back a scream, and tried hard to hold back her tears. What had happened? What had she done? She could remember, and yet she couldn't.

Near hysteria, Kit shifted from beneath Justin's touch. She was shaking as she silently looked around the room for clothing. She didn't dress there, but escaped downstairs to stumble into her jeans and sweater. It was cold and miserable in the cottage, yet she welcomed the misery. She had never felt so ashamed in her life. Michael was dead, and she had betrayed him.

What had happened? A groan of agony escaped her. She didn't understand it. She clutched the gold Celtic cross, her talisman. Michael's talisman.

She had even worn Michael's cross.

She didn't understand anything. Michael had died

here. They had all claimed that it was an accident, but she had bent down beside him, and he had whispered that one word to her just before he had died. And then that poor girl had been murdered on the same night. There were secrets here, and a legend-filled past. And she dreamed here. Oh, God, how she dreamed! About the horned goat-god and the priests and the sacrifices offered over the cliffs.

And Justin. His scent was still on her body. She dreamed about Justin, and she had slept with him, when Michael...

She had to get away.

Kit hurried to the hall closet, where she got her heavy coat and her boots. She was barely able to stumble into the boots, crying and cursing, but at last they were on her feet. She pulled on her coat, then grabbed her purse—and the keys to the rented Toyota.

At the door she paused. She didn't want anyone looking for her. She scribbled out a quick note. *Justin—as you've suggested all along, I'm going home. I want to forget this place.*

When that was done, she walked to the door. She didn't look back as she fled, at last, for home.

Away from Ireland—and Justin O'Niall.

Chapter 1

Kit should have known that morning on the last day of August that circumstances were conspiring against her.

In her apartment east of the park, she sipped a cup of coffee and stared down at the children playing along the tree-lined street. She stared at them, not seeing them, for a long time. Then, at last, she returned to the kitchen table and stared down at the newspaper again.

Irishmen didn't often make the social pages of the *New York Times*, but there he was, just as she remembered him. A little silver now touched his temples, but otherwise Justin O'Niall appeared exactly as he had almost eight long years ago.

"Good luck to you, my friend," Kit murmured softly. She meant it. The events of that short period of her life in Ireland had never left her, but what she had come to feel, and continued to feel when she allowed herself to

do so, was a strange sense of confusion and loss. Well…
that wasn't quite true. Her heart always seemed to give
a slight thud when she thought about Justin. Nothing
major, of course. It had been eight years. But there was
still that flutter…and a certain pain.

As distinguished a bachelor as Justin might be, he
wouldn't have made the *Times* all by himself. According
to the article, he had just become engaged to Susan Accorn, heiress to one of the multimillion-dollar disposable-
diaper companies.

Well, Kit thought philosophically, if and when Susan
and Justin decided to start a family, they would be able
to save an absolute bundle on diapers.

Kit closed the paper. Reflexively, she wound her fingers around the little cross that she still wore about her
neck.

She stared up at the bulletin board above the table.
It held a profusion of newspaper articles and clippings,
her grocery list and other odds and ends. She lifted one
of the articles and looked at the scrap of paper with a
single word written in her own handwriting that hung
beneath it: Kayla.

She stared at it pensively, then shrugged. In college
she'd had an Irish professor whose first language had
been Gaelic, but he'd never heard the word.

Kit dropped the clipping back into place and wandered restlessly to the window, cradling her coffee cup
in her hands.

Mike was playing down below. It seemed that all the
boys were wearing worn blue jackets, but she could pick
Mike out in a second. His hair was a blonde that reflected
even pale sunlight like gold. Her mother had always told

her that her own hair had started out that way, then deepened to its darker chestnut hue.

Kit smiled, as always a little awed when she watched her son. The ball the boys had been tossing rolled into the street, and rather than chase it, Mike stopped short on the curb and watched it lodge beneath a truck on the opposite side of the street. As she had expected, his blond head tilted up, and he stared toward the window.

Mike was Kit's one great source of pride. She had never managed to convince herself that he was anything less than a beautiful child. His eyes were neither green nor brown, nor even hazel. They were a truly unique color that seemed to match the gold of his hair, and they had a slight tilt to them. When he smiled, deep dimples showed in his cheeks.

His hair was a little long, but she liked it that way. He was mischievous, but his disposition was sweet, and in things that really mattered—like not running out into the street—he was obedient.

Kit threw open the window, returning her son's smile and wave. "Hang on, guys!" she called. "I'll get your ball!"

She closed the window, left her second-floor apartment and ran quickly down the stairs. She smiled at the boys, rumpling Mike's hair as she passed him, checked the crazy New York street and hurried to retrieve the ball from beneath the truck. She threw it back to the boys, and her maternal soul thrilled a little bit as Mike leaped high to catch it.

He had the makings of a fine ball player, she thought.

"Thanks, Mom!" He rewarded her effort with another dimpled smile.

"Sure thing. But keep it out of the street, huh?"

Mike nodded and turned back to his friends.

Her son, she decided, also had the potential to grow into a heartbreaker. People—teachers, neighbors, other children—fell very easily for his golden smile.

When her foot touched the first step, she heard a phone ringing. She paused a second, listening, then realized it was her own. She raced up the stairs, threw open the apartment door and hurried to the phone.

For all her effort, the line was dead when she picked it up.

Frustrated, Kit eyed her pack of cigarettes. She was trying to quit, but missing that call had irritated her, and with a sigh she knocked a cigarette from the pack and lit it. She exhaled a long plume of smoke.

She stared at the cigarette, grimacing. She had never smoked in high school, when most of her friends had started. She hadn't started smoking until she'd come back from Ireland.

She'd taken it up because of the dreams. She'd never been quite able to shake them. The suave psychiatrist down on Park Avenue had told her that the dreams were natural—she'd lost her husband, she'd been alone in a strange land, and she'd been very young. They would stop, he assured her, in time.

Maybe she hadn't really explained the situation to him. Her parents had paid the man a fortune, but she'd never been able to tell him the whole truth. She'd never been able to tell him what had happened between her and Justin barely three months after her husband had died, nor had she said anything about her dreams, in which Michael had melted into Justin, who had donned the strange mask of the horned goat.

The psychiatrist would probably have told her that she was crazy. At the least, he would have called her paranoid, especially if she'd told him that she was sure she'd been drugged. Finally she had stopped seeing him, since there didn't seem to be any point.

Kit started violently when the phone shrilled again. She grabbed it after the first ring. "Hello."

"Hi, sweetheart. This is your hardworking and brilliant agent."

"Robert! Well?"

"How about lunch?"

"Robert." Kit tried to sound annoyed. "Just give me an answer. Did they say yes or no?"

"It isn't as simple as that, Kit. Lunch?"

She sighed. "Only if I can bring Mike. School doesn't start until next week."

"You know I love Mike, Kit, but see if you can't get a sitter for a couple of hours. You've got some decisions to make."

A curious frown puckered her brow. Robert did care for Mike, and if the conversation was going to be a simple one, he wouldn't have minded in the least if she brought her son along. At first she had thought that Robert was only trying to lure her into having lunch with him, but now it didn't sound like that at all.

"The Italian place on Madison—on the agency, Kit."

"Let me call you back, Robert."

Kit hung up, hesitated a minute, then called her across-the-hall neighbor. She frequently kept Christy's son Tod, so Christy shouldn't mind making an extra sandwich for Mike.

She didn't. When Kit got off the phone, she went to the window and threw it open. "Michael!"

He looked up at her, shading his eyes with his hands.

"I've got to see Robert for lunch. Be good for Tod's mom, okay?"

He nodded, then shrugged and turned his attention back to the serious business of the ball game.

Kit called Robert, changed into a knit suit and locked up the apartment. She gave her son a kiss on the head, waved to the other kids, and started walking.

Mike called her back. She paused and waited as he ran down the street to catch up with her.

"What is it, Mike?"

He hesitated, then shrugged, looking down at the ground.

"Mike?"

Hands in his pockets, shuffling his feet, he looked back up at her.

"You're not going to leave again, are you, Mom?"

Something caught at her heart. Last May she had accepted an assignment in the Caribbean. Mike had been in school, so she had left him behind, in her mother's care.

He was an only child, and sensitive, and she knew that her leaving had hurt him.

"No," she said, softly but firmly. "I won't leave you again, Dickens. I promise."

He smiled, accepted a hug with only a little squirming, and ran back to his friends.

Kit had intended to take a taxi, but Mike's question put her in a pensive mood. The day was pleasant, and before she knew it she was halfway to the restaurant— still fidgeting with her little Celtic cross as she walked. She kept walking and reached the restaurant only a few minutes beyond her appointment time. Robert Gruyere was standing by one of the checked-cloth-covered tables, waving her in the right direction.

She hurried to him, accepted his kiss on her cheek and took the chair opposite him. "Okay, Robert, the suspense is killing me. Do I have a sale or not?"

"White wine or red?"

"Robert!"

"White or red?"

"White."

Robert signaled to the waiter and ordered a bottle of white wine. Kit fumed as she waited for the wine to be poured.

"Robert, is this a celebration?"

"That depends on you, Kit."

Robert had been Kit's literary agent since she had come to New York City four years ago. She'd had nothing to go on except a degree and a desperation to succeed. Robert had been the youngest member of an old and established agency, and as the new kid on the block he had seen something in Kit. She hadn't gotten rich, but she had managed to stay afloat and gain a certain reputation in her field, which was travel books.

"What do you mean?" she snapped.

"Heinze and Brintz have turned down the idea for the New York book, Kit."

She lowered her eyes and sipped her wine, trying hard not to show the extent of her disappointment. Heinze and Brintz was a new hardcover house, already drawing critical acclaim for the quality of their nonfiction. They had shown an interest in Kit's work, and she had allowed herself to daydream that she could spend a year in the city working—without having to worry about time away from Mike.

She also needed some advance money soon—from somewhere.

"Why didn't you just tell me that at first, Robert?" she asked, reaching into her bag for a cigarette.

Robert flicked his lighter for her. "Because," he said, "they do want you to do a book for them."

Kit inhaled, watching him suspiciously. "On what?"

"On Ireland."

"Ireland!"

Her dismay must have been obvious, because Robert made a disapproving sound. "Kit, I know your husband died in Ireland, but for heaven's sake, that was eight years ago. And, Kit, you can't afford to turn down this advance."

She tapped her cigarette distractedly. "What about Mike?" she asked in a tight voice.

"If you're so worried about him, take him with you."

"There's school—"

"Hire a tutor."

Kit fell silent. The waiter came by again. Robert suggested something, and Kit waved her hand in the air, barely aware of what he ordered for them.

"Well?" he asked after the waiter had left.

"I don't know, Robert."

"How can you not know, Kit? Most writers would sell their souls for an opportunity like this. If you haven't forgotten, publishing is a tough industry."

"I know."

"Look, Kit, I'm half convinced they're fools to offer such a large advance on this kind of book, but they've hired a new managing editor, and she's one of those fanatical Irish-Americans herself. She was impressed with your credits, and with the fact that your senior thesis was given such attention. She wants something not just on the country, but on the ancient times, the legends, the old customs, all that stuff. Talk to her, if nothing else."

Kit nodded. The waiter put her plate in front of her, and she automatically began eating, realizing only then that Robert had ordered calamari. And she hated squid— no matter what you called it.

She set her fork down and began to play with a roll. Robert kept talking. She kept nodding.

Eventually their plates were taken away, and they ordered coffee. Robert took out a pen and began luring her with the sums he wrote down on a napkin. Somehow she wound up with the pen herself, and the sums she wrote down continued to sound astronomical.

"Kit." Robert leaned across the table. "Kit, you don't have to go anywhere near the town where your husband died."

"I know," she murmured.

He stared at her piercingly, and she flushed and lowered her lashes. He reached his hand across the table, his fingers curling comfortingly around hers.

"Talk about it."

"What?" she said, startled.

He leaned back, releasing her hand, watching her more gently now. "Tell me about it. Okay, I'll start with what I know. You graduated from high school and married Michael McHennessy, a young man with a master's in literature from Princeton. You went to Ireland for your honeymoon, and he died the day you arrived. Fell off the cliffs. Tragic, Kit, but no reason to hate a whole country."

"I don't hate Ireland. I love it."

"Then...?"

She shrugged.

"Kit! Tell me what really happened. Why did you stay

there so long afterward? What is it that has stayed with you so long?"

"I…" She lifted her hands. "I—I don't know!" That was a lie; she owed him some kind of an explanation. After all, he was working so hard for her. She couldn't tell him the truth, but maybe it wouldn't hurt to try to talk out some of the confusion. She sighed.

"Michael grew up in an American orphanage," she began, nervously lighting another cigarette. "He did have his birth certificate, though, and he knew he'd been born in Ireland, in a place called Shallywae, on the southwestern coast. He wanted to go back." She smiled, remembering those first hours when she'd been such a radiant bride. "He teased me all the way out. He could feign a marvelous brogue, and he spent the drive talking about leprechauns and banshees and druids." Her smile faded, her voice faltered, and she was suddenly looking at Robert a little desperately, as if he could give her some kind of explanation. "Michael had studied all the ancient writing in Gaelic. I remember that when we reached the cottage he was fooling around, teasing me. He was talking about a time before Christianity when the people worshipped a fertility god from the sea. They called him Bal, and he was supposed to have been a man with a goat's head. Michael told me that every year they would offer up a virgin to Bal and—"

"She was sacrificed?"

Kit flushed slightly, sadly, remembering Michael's twinkling eyes when he'd described the rite. "Not at first. You see, they'd gather on All Hallows' Eve, and the high priest would take the virgin."

"Aha! And then she wouldn't be a virgin anymore."

"It's not funny, Robert."

"Oh, my God, Kit! We're talking about centuries ago!"

Kit ignored him. "The girl was supposed to bear a son to be the new 'god.' Then she was sacrificed."

"Kit, what does this have to do with Michael? You told me that he fell off a cliff."

"I know." Kit stubbed out her cigarette and picked up her wineglass. "But you see, the same night that Michael died, a girl named Mary Browne—a girl with an illegitimate, newborn baby boy—was murdered."

"And you think the two deaths were connected?"

"Yes. No. Oh, I don't know! I never did understand what happened. They all came out for Michael's funeral. Even the poor murdered girl's mother. And she kept muttering about how they belonged to the land in death. I don't know. Maybe I was just too young and impressionable. My parents were in Europe then, too, and I didn't know how to reach them. I had to leave everything up to Justin O'Niall, and that was strange, too, because I first met him in the middle of the night when I was wandering around looking for—"

"Justin O'Niall? *The* Justin O'Niall? You know him?"

Kit looked at Robert with a frown. "'The'?"

"The architect!" Robert said impatiently.

"Well, yes, he's an architect."

"The one marrying the 'Love Buns' heiress."

"Yes."

"You know him?" Robert's voice squeaked a bit.

"Yes, well I did," Kit said uneasily. "Is he that famous?"

"Right next to Frank Lloyd Wright. He's brilliant! He was here about three years ago. My God, you could have introduced me to him! Shallywae, yes! I had heard that he came from some little village! That he's the hereditary lord or something like that."

"Oh, yes, he's quite the lord," Kit said with a surprising trace of bitterness. Robert arched a curious brow. Kit lowered her head; she wasn't about to tell him the whole truth.

"It's like going back hundreds of years, Robert," she murmured. "The people…they go by his wishes. That night, Michael was in the living room, and suddenly he was gone. He must have—I think he saw or heard the murderer. He must have run out quickly. He didn't take his coat or anything. I came back in from the kitchen, and he was gone. I ran out to the cliff looking for him, and I stumbled into a man. Justin O'Niall. I remember that there was music from the glen, and bonfires, and Justin was there, listening, I guess. And I was lost and alone and afraid, so he said that he'd help me find my husband and he—he was with me when I did. I found Michael. I saw him down below, and I scrambled down all those rocks and…"

"And then?"

She shook her head, swallowing. "He whispered something to me, and then he died."

"What did he whisper?"

"Kayla."

"Kayla?" Robert repeated. "What does that mean?"

"I don't know. It isn't Gaelic, so I've never been able to discover what it means. Anyway—" she straightened in her chair, and her voice hardened "—I think I passed out. I woke up at Justin O'Niall's castle—"

"You've been in the castle?"

Kit hesitated, looking wryly at Robert. Nothing that she had written had impressed him this much.

"Yes, I've been in his castle. He took me with him—he probably had nothing else to do with an unconscious woman. He called in the constable, his housekeeper looked after me, and he made the arrangements for the funeral."

"My goodness," Robert murmured, fingering his wineglass. He leaned forward. "So go on!"

"There's nothing else," Kit said, and she could have bitten her tongue. She sounded so defensive.

"You stayed, though, didn't you?"

She lifted a hand vaguely. "I, uh, yes, for a while. I stayed in the cottage for about three months."

"And?"

"And nothing. Then I came home. I took care of Michael. I went back to college. I began writing. I moved to New York. I started a new life."

Robert wagged a finger at her. "Aha!"

"Aha what?"

"Aha, there's simply no reason in the world to avoid a whole country because of what happened eight years ago. It would probably be good for you to go back. You're twenty-six now, not eighteen. You're neither naive nor impressionable. If you do go back to your little village, you can laugh at the past."

"Really?" Kit sipped her wine.

"Really. And if you should run into your old friend Justin O'Niall, you could maybe suggest that he write a book."

"And hire you for his agent, I assume?"

"You wound me, Kit."

She grinned. "I'm not going to run into him."

"But you *are* going to go. You need the money."

Kit took out a pen and idly wrote down figures on her napkin. She really could use the money. In fact, that was an understatement.

"I'll do it—if I can take Mike."

"Great!" Robert called for the check. While he pulled out his credit card, Kit glanced down at the napkin where she had been doodling. Kayla.

A shiver ran along her backbone.

Kayla. The word Michael had murmured before he had died. What did it mean? Probably nothing. He had probably been incapable of real speech....

Robert stood, pulling back her chair for her. He passed her a business card. "Call your new editor today. Her name is Kelly O'Hare."

"Nice and Irish," Kit murmured.

"So is Katherine McHennessy," Robert reminded her with a grin.

She grimaced in return. "I'll call her. But I'm still not sure why she's so convinced I'm the writer she wants. If she wants someone who can research the real Irish literature, it's in Gaelic—and I don't understand a word of it." She fell silent for a moment. "Michael did. He was fluent."

"I'm sure you'll be able to find what you need. Anyone can read books, but what Kelly wants is something with the personal touch. You'll need to leave within a month, you'll have a May or June deadline, and you're going to need your time for research." He gave her a little tap on the chin with his knuckles. "Okay?"

"Yeah, sure," she murmured. Robert led her out to the sidewalk. The sun was brilliant, almost mocking. The sun was never bright in New York. It figures. She was planning to leave, so now there was sun.

"Want to have dinner tonight?" Robert asked her.

She smiled. "No."

"Ah, well, you can't blame me for trying."

"You're my agent, Robert."

"Hey, lots of agents have married their clients."

"I have a seven-year-old son—"

"And last year you had a six-year-old son. The year before that he was five. And next year he'll be eight. Ten years from now he'll go away to college. You've got to start living, Kit. I may be a bit of a lech, but, hey—what normal, heterosexual man in New York City isn't?"

Kit smiled and lowered her lashes. "All right, Robert. We'll have dinner—as soon as I come home, all right?"

"Better than nothing." He gave her a jaunty grin and started down the street. Kit turned and started off in the opposite direction, walking more slowly.

It was a long walk home, and she took her time. When she reached her street, with its prettily planted trees, she had come to something of a realization. She wasn't sure she wanted to go back to Ireland, but she knew that she needed to go back. The past had always been there, in the background, tugging at her.

She stared up at her apartment window for a long time. And then she began to smile, because Mike would be happy that they were going on such a long and exciting vacation together.

She contacted Kelly O'Hare the next day, and to her relief the woman did sound lovely. What she wanted was a book that combined a look at present-day Ireland with a dissertation on the past that had made it what it was. A guide for travelers but more than that, an insight into the land.

Kit was astounded to learn that in addition to her nice-sized advance, she was to be given a hefty expense account. In the spring, a photographer would be sent over to join her. It went way beyond anything she might have expected.

There were a trillion little things to do. Mike had started to pack the moment she had told him they were going. He wasn't packing clothing, though, just his toys and coloring books.

She had to call her parents in Connecticut and let them know what she was doing, and she had to repeat Robert's words to her when her mother expressed concern about Kit returning to a place where she had known such tragedy.

"Mom, Michael has been dead for eight years."

"And we weren't even able to be with you."

"It wasn't your fault."

She could almost see her mother wringing her hands. "Oh, Kit, I don't like it. If only Michael had lived! You'd have a score of children and a beautiful house in the suburbs, instead of that little box in the city—"

"Mother, Michael and I didn't want a score of children. His death *was* tragic, and a waste, but nothing can bring him back, and I've been living a long time without him now." Eons longer than I got to live with him, she added silently. "And I like my apartment in the city."

"It's no good for Mike. He should have a big yard. And a dog."

"Right, Mom. Fine."

"Don't let him drink the water, Kit."

"Mother, there's nothing wrong with Irish water!"

"Yes, well, be careful anyway."

"I will, Mother," she said softly, then added on a slightly forced but cheerful note, "Mike and I will come out for a weekend before we leave, okay?"

After that phone call, she walked into her son's room.

Mike, his hands behind his head, was watching something on cable. He smiled when he saw her.

"We're really leaving, huh, Mom?"

She walked to his bed. "Shove over," she told him. He did so, and she half sat, half leaned beside him, ruffling his hair. "Yeah, we're really leaving."

He was silent for a minute. Then he asked, "Grandma is upset, huh?"

"A little. You know Grandma."

Again he was silent. "Are *you* upset, Mom?" he finally asked.

"No." She was only lying a little. "Why should I be? These people are giving me an awful lot of money, Dickens."

"My father died there," Mike said matter-of-factly. Or perhaps not so matter-of-factly. She saw that he was watching her from the corner of his eye.

"We don't have to go to that town," she heard herself say. But we will, she thought, a little shiver running up her spine. We will. I know we will....

"It's all right," Mike said, and she was surprised that a seven-year-old could sound so mature. "I'd like to see where he's buried."

He said it without pain; he had never known Michael.

"I am part Irish," he added, a touch of pride in his voice.

The normal beating of her heart seemed to stop. She felt a hard thud; then it started pounding normally again.

"Yes, Mike, you are part Irish." She rose, kissed his forehead and pulled up his covers. "Television off now, Dickens. It's late."

He obligingly hit the button, and the room was plunged

into darkness. She was in the doorway when she heard his voice again, very much that of a little boy.

"I love you, Mom."

"I love you, Dickens."

Kit didn't stay up much later herself. But no matter how she plumped her pillows, she couldn't sleep.

Eventually she rose and boiled water for tea. But once she had made her cup of tea, she found herself staring into it, then impulsively splashing the liquid down the drain as if she had seen a bug in it.

She drank half a glass of wine instead, while puffing on a cigarette and staring out the window at the empty street. The distant night sounds of New York seemed comforting to her.

At last she went back to bed and fell into a restless sleep. Then she started to dream, as she hadn't dreamed in years.

Images filled her dreams. Images of Michael, laughing, telling her stories from his book. Leaning over her and tickling her and speaking so mischievously. She could hear his voice as he said, "Ahh, for those pagan days! The goat-god, or the high chief in his stead, was all-powerful. I mean, there was nothing like 'I've got a headache tonight!' She was dragged out to the altar, drugged and acquiescent and sweet, and there she became the bride of the god. And the next year, when she had borne the god's heir, she would be dragged out again and her blood would be shed to feed the land."

"Oh, quit it, Michael! Or *your* bride will have a headache!" she'd told him, breathless, laughing…and scared, too. And she pushed him away in her dream, as she had in life. "I'll get the champagne!"

In her sleep, Kit fought the images, but they came back to her. Slowly, but with incredible vibrancy.

Michael was gone. She called his name, then saw the door swinging in the wind. She ran after him, barefoot and clad only in her sheer white silky nightgown. She ran into the night, across the meadow, into the wind and toward the call of the sea.

She saw the man, then, and she paused, but he had turned to her already. He was tall against the night, like a god himself. She didn't think he was real, but he was, and when she stuttered and stumbled, he answered her with soft laughter against the distant shrilling of pipes and flutes. He gave her his coat and took her hand, and they walked together.

He called her back from the cliff, but she wouldn't go to him. She was already crawling down the jagged rocks. Michael was there. Staring at her unseeingly, whispering...

"Come away, girl, he cannot hear you. Come away..."

Strong arms carried her when she fell.

She awakened in the castle. They were all there: Liam O'Grady, the graying constable. Molly, Doc Conar—and Justin. Arms crossed over his chest as he leaned against the door frame. He wouldn't let them question her when she cried; he calmed her when others suggested that Michael should be taken back to the U.S. He brought Father Pat to her; he arranged for the service and for the burial, and he was there for her throughout.... She saw him standing there in the wind, pointing to the sea, laughing when she innocently asked him if he had seen the subs that had been out there during World War II, and telling her that he might look ancient, but he was really only twenty-eight.

That picture faded. The dream turned into a nightmare.

It was night. Dark and misty and whirling with the sound of the pipes and the banshee shriek of the wind.

She saw the cliff. People were standing there, all the people from the village. They were forming a circle around her. And they were chanting.

"Kayla…kayla…kayla… *Kayla*!"

Molly's face swam before her. Doc's… Liam's. They were forming a circle; they were coming closer and closer.…

Justin was suddenly in her dream. He didn't speak to her; he just smiled. He was naked, walking silently toward her, with a long, slow, sure stride.

She was frightened, and she wanted to run, but she couldn't, because she was tied to a high slab of rock. She wanted to cry, and so she taunted him again.

"The King of the High Hill, the King of the High Hill. You're the King of the High Hill. The O'Niall." Laughter followed. Her own laughter.

Then, suddenly, Justin was gone, and the goat-god was there instead. His eyes were on fire, and talons stretched from his fingers. Talons that dripped with blood. She started to scream as he wrote across her stomach with the blood: "KAYLA."

Kit sat up in her bed, sweating and shaking. As always, she looked around to reassure herself that she was in her apartment in New York. She was. Her heartbeat slowed.

Disgusted, she lay down again, but she didn't close her eyes. She stared up at the ceiling. Had she been a little bit in love with Justin O'Niall, but too ashamed to admit it, so that she had deluded herself into living a dream in order to have him? She hadn't understood much about sexuality then; she had loved Michael very much, and it would have seemed like a tremendous sin to her then to have admitted that her body was as lonely as her soul.

Something strange had happened. Very strange. She hadn't invented Michael's death, nor the death of Mary Browne. And some of those villagers had been awfully weird. Nice, but weird. And very much in awe of Justin O'Niall.

And Justin…

Justin had been a very appealing man, and she had been lonely. There was nothing too hard to understand about what had happened.

She punched her pillow hard and made herself close her eyes. She wound her fingers around her little cross, and in time fell asleep. She didn't dream again.

Kit awoke feeling far more tired than when she had gone to bed. She also felt a little sheepish—and stupid. Her dreams always seemed silly in the morning. Yawning, she stumbled out of her room, glad that her coffee-maker had a timer and that she could quickly give herself a good shot of caffeine.

With her coffee cup in her hand, she glanced into Mike's room and saw that he was still sleeping. She smiled, stretched and decided to enjoy her coffee, her morning cigarette and the newspaper before the apartment was filled with the sounds of mock battle and morning cartoons.

Kit sneaked quickly out her front door in her worn terry robe to retrieve her paper, then carried it back to the kitchen table without glancing at it. She lit a cigarette—yesterday hadn't been so bad, she'd only smoked half a pack—inhaled deeply, sipped her coffee, and spread the newspaper out on the table.

She gasped—inhaling her coffee instead of her cigarette—and went into a spasm of coughing that brought tears to her eyes.

Justin O'Niall had made the front page of the *Times*. The headline seemed to blaze. "'Love Buns' Heiress Murdered in County Cork. Prominent Irish Architect Chief Suspect."

Only Kit's eyes moved; the rest of her was frozen as she quickly scanned the story.

Susan Accorn had been strangled and cast into the Irish Sea sometime during the night of the first of September. That was fact.

The rest, Kit decided, was conjecture.

According to the reporter, Susan and her fiancé, Justin O'Niall, had quarreled at his ancestral home. The engagement had been broken. Suspicion—abetted by the fact that an "acquaintance" of his, a young girl, had also been found murdered eight years earlier—was therefore directed toward Justin O'Niall.

Kit read the article again and again. Her coffee grew cold; her cigarette burned down to the filter.

There was no evidence against Justin. In fact, the article was just short of libelous. The last paragraph included a quote from Justin, asserting his innocence and threatening legal action against anyone who saw fit to slander him.

"Good for you, Justin," Kit muttered aloud. Then she realized that she was shaking, vividly recalled that first time she had seen him.

He had been standing on the cliffs, alone, while Michael had been dying on the rocks far below. She remembered believing—and never quite being convinced that she was wrong—that Michael had seen something and had been pushed to his death for what he had seen. Because a young girl, Mary Browne, had been murdered that night, her throat slit, her body tossed to the waves.

Kit frowned, trying to remember, trying to go back. Yes, Mary had died the same night; Kit could still recall the whispered rumors, since the girl had just been delivered of an illegitimate baby. She could remember Justin's total impatience with some of the talk; he had never been the girl's lover, and he considered it laughable that he could be accused. The rumors had died away—because he had been innocent, Kit was sure. She had come to know him quite well, and his innocence was something she had become convinced of. Still, the memories were coming like a surging tide. His family would have been local chieftains. And before that they would have been the druids, because the druids had virtually ruled the people. Through fear. Through sacrifice and death...

"What am I thinking?" she whispered, threading her fingers through her hair and rocking slightly in her chair. She had known Justin O'Niall, and though she had never understood what had happened between them, she couldn't believe he was a murderer.

Her heart started to pound. She knew that she was going to see him. She'd always known that someday she would have to go back. She could fight it from here to eternity, but it was still there. The haunting, frightening, exquisite, compelling allure.

Her throat constricted. No....

Yes.

Chapter 2

By the first of October, Kit was on her way.

She was determined to make this trip special for Mike, so they didn't fly straight into Shannon, but booked a flight to London, instead. She had decided that he should see something of the city, and he certainly didn't mind.

He liked the guards at Buckingham Palace, and he was fascinated when they wandered around Soho. The Victoria and Albert Museum didn't impress him much, and she forced herself to remember that he was only seven, and not really old enough yet to appreciate the arts, or the wonders of history.

He did like the Tower of London—she was sure he was imagining knights in armor and all the poor wretches who had been prisoners there. He liked Westminster Abbey, too, and it was there, among the tombs and the monuments to England's kings and queens and great men, that he asked her when they would leave for Ireland.

"Aren't you having a good time?"

"Sure. But when are we going over to Ireland?"

Kit shrugged and ruffled his hair. "It's a short flight to Shannon. We can go anytime."

"When?"

"Soon," she promised.

They went the next day. She was still determined to make the trip special, so when the car-rental agency offered her a new Toyota—like the one Michael and she had rented—she turned it down and insisted on a serviceable, much older Volvo, instead.

Before setting off, Kit studied her map and smiled at Mike. "Hey, want to see Blarney Castle today?"

"Do we have to?"

She had been certain he would want to see the castle. He was a normal kid, and normal kids loved that kind of thing. Kit frowned.

"Don't you want to?"

"Yeah, just not today. I want to see where my father is buried."

Well, I don't! Kit wanted to snap. But she had known she would be going back, so she might as well do it now and get it over with.

She studied the map again. "All right, Mike. There's a little town just before the coast called Bailtree. They advertise a few bed-and-breakfast places. We'll check into one, get something to eat somewhere, and if it's still light I'll take you to the cemetery."

"Will we get to the Irish Sea?" Mike asked excitedly.

Kit hesitated. "Probably not today. It will get dark early and…the cliffs aren't safe."

"Mom…"

"Michael! They're not safe!"

He crossed his arms over his chest and fell silent, staring straight ahead. Kit started the car, ignoring him. It wasn't difficult, she had to concentrate on staying on the left-hand side of the road.

About twenty minutes later, they left the city behind. Kit saw that her son was no longer sitting stiff-necked but was staring avidly out the window.

He glanced her way, his growing excitement alive in his eyes. "Look how green it is! So much grass!"

"You've seen grass before, Mike."

"Where?"

"Connecticut. And Central Park is full of grass."

He laughed; it had sounded as if she was trying to dampen his enthusiasm. Kit smiled a little sheepishly, wondering how she could begrudge him his pleasure in the seemingly endless countryside.

"It is very beautiful, Mike," she told him, then turned her eyes back to the road. The tense time between them was over; she should be happy.

Perhaps not completely. She was taking exactly the same road. Heading exactly the same way. She wouldn't be normal if she didn't feel a certain sense of dread, of nostalgia, of pain.

Kit had forgotten how long the winding Irish miles could be. Long before they neared Cork, Mike started saying that he was thirsty. "Can you wait till we reach the city?" she asked him. "I can fill the gas tank there, too."

He grumbled a little, but agreed. Kit promised it would only be another ten minutes, but it ended up being closer to thirty.

Eventually she found a cute little pub that catered

more to families than to the drinking man, and Mike was happy enough to sit down and order a hot chocolate and a bowl of vegetable soup.

Kit ordered soup herself, and a Guinness. The room-temperature beer made her lip curl a bit, but she told herself that she would learn to enjoy it.

"I like it here," Mike said. "So much grass!" He kept talking about all the sheep he had seen. Kit listened to him with half her mind; with the other half she paid attention to the conversation at the next table.

"It's disgraceful."

"Shameful!"

"And all because the man has money. I tell you, Mabel, money can buy anything in this world, even innocence."

Kit tried not to stare at the two women in their furs and pillbox hats, but she was consciously straining to hear the rest of their words and to place their accents. They didn't seem to be Irish—at least not from this part of Ireland.

Mabel, who appeared to be the older of the two, was viciously stabbing her spoon in the direction of a newspaper article. "Look at that, will you, Gladys. They haven't even brought O'Niall in for questioning. And there's no doubt he murdered the poor girl. None at all. He had that awful row with her for all to see; then she turned up dead, practically on his doorstep."

"And the police claim there's no evidence!" Gladys said indignantly, shaking her double chins.

"Mark my words, those townspeople defending him probably know he's a murderer. They're just protecting one of their own—because she was an American. Of course, American women..."

Mabel went into a long discourse on the total lack of

morals to be found in American women. Kit decided at last that their accents were British, rather than Irish.

Gladys lowered her voice, and Kit leaned closer to listen. She couldn't help herself.

"Yes, but, Mabel, the Irish all have a temper—the whole world knows that. He probably went into a rage and strangled her without thinking." She folded her hands primly and nodded with great wisdom. "Manslaughter, Mabel. Not first-degree murder. The man is so good-looking, she probably drove him to it. Striking, and passionate! Why he's as compelling as sin."

"Hmmph!" Mabel obviously disagreed. "Vampires are notoriously compelling, too, my dear. But deadly! What about that other poor girl, all those years ago? Her throat slit! He did it—and that was no case of manslaughter. Do you know what they say—" Mabel looked around, as if finally realizing that she was sitting in a pub full of people. She lowered her voice. "They say, Gladys, that a lot of the coastal people and farmers are almost…well, *pagan*, to this day! I've even heard it rumored that they practice strange rites. Now, I heard this from Barbara Sawyer, and you know how reliable she is. She says that Justin O'Niall is the head of that town just as his grandfathers were before him. That means he's some kind of a head priest. Who knows? It's quite possible that both those poor girls were offered up as sacrifices. O'Niall could very well be half-insane and convinced he's the devil's servant." She leaned closer to her friend. "And tourist women are their very favorite sacrifices!"

Kit wanted to speak up. She wanted to say something. Anything. Oh, the power of rumor and wagging tongues!

"Didn't you hear about the bodies?" Mabel asked.

"Mom!"

Mike—almost shouting her name—kept Kit from hearing the rest. For a minute she wanted to shout at him; then she realized that she had spent years teaching him that it was rude to listen in on other people's conversations, yet here she was, doing that very thing.

"What is it, Mike?"

"Shouldn't we keep going?"

"Yes, we'd better go," she said resignedly. "I've got to pay the check, Mike. Go on out and wait for me by the car."

He smiled, eagerly standing and obeying her. Kit gathered her purse and dug out a few of her Irish pounds. She felt Mabel and Gladys watching her as she walked to the bar and paid the affable innkeeper.

When she had received her change, she turned around. Mabel and Gladys were still watching her. They offered her grim smiles, but she could read their eyes. They didn't approve of her. They obviously didn't like her jeans, or her knit sweater—or the tennis shoes she was wearing.

She smiled back anyway and walked by their table. "I would be very careful here if I were you, ladies. I understand that the whole country is filled with ancient druid cults, and that they're constantly offering up sacrifices!"

She was rewarded for her efforts with a pair of pleasing masks of horror. Gladys actually let her mouth fall open. "Oh!"

Kit nodded at her sagely, then hurried out to meet Mike at the car.

"All set, Dickens?" she asked, turning the key in the ignition.

"What were those women talking about, Mom?"

Kit watched the traffic as she pulled out into the road. "They were gossiping, Mike."

"About a murder?"

She hesitated. Seven-year-olds knew all about murder these days. They had to. All the terrible things that could happen to children were drilled into their heads—at school, at church and at home.

"Yes."

"Was the man caught?"

"No. Mike, I really don't know anything about it. Oh, look!" It had taken them only a few minutes to get out of the city of Cork, and now they were passing pastureland again. They would only be on the road another half hour or so. "Mike, look at that little pony! Isn't he adorable?"

"Do you think I could have a pony, Mom?"

"Sure. Someday." It was her standard answer.

She found Jamie's Bed and Breakfast right where the map said it would be, off a side road in a town that was just a little bit bigger than Shallywae and not ten minutes from it.

Jamie himself greeted her and told her the place was empty, and that she and Mike were welcome to stay as long as they wanted—at a ridiculously low price.

Kit paid for two nights, allowed Mike to accept a soda from Jamie and headed back to the car for their overnight bags. She dug around in the trunk for a minute, then went perfectly still as an unaccountable chill washed over her. She paused, pulling her head out of the trunk to look around. She didn't see a thing, just the dirt road and the forest beyond it. A few sheep were grazing off to the right in a small field.

Kit cocked her head curiously, frowned with annoyance at herself and started back to the house. But a little bit of the uneasy cold remained. She had been sure that she was being watched.

Jamie—James Jameson, she quickly learned—was a friendly sort. His accent was deep and delightful, and Kit saw that Mike was hanging on his every word as the old man led them up a narrow stairway. "'Tis the perfect place for ye and the boy, ma'am. I've got this big room here, leadin' into a smaller one. Ye can make all the noise ye like, laddie. I'm hard of hearin' meself, and the sheep don't care none at all!"

It was nice. Sparsely and simply furnished, but spotlessly clean. They even had their own bath, which was an uncommon treat.

"It's lovely, Jamie. Thank you very much."

"'Tis a quiet place," Jamie said, scratching his almost bald head. "Nice to have ye, 'tis. Nice to have ye!"

Jamie went on down the stairs. Mike started talking excitedly as he wandered into the little room beyond Kit's, carrying his nylon duffel bag. Kit paid scant attention to him and began to unpack her own bag.

Suddenly that eerie feeling settled over her again. It was strong this time, so strong that for a moment she was afraid to look up.

When she finally did, she had to choke back a scream—because she *was* being watched. A man was staring at her from the doorway. An old, rumpled man with rheumy eyes and a face as wrinkled as a bulldog's.

"It is you, then. Y'er back, Mrs. McHennessy."

Her hand fluttered to her throat, but then she let out a long gasp, relieved.

"Old Doug!" she exclaimed. Old Doug and his son— Young Doug—had prepared Michael's grave. Old Doug's wife, Molly, had been Justin's housekeeper, and they had all been tremendously kind to her when Michael had died.

Kit stood and walked to the doorway, offering him

her hand. He didn't look well, she thought with a tug of pity. Old and worn and not of this world.

"Ah, girl, y'er back!"

"I'm a writer now, Old Doug. I'm doing a book."

"Where's the bairn?"

"Bairn? Oh, my son! How did you know?"

"I always knew, lassie. I always knew," he told her with a little wink.

Kit smiled. She *had* been watched at the car. Old Doug had seen her, and he had seen Mike.

"Mike!" Kit called her son, but when she turned around, Mike was already behind her. She hoped he would be nice to Old Doug. Children were often repelled by older people.

But Mike was stepping forward with the same enthusiasm he had shown for everything since he had arrived. "Hi. I'm Mike. Michael Patrick McHennessy. Do you know my mother?"

"Sure, lad, that I do!"

Mike looked at his mother with a little bit of the awe he had been reserving for the Irish. "He remembers you, Mom!" He looked from her to Old Doug. "It's almost like coming home, isn't it?"

His words touched another note of uneasiness within her, but she kept on smiling and tried to talk her way past it. "It is nice of you to remember me, Old Doug. I wasn't here all that long."

"I always knew ye'd come with the bairn, lass. I always knew."

Now he was definitely making her feel creepy. But weren't gravediggers supposed to make you feel creepy? Kit began to wonder how to get him out of her room.

"Pa! Pa, where ye be? What're ye up to?"

The body attached to the voice appeared at the top of the stairs behind Old Doug. Kit had to blink several times, but then she recognized Young Doug.

"Why, 'tis you!" he murmured in surprise, recognizing her at the same instant. Kit nodded. Young Doug had grown from a strapping youth to a very handsome young man, with a debonair smile, nice gray eyes and a thatch of sandy hair. They were, Kit realized, the same age—she had just been a much older eighteen than Douglas had needed to be.

"Young Doug!" She laughed.

"Mrs. McHennessy!" He chuckled in return. "My apologies. I didna mean to be rude!" He gripped his father's arm. "Nor did Pa, I'm sure." He dropped his voice, as if by doing so his father wouldn't hear his words. "Pa's been…slipping a little bit lately."

"It's quite all right," Kit assured him. Was it? She placed her hand on Mike's shoulder. "It's very nice to see you both. Mike, this is—" She was about to say "Young Doug" again, but the name didn't seem to fit anymore.

"Douglas Johnston, son. And what, might I ask, are you doing out of school, lad?"

"Traveling with my mom." Mike wrinkled up his face. "But I'm going to have to get a tutor."

"Not if you stay here, lad." He winked at Kit over the boy's head. "I'm the teacher at the grammar school. You could start classes Monday."

"The teacher?" Kit asked in surprise. "That's wonderful, Doug. But Mike and I won't be staying more than a day or two."

"A pity." This time Doug winked at Mike. "We'll have to convince her to stay on, eh, Mike?"

"Yes!" Mike breathed.

Kit smiled, but her stomach tensed. "I have a book to write, Mike. You know we can't stay in one spot."

Old Doug spoke up. "'Tis no better place on God's own earth to write, lassie. No better place at all."

"Well, Pa and I will take our leave, Mrs. McHennessy, and let you and the boy settle in. I do hope ye'll spare me an hour or so afore ye leave, though."

"Certainly," Kit murmured.

"Come now, Pa."

Young Doug—Douglas, as he was now calling himself—turned his father around, waved to Kit with a warm smile and headed down the narrow stairs.

Kit closed the door—and locked it.

"They remembered you, Mom!" Mike exclaimed, that look of new respect still in his eyes.

"Yes, they were very nice," Kit said, a little impatiently. She had thought they were staying far enough from Shallywae, but she had been wrong. Suddenly she wished they could leave right away. If not for Mike, she would have done so.

"Hey, Dickens," she said, a little weakly, "finish unpacking if you want me to show you the cemetery. It gets dark early here."

He ran off obediently. Kit mechanically unpacked the remainder of her things and dragged a brush hurriedly through her hair. Before she was done, Mike was sitting on her bed, waiting for her.

A few minutes later, they were back on the road to Shallywae.

"My father wanted to be buried here, right?" Mike asked her.

"I don't know," Kit answered, keeping her eyes glued to the road and feeling more uncomfortable every minute. It had been a mistake—a very big mistake—to come. "Michael loved Ireland, though. And so… I had him buried here."

"Because it seemed right," Mike supplied cheerfully.

"Yes."

A few minutes later, they were there. Kit had to park the car at the base of a hill, and it took her several minutes to remember just where in the overgrown, ancient cemetery Michael McHennessy had been laid to rest.

"This way, Mike," she murmured at last, starting up the hill.

He followed her, scampering around a number of the monuments.

"Mom! I can read the date on this one. One-six-nine… Well, I can almost read the date! Boy, are these things *old*!"

"Yes, they are," Kit murmured. She paused, puffing a bit. She walked a lot in New York, but not uphill. She looked around and at length saw a large, weathered stone angel rising from the ground. Michael was near the angel, she knew.

She started checking the names. She had thought Michael's tombstone would be easy to find, but in eight years it had weathered to match the rest. She found a fairly new monument, but it wasn't Michael's. Then she found an old one with the name "McHennessy" barely legible, and she knew she was very near—she remembered trying to bury him near people who might have been long-lost family.

Mike was roaming nearby, fascinated by the ancient monuments. She was about to call him back, then decided that no harm could come to him on the grassy hill.

She closed her eyes for a minute, remembering the day

of the funeral. All the townspeople had been dressed in black. Michael had been laid to rest in a simple wooden coffin. She remembered watching it being lowered into the earth, with Old Doug and Young Doug shoveling dirt on top of it when she looked back.

Justin O'Niall had escorted her, supporting her in her torrent of sobbing.

Michael had been so young.

At last she found it. Kit dropped to her knees. Grass and weeds had grown over the spot, half covering the stone. She ripped them away frantically, not caring that she broke a nail down to the quick in the process.

MICHAEL PADRAIC MCHENNESSY
WELCOMED IN CHRIST'S OWN ARMS

"Mike!"

He didn't answer, and she tore her eyes away from the marker to look for him.

He was on the far side of the hill, talking to a man. Kit frowned. He knew he should be wary of strangers. Just because this wasn't New York…

She stood up, dusting off her knees. She started to hurry toward the pair, then stumbled on a stone that was almost hidden by weeds, cursed softly to herself and continued.

The man's back was to her. His head was bare, and slightly lowered. He was tall, and his shoulders were broad beneath a dark trench coat. She quickened her pace, and she could hear Mike talking.

"Oh, I am American, but I'm part Irish, too. My mother told me so. And my father is buried here. That's why we're here."

Kit heard the man chuckle pleasantly, and her heart seemed to catch in her throat. She knew, even before he turned around, who he was.

"There's Mom!" Mike said excitedly.

The man turned around. It seemed to Kit that he was moving slowly, but he wasn't. It was just that her mind was moving so fast.

Then he was facing her. She wanted to say something, but she couldn't find her voice.

He stared at her for a long time, assessing her dispassionately. It was as if he had known that she would be here.

He had changed very little. There were those slight touches of silver at his temples, but his dark hair was as abundant as ever, though unruly now, lashed about his forehead by the wind. He still had his striking tan. His eyes were narrowed, one brow slightly lifted. His mouth was tightly compressed, severe, and his eyes looked black, though she knew they were blue. They were glinting, now, with anger.

Kit swallowed. Finding him there seemed so much like the first time, when she had been running out into the night, calling for Michael. She'd been so young, so frightened, barely clad. She could still remember how he had turned to her that night, so tall and dark and powerful. He had taken her hand and promised to help her. No one had told her then that he was "the" O'Niall. She had known only that he was strong and capable of protecting her. After Michael had died in her arms, he had dragged her away. Through it all, he had been there for her. She had been inexplicably angry at his power, though she had needed his strength. And, against her will, against her every concept of morality, she had been fascinated.

Kit started to tremble. Eight years was a long time. A long enough time in which to forget. But she had never forgotten him. Kit felt his eyes on her, and warmth rushed through her, as if her blood had been set on fire. And he hadn't said a word.

"Michael McHennessy, lad?"

Just his voice sent a new rush of tremors racing through her.

"Katherine," he said then, and he stared at her with such fury that she couldn't begin to fathom its source.

"Justin." She tried to sound casual, but her voice faltered, leaving her furious with herself. She wasn't eighteen anymore. He could be the great lord of anyone here, but not her.

"Kit," Mike offered innocently. "Friends call Mom 'Kit.'"

"Do they now?" Justin replied. His gaze was on her again, his eyes raking her with a crude and negligent interest from head to toe. She flushed despite herself. To her horror, she could remember him so clearly—in the flesh. She remembered not the gentle and tender times, when he had eased away her pain.

No… She remembered the last time she had seen him. In the flesh… The thought made her hysterical, but it came nevertheless, and she could see her hands against his naked chest, her fingers winding into the dark hair there, her skin so pale against his. She could remember the feel of his hands on her, could see the muscles in his arms when he braced himself above her, and the hard plane of his belly, and…

Kit wished she could disappear, that she could sink into the ground, that she could do anything to hide from Justin O'Niall.

Because he was remembering, too. She knew it; she

could see it in his eyes. She could feel his mocking expression.

"You—you knew I was here," she rasped out.

"Of course," he said smoothly. "I am the O'Niall."

Without uttering another word, he turned his back on her and walked away down the hill.

Chapter 3

"Who was that?" Mike asked Kit curiously.

"Justin O'Niall," she replied, watching the man's retreating back instead of meeting her son's eyes.

"You knew him, too?"

"Yes," Kit said slowly, trying to stop shivering.

"He's neat," Mike decided.

"Yeah. Real neat," Kit murmured bitterly. "Come on, Mike. I'll take you to the grave. Then we'll go and get something to eat."

Bailtree wasn't much larger than Shallywae, but like its coastal sister, it had a town center with a few shops, a post office, a town hall, a garage, a grocery and three restaurants. One was the local men's pub, and Kit steered away from it, not certain if a woman and child would be welcomed or not. "Mary MacGregor's" turned out to be a nice home-style restaurant that catered to the tourist trade, since they weren't far from Blarney Castle.

The seating was family style around trestle tables, an open hearth warmed the room, and the service was quick and friendly. There was a bar, too, and a number of old-timers stood around it and in front of the hearth, a few of them whittling small dolls out of wood as they drank their pints.

Kit suggested to Mike that they split an order of lamb chops and boiled new potatoes. He agreed quickly. It was beginning to look as if he might lay his head on the table and fall asleep at any moment.

They were served a beautiful fresh garden salad, which their waitress had affably split onto two plates. Kit, tired herself, showed her appreciation with a warm smile.

"Och, 'tis nothing. I've a household of five meself, and I know it can be difficult eating out with the loves."

Mike ate his salad. He was very quiet, but appeared content enough. When their entrée came, Kit noticed that he was watching one old man in particular, who was whittling away at a piece of wood about five inches long.

Kit also noticed that the old man was aware of Mike's intense scrutiny. He didn't smile, but he nodded to Mike, as if in acknowledgment.

The lamb chops were delicious, and when she had finished eating, Kit was pleased to discover that "Mary MacGregor's" also served a nice strong cup of coffee. Mike, to her surprise, was awake enough to want a piece of cherry pie.

It was then that the old man muttered something to his cronies, left his place by the hearth and approached her with his pint in one hand, his stick of whittled wood in the other.

"Evenin', ma'am." He was very tall and thin. His eyes were a watery green, and although his hair was as white as foam, it was thick and abundant. He seemed all bones, but Kit liked the multitude of smile lines around his eyes and his lean, hollow-cheeked face.

"Good evening," she returned.

"Hi!" Mike said.

"Barney Canail," the man offered, stretching out a weathered hand to Kit. At last he smiled, and she liked his smile.

"Kit McHennessy, and my son Mike." She hesitated only a moment. "Won't you join us, Barney?"

He had obviously been expecting the invitation, and he slid in next to Kit, watching Mike with warm eyes from beneath his bushy white brows. "Y'er American, then?"

"Yes, but part Irish," Mike supplied. Kit was beginning to feel that her son's assertion sounded like a tape recording.

Barney stretched his liver-spotted hand across the table, offering Mike the stick of wood.

"This is Irish, too, son. A flute. Ye might enjoy havin' it; the hills can be lonely."

"Oh! He can't accept it—" Kit began, but Barney interrupted her quickly with a tisking sound.

"'Tis nothing, nothing at all. Ye sit about and whittle many a night away at my age. I'd like the boy to have it, if ye don't mind."

"I don't mind, it's just—"

"Oh, Mom, can't I keep it?"

Barney's eyes were clear and kind. Kit shrugged and smiled. "Thank Mr. Canail, then, Mike."

Mike did, enthusiastically.

"Do ye like dogs, son?" Barney asked him.

"I love them, but Mom says we can't have one in the city."

"That's true, Mike, that's true. The city's no place for a dog. But if ye'd like to see a good one, my sheepdog Sam is waiting fer me outside the door. He'd be grateful, for sure, were a boy to rub his ears fer a spell."

"Can I, Mom? Can I?"

"All right, Mike."

He left the table eagerly. Barney Canail shifted to sit across from Kit, then stared directly at her and spoke. "Would ye be the same young Mrs. McHennessy who lost her husband in these parts?"

Kit shivered as she lifted her coffee cup to her lips, then nodded.

"I thought so. I hear tell y'er here to write a book, lass."

"Yes, I am."

Barney nodded slightly, his old eyes on the fire. "Y'know there's been another murder, lass."

This time she managed to sip her coffee. "I know. I read about it in the paper at home."

"I'm the constable for Bailtree, lass."

"Are you? Then you must know Constable Liam O'Grady over in Shallywae."

"Aye, that I do."

"How is he?" Kit asked, remembering Liam O'Grady's kindness to a very distraught young girl.

"Well as a man can be, girl." He looked back at her again. "The town's all well, lass. 'Tis easy to say, for between the two o' us—Shallywae and Bailtree—we haven't a population of so much as two thousand."

Kit laughed. "I didn't know the population was even that large."

He smiled vaguely, but still seemed bothered by something. He took a long draft from his pint, and when she reached into her bag for a cigarette, he quickly struck a match on the table and brought it to the tip of her cigarette.

"We've had media folks by the scores drifting around here lately. Private detectives, authorities from Cork, even as far as Dublin."

"I assume," Kit murmured, "it all has to do with comparisons to that poor girl who had her throat slit all those years ago. I mean, you know, now…another woman, this one strangled…" Her voice trailed away.

"What has surprised me," Barney said, "is that they've never mentioned your husband."

Kit felt her heart quicken. "He…he…they never found any reason to believe that Michael was murdered. The assumption was that he wandered too close to the cliffs. He was a stranger in a strange land, you know."

"Do you believe that?"

Kit held her breath for a long moment. When she exhaled, she felt Barney's astute gaze upon her. "No, I don't," she finally said.

"Neither do I, lass."

It was foolish to be having this conversation with a stranger, Kit thought, even if the stranger was a constable. This was a land of strange legends, where secrets were best kept quiet. But she couldn't help blurting out a question. "Do you believe that Justin O'Niall is a murderer?"

Barney smiled, then chuckled. "Girl, there's few who don't know Justin was the man who befriended ye in y'er troubles, so I'm thinking that you don't believe it's so. But I agree with ye there, lass. Justin is a hot-tempered man, I'll not deny, but one to slit the throat of a defenseless lass? No, 'twouldna be his way."

Kit lowered her voice. "I read that his fiancé was strangled."

"You read right."

"And then thrown into the sea."

"Aye."

"But no one knows who did it?"

"No one who's sayin' so, lass."

Kit sighed. She had hoped that she might learn something. Now she stubbed out her cigarette and leaned across the table. "Barney, is there any possibility that…"

"That what, lass?"

"I don't know," Kit murmured weakly. She had been thinking that Mike had died on Halloween, and that the first murdered girl, Mary Browne, had also died that night. But it was only the first of October now, and Susan Accorn had been killed a month ago.

"Nothing, really. Just a vague idea. I was…just wondering if you thought all this might have something to do with a—"

"A devil cult?" Barney queried.

"I—I guess," Kit muttered, lowering her eyes and feeling a bit ashamed of herself for saying such a thing to a man like Barney.

He, too, leaned across the table. He smiled. "There never were any 'devil' cults in the district, Mrs. McHennessy."

"But I've read—"

"Not devil cults. Long ago, long before Christianity came to the land, the Tuatha de Danann invaded. They were worshippers of the goddess Diana—the moon goddess. The Celts came, and their god of the sea was Mannanan MacLir, and Crom was the thunder god. They were ancient times, lass. The people were primitive. They worried about the sea and the earth, from whose bounty they survived. They made their sacrifices for good fishing, fair sailing, strength in warfare—and for good harvests. The devil came to us as a Christian notion."

Kit listened, a little fascinated, a little impatient. "But there was a rite, I know, here on Halloween. All Hallows' Eve—"

"Aye, lass, that there was. But All Hallows' Eve just combined with an ancient day of homage to the harvest."

"Still…"

"Girl, I know this part of God's earth as I know me own hand. I attend the celebrations each year on All Hallows' Eve. There's a bonfire, lass, a lot of drinking and a lot of eating of homemade specialties. Nothing more." His grin deepened. "The only thing like the ancient times is this: with all the dancing, the excitement—and imbibing of home-brewed Irish whiskey—there will be a multitude of procreation taking place on such a night."

Kit smiled but she still felt uncomfortable.

"Ease yer mind, lass, there's nothing frightenin' that occurs up on the cliffs. The days of the druids are long gone. And, as ye should know if y'er writin' a book, girl, in pagan days, the kings were just."

"I know," Kit murmured. "Actually," she admitted, "I should know much more than I do."

"Then ye should meet with Mrs. McNamara at the Shamus Bookstore in Cork," Barney told her with a smile.

"Mrs. McNamara? I'll do that," Kit promised. She paused, smiling as the waitress refilled her coffee cup. "You sound a bit like a history book yourself, Barney."

His rheumy eyes took on a merry twinkle. "I studied

Irish history afore I turned to the law, girl. Long afore ye were born, lass, I thought I'd like to teach in one o' the big universities. But there's something about our part of the land. It seems to draw us all back here. 'Tis where I was born, 'tis where I'll die. How long are ye stayin', lass?"

"Oh, only a day or so more, I think," Kit murmured.

Barney rose. "That would be a mistake, lass. Ye may not want to know it, but ye've been called back yerself, in a sense. Ye'll not be happy until ye understand yer own past."

Kit smiled weakly, unwilling to dispute him. She placed some money on the table—including a generous tip for her helpful waitress—and allowed Barney to escort her to the door.

Outside, in the crisp night air, Mike was happily scratching away at the sheepdog, Sam, who had all four legs raised euphorically to the star-speckled sky so that Mike could freely rub his belly.

"He's a great dog!" Mike told Barney enthusiastically.

"Aye, he's a good old friend."

"Mike, say thank you to Mr. Canail again, then we'd better get you into bed."

"Thank you, Mr. Canail," Mike said dutifully.

"Nothin' to thank me fer, boy. And I'm just Barney, to young and old alike."

Mike talked all the way back to the inn. He was excited about Barney, and he was excited about Sam the sheepdog. He was, in short, excited about everything.

"Can't we stay here a while, Mom? Can't we, please?"

Her head was pounding. She didn't have the strength for an argument with her son. He was excited but tired, and if she gave him a flat no, he would get teary and keep arguing.

"We'll see, Mike."

After a few minutes she realized that Mike had fallen silent. She gazed at him quickly and saw that he had fallen fast asleep in his seat.

A few minutes later they were turning into Jamie's place. Kit parked the car and decided to try not to waken her son. He weighed about sixty-odd pounds, though, and she was grunting as she lifted him from the seat. He stayed asleep, though.

The front door was open, but old Jamie was nowhere to be seen. Kit made her way up the stairs, struggled for a minute to fit her key into the lock, then went through her room to the little chamber beyond it. A second later she half fell onto the bed with Mike as she tried to lower him to it. She thought for sure that she had awakened him, but all he did was issue a tired little sigh and curl on his side.

Kit pulled off his jacket, shoes and pants, then decided he could sleep quite well in his knit shirt and pulled the covers up to his neck. With a last glance at him, she flicked off the overhead light, backed into her room as she closed the door, and then choked back a scream, her hand flying to her mouth, her eyes widening in fear and astonishment.

She hadn't been able to close her door behind her when she had entered, and now there was a man standing in the doorway again. This silhouette was tall, broad in the shoulders, dominating the room. She caught her breath and kept herself from screaming—because she knew him.

He took a step forward into the light. "All right, Kit. What the devil are you doing here?"

She should have told him it was none of his business,

that she had a right to be anywhere she chose—and that *he* had no right to enter her room unasked. Instead, she clenched her hands behind her back to keep them from shaking. "I'm writing a book—" she began feebly.

"The hell you are!" he exclaimed, so sharply that she took an involuntary step backward.

And then she was angry with herself for allowing him to intimidate her. "Justin, I was hired to write a book, and I really don't give a damn what you think. It's the truth."

"Oh?"

Her heart quickened its beat as he took off his trench coat. It appeared as if he intended to stay a while—invited or not.

He draped his coat over the foot of the bed, pushed up the sleeves of his tweed sweater and stuck his hands in his pockets, staring at her with eyes that were politely questioning—and very cold.

"A book on Shallywae? Or on Bailtree? Such large towns!"

The depth of his sarcasm wasn't lost on her. She also noticed that his accent seemed very strong tonight. She remembered clearly that it had always been that way when he was angry. "Since I had to come to Ireland anyway," she replied coolly, "I promised Mike that I would bring him to see…the cemetery."

"Did you really?"

"Yes, of course!" Her palms were sweating, and she realized that she should order him out of the room. If only she could!

"Haven't you heard?" he asked her. "There's been another murder."

"Yes," she said faintly. "I've heard."

"Get out of Shallywae, Kit."

"This isn't Shallywae. It's Bailtree—"

"Get out, Kit!"

"Are you threatening me, Justin?"

She had been wrong when she had thought he hadn't changed much. He had. His face was gaunt. Lines of strain were etched deeply around his mouth, which now appeared to be nothing more than a thin line. He was very tense. As she watched him, she could see a tic in his jaw and the furious pounding of a vein in his throat.

He took a step closer to her, and she clenched her teeth. She had forgotten that he was such a big man.

She hadn't expected him to react to her one way or another. It had been a long time. She had run out on him, true, but she had left the note. And he must have understood her feelings about what had happened. He shouldn't be so angry *now*, so hostile. He shouldn't be looking at her with his eyes so hard and cold. So merciless. She realized that she didn't know him at all.

"Aye, Kit," he said softly, the whispered caress of his words sending sharp chills cascading down her spine. "Aye, lass, I'm threatening you. Take the boy and leave here."

"I—" It was all she could say. She stood mutely staring at him, waiting.

He moved casually into the room, then stretched out on her bed, never taking his eyes from her. He leisurely laced his fingers behind his head. "Do you think I'm a murderer, then, Kit?"

"No."

"Well, that's a relief," he mused. "If it's the truth." His voice hardened again. "Then why are you here?"

"I told you—"

"A lie."

Anger finally drew Kit from her trembling subjugation. "It isn't a lie, Justin. You're welcome to call my publisher."

"I'll do that."

"You bastard!"

"Get out, Kit."

"What I do or don't do isn't your concern, Justin."

"Isn't it?"

"Of course not."

"But it is," he said gravely.

She laughed, feeling a little hysterical. "How could *I* be in danger, Justin? Wouldn't I be under your protection? Who would dare to assault a friend of the King of the High Hill?" Why didn't she just tell him that she fully intended to leave the next day? she wondered. For that matter, why couldn't she just shut up? Another laugh escaped her—she really was getting hysterical. "Or is it only your friends who are in danger—at least when they've offended you in some way?"

He spat out a furious expletive, then suddenly stood with startling agility. For a moment she felt fear, a weakness, as if she might pass out. His hands were very strong.

She remembered their touch. Inside she seemed to shake and shiver; she didn't know if she was excited or terrified, attracted or repelled. She wanted to run into Mike's room and lock the door between them, and at the same time she wanted to reach out and ease the lines of tension around his eyes, his mouth.

He moved toward her, and she tried to back away. She came up against the door to Mike's room and was forced to brace herself there. She lashed out defensively. "I'm not eighteen anymore, Justin O'Niall! I can't be manipulated! Told to leave—"

"You didn't leave the first time I told you to, if I remember correctly," he reminded her.

"Look," she said, a bit desperately, "Justin, you were there when I needed you, and I thank you for that. Very much."

"Do you really? Everyone else is trying to hang me."

He spoke politely, casually. Kit knew then with an absolute certainty that he was innocent—that he really didn't gave a damn what people thought, because he, too, knew that he was guiltless. But she also knew that he hadn't forgotten the past any more than she had, and that there was something there that he hadn't forgiven, either.

And he was moving closer to her.

"Justin, stop it! You have no right! You're the one who has to get out of here. This is *my* room, and you're interfering in *my* life."

He paused, laughing, and despite herself she was enchanted by the sound. He probably hadn't laughed much lately.

"Aren't you forgetting something, Kit? In your own words, I am the King of the High Hill. I can do anything I choose, and I choose to be here—interfering in your life."

"Justin—"

"You shouldn't have come here, Kit, if you didn't want me to interfere."

"I don't see what—"

"Then you're either blind or stupid, or you think that *I* am."

"I don't—"

"Oh, stop it, will you? This is insane."

He was walking toward her again, and she had nowhere to go. She would have melted into the wood of the door if she could have, but she couldn't, so she simply stiffened her spine against it.

And then he was there, so close that he was almost touching her. He rested his palms against the door on either side of her head and stared into her eyes.

"We have to talk, Mrs. McHennessy."

"We have to talk?" She felt nearly hysterical. "Justin, you're being accused of murder, and you're acting as if you're not even concerned!"

"Kit." He simply said her name, nothing more. Then he shifted his weight, and she felt his warmth running over her like a tide. He was striking. From the power of his eyes to the sensual, self-mocking curl of his lip. His features were as ruggedly chiseled as the cliffs that faced the sea, as proud, as strong. He was and always had been a law unto himself. The O'Niall. And when she had first known him…

He had been the gentlest man she had ever met, sensitive to her pain and to her youth. She'd seen him angry, true, but only against injustice. He'd been ruthless and determined—but only to send her home. He'd never touched her. Never come near her like this.

Until she had touched him…that night.

He ran his knuckles lightly over her cheek.

"Why are you here, Kit?"

"I told you—"

"Why?"

She felt like molten liquid, her knees unable to support her. "Because," she rasped out at last.

"Because of what happened in the cottage?" he asked softly, and if anything, she began to tremble even more violently, because in his gentle tone she heard the same sensitivity she had once clung to for her life.

"Yes."

She didn't know that she had touched him, but suddenly her palms were against the soft wool of his sweater. She could feel his heat beneath the fabric, along with the pounding of his heart. She felt the tension coil in his muscles and the vibrancy of his life.

"Justin, that night... I was—I was drugged."

"On passion?" he queried cynically. "What a wonderful excuse."

"You son of a bitch!" she hissed at him. "I was young and innocent, and you seduced—"

"I beg to differ!" he interrupted curtly. Then his voice filled with softness again, softness and tenderness.

"I'd not have touched you, Kit. I tried to help you. You were young. Too young. But I was no saint; you seduced me."

She felt the blood rush to her face. "Justin, something strange happened that night. Listen to me—I was drugged!" She was convinced that it wasn't imagination or conjecture. It was the truth. Merely being here, seeing this place again, had convinced her of it.

"Something *was* strange that night. Maybe you're right. Maybe—"

"There are no maybes!" Kit asserted furiously. "Oh! Why on earth are we having this conversation?"

"We're going to have lots of conversations, Kit. But not now. Now, my love, you're going to get away from here."

"No one can make me—not even you!"

He stared at her for a moment, a curious mix of emotions flashing through his eyes before the cool shield fell over them once again. "Mrs. McHennessy, I'm no longer so taken by your youth or innocence, no longer beholden to protect you, as it were. In fact, I'm well aware of your lies, and I find myself thinking that no quarter should be granted."

"I don't know what—"

"But you do. You do. For now, though, get out. Go home. Run."

"I don't have to listen to you."

"But you should." His voice was soft again, and his words sounded like a warning.

"Don't threaten me, Justin."

"I'm not threatening you, Katherine. I'm asking you; I'm pleading with you!"

His voice was deep and fascinating; there was more command than pleading in it, despite his chosen words, but something in his tone brought her eyes to his. He watched her in return, and it seemed as if the years passed away. She knew him so well.

He touched her, and she didn't resist. His left hand was at her nape, his fingers in her hair. The callused palm of his right hand was against her cheek, lifting her face.

And then his mouth descended to hers.

There was no denying the power of his kiss. His lips covered hers, and she felt his sweet persuasion. His body was hard, and his muscles rippled beneath her fingers. His tongue moved deeply and intimately into her mouth, filling her with longing all the way to a coiling recess of desire deep inside of her.

She'd kissed other men. But drugs or no drugs, no man kissed like Justin. No man could touch her as Justin could.

She broke away from him at last. She wanted to say something, to curse him for what he'd done—for what he'd made her feel—but she couldn't.

He smiled, and for a moment his dark lashes shadowed

his cheeks. When he gazed at her again she felt weak all over, and then she was gasping for breath, because he had suddenly lifted her and deposited her on the bed, then lain down quickly beside her.

"Justin!"

Tenderness streaked through the darkness of his eyes, and he kissed her again, but this time his lips just brushed against her forehead.

"You grew up to be beautiful, Kit."

"Justin…"

He sighed, started to move, then paused. Kit knew why. She could feel the pressure of his chest against her breasts, and she almost cried out herself, begging him not to move. It was absurd, though. So much stood between them.

He stood up and grabbed his trench coat. "Will you listen to me, please? Kit, go home. For God's sake, go home."

"I can't. I have to know what happened that night. Why I was drugged—"

"I know why," he interrupted quietly, resignation in his voice.

"You do?"

"It was in the tea," he told her.

"You know for sure? You had it analyzed?"

"Strange thing, Kit. The tea disappeared, too," he said. "Now you know, so go home."

"I…can't."

His back was to her. He hesitated, then turned and spoke again. "The cottage on the cliff is empty, Kit. And if you stay, I'll be close. Don't ever doubt it."

"This is absurd!" She tried for lightness. "I'm still amazed that you even remember me."

His expression unreadable, he said, "Oh, I remember you well." His eyes met hers briefly. "Very well. And since you've chosen to return…" He shrugged.

"What are you talking about?"

"Good night, Mrs. McHennessy."

He closed the door sharply behind him as he left.

Kit started shaking, and all she could do was stare stupidly at her trembling hands. Finally she stood up and lit a cigarette, but after only a few puffs she coughed, then crushed it out.

What was she doing here? she asked herself over and over again. The hell with the past. She should just get out. Justin himself had told her to. He didn't want her here. Eight years had passed since she had seen him last, but that last time…

What had she been doing in bed with him? True, she had been drugged, but even so, it had made no sense.

He had agreed with her! she suddenly realized. They *had* been drugged. It had been the tea.

Kit closed her eyes. She didn't want to think. She was tired, and she was going to undress and go to sleep. She had to go to sleep. She had to stop thinking—or go mad.

It was easy to get ready for bed, but sleep was another matter entirely. She was tired, but all she could do was toss and turn, until she finally fell asleep. And then she began to dream.

It was an instant replay of a past that would not be put to rest. She could see the cliff; she could hear the howling of the wind. She dreamed of death, of ghosts, of laughing banshees….

The cottage was there, surrounded by darkness, eerily lit by the strange reflections of a glowing moon. Bagpipes played a mournful note, and the wind rose and fell, rose and fell....

There was firelight. Michael was laughing, teasing her, holding her, pinning her to the bed. Telling her of ancient rites. Of a druid, clothed in a black cloak, of the horned mask of the goat-god, the fertility god...

Then Michael was gone, and the goat-god stood before her in his mask and cape. She wanted to scream, to fight, but she couldn't move from the bed. The goat-god touched her, and to her horror and shame, she wanted him....

And then the goat-god wasn't a goat-god at all, but Justin O'Niall, rising above her in the darkness. She saw his face in the moon glow, determined and satanic, his features taut with naked purpose...and desire.

She wanted him. Wanted his touch against her bare flesh. But when she looked at him again, the mask was back. All she knew was the pressure of his hands on her flesh, lifting her hips, caressing her....

Only his eyes remained visible to her, on fire with the light of the moon. She opened her mouth to scream. She was suffocating...choking....

Kit jerked upright in the darkness.

She was soaked with perspiration, trembling.

The clock at her bedside was ticking steadily away, and the moon was casting a gleam of silver through the window, illuminating her simple room. Not far away, Mike was sleeping in his own bed.

Kit leaned back against her pillow, glancing at the clock. It was three o'clock in the morning.

Eight years wasn't really such a long time. Not such a long time at all.

Chapter 4

The phone was ringing. Kit threw her hand out, barely opening her eyes, as she fumbled for the receiver. It was morning; she could tell by the brightness assaulting her eyes. She was exhausted, as if she hadn't slept at all.

"Hello?" she managed to mumble into the receiver.

"It's Douglas, Mrs. McHennessy. Douglas Johnston."

"Oh! Good morning, Douglas."

"I woke you. I'm sorry. But it's Monday morning, ye know, and I was thinking about your son. I thought you might need some time to yerself to work, and that ye might be willing for the boy to come to school with me."

"Oh," Kit murmured. "Ah…thank you, Doug; that's very thoughtful of you…." Her voice trailed away as she tried to think quickly. She wasn't sure she wanted Mike out of her sight. He was awake, though, and hurtling himself onto her bed.

"Who is it, Mom?"

"Mr. Johnston."

"What does he want?"

"Kit?" Doug's voice came to her over the phone.

"I'm sorry, Doug, excuse me just a second." Kit covered the mouthpiece with her hand and stared at her son. "Would you like to go to Mr. Johnston's school for the day, Mike?"

"Oh, boy!" Mike was off the bed before she could say any more. "I'm getting dressed right now," he called to her, racing back to his own room.

Kit lifted her hand away from the receiver. "Douglas, Mike is very eager to come to school with you. Thank you very much. Where is the school? Shall I drive him?"

"No, no, Mrs. McHennessy. I'll stop by in say, twenty minutes. And I'll have him back to Jamie's by three."

Kit thanked Doug, then hung up. Actually, it was perfect. She could go into Cork and visit the bookstore, then be back by three. After that, she and Mike could go to the cliffs he wanted to see so badly, and still be back by five.

Then she could decide whether to stay another night or not.

"I'm ready, Mom!"

Kit's gaze traveled to the connecting door. She lowered her eyelids with a little smile. Mike *was* ready— after a fashion. His shirttail was half in and half out, and his socks didn't match.

"Mike, you've got a minute or two. Tuck your shirt in right and please—! Dig out some socks that match."

Kit scrambled out of bed, silently swearing at Justin O'Niall. He had cost her a good night's sleep. She washed her face, brushed her teeth and crawled into beige slacks, a woolly sweater and a blue blazer. She quickly put on a minimum of makeup and glanced at her watch, shaking her head with amazement. Only eight minutes had passed since Doug had called.

"Mike, let's get downstairs and see if Jamie can give you something to eat."

Jamie already had breakfast set out on the table in the sunny kitchen. He told Kit that Douglas Johnston had called him, too, to make sure that Mike had something to eat.

"He's a thoughtful lad, our Douglas!" Jamie told Kit proudly.

Mike—who usually ate only a bowl of cereal for breakfast—obediently wolfed down toast, eggs, bacon and a serving of porridge. Then Douglas was at the door, and Kit was thinking again that he'd grown into quite a handsome young man.

She set down her teacup when Douglas entered, and stood to thank him again. She walked outside with him and Mike, noting with approval that Douglas immediately reminded Mike to fasten his seat belt. Kit stood by the driver's side of the car.

"This really is nice of you, Douglas."

"Not at all." His eyes sparkled. "But, I will admit, I'll be much obliged if the lad's mother would consider havin' supper with me, somewhere along the line."

"That would be very nice," she said, for the moment ignoring the fact that she might not be there beyond today. "Oh, Doug! Speaking of mothers, how's yours? I've been terrible not to ask; Molly was so kind to me when—"

"Me ma is doin' just fine, Mrs. McHennessy. She's heard you're in town, and she's anxious to see you. She's still working fer Justin during the day, if ye've a mind to drop in during the afternoon. She'd be anxious to see the lad, too, I know."

Kit nodded, a smile glued to her face, as she stepped away from the car.

"Bye, Mom!" Mike called, waving happily, and she waved in return.

Back inside, she sternly reminded herself that she was writing a book, so she gathered her notepad and pocket tape recorder and started off for Cork.

It took her longer to find the Shamus Bookstore than she had expected, and she could have kicked herself for not getting decent directions. But once she had found it—and met Mrs. McNamara, a pretty young woman with wonderful enthusiasm and energy—she was glad she had made the effort.

"I think we have everything you could want, Mrs. McHennessy," the other woman told her, excited at the prospect of helping someone research a book. She led Kit to the rear wall, where the shelves were overstuffed. "Here are all our books about the early tribal invasions. This one is on the Firbolgs—legends say they came from Greece. Then there were the Tuatha De Danann, the Milesians—the family of Gaels who came. Here are the centuries following the birth of Christ. And there are at least ten different books on the old Brehon laws. Plus we have the Viking invasions, the Norman invasions, the Tudor years, Cromwell's atrocities, James the Second in Ireland and the Battle of the Boyne. Down here are the wars with the British, the potato famine and the forming of the Free State."

"You do have everything!" Kit laughed.

"Just about. Oh, I see a customer up front. Please, browse all you like, and if I can be of any assistance…"

While Mrs. McNamara hurried to the front of the

store, Kit simply stared at all the books. One from each section would start her off very well.

She forced herself to begin with the bottom shelves first. Cromwell, she knew from her college thesis, had come down on Ireland like a deadly storm. She flipped open a book about him and grimaced as she read that he had ordered the burning of the priests' hands before executing the tortured men.

"Not a nice guy," she murmured aloud. She started stacking books on the floor. She chose a beautiful book on the Sinn Fein, the Irish political party, and then one on the Tudor and Stuart influence on Ireland.

How far back did she want to go?

It didn't matter what she wanted to do. She found herself piling up books on the Firbolgs, the Tuatha De Danann and the Milesians. With a stack of about twenty reference books piled in her arms, she walked to the front of the store.

"I'm going to like having you as a customer!" Mrs. McNamara laughed.

"Good," Kit said with a smile. "Because if I get confused, I'll feel free to call you."

Mrs. McNamara told Kit that her name was Julie, and that Kit was welcome to call her anytime. "Where are you staying?"

"In Bailtree, at the moment," Kit said.

"Oh," Julie murmured, a little disapproving. She gazed at Kit over the register as she rang up a book. "You're sure you're not a reporter?"

Kit shook her head. "No, I'm not."

Julie shrugged. "Our small towns can be strange. You should be careful; we've just had a murder."

"Yes, I've heard about it." Julie kept ringing up books,

and Kit remained silent for a moment. "Do you actually think it's dangerous for me to stay in the area?"

Julie shrugged, watching the figures on the register. "Well, they haven't caught the murderer yet."

Kit pretended to study a book cover. "Then you don't seem to think that…the fiancé did it?"

"Justin O'Niall? Never," Julie said steadfastly.

Kit felt herself smiling and she wanted to kick herself. No, she wanted to kick Justin. Why was she so pleased that this young woman believed in his innocence? "Why do you say that?" she finally asked.

"There never was any evidence against him. And his housekeeper swore that he was sitting at his desk the whole time."

"I hear they're comparing the murder to one from a few years ago," Kit said slowly.

"Oh, aye, Mary Browne," Julie said dismissively. "They never did solve that one. And some tried to pin that one on Justin, too. All because she'd been running around saying that baby of hers was his. I tell you, none of us believed that for a second!"

"Why not?"

"Because it just couldn't be," Julie said after a moment. "You'd have to know us better to understand, I suppose," she said ruefully. "It just wouldn't be Justin's style. Oh, he has a temper, and he has an incredible way with women—but he's the O'Niall, you see." She offered Kit a dimpled smile. "He owns almost everything around here, as his father did. And everyone reveres him. It's almost inbred, you see. I know this sounds archaic, but…the people honor the O'Niall, and the O'Niall takes care of the people. Justin is always there for everyone. When the harvest is bad, he feeds those who are starving." She lifted her hands, trying to explain. "If a boy deserves to go on to college, but there's no money—the O'Niall provides."

"It sounds as if he has a champion in you, Julie. I take it that you know him."

"Oh, aye! I was madly in love with him for years. He was everything to me. Tall, dark, handsome, vaguely mysterious and all-powerful. And sexy as hell."

"And you never…?"

Julie laughed. "No, *he* never. And that's why I'm so sure about Mary Browne. Justin has had his flings, but never with the young village lasses. He plays hard, but only with hard players, like that Susan Accorn. Do you see?"

"I think so."

"Anyway, if you're still interested in the murders, take a trip over to the library. They've all the newspaper reports on microfilm."

"Thanks," Kit murmured. "Maybe I'll do that." She picked up her box of books, straining to manage its weight, then nodded to Julie. There was no "maybe" about it; she knew she was going to the library.

The young man at the library wasn't as cordial as Julie McNamara had been. He seemed to disapprove of Americans snooping through Irish newspapers, but whatever his attitude, he still steered Kit in the right direction.

She had no difficulty finding articles on the murder of Susan Accorn, since it was very recent history, and these stories told her much more than the *Times* had. She learned that Susan Accorn's body had been naked when found, but the coroner had reported that there had been no sign of rape or sexual abuse. There was talk of the family's fury, and of their determination to send private detectives in to ascertain if the Irish were really doing all they could.

It was apparent that the Irish authorities had resented such an insult. The Accorns had almost accused Constables Liam O'Grady of Shallywae and Barney Canail of Bailtree of being bumbling idiots, determined to obstruct justice rather than uphold it.

The words on the microfilm blurred before Kit's eyes. It seemed as if the reporters really did want to hang Justin, but she knew he was innocent, just as Julie did. In that case, though, someone else had to be a murderer.

Kit began searching through the files again, watching the past slip by until she had gone back eight years.

Michael's death was there in black and white. "American Man Plunges to Death from Cliff." It was a sad story, telling about Michael's yearning to come to Ireland and how it had caused his tragic demise. Kit was mentioned as the "grieving child-widow."

She didn't stare at the story for long; it hurt too badly.

She went on until she found all the articles on Mary Browne's murder. Understandably, she hadn't paid much attention at the time.

She inhaled sharply and held her breath when she came to the description of the dead girl's body. Mary Browne had also been found naked—but once again, though her throat had been slit from ear to ear, there had been no evidence of rape or sexual abuse. No motive had ever been found for her murder, and although the case was still officially open, reading between the lines assured Kit that the police had decided she had been murdered by a roving lunatic. No doubt the man was behind bars in an asylum now, locked away for other crimes.

Kit glanced at her watch and saw that the time had

passed quickly. If she didn't get moving, she wouldn't be back when Douglas dropped Michael off after school.

Despite his rather abrupt attitude, Kit went to thank the young librarian who had helped her. While they spoke, she noticed that a small crowd had gathered at the far end of the library, behind a display wall.

"What's going on?" Kit asked.

"We've a few things on loan from the museum in Dublin," he replied absently as he checked in a pile of books. "You might want to have a look, if you're interested in history. One of the local ladies is giving a bit of a tour."

She knew she was already running late, but the lure was too strong. Kit decided she would take a quick glance, then hurry back to Bailtree.

The crowd was grouped around a young woman who was describing each article on display. In one case there was a mannequin with fierce features elaborately painted on its face. The clothing was obviously authentic, shredded and torn by time, and the figure carried a huge battle-ax, which turned out not to be surprising, since Kit quickly ascertained that this was intended to be the great Brian Boru.

Kit forgot the time and listened with interest, following along with the group.

There were an assortment of figures dressed in remnants from the ages. Ladies from the eight-hundreds; royal princesses of Tara, decked in gold trim and furs. All sorts of additional items, like combs, purses and hairpieces, were on display, as well. It was wonderful. Kit dragged her notebook out of her bag and began jotting things down. Then the crowd shifted, and she looked up.

She felt as if a cold breeze had suddenly risen. The guide's voice faded, and all Kit could see was the last display case, at the end of the corridor, isolated and alone.

There was a dummy, she was certain, beneath the clothing, but no features had been painted on it. They weren't necessary. The figure was wrapped in a cloak, which had been faded brownish green by time, but undoubtedly it had once been pitch-black. The figure wore a mask, with horns like those of a huge goat. It was the same tarnished color as the cloak, but little splotches of red and gold remained to hint at how it had once been painted. The eyes were empty, slanted pits, hollow caverns that were the essence of something evil. Of promised malevolence...

She had seen a picture of the goat-god once, in Michael's book. And in her nightmares she had seen him a thousand times since.

But here, now, he seemed so real! She started to tremble, feeling her throat constrict. A shaft of cold seemed to run along her spine.

"...from two hundred B.C. through the early centuries after Christ's birth. The goat was, to our ancestors, a creature of fertility. Fertility for the harvest, without which they could not survive. Fertility for their race. Prisoners of war were often used as sacrifices, but to be the bride of the goat-god was considered a great honor. The chosen woman would bear a child who would become the 'god' for the succeeding generation. That her own blood was to be shed meant little—the sacrifice of her life to feed mother earth and the child it must cherish was also a privilege. Nor were such rites unique to our shores...."

The young woman was still talking, but Kit didn't want to hear any more. She dropped her pencil, but she didn't even notice as she walked hurriedly away from the library.

By the time she reached her car she felt as if her sanity had come back to her. It had been ridiculous to be so frightened by a costumed mannequin. Okay, so she'd had a few nightmares about such a mask, but she had a vivid imagination, which, it seemed, was determined to run amok when she slept. It all made perfect sense, psychiatrically speaking. She had been very young when Michael died, and just before his death he had been talking about ancient rites and sacrifices. Of course that conversation would be embedded somewhere deep in her subconscious.

And, embarrassing as it was to admit, she had felt a deep sexual attraction the first time she had seen Justin O'Niall on the cliffs. She'd taken classes in human behavior. It had been unacceptable to her moral sense to recognize that attraction for what it was, so she had made it into something diabolical to excuse what had happened.

It wasn't until she had almost reached the old farmhouse that she was struck by another thought. She might have been young, she might have been confused, hurt and alone, but even taking into consideration Justin's care and kindness, as well as his electric attraction, she had loved Michael deeply. No matter what her attraction to Justin had been, she would never have jumped into bed with him at that point, or even a year later. She had been drugged. She didn't know why; nothing she could think of made any sense. But it had happened. She knew it— and now she knew that Justin knew it, too.

She was late.

Kit saw Douglas's car parked by the roadside. She parked beside it and hopped out, then rushed to the farmhouse. But before she could enter, she heard laughter coming from the back. Mike's laughter. She hurried around the house.

Mike and Douglas were there, and so were Jamie and Barney Canail. Mike was laughing because Douglas was on the ground, struggling to retrieve a rubber ball from Sam the sheepdog's teeth.

Barney Canail saw her first. "Afternoon, Mrs. McHennessy," he called out.

She waved to the group, then started walking toward them apologizing. "I'm so sorry I'm late. The time—"

"Kit McHennessy!" Douglas laughed, his grin charmingly boyish. "Y'er not but five minutes late, and havin' Mike here has been the pleasure of our day!"

"Aye, old Sam's day, fer sure," Barney agreed, bending to scratch the dog's ears. "Was yer trip profitable?" he asked.

As Kit gazed into his watery green eyes, she wondered if the question meant more than the obvious. It was almost as if he had been expecting her to find something out. Something that concerned a lot more than history.

"Very profitable. Thanks so much for the tip." Maybe Barney had known that Julie McNamara would send her to the library, she thought, and maybe he had known that the goat-god would be on display.

She was letting her imagination run wild. There was very little she could do about her dreams, but she refused to think so hysterically in broad daylight.

"Mike," she asked, "how did you like school? What did you study?"

"A lot of math. I was good at it. Really. Ask Mr. Johnston!"

Kit ruffled his hair and smiled at Douglas.

"He was an excellent student. The others loved havin' him. He taught the class all about New York City."

"Well, now that yer back, lass," Barney Canail said,

grimacing a little as he struggled back to his feet, "Jamie and me were thinkin' of headin' in fer a pint."

"Mom's taking me to the cliffs," Mike told them.

"'Tis a beautiful day fer a walk," Douglas said. "Ye'll have a grand time, boy." He turned to Kit again. "Would you like me to pick him up again tomorrow mornin'?"

"I…that's a lot to ask of you."

"I don't mind. 'Tis no trouble. Really."

For a minute Kit felt uncomfortable, as if control was slipping from her grasp. As if an unseen force were sinking cold talons into her shoulders. Then she realized how ridiculous that was. "Thank you, Douglas. That would be great," she said.

"Then I'll see ye agin in the mornin', lad," Doug said cheerfully. He nodded to Kit, waved to Jamie and Barney and whistled as he walked around the corner of the house.

Mike began tugging at her arm. "Can we go to the cliffs now, Mom? You promised."

"Yes, Mike, we can go now." She glanced at Barney and Jamie. Were they watching her peculiarly? "I guess we'll see you in town later," she murmured.

"Aye, most likely. Have a nice time, now," Barney said.

Her smile felt strained as she waved again and followed Douglas Johnston's trail around the house. His little Datsun was already gone.

Mike crawled eagerly into the car, chattering away about the kids at the school. Kit answered him in monosyllables, which were the only replies he seemed to need.

The drive seemed short—too short. And no amount of logic could keep her heart from feeling heavy.

Nothing had changed. Nothing.

Down the rutted and twisted road stood the cottage, whitewashed, thatch-roofed. Wildflowers were there in abundance, and, beyond the cottage, high grass and bracken grew in passionate disorder, waving and flattening with the wind like an ocean of green and mauve and shimmering blue. Far to the left and right, sweeping downward into the fertile valleys, were the forests, shadowed, intriguing, beckoning her to come explore their secrets.

Where the greenery ended, the cliffs began. High, sheer, strewn with rocks and pebbles, they dropped to the sea below. The sky, which was a dismal gray and filled with capricious clouds, stretched above. Kit knew that she could look down and watch the sea pounding against the rocks. The spray would rise, crystalline, catching whatever sun escaped through the roiling clouds. The roar of the waves would rise to mingle with the whine of the wind; seabirds would shriek, and it would be as it had been eight years ago.

As it had been centuries ago.

Kit hadn't realized that she had already parked the car along the road that led to the cottage. She was sitting with her hands folded together, clamped hard in her lap, and she was shivering. She had forgotten how much colder it could be along the cliffs.

"Mom?"

She glanced at Mike, who was staring at her with curiosity and concern.

"Can we get out now?"

"Sure. I was just…cold. Are you sure your jacket is warm enough?"

"Yeah. I'm plenty warm."

Kit nodded and stepped outside, vaguely hearing Mike's door slam shut. She hadn't closed her own door.

She was hanging on to it, staring out at the cottage—and the cliffs beyond.

It had been nighttime when she had come here that first time. The wind had been vicious, the sky pitch-black, except for a full moon that cast glowing light and mysterious shadow. It was a place that seemed to have a life of its own, sometimes lonely and forlorn and brooding, sometimes wild and menacing, as if it were waiting to trap the unwary....

Watching...

Always she had a sense of being watched, as if the rocks and the distant trees had eyes, as if they lived and breathed and watched her every move....

Kit gave herself a little shake. She was giving a personality to a pile of rock, and that was ridiculous. She had never been afraid of the cliffs. She had walked along them often after Michael had died.

She closed her door and started walking now, shoving her hands into the pockets of her pants. "You coming?" she asked Mike.

He nodded and hurried to catch up with her. She slipped an arm around his shoulders as they walked.

"You've got to promise to stay away from the edge," she said lightly, just like any mother warning her child to be careful.

His answer came with a little sigh—any child's response to a parent who seemed to think that being a child meant you had no intelligence.

Mike pulled up the hood of his jacket. "It's windy here," he said.

"Yes, it is," Kit agreed. She glanced at the sky. She could see the clouds moving, seeming to consume the open sky. It would be dark much sooner than she had expected. The clouds were definitely the warning of a coming storm.

"Can we go into the cottage?" Mike asked curiously.

"No. I'm sure it's locked."

"Oh," Mike said. She didn't know if he was disappointed or not.

They walked past it, and then everything seemed to be exactly as it had been eight years earlier. Because she could see the tall silhouette of a man standing on the grassy section of the hill that led to the treacherous rise of rock.

Her heart skipped a beat; her footsteps paused for a fraction of a second. But then she kept walking, because she realized that she had almost been expecting him to be there, that she would have been disappointed if he hadn't been.

"It's the man from the cemetery," Michael murmured excitedly.

"I know," Kit said.

Justin turned then, aware that they were coming. His feet were planted firmly apart; he was a man who had long known the cliffs and the wind, and who challenged them with little thought. His dark hair was slashed across his forehead by the wind, and his hands, too, were shoved into his pockets. He stood very still, watching her approach. The woolen scarf he had wrapped around his neck drifted about him, floating on the wind, then falling again to lie against his mauve sweater.

His eyes were on Kit as she neared him, his gaze unabashed and offering no apology. Only when she stood practically in front of him did his gaze flicker and fall to Mike.

"Hello, Mr. Michael Patrick McHennessy. Have you come to see our cliffs, then?"

Mike nodded eagerly.

Justin's eyes rose to Kit's once again. There was a questioning look in them, and a certain patient amusement. "Mind if I walk along with you?" Though he dropped his gaze and asked the question of Mike, Kit knew it was directed to her.

"Mind? No!" Mike said.

Justin placed a hand on Mike's shoulder, and the two of them started walking ahead of her. She followed, staying about three feet behind.

She heard Justin tell Mike that the rocks were the very type known to house the "little people," or leprechauns.

"Have you always lived here?" Mike asked Justin.

"Not always, but mostly."

A few minutes later they were at the edge of the cliff. They could see the water below, rushing and swirling, battering and lashing rocks, receding and leaving little pools that sparkled in the weak sunlight passing through the clouds.

Kit was glad to see that Justin had positioned Mike several feet from the edge at a section where the rock sloped gently, instead of dropping off abruptly. He warned Michael that the rocks were known as the Devil's Teeth.

"I know," Mike said solemnly. "They killed my father."

Justin didn't reply. Kit backed uneasily away from the two of them, her eyes on the ground, but she felt Justin watching her. She didn't need to see him to know that he was staring at her.

Justin bent and collected a handful of pebbles. He

tossed one over the edge. It fell and was lost in the tumult below. Then he handed the pebbles to Mike.

Mike grinned with sheer pleasure, and Justin stepped back to stand beside her. He looked at her, and she thought she saw a hint of tenderness in his eyes. She knew that he was searching for the changes that the years had wrought. Curiously, she didn't mind; she felt as if she was coming to know him again, as if the time that had changed them and made them strangers was fading until it was gone.

"I've been here half the day, waiting," he told her.

She tried to shrug casually. "If you wanted to see me, you could have just called."

"I did. You were out."

"I went into Cork." Kit hesitated, and when she spoke her voice was both defiant and reproachful. "I *am* writing a book."

He grinned and deep creases etched themselves around his eyes and mouth. "I believe you."

"Did you call my publisher?" She couldn't keep herself from asking the question, but she couldn't keep herself from smiling, either.

He didn't answer her right away. Instead he sat down in the long grass, plucking a piece and chewing it idly. With a little sigh of exasperation, Kit sank down beside him.

She felt her heart contract with pain. He had told her to go home, yet he had also told her that they needed to talk. Did he suspect the truth? She felt as if he were some sort of predator—and she his only half-suspecting prey.

"Did you?" she repeated irritably.

"Well, now, I don't know who your publisher is, do I?"

"I *am* doing a book on Ireland!"

"I'm sure you are."

"About ancient superstitions that linger to the present day!" she snapped.

He was still smiling as the wind ran riot about them and began its banshee moan. "Well, then, All Hallows' Eve should interest you. You can attend the…pagan rites."

"Stop it, Justin!"

He frowned. "What's the matter with you? I was merely teasing. It's simply a party."

"Is it?"

"Of course."

"Oh, Justin…" She sighed impatiently. "Don't you see?"

"What am I supposed to see?"

"Justin, you said yourself that the tea was drugged—"

"Aye, it was, Kit. But I don't see any evil in it."

She sprang to her feet. "You don't? Well, you weren't the one with such a horrible thing on your conscience."

"It bloody well was on my conscience!" he retorted, and then he was standing, too, facing her in anger. His smile tightened as his blazing eyes narrowed. "And there was nothing horrible about it. The moral issue aside, I had a damn good time!"

"What are you arguing about?"

Mike's voice broke through Kit's anger, and she spun around, stunned that she could have forgotten how close he was. "Nothing," she assured him quickly.

"And everything!" Justin said laughing. He ducked down to Mike and grabbed his shoulders.

"How would you like to go to a castle for dinner?"

"Oh, boy!" Mike said excitedly.

"We're not going!" Kit snapped.

"Oh, but you are," Justin told her. Mike turned around to stare at her hopefully, and Justin kept his gaze steadily on her. His hands were still resting on Mike's shoulders—as if he had the power to take the boy away from her.

I should tell him to jump in a lake! Kit thought furiously. But she hesitated, her throat dry. "You might have asked me first," she finally said coldly.

"We can go! Oh, boy! Oh, boy!" Delighted, Mike started running through the high grass.

Justin shrugged, undaunted by her reproach. "Molly wants to see you. She's staying for dinner herself." He hesitated for a moment, then said softly, "You have to come, Kit."

She lowered her eyes, her palms damp, her heart beating too quickly. There was a power here. A power that had drawn her back after eight years. The power of the hills and the cliffs. The power of the wind, whistling, crying, whispering in soft tones that she should stay…

The answers were here…and Justin was here.

She looked into his eyes. They were very dark and had taken on the cast of the gray-clouded sky. Like the forests around her, they compelled her with their secret depths. And he knew exactly what she was thinking. The curl of his lip betrayed his amusement.

"I've been wanting to see Molly," she said with an exaggerated sigh of resignation. "And I suppose we have to eat dinner somewhere."

Justin laughed. "Is that a yes? Well, thank you so much, Mrs. McHennessy. How gracious."

He turned and started walking. Swearing under her breath, Kit followed him.

Justin caught up with Mike, and as they walked he asked about the airplane ride, and he listened intently when Mike told him proudly that he had already spent a day in an Irish school.

Justin stopped when they reached the cottage. He stuck a hand into his pocket, then took Kit's hand and pressed something into her palm.

She stared into her hand. He had given her a key.

"It's to the cottage," he told her. She met his eyes again. He was staring at her intently, and an inner chill gripped her. Then something hot and mercurial seemed to quiver along her limbs. He had told her to go, yet he was trying to get her to stay....

"The cottage?" she mumbled stupidly.

"Yes," he said flatly. "I own it, you know."

No, she hadn't known. "Why not? You own everything else," she muttered. She looked quickly around for Mike. He was already heading toward the car, so she lowered her voice and said vehemently, "But you don't own me, Justin O'Niall."

He caught her arm, pulling her against him when she would have followed her son. "Don't I, Kit? Don't I own just a piece of you?"

The deep, husky whisper was filled with insinuation. Despite herself, Kit was trembling as she jerked herself away.

She watched Justin join Mike at the car. The two of them had their heads together and were talking animatedly, seemingly unaware of her existence. Kit hugged herself as the wind rushed around her, taking her breath away, seeming to grip her with cold gray fingers.

She pressed her hands against her cheeks. She had thought she was mature and sophisticated, but she was still no match for Justin O'Niall. Not for his strength, nor his will, nor his determination.

Nor his appeal to her senses—and her soul.

Chapter 5

"So," Justin said at last, a slight smile curving his lips as he leaned back in his chair, striking a match to his cigarette and staring at her over the flame, "what have you been doing for the last eight years?"

Kit sipped her coffee. He might have been asking her what she had done last week. "Not much," she murmured, shrugging in response to the cynical hike of his brow. She lowered her eyes, curious that she could be so comfortable here. His home was a castle in the true sense of the word. He'd told her once that it had originally been nothing more than earthworks, then a wooden defense post; then, after the Viking invasions and the Norman conquest of England, the people had rebuilt it in stone. It was small, as castles went, and the arrow slits had been enlarged to make normal windows. The outer walls were nothing but rubble, but the great hall remained, and there were three towers with wonderful old curving stairways. Kit was certain that Justin had spent a small fortune remodeling the place to include all the contemporary comforts: brand-new kitchen, central heating, an intercom system—but then, if Justin was as famous as Robert claimed, he probably had an income that could handle it easily.

It was a wonderful place, she realized. She had adored it eight years ago, and she felt the same way now. She wondered if Susan Accorn had been enchanted by it.

The great hall had changed very little. The dining room table, with its carved high-backed chairs, still sat on a low dais looking out over the rest of the room. In front of the fireplace were the same chairs where she had once sat with Doctor Conar, Liam O'Grady, Molly and Justin, when they had told her that she had to decide what to do with Michael's body.

Kit trembled and set her cup down. This room brought back memories, but it was nice to be here. The fire in the hearth warmed her, and the whiskey sours Justin had made before dinner had softened the rough edges of her nervous system. Molly was giving Mike a tour of the house, and Kit and Justin were alone, acting curiously like old friends who had been apart for a long time.

"Kit? Are you with me?"

"Yes. Yes. The last eight years," she murmured, leaning back. "I went to college. I graduated. I went to New York. I started writing."

"Sounds very simple for eight years," Justin commented.

Kit shrugged. "It was a simple life."

"You forgot to mention that you had a child," he reminded her.

"Oh, yes. Mike. Well, I suppose that's obvious," Kit murmured, suddenly fascinated by her coffee cup. She looked up at Justin and smiled. "Mike made my life very simple. I worked, and I took care of him."

"You never remarried." It was a statement, not a question.

"No." Kit hesitated. It was her turn to ask questions now. "What about you?" she murmured at last.

"Oh, I murder someone every few years," he said dryly.

"Justin!" Kit snapped. "That's not amusing!"

"But that's what you meant, isn't it?"

His accent was growing stronger, a sure sign of simmering anger. Too bad, Kit decided irritably. She wasn't going to watch every word she said—especially since no one ever received any answers that way.

"All right," she said evenly. "Maybe that *was* what I meant to say. Want to talk about it?"

"Not particularly."

"Justin…"

"I said not particularly. But if you've got questions, go ahead and ask them. God knows I've answered enough already."

"Well, it does seem strange," Kit said defensively. "Your fiancée has been dead just over a month, but you hardly appear to be grieving."

He watched her for a long moment, his features expressionless. Then his eyes narrowed slightly. "I remember a certain time, Mrs. McHennessy, when your husband hadn't been dead all that long, but you certainly weren't behaving like a woman in mourning."

The blood rushed to her face, and her palm itched to

slap the patrician arrogance from his features. "You knew damn well that I was grieving!"

He shrugged, lifting a hand absently. "Well, it was a long time ago, wasn't it?"

She should have said something dismissive, should have shrugged off the incident. Instead, her words carried a defensive tone.

"I was drugged, and you've admitted that you know it. I'd never have—"

He was suddenly leaning across the table, his eyes dark and probing. "Wouldn't you?" he asked in a harsh whisper.

"I—" Her voice broke, and her face flamed. She felt as if he could look through her, as if he sensed the devastating sensual effect he had on women. On her. "No!" she snapped.

It might have been the best joke Justin O'Niall had heard in ages. His laughter rang out loud and true, and the smile that remained to light his eyes was open and honest.

"I don't know who you think you are," she told him flatly, lowering her voice as she remembered that her son was somewhere around, possibly within earshot.

Justin brought his sparkling eyes close to hers. "Don't you?" he asked musingly. "Imagine. You ran away, and I let you go. I should have scoured the earth for you."

She didn't like his whimsical tone; she couldn't tell if he was mocking her or not. "I was very young, and very hurt," Kit told him, trying very hard to keep her voice low and her temper in check. "You were older, experienced, and well aware that something wasn't right. You—"

She broke off, because he was laughing again. She had never seen such genuine amusement.

"Kit! When you find a very attractive woman smiling

away in a bubble bath, as naked as the day she was born, it's difficult to ignore the situation. But I did. Until…" He shrugged. "Still, I was above reproach for a laudable amount of time. Then you threw your arms around me. You dragged me down. You insisted."

"But…" she said weakly.

"I think it's rather like hypnotism, don't you? If it wasn't something you wanted to do…"

"Justin!"

"Well, there won't be any drugs this time, will there?"

The question was soft, but there was still a trace of laughter in his voice, and Kit still had no idea if he was serious or not.

"There won't be a next time."

"I think there will—and so do you."

Her throat felt suddenly dry. She lowered her eyes, afraid that he would see that she was protesting too much. Protesting the truth.

"Justin," she said softy, sitting very still, "listen to me, please. I don't deny that I felt an attraction to you." God help me, she added in silence, I still do. "But I loved Michael very much. I wouldn't have betrayed his memory like that—and I think you know it. And that's why I ran, Justin. I was too young, too confused—too everything—to deal with the situation. I'm still confused. Why would someone do such a thing? Why would someone drug my tea?"

He reached across the table, and his fingers played gently over her palm. "Kit, I'm sure no one meant to harm you."

"Molly gave me the tea."

He nodded, obviously not surprised. Molly had treated Kit like a daughter all during that sad time, and had greeted her tonight with tears. "Molly would never hurt you. She adored you."

"I know that. But maybe there was something in the tea meant just to relax me."

"I thought of that. I even asked her about it, but she said she knew nothing."

"And you let it rest?"

"Aye, Kit, I did. No one meant you harm. Someone meant only to ease your spirit."

"Oh, Justin, you're so blind!"

He hesitated, then stared at her so piercingly that she felt a cowardly quivering begin to take root deep in her abdomen. "No, I'm not, Kit. I keep telling you that."

"Justin, you should be concerned—"

"I am concerned."

"About the murders!"

"I'm hardly involved, am I?"

"Justin, what happened with your fiancée? I've heard that you had a terrible fight just before she was murdered."

He wasn't looking at her anymore. He was gazing across the hall at the fire. He answered distractedly. "Aye, that we did."

"Why? What was it about? Did she want to break the engagement? Or did you? What was going on?"

He glanced at her sharply. "You'd do just fine were you to join the police, Mrs. McHennessy."

She didn't flush, and she didn't back down. "Justin, please, answer me."

He shrugged. "Why not? I've answered everyone else. We fought over the newspaper."

"The newspaper?"

He looked at her steadily, a rueful smile playing over

his mouth. "You don't understand my lack of undying grief, do you? Of course it hurt when I heard Susan was dead. But I never asked her to be my wife."

Kit shivered at the familiarity of it all. Hadn't she once heard him deny that he had known Mary Browne intimately?

"But you were…you were…"

"Involved with her, yes. I met Susan in London, while I was working on a project there. She was a very lovely woman. I was attracted to her."

"But you weren't interested in marriage. Just…an affair."

He laughed. The sound was brittle, like crackling leaves. "You're thinking like a soap opera. Was I to spend my life pining for you to return? I never married because I never met the woman with whom I wished to spend my life. And yet, I'm fond of the weaker sex."

"Would you stop that, please?"

"What?"

"Sounding so… Irish!"

He looked startled, and then he smiled. "You don't mean 'Irish,' do you?"

"No! I mean like some ancient lord and master. But please excuse me. Go on."

"All right. As I was saying, I met her in London. We were together frequently, and I asked her to come here and spend a week with me. We arrived separately—I had to stop in Dublin overnight on business. I saw the announcement of my engagement in the paper, and when I got home, Susan was in the process of refurbishing my house. She had also acquainted herself with a number of the townspeople."

"And?"

"We had a fight. A serious one." He grimaced. "I liked Susan. She was fun; she had a passion for life. But she could also be cruel, vindictive—and spoiled. She liked to play with people. I think I was part of a collection to her. The idea of adding an Irishman to her string of suitors appealed to her. She'd been dating a Belgian trapeze artist before she met me—haven't you read that anywhere?"

"No, I hadn't," Kit said. "But I didn't think the papers said everything anyway." She stared into his eyes. "That's why I'm asking you."

"The American way," he said, a little bitterly. "Give a man a fair shake."

"If that's the way you want to see it."

He shrugged. "Well, then, you've gotten your answers. Susan couldn't believe that a man wouldn't choose to fall down on his knees in gratitude if she deigned to marry him. She was also quite convinced that men made more than adequate punching bags. She slapped me, leaving a couple of very nice scratches along my cheek."

"And?" Kit queried, swallowing hard.

"And later she was murdered. But not by me."

Kit looked at him steadily, but she said nothing.

"Do you believe me?" He still sounded amused.

"Yes. I—I wouldn't be here if I didn't." Was that the truth? Or was she there only because he had asked her, because he had beckoned? Would she follow him blindly to the brink of death just because he possessed such a raw—and fatal?—attraction? She didn't want to think so. She wanted to believe that she was interested only in the truth.

He smiled, lowering his eyes.

"So who murdered her?" she asked at last.

An oath of irritation escaped him. "How would I

know? Do you think the murderer is going to come to me with a full confession? Maybe the Belgian trapeze artist—I don't know. Susan was capable of acquiring enemies."

"Justin! How can you ignore things? Another girl was murdered eight years ago, on the same night Michael died."

He sighed. "And you're quite certain the two are associated?"

"Yes, I am—and so is half the world."

He was silent for a moment. Then he said coldly, "You should go home, Kit."

"You just gave me the key to the cottage." He didn't reply, so she went on. "Why didn't you ever tell me that you owned the cottage?"

He shrugged. "What difference does it make? I own half the land around here."

It makes a difference, she wanted to scream. It makes a tremendous difference.

Kit shivered suddenly. The wind outside had risen abruptly, and now it sounded like a hundred women moaning in the night. Here along the cliffs, where the air never seemed to be still, it was easy to see how legends about banshees had grown.

She didn't believe in banshees, but she couldn't escape the chill as she gazed at Justin. His features had been cast into shadow by the flickering blaze in the hearth, and his eyes were dark…bottomless.

Kit swallowed fiercely. She didn't believe in banshees or spirits. But something was going on.

"More coffee?" Justin asked.

She nodded. She needed something warm.

He walked around to the coffeepot, which had been

left at the far end of the table. Kit watched him as he moved. His hands looked very strong. In general, he was a powerful man, well over six feet, trim but broad-shouldered, and fit. Physically he could have performed any or all of the murders.

She jumped when his hand came down on her shoulder, and she couldn't help the fear in her eyes when she looked up at him.

She saw his features tauten, his mouth compress, but he said nothing as he set the steaming cup down in front of her. Then he refilled his own cup and sat down again. His eyes were cold when they fell on her. "You can run again…if you're frightened."

"I'm not afraid of you, Justin." Was she lying? She didn't know.

His look said clearly that he doubted her words. Kit reached nervously for a cigarette. She watched him as he lit it for her, then tried to put her nebulous feelings into words.

"Justin, you have to be concerned. Two women have been murdered, and I believe that Michael was murdered, too. He wasn't stupid. I just can't see him falling off a cliff."

"There was an autopsy, Kit. There was no sign that he had fought with anyone. His death has a perfectly logical explanation. He wandered out on the cliffs. It was dark. He didn't know the area, and he fell."

"I'm not the only one who thinks he was murdered," Kit murmured resentfully.

"Oh? Who else?"

She probably shouldn't have spoken, but she met Justin's eyes squarely. "Constable Barney Canail from Bailtree believes the same thing."

"Does he now?" He appeared to be only vaguely interested.

Kit rose, stubbing out her cigarette, then carried her coffee cup as she wandered over to the mantel. She stared into the fire as she spoke again. "Haven't you noticed that it's only women associated with you who are murdered?"

When he replied, his voice rang out harshly behind her. She was startled to see that he, too, had risen and followed her.

"You've just told me that your husband was murdered, and he wasn't a woman 'associated' with me. If it's accusing me of murder you are, then do it and be done with it."

For a second, she couldn't speak. "I'm not accusing you of anything, Justin; I just can't understand how you can be so unconcerned."

"Unconcerned? By God, woman, you do sound daft! My home's been prey to every constable, sheriff and bobby this side of the Atlantic, not to mention private detectives and sniveling reporters. I'm concerned, all right. I'm just a wee bit weary, that's all. I never did see your husband alive, Mrs. McHennessy. And I had no association at all with young Mary Browne. I had no help for anything the girl chose to say. Now, if you think I'm a madman, the door is open."

Kit swallowed and turned back to the fire, watching the flames dancing before her. "I don't think you're a madman. But someone is."

"That's why you should go home."

"Justin," Kit began a little weakly, "I think it has something to do with All Hallows' Eve. That's when Mary's throat was slit. That's when—"

"Give it up, won't you? All Hallows' Eve is nothing but a picnic in the hills. A bonfire. Men play their pipes, and they drink themselves out cold. The time is coming; you'll be able to see for yourself. We Irish are the ones who are supposed to be hung up on the old legends, not you Americans. You've been reading too much, girl. Seeing too many movies."

That could be true. She couldn't deny that the subject had preyed on her mind, so much so that she saw demons where men stood, and was ready to find evil in a village of kindly farmers.

She turned to face him, feeling frustrated. "Justin, don't you understand? You'll never be in the clear—not until the murderer is found."

He ran his hand through his hair. "Kit, don't you think we've been through it all a hundred times? Liam and old Barney and I, turning it over and over in our minds. There aren't any answers. None that we can find, anyway." He grinned at her. "Not unless the ancient druids are risin' up from the earth."

"That's not funny, Justin."

"Ah, surely, Kit, you canna take such things seriously."

"Then this murderer will never be caught."

"Not unless he strikes again."

"Do you think he will?"

Justin's eyes narrowed. "You're asking me? There are some as think I should know."

"Why did you give me the key to the cottage? Why, when you've already told me to leave?"

"If you're going to be here, I want you near. I told you that. I can reach the cottage in ten minutes from here."

"But do you *want* me to stay, Justin? Or to go?"

He shrugged, but his gaze never faltered. "I would rather you left—for your own safety. You see," he said lightly, mockingly, "this time I *will* find you."

Why? The word seemed to scream inside her mind, but she swallowed it back, because she didn't have the nerve to ask the question.

Kit watched him as he came toward her. It was a matter of only a few steps, and then he was standing before her, his hands on her shoulders. Her bones felt very delicate beneath them. She looked up into his eyes, so full of secrets, and the flames danced and crackled, sending shadows over his features. Her heart was beating quickly, but she couldn't have said whether she was frightened or excited.

He smiled slowly, a secret smile, a little bit arrogant, a little bit amused. He knew the effect he had on her, he knew that he frightened her, and sometimes that amused him. He also knew that she was attracted to him, and that, too, amused him.

Kit felt humiliatingly weak. If he had asked her into that bed that minute, she would have obliged him, then wondered later why she had.

"I *think* you should go," he told her. "I *want* you to stay."

Kit cast her head back, cocking it slightly. "You should be a grieving man, Justin," she said softly.

"I wasn't in love with Susan."

"Nor are you in love with me."

The corner of his mouth lifted in what might have been a wistful smile. "I might have been. Had you stayed."

She needed to answer him. To say something that would break the spell he had cast over her. Justin was a man who needed no illusions. She was certain that he could meet any attractive woman, assess her, and decide in moments if he wanted to make love to her or not. For him, it would be that simple. The message would be in his eyes, and Kit was certain that most women would respond to it.

But she didn't want to be just one more in a long string of casual lovers. She didn't want to have a fascination with him that bordered on obsession. But she did, and she could only stare at him when he spoke.

"Do y'know, Kit, I fell a little bit in love with you that first night I saw you. You had on that gauzy shift, and your hair was flying about you like waves of silk. I knew ye'd just come from some man's bed, and that ye'd liked it there, and I felt an envy in my heart for that man. You were so fresh and innocent. I wanted to touch you then. And I wanted to touch you when I finally did, although I knew it wasn't right, because you were everything that you said—young, hurt, and too much alone. I'm not a fool, woman, or a celibate. I haven't spent these eight years living like a monk. But I've thought about you—often. And, seeing you now, nothing has changed. There's still an innocence about you that makes a man want to protect you, but there's something else, too. It's in your smile, in the way you move. Something that brings out all that's primitive in a man and makes him tremble with longing."

"No, Justin, there's nothing. There can't be."

"There will be," he said, and the words were a warning.

"Mom!"

They snapped to attention when Mike burst into the room.

"Mom! Come see what Molly made. They're really neat! And she says she'll show us how to make them!"

Kit breathed deeply. Mike had made the room ordinary again. Even Justin was ordinary again, not a demon—or a diabolical god. He was smiling as he looked at Mike, his arm resting on the mantel. He was just a very attractive man, intrigued by the antics of a boy.

"What are you talking about, Mike?" Kit asked her son.

"The faces, Mrs. McHennessy." It was Molly who answered her, following Mike in from the kitchen. She smiled broadly, a tall woman with iron-gray hair and a warm smile. Douglas had her smile, Kit thought.

"Come see for yourself, me girl!" Molly urged.

Mike took her hand and dragged her along. She caught Justin's eyes; he grinned and shrugged. She could hear him walking behind her.

They were lined up on the long kitchen worktable. At first Kit thought they were only an assortment of vegetables: turnips, beets, potatoes. Then she saw that they all had faces carved into them. Macabre faces, with slanted eyes and broad, toothless grins. They made her uneasy, but she couldn't draw her eyes away from their evil grimaces.

"They're jack-o'-lanterns!" Mike exclaimed. "Molly let me help her—but just a little."

"Jack-o'-lanterns?" Kit murmured stupidly.

"Why, 'tis almost All Hallows' Eve," Molly said, her tone slightly chastising. She picked up one of the potatoes and traced the toothless grin. "This lot is for the church fair on Sunday. They will'na last the month, of course. We'll do another lot before the night is on us."

"Potatoes?" Kit asked.

Behind her, Justin laughed. "I'll have ye know, Mrs. McHennessy, that the potato is the original jack-o'-lantern. You Americans came up with the pumpkin."

"Really?" Mike demanded.

"Oh, aye, really!" Justin replied. He sat on one of the old kitchen chairs and drew Mike to his side, handing him another of the potato faces. "The Irish began carving these little faces centuries ago for All Hallows' Eve. They were done to drive away the evil spirits that might have been about. That's why they're so ghoulish."

"'Tis even an Irish legend that supplied the name," Molly inserted proudly.

"Really?" Mike repeated, his eyes wide and fascinated.

Justin laughed. "Really. 'Tis said there was a man named Jack, and a miserly fellow he was. So miserly that he denied God, and he denied the devil, and lived out his days believin' in none other than himself. Came the day old Jack died, he was barred from heaven. But neither would the devil take note of him, and he was also barred from hell. So Jack's spirit was doomed to roam the earth forever, with never a place to call home."

"Wow!" Mike murmured. He looked at Justin and grinned. "So people put little candles inside the faces, and then they were lanterns!"

"Right!"

Mike looked at Molly. "Could I keep this one? Could I, please?"

"Aye," Molly agreed.

"Mike, I don't think—" Kit began.

"'Tis just a potato!" Justin protested with a laugh.

It was indeed only a potato. In a few days it would start to rot, and Mike would have to throw it away. She would be an idiot to cause a fuss over a potato.

"When it starts to smell," Kit said, "you're going to have to get rid of it."

"I know, Mom."

All three of them were staring at her, as if she was behaving peculiarly. She hadn't thought she'd given her feelings away, but apparently she had. She would have to be more careful.

She smiled, then gave Molly a little hug. "Molly, Justin, thank you so much for the lovely dinner. I think I should get Mike into bed now."

"Ach, 'twas nothing. Such a pleasure to see ye, lass. I'm hopin' ye'll come agin," Molly said.

The older woman's hug was as warm as her words. Kit drew away, a little guiltily. "I'm not sure how long we're staying yet, Molly, but I promise I'll come to say goodbye."

"I'll walk you to the car," Justin said.

Mike held his potato tightly as they walked along the path to Kit's car. There was only a sliver of a moon, but it was enough to cast an eerie glow on the carved face, and suddenly Kit realized why the jack-o'-lanterns had frightened her. There was something about the face that reminded her of the mask of the goat-god, Bal. Something about the grin, something about the slitted eyes.

She swallowed. It was only a potato, she insisted to herself.

Mike crawled into his seat. Justin opened the driver's door for Kit, but he didn't touch her.

"I'll help you move into the cottage tomorrow," he told her.

"There's no need. I'm not sure what I'm doing."

"Well, then, you can tell me in the morning. I'll be there early."

"Justin—"

"Good night, Kit." He stared into her eyes. "You will see me. We've still got things to settle, don't we?" He didn't give her a chance to answer as he smiled across at Mike. "Night, Mike."

"Good night, Justin. Thank you."

"Justin," Kit said irritably, "we don't—"

"We do."

She shivered as she slid the key into the ignition. Though she didn't look at him again, she felt him watching her. She trembled all the way back to Jamie's, and far into the night.

Chapter 6

Kit leaned closer to the wavery mirror over the sink and studiously blended her blush over her cheeks. She moved back anxiously to view the effect of her artistry, wondering at the jittery feeling that wouldn't leave her.

Good God! she chastised herself. It didn't matter if her makeup was perfect, nor if her outfit—a soft, tawny knit outfit, with the skirt falling to midcalf in a gentle swirl over her boots—was attractive. There was no reason to fuss, no reason for this anxiety, for her feverish excitement. She had left Ireland and Justin years ago, then closed him out of her life.

He shouldn't matter—but he did.

She shouldn't have come back. She shouldn't have seen him again.... But she had. And the feelings, the needs, the confusion, that she had felt eight years ago were back. But there was an even sharper edge of danger now; there were no walls between them. She was no longer young and innocent, and her tragedy was long in the past.

Kit swallowed fiercely and gripped the sink, fighting a wave of dizziness. She was blowing things all out of proportion. Justin had not—by his own admission—spent his life waiting for her. She just happened to be there now, an available diversion when everything else in his life had become chaotic. The magic was all in her mind. Once upon a time they had shared a single passionate moment, and that had been that. It happened all the time. There was nothing special between them....

But there was, of course. Something very special, but she didn't know if she could ever tell Justin or not. Or if he would care.

"Oh, stop!" she said out loud. She was driving herself crazy.

She stared steadily at her reflection again. "He's being suspected of murder—and he isn't guilty. You owe him your support and help, but that's all."

"Owe" was a curious word, and it had nothing to do with the way her heart was beating, or with the way that she was wishing he would show up this morning, ready to insist, in his autocratic manner, that she moved into the cottage, that she see him again and again.

She ground out a sound of irritation and turned away from the mirror. She was going to go downstairs and have breakfast and a nice conversation with Jamie. Then she was going to drive around the countryside, before beginning to study the books she had bought from Julie McNamara. She was here to work. And since Mike had gone off to school with Douglas again, she had the whole day in which to do it.

Kit left her room and started quickly down the stairs. She burst into the kitchen with a cheerful smile for Jamie glued to her features and a happy "Good morning" on her lips, but she never uttered the words.

Justin was there.

She stopped dead just inside the door and stared at him, wondering whether time could stand still, whether it could create aeons out of a single moment. Maybe Justin hadn't waited for her, but suddenly she felt as if she had been waiting for him all these years, no matter how much she had tried to delude herself that he was entirely in the past.

He was seated at the table, holding a cup of coffee. She wondered if he was feeling all the things that raged through her; curiosity so deep it was a poignant ache; need so rich that it caused her heart to shimmer. She shouldn't feel such things, but she did.

And then the moment passed, and time began to tick again. Kit felt embarrassed, as if she had been standing there with her emotions obvious to both of them.

"Justin," she said in what she hoped was a casual tone, trying to hide the excitement she felt at seeing that he had come for her, that he wanted something from her, too.

"Good morning, Kit. I was just telling Jamie that you were moving into the cottage."

"I—"

I never said I was. She wanted to say it, but the words wouldn't come. She was barely aware that Jamie was in the room, because Justin had moved closer and taken both her hands in his. She felt his eyes on her like a caress— a bold caress, but intimate and caring—and she felt his fingers curling over hers like a promise, strong and sure.

He grinned, crookedly and a bit awkwardly. "Am I acting 'Irish' again, Kit? Too autocratic?" he asked softly.

She pulled her hands away without answering and turned quickly to Jamie instead.

"I think Mike and I *will* take the cottage, Jamie. I've decided to stay around for a while, at least until Halloween. The celebration should be just what I'm looking for."

"Oh, aye, 'twill be just what you want fer that book o' yours," Jamie told her with a pleasant smile. He didn't seem to mind the loss of two guests. "But ye'll have your breakfast first, lass."

She smiled. "Yes, thank you, Jamie." She still couldn't look at Justin.

"Bacon and toast and eggs over easy," Jamie said. "Coffee's in the pot, and porridge is on the table."

"Well, I'm not eating alone," Kit protested, beginning to feel a bit more normal.

"Justin?" Jamie asked.

"I'll have the same, then, Jamie. Hand me the bread, and I'll be in charge of toast."

Kit felt awkward letting the two of them do all the work, so she poured out the last of the coffee and started another pot. She couldn't help brushing against Justin occasionally, and each time it felt sweetly warm and wonderfully natural and intimate all at once.

Even the conversation became easy. Jamie told Justin that he'd seen some pictures on the news about Justin's latest office building in Dublin, and once they were all sitting at the table, Justin sketched out the design for Kit with such enthusiasm that she was enchanted by this whole new side of him.

"I'm working on a very similar one in London," he told her, then went on to explain that the design was not only aesthetically pleasing but incorporated an unusual plan for escape in the event of a fire. "See, Kit," he said, rising to point over her shoulder while she studied the drawing on the napkin before her. "If you were forced to, you could come down all forty stories by way of the outside balconies."

"It's wonderful, Justin. It really is," she said enthusiastically, turning to face him. He smiled, and it was there again, that hint of the diabolical, of mischief. Suddenly they were both caught by that sense of intimacy, and she knew he could read her mind. She'd never experienced anything like it, and it was so strong that it was frightening.

She knew that she was blushing—and that he saw it—and she hurriedly turned her attention back to the paper. She made her voice as cool and courteous as possible when she said, "I must say, I'm rather proud to know you. Few architects seem to be as concerned with people's safety as you are. I think what you're doing is wonderful."

"Thank you." His fingers closed over the napkin and crumpled it. "Want more coffee, Kit? Or shall we get going?"

He had put some distance between them again, and Kit was grateful. "Maybe I should wait for Mike to come home from school."

"Oh, I wouldn't worry, Kit," Jamie asserted cheerfully. "Douglas can bring him on over to the cottage."

Kit smiled weakly. She could feel Justin's eyes on her again. It was almost as if he was holding his breath. Was it possible that he was worried she would change her mind?

He had nothing to worry about: she couldn't. Destiny was driving her. Almost in resignation, she pushed her chair away from the table and stood. "I'll just run up and get our things," she murmured weakly.

"Take your time," Justin told her.

It didn't take long to pack. Even when she tried to dawdle over Mike's things, she couldn't seem to make the job last.

She could still run, she told herself. She could get her things together, go downstairs and tell both Jamie and Justin a firm goodbye, then hop in the car, drive to the school and take Mike away.

And then they could leave this part of Ireland forever.

But she wasn't sure that she could face herself if she ran away. She didn't know whether she loved Justin, feared him or despised him, but she had never felt anything as intense as the emotions that surfaced when she was around him. She didn't know where they might lead, but whatever lay between them had to be explored.

Kit heard footsteps on the stairs. In a wild panic, she rose and rushed out—she didn't want to be alone in the room with Justin. But it wasn't Justin coming up the stairs; it was Jamie.

"All set, Kit? Can I help ye, lass?"

"Yes, thank you, Jamie. If you'd like to take Mike's duffel bag there…"

Jamie didn't take the duffel bag; he took her heavier suitcase. She worried about the weight being too much for him, but as soon as he reached the landing, Justin was there, ready to take the heavy bag.

In what seemed like no time at all, their things were in the trunk and she was ready to go. She really hadn't been at Jamie's long, yet she had the strangest feeling that she was leaving home. Jamie seemed like a father, watching his hatchling leave the nest.

"Jamie…" she began, but he brushed aside her thanks and anything else that she might have wanted to say.

"Ye'll be seein' me, lass, that ye will!" he promised. "And don't fret for the boy; young Douglas will bring him along when he comes."

"Be seeing you, Jamie," Justin said. He was standing by the driver's side of her car. For the first time, Kit realized that his own car was nowhere in sight.

"How did you get here?" she asked.

"Molly dropped me off. Let's get going, Kit."

Jamie came around to open the passenger door for Kit, but, though she didn't mean to be rude, she ignored him. She was suddenly determined not to let fate blow her where it would.

"Wait a minute, Justin O'Niall. You just had her drop you here, did you? Pretty damn sure of yourself!"

"Ah, Kit! For the love of God, will you get in the car, please?"

She stared at him stubbornly.

He sighed in exasperation, and said, "Katherine, if you hadn't wished to come, I could have called Molly to come back."

"I rented the car; I'll drive it."

"Kit, please—"

"I said I'll drive."

He threw up his hands and spoke not to her but to Jamie as he came around the car. "May the saints preserve us from fools—and women!"

He slid angrily into the passenger seat while Kit got in on the driver's side. She waved cheerfully to Jamie while she snapped at Justin, "I heard that!"

"Well, it's the truth," he said heatedly, staring at her. "You wanted to drive—so drive!"

She slammed the car into reverse with such vigor that Jamie jumped back. She wanted to tell him that she was sorry, but decided that it would look like an admission of guilt, so she merely took it more carefully as she turned the car around and headed for the road.

"I don't even know what I'm doing," she muttered.

"You never did," he commented dryly.

"If this is supposed to be a charming seduction, you're not doing very well."

"Ah, yes, I'm acting 'Irish' again."

"No. Just like a drill sergeant."

"Honest to God, Kit, I didn't start this. I didn't say a single negative word. You're picking the fights, creating the argument."

"No—you started it. You presumed."

"I 'presumed.' Ah, come on, Katherine! Damn!" he swore suddenly, his eyes glued to the road, and Kit looked ahead to see that she was about to smash head-on into a delivery truck. She swerved quickly, coming to a halt on the shoulder of the road. Her hands shaking, she covered her face. If they'd been any closer to the gray granite cliffs of the coast, there would have been nowhere to swerve.

She couldn't look at Justin, but she expected his verbal tirade to come lashing against her any second. It didn't. She hadn't realized how badly she was trembling until she felt him gently removing her hands from her face, forcing her to look at him with very wide, very frightened blue eyes.

He smiled and stroked her cheek once with his knuckles. "May I drive, Kit?" he asked softly. "We're both nervous this morning." He gave her a rueful smile. "But I'm familiar with the roads, and you're not."

She didn't answer him. She just opened the door and got out of the car. By the time she had walked around it, he had shifted over in the seat and the motor was humming again.

He was silent when he pulled back onto the road, and the silence seemed to grow louder and louder, tense and electric. Kit looked down at her folded hands; they were still trembling. And then Justin began to talk.

"I read your book on Nassau."

"You did?" she asked, startled.

He nodded, his eyes still on the road. "Actually," he said softly, "I have all of them. I have an associate in New York who sends them to me."

"Oh?"

"I liked them very much."

"Well," Kit murmured, "my things are really rather specialized. They're for the tourist who has an interest in history, rather than suntanning or gambling."

"Oh, I imagine a number of people would really enjoy learning some of the history of what they're seeing."

"Well, I hope so."

"Had you been planning to work today?"

Kit hesitated. "I was going to drive around and try to absorb some local color; then I was going to read."

"How about if we get your things into the cottage, drive south to a pub I know for lunch, and then I'll bring you home again in time to meet Mike when he gets here?"

He glanced her way quickly, smiling. Kit nodded, suddenly grateful for the casual conversation, the return to normalcy between them. "Lunch sounds nice."

As she turned away to look out the window, she saw that the landscape had already changed. They were nearing the coast. The emerald-green fields were gone, and the crags and cliffs were rising, along with the moan of the wind. Mauve flowers were interspersed with ragged tufts of grass that clung to the rocky ground, and the air smelled of salt.

The cottage lay before them.

Justin brought the car to a stop. Kit clamped her hands tightly together in her lap and stared at the small house. It hadn't changed, of course, but she already knew that. She'd seen it yesterday when she had brought Mike here. But this was different. She hadn't intended to go inside then, and now she was going to stay.

Justin got out of the car, slamming the door behind him. He went up to the door and unlocked it, and Kit thought dimly about the fact that he was opening the door when he had already given her the key.

All landlords probably had extra keys, but clearly it would never have occurred to him that she might object to him using his own key while she was staying there.

He walked back to the car and opened the trunk; then, with her suitcase in his hand, he walked around to her.

"Are you all right, Kit?"

She nodded.

"Are the memories of Michael...too strong?"

She lowered her head, ashamed. She hadn't been thinking about Michael at all; she had been remembering her last night here.

"No, I'm fine."

To prove her point, she stepped out of the car and started up the walk. She noticed the beautiful wildflowers growing along the front. And then she stepped into the cottage, and it was as if eight years of her life had never been. She knew it so well. The kitchen to the right, the parlor to the left. And the stairs that led to the bedroom.

Justin was behind her, nudging her slightly. She had to move, so she walked into the parlor.

A beautiful arrangement of fresh flowers sat on the lace-covered table, and a warm fire burned in the hearth, giving the room a welcoming, lived-in feeling.

She walked over to the fire and put her hands out to feel the warmth of the low blaze. She was shaking, and she knew it. She prayed that the warmth would calm her, yet she wondered if anything could. Inside, deep inside, she was hot and then cold, and she felt as if she could never be still. She was nervous and excited and afraid, and her throat was bone-dry.

Justin stood behind the chair, his fingers curled over the back of it. "There's milk in the refrigerator, along with butter, eggs, bacon and bread. Not much, but a start."

"That was thoughtful of you. Food, flowers…a fire. It's all very nice."

"Well," he admitted, "I ordered the food, but you've Molly to thank for the flowers."

"Oh. Still, it's all very kind."

"Not presumptuous?"

Kit nodded, her back to him. "Yes," she whispered. "Presumptuous, too—but kind. Thank you."

"Shall we have something? Tea—?"

"No!" Kit whirled around in horror. Her eyes met Justin's just as he realized what he had said, and he smiled, shaking his head.

"Normal tea, Kit. Irish breakfast tea."

She looked down, suddenly embarrassed, and turned to the fire. It cracked and popped, and the room seemed very small. He was silent, and she suddenly felt as if she had to talk.

"Justin, lunch sounds lovely, and all this is very nice,

but we're missing the whole point, and you just brought it up."

"I did?"

"Justin, eight years ago—God knows why!—someone put something into my tea. Michael went over a cliff, and a young girl was murdered. And now you're being accused of murder again, and we're talking about books and flowers." She spun around to face him close to tears. "I know you didn't do it, and—"

She hadn't really been aware that he had moved. Suddenly he was just there, in front of her, one hand on her shoulder, the other on her chin, and he was lifting it, very gently, staring into her eyes.

"Kit… Katherine, you mustna' worry about me. I *am* innocent, and I want you here, near to me, because someone *is* a murderer, and I'd not have you hurt. I'll discover the truth; I promise you that. Kit…"

"Justin…"

It was barely a whisper, and it was quickly silenced as he lowered his mouth to hers. His lips met the quivering softness of hers, and their breath mingled with the bittersweet beauty of the kiss. A sudden rush of tenderness had brought him to her, but then it passed and a storm began to rage, stripping away time and pretense and inhibition.

Justin had been waiting for eight years. For a lifetime.

Her lips parted beneath his, and his tongue began to delve and probe, to cajole and explore, while his arms, trembling, swept around her, dragging her against him. She was soft and warm, her heart pounding, and through the soft knit of her shirt and the cotton of his shirt he could feel her breasts against his chest. He could feel her nipples harden, and it was as if something inside him soared and exploded. His fingers were in her hair, and it

was like silk cascading down around him. He had to let
her go. He had to step back, to lift his mouth from hers.
He had to put some distance between them or…

"Oh…"

It was the softest, most provocative sound he had ever
heard. He did draw away, but only an inch, and only for a
second. He stared into her eyes and thought of what she
had done, and of all that she was still hiding from him,
and then those thoughts fled, because only one thing really mattered to him now, and that was raw desire. But
it was more, too, because despite all the fever and gut-
wrenching need he felt, he could never see her, never
touch her, never inhale the sweet scent of her, without
being overwhelmed by tenderness.

And now…

Her hair was wild and beautiful, a halo to frame the
lustrous magic of her eyes. Her neck was slender, and he
could see the beat of her pulse, a throbbing that caused
him to wet lips that had gone dry, to straighten and feel
as if his body had tautened to steel.

"Lunch." She merely mouthed the word; there was no
sound to it. Her lips were still parted, her immense eyes
were still on him, and her mouth was ever so slightly
damp and shining from his kiss. Her breasts were rising
and falling rapidly, and the velvet whisper of her breath
fell against his cheek.

This can't be right, Kit thought, but she couldn't move,
and she found herself praying that Justin would be as arrogant and confident as she accused him of being. She
prayed that he would touch her again.

"Lunch." His voice faltered, and the rich baritone was
husky, but at least he managed to give substance to the word.

His lips against hers, the flagrant foray his tongue had

made deep into her mouth, had stolen breath and sanity from her. She could still feel his body against hers, and she thought she would die if he didn't touch her again.

And then he did.

He smiled, slowly, ruefully, and stretched out his arm, his fingers lacing into the hair at her nape, pulling her toward him. He brushed a kiss against the top of her head and whispered, "Who are we kidding?"

And then his touch was no longer gentle. His finger caught her chin and lifted it, and when his lips seared hers again she nearly cried out at the intensity of the hunger, the need, he aroused in her. She clung to him, eager to meet and savor each thrust of his tongue, to luxuriate in the strength of her passion for him.

She felt his hand sliding beneath her shirt to the bare flesh of her midriff. Her skin seemed to burn with his touch. Then his hand covered her breast, his fingers teasing over the lacy fabric of her bra, then slipping beneath it, too. His thumb coursed over her nipple, and she leaned against him, hungering for more of his kiss, of his touch.

Then he drew them both down to the soft hearth rug, and as he placed her there, he spread her hair out around her, smiling. And then she missed his kiss, missed that ardent pressure of lips against hers. He had drawn back and begun stripping away his tailored shirt, and when he spoke, his voice was rough with emotion.

"There's nothing between us now, Kit. No drug, no force—and no pretense."

She nodded, because she couldn't speak. And because his shirt was gone and she had to put her hand out, had to place her palm against the rippling muscle and crisp black hair on his chest. She had to move her fingers in fascination over his flesh, his nipples, his ribs, until he grasped her fingers and brought them to his lips. He kissed them and suckled them, and she inhaled sharply. He was wrong, she thought. She *was* drugged; no force on earth could affect her more potently than the sight and feel of him.

Groaning, he quickly kicked his shoes and socks away, then hurriedly shimmied out of his jeans and briefs. And then he looked at her with amazement, as if he couldn't believe she was still clothed when he was entirely naked.

Magnificently naked, she thought, and she couldn't even tell him that just the sight of him was enough to paralyze her. His body was sleek and muscled, lean and fascinating. And his desire for her was completely evident. He wasn't even blushing, while she was sure she was turning a dozen shades of red.

"Katherine…?"

It was both a question and a reproach, but it was spoken with tenderness and humor—and hunger. No one else ever said her name quite that way, in that deep, haunting tenor and with that trace of a lilt that proclaimed him Ireland's own. Her name became a sensual caress on his lips.

And then he touched her again.

He slipped off her boots, then arrogantly stripped away her skirt and stockings and panties with one sweeping gesture. His hands against the flesh of her thighs were hot, and she gasped for breath as she reveled in the sensation. He pulled her up to lift the shirt over her head, but suddenly he became fascinated with her kneecap. And his kiss didn't stop there. It grazed against her inner thigh, and she was suddenly neither silent nor still, but whispering his name urgently, fumbling out of her shirt and moving into his arms.

His fingers found the hook of her bra, and her breasts

fell into his hands like a gift of ripe fruit. His kisses tarried there while she wrapped her arms around him and nipped his shoulders with a shuddering, quivering rapture. This couldn't be true. It felt so good to be here, to be in his arms, to give herself up to sensual fires raging through her....

She felt as if this was the most beautiful moment she would ever know in her life. It was as if they had both been deprived forever.

Justin marveled at the silkiness of her hair, the way it fell over his flesh and caressed him. He savored the taste of her flesh, the rounded weight of her breasts, the supple shape of her calves and her thighs, and the sensual curve of her hips.

To him, their lovemaking was like a miracle, as she wound her long legs around him and stared at him with eyes that were both sultry and innocent. She shivered and gasped and wet her lips, closing her eyes with the depth of her passion, and closing her body around him as he thrust into her. He felt sheathed in silk, hot and wet, sheathed in her body. Her eyes met his, matching his urgency, matching his need. And that honesty had cost her, he knew, and that made the moment even more beautiful.

She was incapable of holding back. She had to touch him, had to run her fingers along his back, had to cling to him while he moved within her, filling her with pleasure so intense that she could scarcely bear it. She kept her eyes on him, because she had to see his face—taut, teeth clenched, muscles straining. His eyes, too, were burning with the heat of his desire. Then her vision blurred, because he kissed her. His tongue filled her mouth as his body filled hers, and then the molten pleasure burst through her. Volatile shudders swept through her with the force of her release, and she moaned his name aloud as he joined her at the peak.

It was long minutes before he pulled away from her. They were both damp from the passion they had generated, and she flushed slightly, but she didn't look away from him. She merely smiled shyly and stroked his cheek.

He caught her hand, kissed the back, then held it against his cheek. "Promise me one thing, Katherine."

"What?" she asked hoarsely.

"That you'll not run away again. Promise me. Swear to it. Because I'll find you this time, you know."

She smiled at him. She was afraid that she was going to cry because it had been so good between them, and because it was still so good to be here with him, both of them naked and comfortable and not at all afraid.

"I swear it," she vowed. But he was staring at her so intently that she was a little bit nervous, and she murmured, "Do you...do you still want to go to lunch?"

He didn't laugh; he only kissed her lips. "What is it? A loaf of bread, a jug of wine—and thou?" He smiled. "Nay, lass, it's not lunch I want. I want time. Time with you. All the time that I've lost."

There was nothing for her to say—because all she wanted was him.

Chapter 7

Justin lay on the bed, his bronzed torso very dark against the crisp white of the sheets. His fingers were idly laced behind his head, and he was leaning comfortably against two plump pillows. His lashes fell over half-closed eyes that appeared lazy, but were in truth narrowed in speculation. He hardened himself against emotion as he watched Kit.

It had been a week since they had first come here to the cottage. A week in which they had spent nearly all their time together. Discreetly, of course, since she did have a young son. And they both had work that couldn't be ignored. But not a day had passed in which they hadn't seen one another, hadn't given in to the strength of the feelings that lay between them.

It had been a week of discovery. By silent agreement, nothing ugly and nothing frightening—and certainly nothing painful—had been discussed. Even when he had shown Kit the bolts on the door and explained the window catches, neither of them had mentioned the reason why it was so important for her to keep everything locked. Nor did they do so when he showed her the instant-dial lines on the phone: one instantly rang his house, a second got Constable Liam O'Grady's office, a third would reach Barney Canail, and as a last safeguard, a fourth contacted Jamie Jameson.

They hadn't talked about the past, only the present. Kit had made no confessions, nor had she even intimated that she might need to confess, and that made Justin angry.

At times he felt wearily resigned, so he watched her, as he was doing now. It hadn't been so long, he told himself. Not really. They'd seen each other daily, but only twice had they had a chance to throw caution and discretion to the winds and give in to their desire.

And now they had tonight.

Mike was away on a school field trip. It had been difficult for Kit to let him go, Justin knew, and he had felt a few twinges himself. But not only was Douglas Johnston in charge of the group, Molly had gone along with them, and so had Barney Canail, who had left his deputy in charge of his department.

So they were alone. Completely alone. And again, by tacit agreement, they had planned a quiet evening, a domestic evening, just like an old married couple. He'd brought flowers and wine, while Kit had prepared a wonderful beef Wellington with parslied potatoes and a green salad, and they'd eaten by candlelight. Dinner had been wonderfully romantic, their knees touching beneath the table, one of her stockinged feet occasionally brushing over his ankle, his fingers curling over hers where they lay on top of the tablecloth. She had laughed a lot, but nervously, filling him with desire. Vivaldi had played softly on the stereo, and they had discussed movies and plays and music, and been delighted by both their shared likes and the spirit of their disputes.

She'd worn silk, a floor-length gown in soft violet, trimmed at the bodice and hem and sleeves with blue. It highlighted the fire in her hair and the color of her eyes, and it made it difficult for him to open the wine, to play the part of the civilized gentleman.

That role had come to an end after dinner. He had been tied in knots, and she had suggested coffee before the fire. He'd caught her hand and said that he'd rather have his coffee later, and in spite of the fact that they were coming to know one another very well, Kit had flushed the color of a winter apple. Her lashes had fallen over the dazzle of her eyes, and she had demurely excused herself to disappear up the stairs.

And she was still where he had found her ten minutes ago, sitting at the dressing table, brushing out her hair. The blue silk was gone, and she was wearing an even more provocative costume, some kind of shimmering gauze in a soft shade of mauve. It revealed more than it concealed. The lights were low, but he could see her breasts with each movement that she made. She had beautiful breasts, full and exquisitely rounded, but firm and crested in the most exotic shade of rose that he had ever seen, a shade heightened to a dusky mystery by the mauve that lay against her skin as softly as a cloud.

Enough was enough, Justin finally decided. He had tossed his own clothing in a haphazard pile in the corner, and if she didn't get up and come to bed soon, he was going to attack her like a maddened animal.

He smiled slightly, remembering the first night he had seen her, running across the moor in gossamer white. She had been like a fantasy come to life, hauntingly young and innocent and beautiful, an enchantress out of the mist. He would never forget her eyes that night, shy and embarrassed and huge, with a sheen of tears and a touch of fear. And then, of course, they'd found Michael.

Everything that had followed had been bittersweet. He'd never meant to fall in love with her. He was the O'Niall—and the name brought responsibility with it. That was an old-fashioned idea, perhaps, but it was still something that came along with the castle, with the land, with the inheritance of his blood. He had been twenty-eight, too old for an innocent eighteen-year-old, even if she was a widow.

Especially because she was a widow. She had been hurt and lost and confused, and he had meant to be her friend. For a while he had succeeded. But only for a while. God, it was so difficult to look back.

Why did you leave me? he wanted to ask. Why didn't you come back?

He hadn't meant to fall in love with her. Not then, not now. But he'd spent the last eight years as a free man, refusing to tie himself down, almost as if he'd known, as if he'd been waiting for her to come back to him. He'd never wanted anyone so completely. Never ached to hold a woman, to know her spirit, to hear her laughter, to wake beside her time and time again. As soon as he had seen her at the cemetery, he had known that he had to touch her again. Even when he'd told her to leave, he'd never intended to let her get very far, because there was still the other matter, of course.

He understood why she had left him. He had known

that she had loved her husband and had been too young to understand that letting herself feel again wasn't treachery, that desire and the need to touch could not be buried forever.

True, they had been drugged. He knew that. But he wasn't as perplexed as Kit. He was sure that the tea had been meant only to give her a gentle sleep and sweet dreams, to ease away the anguish in her soul.

He tightened his fingers behind his head. She was staring into the mirror, but he could tell that she wasn't really seeing anything. Her brush was held idly in her hand, and he wondered whether she, too, was reflecting on the past and wondering at its part in the future.

She hadn't really changed much. She had a veneer of sophistication now, and stylish clothes. Her hair was still long, but layered slightly and streaked with blonde. She was independent; after all, she lived in New York City. But her eyes...

They were still the same. Beautiful, innocent, exotic. They could sizzle, could caress. They were like the sky, wide and honest, yet he knew that the honesty wasn't real. And oh, how that hurt.

She moved, just slightly. The slinky nightgown caught the light, and she was so erotically outlined that Justin exhaled a soft oath and tossed the covers away, then got to his feet. Alarmed, she lifted her eyes to his in the mirror.

He smiled, but it wasn't a friendly smile. It was slightly menacing, because he didn't think he could take any more of the torture she was putting him through.

"Justin..."

His hands fell to her shoulders. He bent down and pressed his lips against her, savoring the taste of her flesh, running the tip of his tongue over the delicious satin of her skin. He kissed her throat, grazing his teeth against it. He felt her tremble, heard the sharp intake of her breath, and felt his own body surge and tighten in response.

Their eyes met in the mirror again, and he smiled, sliding his palms over her shoulders and then lower, until he cupped her breasts. A flush rose to her cheeks, but she seemed unable to break their mirrored gaze. He rubbed his thumbs over her nipples, which hardened beneath the fabric of her gown, and swallowed sharply when her head fell back against his belly and her hair swung tauntingly against his arousal.

"What are you doing?" he managed to ask with soft humor.

"I—I thought we should talk," she whispered.

"Can't we talk later?" he asked.

"I—"

He bent over her, taking her left nipple, fabric and all, into his mouth, laving it with erotic strokes of his tongue. He heard her breath catch in her throat and reveled in the way her nipple hardened like a luscious pearl.

"I…oh…"

She twisted against him; he raised his head, and she buried her face against his belly, thrusting kisses against it, making him shudder with the intense pleasure that swept through him as she darted the hot, wet tip of her tongue across his flesh. He threaded his fingers through her hair, his muscles tightening, his face a mask of desire.

"Katherine…"

She rubbed her head against him, covering him in the silky cascade of her hair, boldly exploring his reactions further and bringing the provocative allure of her damp kisses and caresses ever more intimately against him until she knew all of him. He whispered her name wildly, then wrenched her from the chair and into his arms. He tore heedlessly at the gown she was wearing, and she protested breathlessly.

"I bought this just for you! To be seductive and—"

"You've achieved it," he said briefly, and the mauve gown fluttered to the floor. His lips seared hers, while he crushed his body to hers and his hands moved everywhere. She didn't remember falling onto the bed—she was just there, and he was with her, over her, blanketing her. She adored the feel of him, the steely hardness of his body, the wonderful way they fit together. She cried out softly when he entered her, because it felt so good, so shattering, so complete. And when he began to move she lost all thought, eager only to meet each stroke, each thrust, to climb with him toward the peak, the culmination of all desire.

When she thought that she would explode with the sweetness, he was suddenly gone. Bereft and astonished, she gasped again, then shuddered when he caught her foot and knelt to kiss her sole, her instep, her knees, her thighs, then higher and higher until she was nearly sobbing. Only then did he sheathe himself once more within her softness, and then Kit felt herself shatter, shaking with the ultimate sensations that swept through her.

Justin was watching her, his forefinger moving lazily over her cheek. He was smiling, and she felt just a bit furious, because he knew the extent of his power.

She lowered her lashes, still gasping for breath, annoyed that she was blushing. "You're a torturer," she accused him.

"Me!"

"You…you…what you did. I was already…"

He laughed, and the sound was rich and sweet and intimate. "Me!" he repeated. "You sat there with that damn brush for half an hour."

"It was only ten minutes."

"And then, when I went to you—in pathetically desperate shape to begin with—you turned around and drove me nearly through the roof."

"You didn't…like it?"

"I adored it—but you deserved exactly what you got in turn." He arched one brow and repeated her own words. "You didn't like it?"

She opened her mouth, hesitated, then smiled and admitted, "I think I died a little bit."

He smiled, leaned forward and kissed her lips. Kit curled contentedly against him, running her fingers over the fascinating whorls of dark hair on his chest as he slipped an arm about her, cradling her against him. For several minutes they were silent. Kit didn't want to break the beauty of the moment. She wanted to pretend that there was nothing wrong, that no mysteries lay between them.

Finally, though, she spoke. "Justin?"

"Hmm?"

"We have to talk."

"Aye, we do."

She felt as if he was watching her intently, but she didn't know why. She raised herself against his chest and stared into his eyes. They were so dark, dark and elusive.

She was in love with him, but she didn't know what he wanted from her, only that, like her, he had his secrets.

She splayed her fingers over his chest and rested her chin on them. "Justin, when I was here before, I always felt like someone was watching me." She raised herself again. "As if the trees had eyes. As if someone wanted to know…every move I made."

She didn't like his expression. He was smiling, as if he was thinking she had a very vivid imagination.

"The trees?"

"Damn it, you know what I mean!"

He sighed. "No, Kit, I don't. I assure you—when I wanted to see you, I came to you. I was not in the trees spying on you!"

"I didn't say you were!"

"Kit, you were very upset. Your husband had just died."

"It didn't make me crazy!" she snapped.

He sighed again. "Okay, so someone was watching you. What's the point you're trying to make?"

"I don't know."

Angry, she turned away from him and got up to find her gown. Having it on didn't make her feel at all dressed, so she mumbled something unintelligible and slammed open the closet door to find a robe. Justin watched her in cool silence. She slipped into her robe and walked over to the window, where she drew back the curtains. The night was black, and the ceaseless wind moaned softly. She could see the gorse and bracken flattening against it. Beyond, the surf would be rising and falling angrily against the rugged, timeless cliffs.

"Kit?" He spoke softly at last. He didn't move, but watched her from the bed.

She didn't turn to him, continuing to stare out pensively at the night. "What?"

"I'm not trying to make you angry. I'm just saying that you were very young and upset—"

"I wasn't stupid or psychotic."

He hesitated. When he spoke, his voice was low and even. "I'm not trying to pick a fight, Kit."

Kit gritted her teeth. "Justin, you're refusing to take any of this seriously."

"I take it very seriously. After all, I'm the one who's suspected of murder."

He fell silent, and suddenly she walked back and knelt upon the bed. "Justin, something was going on. Agreed? On the night I came here with Michael, a young girl—who had been claiming that her illegitimate child was yours!—was murdered. That same night, Michael died on the cliffs. You say he fell; I say he was murdered. And then, three months later, someone drugged the tea in my kitchen so I would seduce you—"

"Kit, now you're pushing the line between fact and supposition!"

"You said yourself—"

"Aye, the tea was tampered with; we both wound up under its influence. But, Kit, I think some poor soul meaning only the best for you fixed that tea. Someone meaning to give you rest and oblivion and ease from your grief. Think about what you're saying. No one even knew that I'd be there! And what is this leading to, anyway?"

"To the O'Niall."

His eyes narrowed sharply, and his fists clenched on the sheets. "I'd thought you'd decided I was an innocent man, Mrs. McHennessy."

"Don't put words in my mouth!"

"It doesn't appear that I need to; you've spoken quite a mouthful without my help."

"You're impossible!" she flared, leaning back against the headboard in disgust. "I'm trying to help you—"

"But I don't need any help, Mrs. McHennessy, and I'll thank you to be remembering that!"

Kit muttered something about exactly what he could do with himself and leaped out of bed. She didn't stop for slippers, but charged down the stairs to the kitchen. She poured herself a cup of still-warm coffee and splashed a generous dose of brandy into it. She was close to tears. It seemed as if they got so close…and then he blocked her out. He had to care; he had to be worried. Why couldn't she get through to him?

Suddenly she screamed as a pair of arms slipped around her waist.

"Kit, I'm sorry, lass. I didn't mean to scare you, just to apologize."

She turned to face him. His chest was still bare, but he had a towel wrapped snugly around his waist. "May I join you?" he asked. He poured himself a cup of coffee and poured some brandy into it. "Irish whiskey would be better," he murmured lightly, flashing her a smile that went unreturned.

He walked into the living room, setting down his cup so he could put another log on the fire. Then he reached for his coffee and sat down cross-legged before the fire, patting the space beside him and nodding to her.

Kit hesitated, then sat stiffly next to him. She lowered her head. "There's nothing left for me to say if you won't take me seriously, Justin."

"I do take you seriously. But, Kit, you're talking madness."

"Just listen to me, please," Kit beseeched him. "Justin, I think that someone *else* might be mad. In ancient times your people, the O'Nialls, were the local kings. And after that they were political and religious leaders.

Fact, not supposition. The goat-god—in the person of the O'Niall—took his virgin and conceived his son, and then his bride was sacrificed the next year so that her blood could feed the land."

"Kit, you're talking ancient history."

"And *you're* getting angry again."

"Well, I don't always care to be reminded that I can actually trace my ancestors to people who did such things."

"You always laugh about it."

"Sometimes, aye. One has to wonder what happened if he chose a barren virgin."

"Now you're laughing again."

"Well, you were just complaining that I was angry. Make up your mind."

"Justin—"

"I'm sorry, Kit, I just don't believe it. It's too preposterous."

"You wanted me to leave," she said accusingly. "Why? And why the bolts on the door? You're afraid of something."

"Well, of course I am!" he snapped. He drew in a breath and sipped his coffee, staring at the fire. "Kit, if a shark attacked a child at a beach, it would probably have swum far away by the next week. But I'm willing to admit no parent would allow his child to play on that beach for a long, long time."

Kit watched him for a minute, then shook her head gravely. "I know I'm right, and I think you know it, too. There's too much going on here for coincidence. The next murder victim was your fiancée—"

"She wasn't my fiancée."

"But the world thought she was."

He turned to her. "And there goes your theory, shot

to hell. Susan certainly hadn't had my baby. She didn't create the new O'Niall. Nor was Mary's child mine, and anyone with a brain in their head knew that."

Kit stood up restlessly, sipping her coffee, retreating to the safety of a chair. "We have to find out—"

"Kit, the police have been through all of this. Dozens of police, from here, from Dublin. The Accorns have had private investigators working here—and no one has learned a damn thing. Look, I appreciate your concern for me; I really do. But I don't want you running around trying to find a murderer. If you're right, and the killer is from around here, you could put yourself in real danger. If I had a brain in my head, I wouldn't let you stay here at all."

Kit felt a shiver inch its way along her spine. She lowered her eyes and stared into her coffee cup. "I'm all right," she murmured.

"Are you?"

She glanced back at him and found him staring at her with a penetrating intensity. She couldn't meet that gaze.

"Of course. The bolts are on the door. I'm sensible and I'm careful."

"Well, be sure you are," he muttered dryly. His gaze left her as he stared into the fire.

Suddenly he threw his cup into the fireplace, shattering it against the brick, sending the flames lapping and hissing to new heights. And then he was on his feet, very much the pagan lord, with the golden firelight playing over his shoulders and torso, his arms braced tautly across his chest. Kit had started violently at the sound of the cup crashing; now she saw the look on his face and dropped her own cup with a little cry, unable to move, unable to escape.

He walked over to her, pinning her in her chair as he leaned over to brace himself against it and stare into her eyes.

"You're the prime candidate, you know. According to your theory, that is."

Her lips were dry, and she couldn't talk. She shook her head in confusion.

"What…what are you talking about?" she managed at last.

"What am I talking about? When the hell are you going to tell me?" He was shouting, and she could see him trembling with the force of the emotions sweeping through him. "Damn it! Why did you come back then? What are you waiting for?"

"What are you talking about?"

"How can you pretend not to know? I've given you every opportunity to tell me truth."

"I've never lied to you!"

"But you haven't told the truth, either!"

Kit stared at him and felt the heat that flowed between them. She knew…she knew that *he* knew. She didn't know how he had discovered the truth, but she couldn't face him this way. She was afraid. She lowered her eyes quickly. "Get out of here, Justin."

She tried to speak imperiously. And then she tried to rise and brush past him, but he wouldn't allow it. He grasped her hands and pulled her hard against him.

"Justin—"

His fingers threaded into her hair, and tears stung her eyes when she was forced to look up at him.

"Mike, Kit. Mike. When were you going to tell me that he's my son?"

She gasped. She hadn't realized that he'd had any suspicions.

"You're wrong!" she lied desperately.

"No, Kit. No good. I made a few calls the moment I left you in the cemetery that very first day. He was premature, Kit. Very convenient for you, because you wanted him to be Michael's. You even tried to lie to yourself."

"Michael could have—"

"Stop it, Kit. Stop it." She realized that tears were streaming down her face only when he gently brushed them away and pulled her tightly against his body, wrapping his arms around her and holding her close. And then he was whispering words she barely understood, soothing things, gentle things, caring things. He picked her up and carried her back to the chair, where he sat down and held her on his lap, breathing tender kisses over the top of her head.

"He is my son, Kit. Mike is my son."

She gave a small sob, and her answer was barely audible. "Yes. I—I *did* want to believe he was Michael's. I was so young then. Alone. Afraid. I didn't know what to do. I had to live the lie."

"I love you, Kit. I loved you then, and I love you now." He hesitated. "I know that you loved Michael McHennessy. But he's gone. You can't bring him back by living a lie."

She didn't answer him. She was shivering and she didn't know what anything meant anymore. She was still too stunned that he had guessed, and then she wondered if she had been blind not to have realized that he might.

But then, at the beginning, she hadn't even known if he would remember her....

And maybe, in the deepest recesses of her mind, she had told herself to come here on purpose. Maybe she had thought that Michael had a right to a living parent, rather than a hallowed memory.

But what did it mean…?

She leaned back, searching Justin's eyes. She was looking for something, but she didn't know what, and she was afraid that she would start crying again.

"Us…you and I… Justin, was it all because you wanted to know about Mike?"

He stroked her cheek, smiling tenderly. "No, love, I swear it. 'Us' is because it was always meant to be. 'Us' is because I couldn't stay away from you. Because you're incredibly sexy and beautiful, and because I've spent my life dreaming about you since we met. I love you, Kit."

She dared to reach out then and touch his face. The words were difficult to form after so many years, but the emotion was there, deep and rich, when at last she said, "I love you."

For a moment he was silent as he continued to watch her with the utmost tenderness, but then his smile faded, and his arms tightened around her. "Do you understand now why I want you to leave?"

She shook her head.

"Kit, according to your own theory, you're the one who should die. You're the one who was taken by the O'Niall. The one to give the land a son."

"The one who's supposed to be sacrificed."

Chapter 8

"**M**om! *Mom!*"

Mike's frantic cry penetrated Kit's worried thoughts as she flipped an egg in the frying pan. She shoved the frying pan away from the heat and rushed out the front door, frowning. Mike was still yelling for her, bent over something on the walk.

"Mike?"

She went to join him, crouching to look down herself. When she did, she was so startled that she clapped her hand to her mouth, holding back her own scream.

Lying on the stone walk was another stone, shaped into a miniature altar. And on the stone was a naked doll. It was almost a foot in length, with long, wild hair. It was on its back, and across its throat was a blood-red line, and some sticky red substance had been splashed all over the stone.

"Oh, God!" she gasped.

Mike looked at his mother's white face, stricken. "I'll throw it away, Mom. You look so upset."

"No!" she screeched. "No, Mike, don't touch it. Maybe there are fingerprints or something. Don't touch it."

"Fingerprints? We're going to call the police?"

"What?" Kit was appalled by the excitement in Mike's face. She shivered, wanting him to understand how serious this was, and also wanting to shield him from terror and ugliness. "Yes, Mike, I'm going to call the constable."

"Barney?"

"No. Liam O'Grady is the constable here," she said. "Barney works in Bailtree. And you—you come inside right now." The doll could easily be a warning, not just an obscene joke. And whoever had left it might still be nearby. "Come on, young man, come inside."

"Douglas will be here any second—"

"And he'll knock on the door! Come inside now!"

She caught his hand and dragged him inside. She caught sight of herself in the hallway mirror and saw that she was very white, with huge purple shadows under her eyes. She'd been upset all weekend, even before this.

Friday night had been exquisite, at least for a while, but then it had become Saturday, and Mike had come home. No matter how she tried, Kit had found herself growing more nervous and distant. Justin knew about Mike. He must have hired a private investigator to check into Mike's birth.

On Friday, as tender as Justin had been, she'd been too emotional to talk. And, as the hours had passed, she had grown more and more worried. She'd felt almost shut out. On Saturday, Justin and Mike had gone into the market together, then stopped to play darts with Barney

Canail and Old Doug along the way. All three of them had had dinner together, but Justin, in a brooding mood, had left early.

By Sunday she had been furious with herself. Why had she confessed anything? She knew that she was in love with Justin, and he said that he was in love with her. But it was so hard to really know. There was something as elementally pagan and wild about the man as about the land. Over eight long years she hadn't been able to forget him. And she hadn't been able to see him again without feeling the same overpowering need to touch him again. But could you build a future on that?

And what was he planning to do about Mike?

Her palms began to sweat. Was he going to say something to Mike? Surely he wouldn't. And he wouldn't do anything to take him away or press his point...or would he?

"Mom?" She spun around. Mike was at her side. "Mom, you were going to call the constable."

"Oh, yes." Her hands flew to her cheeks, and she hurried to the phone. They hadn't fought, yet she suddenly wondered if she was speaking to Justin or not. She hesitated, then decided that, yes, she would call him first.

She dialed the single digit to reach his house and waited while the phone rang. She expected him to pick it up, and was surprised when Molly answered instead.

"Molly, hello. It's Kit. Is Justin there, please?"

"Why, no, dear, he's not. He'd headin' out there fer the cottage already, he is."

"Oh." Kit hesitated. "How long ago did he leave?"

"Well, now, let me see. Why, he should be there. I'm sure I don't know whatever could be keepin' him."

Kit's throat constricted slightly, and she had trouble

saying goodbye. Then she found herself staring at the receiver. Would Justin have done such a thing? He had admitted that he wanted her to leave. If there was anything at all to her theory, she would be the murderer's next victim. Would he do such a horrible thing to scare her away?

How could she love a man and still mistrust him? But where was he?

Frightened tears welled up in her eyes.

"Mom! Justin is here! And Mr. Johnston is here, too! I'm going to tell them what happened!"

"No, Mike, wait!"

She was too late. She could hear the door slam; Mike was already running out to meet the two men.

Nervously pushing up the sleeves of her red sweater, Kit hurried after him, struggling for composure.

Mike had already reached Justin. They were at the far end of the walk. Kit could hear her son excitedly telling Justin what he had discovered. She watched Justin carefully as he hunkered down to be closer to Mike. A frown formed across his forehead, and then his eyes darted to her. They were dark, shielded and speculative. He rose quickly, but he didn't come to her. Instead he paused, bending down again to look at the doll, but without touching it.

Douglas Johnston followed, ducking down beside him. He was the first to speak to Kit. "Mrs. McHennessy, are you all right?"

She swallowed and nodded, then walked down the steps. Douglas stood, smiling with concern. "It's only a sick joke, you know."

"Probably."

"You should call Liam, though."

"Yes, I intend to."

Justin looked up sharply at that, then stood, frowning more deeply. "You haven't called him yet?"

She didn't much care for his tone, but she didn't have a chance to answer.

He had already pushed brusquely past her into the house. He paused only long enough to call over his shoulder, "Don't go touching anything, now."

Douglas Johnston cleared his throat. "He doesn't mean anything by it, Kit, you know. He's just…worried."

Kit glanced at him quickly. He had never repeated his dinner invitation to her, and now she understood why: Douglas, like everyone else in this place, would bow to the desires of Justin O'Niall. She felt as if she were wearing a brand.

"Don't defend him, Douglas. He's being rude," she said dismissively. And she smiled sweetly at him. "Have I ever really thanked you? You've done so much for Mike and me."

"'Tis nothing, Kit. I've told you." He watched her for a long moment, then ruffled Mike's hair. "We should be going."

"You'll be okay, Mom," Mike said confidently. "The O'Niall is here!"

He ran to Douglas's car, and Kit watched him with growing concern. Where had a seven-year-old come up with such a choice of words?

Douglas looked at Kit, smiled ruefully and turned to follow his charge. "Don't be worryin' now, Kit!" he called to her. Then he paused, glanced quickly at Mike, and said more quietly, "Don't be careless, though, eh? Keep the doors locked and don't go wanderin' off alone."

Her throat felt very tight. Was she a fool to stay here?

She tried to smile, but she wasn't feeling very brave. "I will be, Douglas. Thank you."

"I'm sure it was a prank."

"Yes."

"Or maybe a warning."

"A warning?"

"That you should...leave." He stared at her earnestly for several seconds, then cleared his throat. "Well, see you this afternoon."

"Yes, thanks, Douglas."

Justin came out of the house as Douglas waved good-bye. He was smiling, but Kit noticed his eyes narrowed in thought. "Liam O'Grady is on his way," he said when Douglas and Mike were gone.

Kit nodded, but her eyes fell to the doll, and despite herself, she shivered.

"I called the airport," Justin said.

"What?" Incredulous, she stared at him again.

"I've booked you and Mike on a flight out of Shannon at four tomorrow. Straight through to New York."

"Well, I'm not going—"

"You are."

"I'm not! Even if I did leave, Justin, it wouldn't be for home. I know it's beyond your ability to comprehend this, but I am here to work!"

He swore impatiently, settling his hands on his hips and staring at her angrily.

She wished he didn't seem so tall and strong, that she didn't long to forget everything else and move into his arms.

"Kit, is this book worth your life?" he demanded.

"My life hasn't been threatened."

"Well, this is hardly like receiving candy or a bouquet of flowers."

"Justin, you can't tell me what to do. Maybe I can't leave. Maybe I have to understand what happened eight years ago. All this ties in—I'm sure of it—and I owe it to Michael to stay until—"

"Which Michael?" he demanded, suddenly and nastily.

Kit froze. "Michael, my husband," she said coolly, feeling suddenly cold inside, but still aware of him— and painfully frightened. "And just what is the problem with that?"

He shook his head. "Nothing. I was just hoping that you weren't planning on perpetuating this living-legend idea for Mike, that's all."

She gasped, stepping away from him. "What are you planning on saying to him? You can't say anything! You'd destroy him. He wouldn't believe you, I'm certain. He's never seen you before! You can't just come out with something like that—"

"And what do you want me to do?" he said, interrupting and closing the distance between them in a single stride. He didn't touch her; he just towered over her, and she realized faintly that he didn't want to touch her because he was too violently angry at her. "Tell him at his wedding, perhaps? For college graduation? Never?"

She backed away again, clenching her fists at her sides. "No! I don't know! But not now! I hadn't thought—"

"That's right, you hadn't thought! Because you didn't intend to tell me! Why? What was your game? Come here and check the man out? Then, if I was a murderer, if I'd gone daft, or if you simply didn't care too much for my personality, you could just forget all about my role in his birth. Sorry, Kit. You cheated me out of seven years. But you won't cheat me of any more."

"What? Cheated you? My God! How do you think I felt? You might not have remembered me; you might not have cared!" She had known this was coming, but she still didn't know how to deal with it. "You weren't there! You don't know what it felt like. I almost—"

She broke off, paralyzed, knowing exactly how he would react to her next words.

He was still. Dead still. And he was looking at her as if he would love to strangle her, then and there. Then he walked toward her again. She backed away a step, but it wasn't enough. He caught her arms, and she felt the granite hardness of him, as cold and distant as the fall air.

"You almost what, Kit?" he whispered threateningly.

"Damn it, Justin," she swore. "I was eighteen years old! I dreamed about this place, horrible nightmares, and I didn't know what to think or feel. At first I didn't even recognize myself! You can't imagine how horrible that was!"

"I'm trying."

"You're not! You don't understand anything about the real world!"

"It's wonderful to be loved," he said bitterly.

"If you loved me, you wouldn't threaten Mike!"

"I'm not threatening him!"

"You are!"

"You're the one who feels threatened, because you can't begin to imagine that what you did might have been wrong. Or are you still embarrassed over something that happened eight years ago? Well, what about me? I can't even go up to my own flesh and blood and hold him. I have to be a stranger. I have to smile and keep my distance. I—"

He broke off so suddenly that Kit instantly turned, aware that someone must be approaching.

The constable, of course. Or constables. Justin must have called them both.

Liam O'Grady and Barney Canail were perfect opposites, a Laurel-and-Hardy pair if Kit had ever seen one. Where Barney was tall and lean, Liam was short and as heavyset as a champion boxer. He had dark brown eyes the color of mahogany and a full head of graying hair that had once been bright red. His cheeks were perpetually red, giving him the appearance of a jovial Santa Claus.

He was a nice man, too. Kit would never forget how gently he had dealt with her when Michael had died. How softly spoken his questions had been, how he had gone above and beyond the call of duty to accommodate her wishes. He hadn't thought that she should stay on after Michael died—no one had—but he had checked on her welfare almost as frequently as Justin. His gentle appearance was deceiving in one aspect, though; his small dark eyes were as sharp as pencil points, and he didn't miss a thing.

"Mrs. McHennessy?"

She could tell that he was pretending that he hadn't heard a word, though it would have been impossible for either man to have missed her angry exchange with Justin.

Liam stepped forward, stretching out his hand with a friendly smile. "I've been looking for a chance to see you, lass, e'er since I heard you were here. Welcome, welcome. I'm sorry to see you over this, though."

He reached for Kit's hand and pumped it. She swallowed back her temper and her tears and kissed his cheek. "Liam, you haven't changed a bit. You look marvelous."

"I need a diet," he returned gruffly, then looked past her to Justin.

Barney came up behind him, hands in his pockets. He gave Kit an understanding nod while Liam asked Justin where the doll was.

Then they all went to stare at the mock sacrifice. Kit began to feel a bit silly for making such a fuss over it. It was just a prank, because she was an American, a foreigner, and she was seeing their precious O'Niall.

The men were all crouching down together speaking in tones so low that she couldn't hear their words. Then Justin looked up abruptly, as if suddenly remembering that she was there.

"Why don't you put on some coffee, Katherine?" he suggested mildly.

She felt like telling him to make his own coffee, but Barney looked up then, too, smiling. "I wouldn't mind tea, Kit, if ye'd boil a kettle of water."

She couldn't very well be rude to Barney, so she started back to the cottage. Looking back, she noticed over her shoulder that Barney was holding up a plastic bag, and that Liam was picking up the doll and the stone, using a handkerchief. They were going to look for fingerprints. Kit was certain that they wouldn't find any, but she supposed they had to make the effort.

In the kitchen, she dumped Mike's half-cooked eggs into the garbage, set the kettle on one burner and the coffeepot on another. She didn't realize how edgy she was until she jumped at the sound of a movement behind her.

"Easy, lass, 'tis me!" Barney told her quickly, smiling

apologetically as he leaned against the door frame. "It's upset you, badly then?"

She shook her head. "No, no…really. I'm sure it was just a prank."

His face crinkled kindly. "Now, ye don't believe that for a minute, do you, lass?"

"It has to be—no, no, I don't. Oh… I don't know what I think."

"Well, now," Barney murmured, moving into the kitchen. His voice was low again, as if he was afraid that the others would walk in at any second. "I've an idea. And I didna mean ta be listenin' in, but the things I heard might have some bearin'."

She must have flushed, because Barney apologized again. "I do beg yer pardon."

"Please, I—we were yelling. I'm sorry you two were subjected to our private quarrels."

He smiled. "Aye, quarrels. People must matter very much to one another to have them, eh? But supposin' that someone did believe that Mary Browne's child was Justin's eight years ago, and so the lass died. This same person kens that a mistake has been made. Well, then, he'd be lookin' for someone new. Then we've Susan Accorn."

Kit sighed. "I said that to Justin the other night. He reminded me that Susan had no child."

"Aye, and she wasn't really murdered properly."

"Properly? I don't understand."

"Susan Accorn was gotten out of the way. To our murderer's way of thinking, she wasn't fit for the O'Niall. See what I'm saying to you, lass?"

The kettle began to whistle. Grateful for the interruption, Kit turned around to make the tea.

"Someone knows, Kit McHennessy. Someone else knows."

She spun around, nearly scalding herself. "Barney...?" There was a trace of hysteria in her voice.

He quickly took the kettle and set it on the stove again. "Now, don't go gettin' wild on me, girl. Those two out there would be wringin' me neck fer tellin' me mind." He gave her a crooked smile. "It's not that they think ye've no sense, they're just protective, especially Justin O'Niall. He's that sort of man, and ye can't go changin' blood or breedin'. He'll be that way all yer life, girl, no matter how ye try to tame him."

Kit lowered her eyes. "I don't know that I'll be try-ing, Barney," she said, as lightly as she could. "But—"

"Shush, now. I want ye to think. I want ye to think hard about who might be knowin' about yer boy."

Kit shook her head vehemently. "Barney, no one knows." She lowered her head and whispered. "Justin didn't know. Barney, it's impossible. I left here—I never said a word. My God, I stayed away eight years."

He cleared his throat. "Perhaps somewhere ye said something, ye gave some hint."

"No, really."

"Think on it, lass. It could mean yer life."

She started to reply, then saw that Justin and Liam were coming in. She nodded quickly, then asked Barney how he liked his tea.

"Two sugars, lass, thank ye."

Barney took his tea. Liam asked for coffee and smiled reassuringly when he took the cup. "A prank, as sure as day," he said. "Don't let it get under your skin."

"I think she should leave," Justin said.

Kit smiled sweetly. "She isn't leaving," she told Liam.

"Well, now, perhaps you might want to see Dublin fer a spell. Or fly over to London."

"Back to New York would be better," Justin said, his back to her while he poured his own coffee.

"Well…" Liam's eyes met Barney's across the kitchen. He shrugged. "Kit McHennessy, it's true strange things happened when you were here before. And now, well, we do have an unsolved murder once again."

"Liam, thank you for being worried. But I was in New York City when Susan was…when Susan died."

"You shouldna be alone," Liam said.

Justin turned around at last, eyeing Kit over the rim of his coffee cup. "She won't be."

She opened her mouth to protest. Why didn't she just go home? she wondered. She could buy herself some time. It was hard to imagine how she and Justin would manage to get along after their last argument. She had been a fool to come here.

But she'd had to come. She'd always known that she would have to come back sometime. Even if Susan Accorn had lived and Justin had married her and they had settled into pleasant domesticity—she would have had to come sometime. Mike did have a right to know the truth.

But not now…

"I'd best be gettin' back to me own office," Barney said. He set his cup on the counter and winked quickly at Kit. "You call me, lass, if ye've ever a need to talk. Tell yer boy I said hello."

"I will, Barney."

"We'll dust for prints, Justin," Liam said. He lifted his shoulders in a shrug. "I'm not expecting much."

"Thank you both for coming out. I appreciate it," Kit said.

"Sorry it was fer the likes of such a thing." Liam shook

his head. "But then," he brightened, "we'll all be together soon enough fer a happier event. If yer still going to be with us, Katherine McHennessy, you'll be at the celebration."

Kit must have looked confused. Justin, who was watching her, said coolly, "All Hallows' Eve."

"Oh, yes."

"Barney plays his pipes," Liam said with a laugh.

"And I play 'em well, ye old coot," Barney retorted.

"Ye'll hear fer yerself," Liam warned Kit, and she laughed. But when Justin walked the two men to the door, she shivered. All Hallows' Eve. The night of the goat-god.

She was still in the kitchen when Justin returned. She stiffened; she had no idea what to say.

"So you're not leaving?" he said abruptly, coldly.

"No." He turned around and started for the stairs.

Kit exhaled, then wondered nervously what he was up to. He hadn't said a word about Mike. "Justin?" She heard movement upstairs. He didn't answer her. She bit her lip and moved to the bottom of the stairway. "Justin!"

"What?"

"What are you doing?"

"Packing."

"Packing? My things?"

She took the stairs two at a time, arriving at the top breathless. He was in the bedroom; her suitcase was on the bed, and he was haphazardly throwing her lingerie into it.

"Justin! What do you think you're doing?"

He didn't glance her way. "You can't stay here alone."

Instinctively she fought him, taking the things from the suitcase and shoving them back into the dresser. He moved to the closet. She followed suit.

"Justin, I'm not leaving! I have to stay. Don't you see? I don't understand what happened to Michael, and I don't understand what happened…between us. I have to find the answer. Can't you try to understand that?"

She grabbed his arm, forcing him to pay attention.

"I understand," he said briefly, and then he returned to his task.

"Justin, stop it! I'm staying."

"Fine."

"Then what—"

"Kit, you're coming to the castle."

She stepped back, gasping. "I can't!"

"You have to."

"What would people—"

"What would people say? Is that it? Has that been the crux of all this? What would people say if they learned that precious Katherine McHennessy had a child by the O'Niall?"

She opened her mouth and stared at him, then shoved hard against his chest, sending him backward into the closet. "No! No!" she shrieked furiously. "That isn't it— not this time, Mr. O'Niall. You're the one accused of murder! And by your own admission, you've already had police and private investigators crawling down your throat! I was thinking of you, you stupid idiot!"

Surprised, he stepped out of the closet. He tried to put his hands on her shoulders, but she shook him off.

"Kit! I didn't kill her, and, no, I don't give a damn what people say, because I know the truth!"

Kit shook her head. "I don't want to come with you, Justin."

He backed her against the wall. His voice was soft,

though his face seemed ravaged, taut, a pulse beating heatedly in his throat.

"You said you love me, Kit."

"I do."

"Then...?" He whispered the word tensely, bitterly.

"This! This packing! One minute you don't believe me, but the next you're dragging me around, supposedly to save my life."

"Good God, girl, I'm worried about you!"

She lowered her head. She wanted to touch him, but she was too miserable to reach out. *I'm afraid*, she wanted to shout. *I'm afraid of what I don't understand. I'm afraid that you'll take my son away, prove me a liar in his eyes. I'm afraid that I love you too much, that our passions run too deep, that there's no way to cross the distance between us....*

"What is it, Kit? For the love of God, what is it?"

She couldn't speak, and when she finally reached out to touch him, he was gone.

Chapter 9

The air in the pub was stuffy with smoke, but it was warm inside and full of laughter. A dart game heavy with friendly competition was taking place in one corner of the room, and two of the old-timers were deep in a game of chess.

As he watched the action surrounding him, Justin brooded ruefully about his home. He loved it. He knew that he came from a clannish people—any Irishman was passionate, opinionated and clannish—but this went deeper than just being Irish. This place was special. A man never had to lock his car in Shallywae; the elderly were never left to struggle along on pensions, nor were they ever sent to institutions. A man loved and respected his parents and his grandparents here. And a man, any man, was loved for the simple fact that he was one of God's creatures. No hungry traveler was ever turned away; the hospitality of the ancient kings lived on.

But now murder had darkened the air for the second time in eight years. And both murders involved him.

"Think, man, think it over again."

Justin leaned back and took a long swallow of his beer, shaking his head and running his fingers through his hair. "There's no one who knows," he told Barney at last, lifting his hands helplessly.

Barney sighed. "I canna be wrong."

Justin leaned forward across the table again, a shock of dark hair falling across his forehead. "I don't think you are, but, Barney, think about it—it's frightening. Day by day, all our lives, we've been living with a—a madman. Someone who walks and talks and smiles, someone who acts like a friend. Someone psychotic enough to murder innocent women. And we don't know who! Damn it, we don't know who!"

Barney drew a finger up and down his nearly empty glass, looking warningly over Justin's shoulder. Matthew O'Hara and Timothy Dalton, a couple of local farmers, were coming in. They both tipped their hats respectfully to Justin, who smiled and waved in return.

She'd say it was because I'm the O'Niall, Justin brooded with a scowl. He didn't think that was it at all. He'd lived here all his life, and he'd gained a fair amount of recognition as an architect. His name and face had even appeared in several magazines. These were friendly people, and they were pleased when one of their own did well.

Barney raised his pint glass to the busy barmaid. "Meg, ye lovely peg o' my heart! May we have another here?"

Meg Flaherty, fifty-five years young if she was a day, flushed at Barney's warm words and served their drinks.

When she was gone, Barney lowered his voice again. "Liam's watchin' her now?"

"He is."

Barney chuckled suddenly. "Now, ye know the lass would really be panicked if she thought she was bein' followed night and day."

"Then what are we to do, Barney? I can't take the chance of not having her watched."

He shrugged. "No, that ye can't. If we could just put our fingers on the truth here…" His voice trailed away, and he cleared his throat. "Who was around back then?"

Justin arched a brow. "Everyone. Myself, Liam, Doc Conar. Young Doug, Molly." He paused unhappily. "Old Doug, but he's always been…"

"Senile," Barney supplied dismissively. "And Molly has been working fer ye forever. And—"

"Young Doug. Douglas Johnston," Justin murmured, feeling slightly ill. "Mike goes off with him every day."

"Justin!" Barney reached forward to shake his arm. "The boy is in no danger. Never has been. The boy is the next O'Niall."

Justin exhaled. That was true. If there was something to Kit's theory, Mike was in no danger.

He suddenly tightened his fingers around his glass until they turned white. What the hell was going to happen here? He didn't know how much longer he could stay away from her. Nor did he know how long it would be before he went rushing to the boy—*his son*—to sweep him into his arms and blurt out the truth.

A pulse twitched in his chest, and he swallowed quickly, trying to hold down his confusion and despair and anger. What was so wrong between them that it couldn't be righted? He didn't want to say anything; he knew that he was dealing with a child's fragile sensibilities. But she wouldn't be rational, so what was he to do?

She couldn't leave him. He couldn't let her. Not again. But he was afraid that she would. She liked New York, her work, her independence. Would she ever consent to a life in an isolated backwater like Shallywae, however quaintly attractive it might be?

Barney smiled. "'Twould make life easier all around if ye could watch the lass yerself, Justin."

Dark, angry eyes rose to his. "I told you, Barney—"

"Well, son, now surely, ye've devised buildings that defy the earth and sky. Can ye not devise a way back into her good graces?"

Justin didn't answer right away; he leaned back, drumming his fingers against the heavy wooden table. "Am I such an ogre, Barney? Tell me, is it wrong to cherish the life of someone you love?"

Barney chuckled. "Which do I answer first? All right, Justin O'Niall. You are self-confident, determined—well, pig-headed. And no, 'tis not bad to care. What yer lacking, Mr. O'Niall, is the tact to listen carefully and pretend to agree, then do what you think necessary anyway."

"Oh?" Justin arched an imperious brow.

Barney dared to chuckle again. He noticed that Justin's glass was nearly empty again. He lifted his hand to Meg, asking the other man, "Do ye need another?"

"Yes. I'm 'devising,'" Justin retorted.

"And what might ye be devising?"

"A way back in." He swallowed a mouthful of beer. "A stab at humility," he promised solemnly.

The fire crackled in the hearth. Chewing the nub of her pencil, Kit stared into the flames.

It was an exceptionally windy night. The howling wind seemed to hold the small cottage in a vise, like the mouth of a dragon.

Mike was upstairs, sleeping. Kit herself was dressed in a warm, belted velour robe and her fuzzy slippers. She didn't look sexy, she knew. But then, there was nobody to look sexy for.

It had been a week—a full week!—since Justin had walked out the door. At first she'd cried, then she'd gotten angry, and finally she'd gone into a deep depression from which she hadn't yet entirely emerged, though she'd tried.

She had worked like a maniac for the majority of the time. Thanks to Julie McNamara's assortment of books, she'd been able to put together a large number of diverse facts and theories, then form her own opinions. She'd made a list of "must have" photographs for her own book, and an outline for combining fact, fiction and current travel information into each chapter. She was pleased with her work, and pleased, at least in that respect, that she had come here. But on the personal side...

With a sigh, she set down her pencil. She couldn't work anymore tonight. Work was a balm, but when the restlessness settled over her, she knew she had to give up.

Honestly, she chided herself in silence, you don't even have the sense to be afraid! All you do is think about him, not about the murderer who's still out there somewhere.

Kit stood up and wandered over to the fire, automatically stretching her hands out to it. She bit her lip against the sudden onslaught of pain that assaulted her. It was awful, she thought miserably. She missed him so badly, and in so many ways. For years she had just waited, almost like a dormant flower. And she had gotten by, day to day. But now...

She missed him because she wanted to talk to him. To point out something, to ask a question. She missed his slow, lazy—yes, arrogant—smile. She missed his warmth, his fingers curling around hers. She missed his eyes, his voice, the lilt that came back to him in excitement or anger.

She missed being loved.

She felt almost immoral for wanting him. She wanted to run her fingertips along his arms and across his chest, wanted to touch the crisp, enchanting darkness of his hair.

She missed his kiss sliding along her spine...his whisper against her cheeks, his lips covering her breast. She missed him inside in a way that made her ache and yearn, and she marveled at the way that merely thinking about him could make her shiver before a blazing fire.

How many times had she almost forgotten everything and walked over to the castle? And why hadn't she? It would be so easy to apologize. So easy...

And yet...what for? Apologizing couldn't solve what lay between them. Could anything? At this moment she was desperate. If she saw him, if she just had him before her at this very moment, she might forget that they were from two different worlds, that time would be their enemy if what he really wanted was a woman he could rule and command. That her love for him would die forever if he hurt her son—their son—in any way.

Her fingers were trembling uncontrollably. She squared her shoulders, thinking that she could fix herself a cup of coffee with brandy and calm down, at least enough to sleep. Enough to make it through another night.

She didn't quite make it to the kitchen, though. The moonlight falling on the lawn caught her attention, and she walked over to the window. All Hallows' Eve was barely a week away. The thought made her shiver, and she wondered again why she didn't just leave. But she knew why. She had to be here. She had to find out....

Find out what? she wondered wearily. Nothing had happened since she'd found the doll. And Michael McHennessy had been dead for so long now.

Kit looked around the room, shaking her head with regret. The room, the cottage, should have reminded her of Michael, but she could barely picture him here. Of course, they had never sat in the parlor together. They'd barely arrived when he'd disappeared.

She smiled with sweet nostalgia, remembering their few moments upstairs. And then her smile faded painfully, because his words were what she remembered most: the story of the virgin who was given to the priest, to the goat-god.

And then Molly had told her that the O'Nialls had been the kings, and before that, the priests....

Kit walked decisively into the kitchen. She poured her coffee, added the brandy, then moved out to the living room again. The coffee was hot, and she drank it quickly. She needed its solace.

No good. She wanted Justin. Nothing else would do.

A movement drew her attention to the window. Instantly she tensed, set her cup down beside her and ran over to the window.

There was nothing outside but the darkness. Bracken and grass lay flat, crushed by the wind, a wind as old as time.

Kit realized that she was still shivering. She pulled her robe more tightly around her, then closed the drapes and frowned. It wasn't exactly true that nothing had happened since the incident of the doll.

She was certain that she was being watched again. Watched and followed. She never left the cottage in the dark, but on Tuesday she had driven to Cork, and she could have sworn she had been followed. She'd tried to convince herself that it wasn't true. After all, Justin had laughed at the idea.

Damn him anyway! He was supposedly worried about her, but where the hell was he? She had thought that he would come back. She'd hoped; she'd prayed. But there had been no sign of him.

With a weary sigh, she lay down on the couch and watched the fire. After a while, her eyelids began to droop, and she felt herself slipping into a doze.

The dream came again.

She was surrounded by mist, and she could barely see, because it was so thick. The wind was moaning like a hellish chorus, loud and anguished. Beneath that sound, though, she could hear movement: footsteps, coming toward her.

She couldn't move. At first she thought she was paralyzed, but then she realized that she was tied. Her wrists and ankles were bound to a slab of stone....

Just like the doll. The doll with the angry red ribbon of blood around its neck. Like the doll, she was naked and bound on an altar of stone, and someone was coming nearer and nearer....

She opened her mouth to scream, but her scream never came. It was Justin.

He, too, was naked. Naked and graceful as he came toward her through the mist. She could see his eyes, see his striking satanic smile.

He was coming closer, coming to her. She didn't want to scream anymore. She wanted to reach out to him.

Then the mist passed between them again, and he wasn't Justin anymore. He was the creature. The goat-god. The priest in the cape and the mask, with the horns and the evil leer.

The wind had died, and what she heard now was chanting. She realized that they were all around her; Liam and Barney, Molly and Douglas and Old Doug, Meg from the pub and even Julie McNamara. They were smiling, looking at her, saying words in a language she couldn't understand, repeating them over and over....

The god was almost upon her. He towered above her, reaching inside his cape. His arm suddenly rose high into the air, slashing it. She looked up and saw that the moon was glinting on an object. Glinting and glittering...on a knife. A huge broad dagger with a silver edge. A dagger that dripped blood...

"Ohhh!"

Instinct brought her awake before the dagger could fall. Shaking, she lowered her legs to the floor and covered her face with her palms. And then, before she could really react to the terror of her dream, she was jolted into full alertness. There was someone coming up the walk.

Kit stiffened, then jumped to her feet. She felt dizzy, and she wished fervently that she hadn't drunk the spiked coffee. She looked at the clock over the mantel. It was nearly midnight. No one would be coming at this hour to make a social call.

She brought her knuckles to her lips as the footsteps drew closer. Desperately she looked around the room. The only possible weapon was the poker from the fireplace. She grabbed it hastily and waited, her body strung as tensely as wire.

There was a soft tapping at the door.

Compelled, Kit moved toward it, wide-eyed, her fingers wound tightly around the poker.

The tapping came again. Harder. More insistent.

She stepped closer to the door, barely breathing. If it was someone on legitimate business, he would go away when she didn't answer his knock. And if not…

What if the whole village was in on it? she wondered in wild panic. What if Justin was their goat-god and they were all ready and willing to serve him, eager to cast her into the sea?

"Kit! Open the bloody door! Let me in!"

"*Oh!*" Panic and tension eased out of her. She was relieved, because of course she didn't really think that…

"Kit—" he demanded.

She swung the door open, the poker still at her side. Immediately, she got a potent whiff of him. He smelled of cherry tobacco and the dark beer served in Meg's pub. His hair was an unruly mess, with one lock of it almost covering his left eye. His smile, crooked and rueful, was devastating, and he wobbled slightly in the doorway.

"Justin…"

He bowed. "Excuse me. Mrs. McHennessy, please, may I enter?"

"Justin, you've been—"

He cut her off, stepping in, eyeing the poker in her hand with an arched brow. "Please?" He reached for the poker. "I haven't been that rude, have I?"

Still smiling, he walked—or swayed—over to the fireplace and set the poker back where it belonged. Then he turned to see her staring at him, wide-eyed, wearing a pair of absurd red fuzzy slippers that at least matched the color of her velour robe.

"Justin…"

He didn't give her a chance to talk. With startling agility he suddenly swept her a deep bow, falling on one knee to take her hand.

"Justin…"

"Ah, Mrs. McHennessy, I do beg your pardon."

"Justin! You're drunk."

He looked up at her, a satanic light gleaming from the depths of his eyes. "So I am, love, so I am."

Before she had a chance to reply, he was up as quickly as he had knelt before her. Astonished, she watched him amble over to the couch she had just vacated, offer her a crazy grin and fall onto it. He was on his back, eyes closed, dead still.

"Justin?" Torn between anger and amazement, Kit tiptoed over to where he lay, staring down at him.

Drunk! The damn fool had gotten drunk, and then he had come over here to make fun of her. And *then* he had passed out on her couch. Well, he was over six feet tall and probably weighed close to two hundred pounds. She wasn't going to be able to move him.

She sighed and ran upstairs to get an extra blanket. She checked the bed and saw that Mike was sound asleep, as comfortable as…

As comfortable and as dead to the world as his father.

There. She had really, truly admitted it for the very first time.

She bit her lip, found a blanket and walked thoughtfully back down the stairs. When she neared the couch, she couldn't help staring down at him. She loved the way his dark brows arched over his eyes. She loved the straight length of his nose, the fullness of his lower lip, the devilish sensuality of his mouth and the slight smile that remained even in sleep.

With a little sigh, she leaned over to tuck the blanket around him, and as she did, her breasts brushed his chest. Suddenly something warm slipped around her waist, and she gasped, looking at his face and seeing that his eyes were wide open.

"Kit…"

"Justin…" she began warily.

But it was too late. She was suddenly stretched out on top of him, and before she really knew what was happening, her lips were molded to his in a hungry kiss, hot and demanding.

Either he wasn't really drunk, or he was amazingly adept considering his inebriated state. He had untied the belt of her robe and slid the hem of her thin nightgown high on her thighs, and his hands were warm on her bare flesh. He was stroking her hip, her midriff, the heavy undercurve of her breast. When his lips released hers at last, his eyes sought hers. She couldn't have moved if she'd wanted to, because his left arm was still locked around her, while his right hand caressed and roved.

"You cheat," she whispered.

"I need you."

"You smell like a brewery."

"There are worse things," he said, wounded.

"Like what?"

"Well… I don't smell like a sewer."

She started to laugh. He caught her lips again, and by that time his hand had moved between their bodies. Moved low, to a spot where she began to feel a constant throbbing.

He broke off the kiss, and his hand moved, his fingers stroked, penetrated. She gasped sharply.

"I dreamed of you," she said quickly. "I dreamed that you were coming for me. That you were the goat-god."

"You dreamed that?" he asked, stricken. And yet the sweet torture he was inflicting on her didn't stop.

"I am no evil beast, Kit. Just the man who loves you."

She couldn't speak. She felt as if hot honey were rushing through her veins, pooling at the center of her being, at the sweet spot where his fingers wrought their magic.

"M-Mike is upstairs."

"Sleeping."

"What if—"

"He won't."

"But we can't—"

"But we can."

Her eyes went very wide, because suddenly she was straddling his bare flesh. She had never felt more intimately joined in her life. Cool on the outside…burning in the middle. Decadently filled and inwardly stroked with a startling, incredible impact that was erotic beyond imagination…

"I…"

"Kiss me," he urged her softly.

And that was the beginning of the end. She unleashed the dreams and the hunger and the longing and felt with delicious fever the ache being assuaged and assuaged… and assuaged.

Later, when the fire had nearly died and the wind had become a gentle breeze, she laid her head against his chest. "I have to move. Michael might come down."

"Aye." He kissed her cheek, but he didn't release her, nor withdraw himself from her sweet sanctuary.

Kit frowned. "Justin...this can't solve things."

"Not murder, no."

"I meant other things."

"No," he whispered. "No. But I feel so much better," he told her. "So much better just to be with you."

She felt better, too. She felt him in her, and all around her. She inhaled his scent and felt him down to her soul. She was too languorous to dispute him. Too lazy even to move. She would, though, in just a few seconds.

"Mom?"

Kit heard the voice dimly at first. She was so sleepy, so comfortably ensconced in the warmth of the blanket. Then she remembered the night.

In a panic, she opened her eyes, realizing that Mike was standing beside her and that she was still on the sofa and that she had fallen asleep there after...after being with Justin.

"Mike!"

In desperation she looked around, but Justin was gone. She was on the sofa all by herself. Her robe was even rebelted, and the blanket was tucked in all around her.

"Oh!" she breathed in relief. But she wondered where he was.

Mike was dressed and smiling and very pleased that he had gotten himself ready for school. "Mom, can I get some cornflakes? It's almost time for Douglas to come."

"Oh, uh, of course," she said quickly. Justin wasn't the type to hide in a closet, she realized. He had left, carefully, discreetly.

She reached for Mike with a broad smile and gave him a little hug. He squirmed a bit and gave her a peculiar look.

"What's that for?" he asked.

"Nothing. Just that I love you. Come on, I'll feed you whatever you want."

He wanted cornflakes and toast. He'd barely eaten the last of his breakfast when Kit heard Douglas's horn blaring. She walked outside with Mike, kissed him quickly on top of his head, then waved to Douglas, who waved back cheerily.

When they were gone, she fixed herself toast and coffee in a curiously light mood. She half expected Justin to appear, but he didn't, so she bolted the door and went upstairs to take a long hot bath. She caught sight of her reflection in the mirror and smiled at the dreamy quality in her eyes.

"Well loved!" She laughed aloud.

By the time she had bathed and dressed it was almost eleven, and she didn't feel like working. She hesitated, then decided to take a walk through the woods over to the castle. He had come to her last night—no matter in what condition—so she would hold out the olive branch and go to him this morning.

Halfway there, she regretted her impulse. There was only a glimmer of sunshine, and it didn't reach through the dense foliage. And there was a mist. She could barely make out the little trail through the trees because of the low-lying ground fog. For once there wasn't even a wind, and the silence was eerie.

It was only a ten-minute walk, she told herself, but she quickened her pace. She wanted it to be a five-minute walk.

Sweat had beaded her forehead, and she was breathing heavily when she finally saw the walls of the castle rising before her. She began to feel a bit silly.

Molly answered the door and eagerly ushered her in. "Justin's not in, love, but come, have some tea," the older woman urged.

Kit swallowed her disappointment and told Molly that she would love some tea. Molly headed into the kitchen, but Kit hesitated at the door. The counter was covered with potatoes that had been carved into gruesome jack-o'-lanterns.

Molly winked at her. "All Hallows' Eve this week. The young ones do love my potato men!"

Kit smiled and forced herself to admire Molly's work. They went on talking about how much Mike liked school, and Kit was glad to see how proud Molly was of Douglas.

"Old Doug, well, he's a good man, he is, but a grave-digger all his life. I was glad to see me son a teacher."

Kit commented on how much Mike admired Douglas, and how grateful she was that Douglas had taken such an interest in her son. "He's been very kind."

"He's a good man. And he likes the boy. Who would not? He's a well-mannered, handsome lad."

Kit thanked her for both the compliment and the tea. Justin hadn't returned, and she felt too restless to sit.

"I'll tell him ye were here," Molly promised, seeing Kit out.

Once she got outside, Kit noted with irritation that the fog hadn't lifted yet. She toyed with the idea of taking the long way home, by the highway, but that would have taken her half an hour. Swearing beneath her breath, she started down the path again.

The wind was picking up, and Kit was actually glad of it; she didn't like the silence in the forest. But the fog was just awful. She lost the trail for a moment, and when she found her way back onto the path, she had to dust leaves from her sweater. Just then a flash of movement caught her eye, and she screamed.

There, right in front of her, was the goat-god. Clothed in the black cape, tall and malevolent. His horns were long, his eyes were diamond-bright, and as dark as death against the sky.

"No!" she cried in terror.

Because he was coming toward her, gliding over the path, and there was nowhere to run.

Chapter 10

It seemed as if the forest echoed and trembled with her screams. But then, suddenly, he was gone. He had been coming straight at her, and then... And then he was swallowed by the mist and the trees and the bracken.

Kit ran, unaware that she was screaming again. All she wanted was to get out of the forest, out of the mist, away from the creature she had seen. Pain streaked through her calves, and her breathing was loud as she struggled to reach the cottage.

"Kit!"

It was Justin, calling her name, but she didn't know from where. A little spasm of fear swept through her. Had he donned the cape and mask, then cast them aside to come running to her rescue?

"Mrs. McHennessy!"

She reached the road that ran along the forest, running with such speed that she was unable to stop but went crashing into the second man who had called her name.

It was Old Doug, with his fey, watery eyes and gentle smile. Yet even while he spread his arms to steady her, Kit scurried away. If ever there was a candidate for the asylum, it was Old Doug. And suddenly she remembered what he had said when he had first seen her; he had asked about Mike! He had asked about her son, when he shouldn't have known...

No. Maybe she was the one going crazy. He wasn't sweating or panting, so how could he have cast aside a cloak and a mask and beaten her here?

"Are ye all right, lass?" he asked kindly. "Why, ye look as if a score of banshees were on yer trail, child!"

"Old Doug, were you just in the forest?"

He scratched his head. "Aye, that I was. Come to get my lunch from Molly."

She stepped back, gasping. "Did you—did you see it?"

"Kit!"

She jumped as long arms swept around her waist.

It was Justin, his eyes dark, perspiration beaded across his brow, his breath coming raggedly. "Kit! What happened? Oh, my God, you're all right!"

He pulled her tightly against him, holding her against his chest while he rested his chin on the top of her head. The thunder of his heartbeat was very loud.

Tears stung her eyes. She loved him so much, but she was so afraid. He had been in the forest, and he was panting, and he had been behind her.

He set her slightly away from him with a worried frown. "What happened?"

"The—" she began, but then old Barney Canail came crashing out of the forest, too. He took one look at her, saw that she was all right and sat down hard on the ground.

"Lord, Lord, if I'm not gettin' too old for a chase such as that! Where were ye, girl! I heard ye scream."

Then Barney was interrupted by Liam O'Grady, who had come more slowly than the others. His girth wouldn't allow a faster pace.

Kit let herself rest against Justin as she faced the others. She was still shaking so badly that she was afraid she would fall, and it was worse now than it had ever been, because she was forced to be suspicious of men who were her friends—and the man that she loved.

No, she decided firmly. She would not suspect Justin. She had known in her heart of his innocence before she had come here, and she would not waver in her beliefs now.

"The—the goat-god was in the forest," she said hesitantly.

"What?"

The word came flying out to her harshly from three of them. Old Doug just stood staring at her.

"The goat-god—"

"Kit, there is no goat-god!" Liam said softly.

"Someone dressed up like the goat-god was there. Someone in a cape and a horned mask. I was coming through the forest, and he was just…there." Her lip trembled slightly. "Coming at me, out of the mist."

Silence reigned; she couldn't see Justin's eyes, but she knew that the men were exchanging skeptical glances.

"I'm telling you what I saw," she said coolly.

"Are ye sure, Mrs. McHennessy?" Barney asked. "There's such a fog this mornin', and ye've had the creature heavy on yer mind. You might have imagined—"

"I didn't imagine anything. It was there."

"Douglas, did ye see anything strange in the forest?" Barney asked the old man.

"Ah, the forest," Old Doug said, smiling. "Why, 'tis a veritable haven for gods and ghosts!" he said cheerfully.

He would clearly be no help. "I wasn't dreaming things up!" she insisted.

"Mrs. McHennessy—" Liam began.

Justin's arms tightened around her. "If she says she saw it, then she did."

A gentle faith rang from his words. But was it really because he believed her—or because he knew more than he was saying?

"Let's take a look, shall we?" he suggested.

"All right, let's see what we can find," Liam said, taking charge. "Barney, cover the north sector. Justin, you and Kit take the path. I'll search south."

"I know the forest like the back of me own hand," Old Doug offered. "I'll find it." He paused. "What am I looking for?"

Kit smiled. "A cape or a mask, Doug."

He nodded and set off, crashing through the bracken.

Kit and Justin started down the path. The mist was growing thicker, so thick that she could barely see him ahead of her.

"Justin?" she murmured to him. Was she a fool? Was she signing her own death warrant by being here? By asking these questions? "Where were you this morning? What were you doing in the woods?"

He stopped, his back to her, and she saw the muscles tighten beneath his sweater.

He turned to her slowly, his eyes as glittery as the jeweled orbs in the goat-god's face.

"Was I in the woods wearing a cape, Kit? Is that what you mean?"

"No, that's not what I mean!" she retorted, but her voice faltered. "No, but I had just come from your house, and you weren't there. The whole thing seems rather strange, doesn't it? I see this creature in the woods, and then I run into Old Doug on my way out—and you and Barney and Liam are all running around like the Three Stooges."

"I beg your pardon?"

Even in such a remote area, Kit didn't see how he could have missed the Three Stooges. "Never mind. What I'm saying is that it's such a coincidence that all three of you—"

"I see." The glitter left his eyes, and he smiled. Then he looked at her again and pulled her close against him, kissing her forehead. "Kit, you haven't been alone at all for nearly two weeks now."

"What?"

"We've been splitting a vigil, Barney, Liam and I. Watching you."

Anger at such an invasion of her privacy rose up inside her, but it quickly subsided. He had been worried, and he had seen to it that she was safe. Then her smile faded. "I was alone this morning."

He stroked her cheek softly. "I didn't think you'd appreciate waking up beside me."

"No."

"So I snuck out to shower and change. Barney was in the bushes at the cottage, and he followed you to the castle, but he lost you once you started through the forest on the way back."

"Where were you?"

"Heading back to the cottage."

"Oh."

His lips settled over hers, and he kissed her gently beneath the arbor the trees made in the mist. And with that kiss, new faith throbbed into her blood.

"Third degree over?" he asked her.

He started forward again before she had a chance to answer, and she tripped over a root; if not for the strength of his arm around her, she would have fallen.

"Are you all right?"

"Fine."

He turned to her again. She reached out to feel his face through the damp mist, drawing a finger over the line of his cheekbone and the angle of his jaw. "We're not going to find anything, are we?" she murmured.

"I don't know."

They watched one another for several seconds, then were interrupted by the totally unexpected sound of Barney's scream of triumph.

"Why, 'tis true! There's a cloak hidden here, beneath a rock!"

"Where are you?" Justin shouted to him. "Keep talking!"

Barney kept up a steady stream of words until they reached him. He was in a small, sheltered clearing in the midst of dense foliage, a private haven, invisible to the world.

Liam reached the spot just as they did and knelt down beside Barney. "'Tis a black cloak, all right."

"Is the mask there?" Kit asked nervously. She didn't think she ever wanted to see it again, yet, paradoxically, she wanted it to be there.

"No, Kit. Just a black cloak," Liam sighed. "Well, we can try fer fingerprints agin."

"Did you—did you find any on the doll?" she asked, hope rising within her.

"No," Barney said in disgust. "It were wiped clean, and the stone, too."

Suddenly feeling sick, she swallowed, certain they wouldn't find any prints here, either.

"Don't look so upset, Kit," Justin murmured to her. "There might be a hair on it, or something else they can check."

Liam's eyes brightened. "Aye, someone running in the woods might well have stripped off the cloak quickly, and perhaps a hair clung to it. We'll see, now; we'll see."

"I'd best be gettin' back," Barney murmured. He looked at Justin for a moment then turned his gaze to Kit. "You all right now?"

She nodded. She really did feel better. At least she wasn't losing her mind. The cloak existed, and that meant someone *was* trying to frighten her.

"Wait!" she said suddenly. "It isn't old, is it?"

Liam, carefully picking up the material with a long stick, gazed at her curiously. He shook his head. "Looks like satin, new and shiny."

"Why?" Barney asked her.

"Oh… I don't know."

Barney shifted from one foot to the other. "Now, you don't really believe that some ancient god is comin' back now, eh?"

"Barney!" She shook her head. "I was just thinking that—"

"Someone does believe in the legend," Justin provided.

She shrugged. She didn't know what to think anymore.

"I'll take this in," Liam said, and he, too, looked from Justin to Kit. "You're all right?"

"I'm fine. I'm angry, actually. I don't like being frightened."

Barney, Liam and the offending cloak started back through the trees. Justin and Kit, by some mutual agreement, waited until they had gone. Kit looked around and shivered suddenly. The forest was so dense. She would take care not to be here alone again. Suddenly her legs wouldn't hold her any longer, and she sat down on the stone behind which Barney had found the cloak.

"Kit?"

She hadn't realized that she had been sitting in troubled silence until she looked up to find Justin's dark, pensive eyes on her.

"What?"

"I'm not trying to make you angry," he said softly. "But if you still insist on staying, I think you should come to the castle. If I have to be gone, Molly is usually about."

"Justin, I really am here to work."

"You can work at the castle."

"But…"

"But what?" She could see that, though he was trying not to, he was becoming annoyed. She lowered her head and smiled. This was the Justin she knew—and loved. And though she was determined to hold her own against him, she wondered if she wasn't wrong to attack his behavior. His self-confidence, his assurance, even his quick temper, were among the very things that she loved about him.

"But what, Katherine McHennessy?"

"Justin!" She sighed softly. "Justin, you're forgetting

your own home. This is a very Catholic area, and the townspeople—"

"The townspeople here are no different than any others. Some will talk; some will be sensible, and think that you're a bright young lady to take care."

"Justin…"

"Are you worried for me, Kit? Or for yourself?"

"For both of us. For Mike."

He hesitated. "I'm thinking of Mike."

Startled, she met his eyes. "But Mike isn't in any danger! He's the—"

"The what?"

She lowered her eyes again. "He's the O'Niall."

"He's a little boy. Little boys can get into trouble—especially if they find themselves in a situation where they feel they need to protect their mothers."

"Justin, listen—"

"No, *you* listen, Kit. Things seem to be closing in on you. First the doll, now this."

"Someone is trying to frighten me."

"And what if it goes further than that?"

"I keep the doors locked—"

"And you wound up alone here in the forest anyway, the stupidest thing you could possibly have done."

"Damn you, Justin! And you want me to move in with you?"

"It's the only sensible thing to do."

"I…can't."

He stared at her for a long moment, then turned and stood with his back to her, his stance stiff and furious.

"Justin!"

There was a note of panic in her voice, and he turned

quickly, reaching out a hand to her. She rose and took it, then met his eyes, and they kept walking.

She didn't know where they were heading, but in a matter of minutes they had come out on the road that led to the cottage. She wasn't at all surprised when he slipped his own key into the door, then shoved it open and allowed her to walk in first. She went straight to the living room and sat down. The hearth was filled with ashes, and instead of sitting down beside her, Justin set about sweeping it out and stacking logs. He was quick and adept; in seconds a fire was burning against the chill in the cottage.

Finally he sat down across from her, studying her for so long that she grew nervous. Eventually she couldn't keep herself from speaking. "Stop it!"

"Stop what?"

"Stop staring at me that way. After what you did last night—"

"You didn't throw me out," he reminded her.

"I felt sorry for you. I thought you could barely stand. And it was all an act, wasn't it?"

He shrugged. "No, I'd had a few pints with Barney down at the pub."

"Hmm."

He leaned back in his chair, staring at her so intently that she leaped up and walked over to the window.

"You must have something to do," she said irritably. "A building to build. A sketch or a blueprint to work on."

"Actually, I do have something to do."

"Then?"

"I'm not leaving, Kit, until I've gotten you moved into the castle."

"Justin…"

"I've had it with the three of us hiding in bushes and following you around, Kit. And I cannot leave you alone."

"And I can't—"

"You could always marry me now. That would still any wagging tongues."

She lowered her eyes. She didn't know what to say, only that a little thrill of panic was sweeping through her.

She loved him, didn't she? Her life had been a vast, emotionless wasteland when she had been away from him. She'd spent eight years pretending that she just didn't meet the right people, but it had all been a pretense. He was the only right one for her.

Justin would be uncompromising, though. He would demand that Michael be told the truth. He would want her son's name changed. He would want her to move to Ireland.

"I can see the gears in that mind of yours working away," he told her.

She shook her head sadly. "I can't...."

"Kit, just what can you do?" he demanded coldly.

"I need time."

He threw his hands up in disgust. "Time for what?"

"You don't understand, do you? I love this place— even though I lost a husband here, I love this place. The people are warm and friendly and giving, but...but it's not my home. Not yet, anyway."

"All right, Kit, God knows why, but I can never win a single argument with you. I can't get inside your mind. All I know is that this is insane. I love you, and I believe that, despite yourself, you love me. Oddly enough..." He paused, smiling. "Oddly enough, you do seem to have faith in me. You believe in my innocence."

"I do," she whispered.

He walked toward her, and though he was fully dressed, she couldn't help remembering her dream. His gait was the same: sure, slow. He knew where he was going; he could afford to take his time. She watched him, thinking that perhaps she should run, or push him away when he moved to touch her.

But she couldn't do that. She inhaled the clean, heady scent of him as he gazed down at her with a crooked smile.

"It's a pity that you don't have more faith in me as a man."

"I—I don't know what you mean."

"Aye, you do. But I'll let you think on that for a minute."

She knew that the kiss was coming, and she was certain that he intended it to be just a kiss, nothing more. But when his lips touched hers, she tasted the salt of tears she hadn't known she was shedding.

She clung to him, not knowing how else to tell him that what she felt for him was so deep that it was terrifying. That she could all too easily swear to give up everything that she was, everything that she had been, just to be his wife.

But it would be wrong, and it wouldn't work. But because she couldn't put it into words, she put the love she felt into her kiss. Her tongue traced his lips and danced deliciously within the warm, moist cavern of his mouth. She arched against him, putting all her desperation into their kiss.

He smiled at her. "I did have something to do, but it can wait."

She didn't understand why; after all, she had just refused to marry him. But she met his smile with her own.

"I—I wanted to help you, you know," she whispered. "I came here because—because I wanted to help you."

She wasn't sure when she wound up in his arms, only that suddenly he was carrying her up the staircase.

And then she was naked on the bed as the wind cried beyond the cottage and he lowered himself to her in the dim light.

She reached for him because she had no other choice, and she loved him because she was certain it was her destiny to do so.

Afterward, she lay curled in his arms. She didn't want him to speak, yet she knew that he would.

"Kit, you tell me—what do you expect me to do?"

"I don't know."

"Do you really think that I can just kiss you good-bye and watch you take Mike away from me?"

A shiver raked along her spine. "He's not even eight years old."

"Aye. But eight years is a long time. And do you know how hard it has been, Kit? Do you have any idea? I see my own son day in and day out, and I have to keep a stranger's distance. I can only warn you; I won't wait forever."

She tensed, biting her lip, aware of his arm around her and the feel of his chest beneath her cheek.

"What's your problem, Kit? You're an American, and I'm Irish, but that doesn't make us alien creatures from opposing planets."

"Yes, but it does—"

"I won't go through this anymore, Kit. I love you. I want to marry you. I want my son."

"Justin—"

"Hear me out, Kit. I'm warning you—there are things that I can do. Legal things."

She gasped, pushing herself away from him.

"You can't do anything! I'm his *mother*. Don't you dare threaten me!"

"You're threatening *me*," he commented easily, which chilled her even more. He looked so comfortable; legs sprawled out, fingers laced behind his head. She was on the verge of either tears or a tantrum, her hair a tangled mess and her hands clenched into fists.

What did she expect from him? she wondered. He knew that Mike was his son, and someday Mike would have to know, too. Was she wrong to fight him so?

It wasn't that she didn't want Mike to know; she just wasn't sure when. And it would have to be done carefully, while Justin was so accustomed to simply claiming what he wanted.

"You know that I'm right," he said suddenly.

"I can't—"

"You can't, you can't, you can't!" he mocked, his eyes narrowing as anger burned within them. His hands suddenly locked behind her head. "Thank God you don't lie about this," he murmured.

"This?"

"Us."

And then he kissed her. So tenderly, so completely, that a haunting rush of sweetness and honey began to cascade through her again. She sighed and gave in to the overwhelming desire. This feeling needed no reason, no words. This beauty was always there, waiting to be awakened, to be explored.

Could this be a love to last forever? Kit wondered, feeling herself become complete in his arms.

He was leaning against her now, his fingers entwined

with hers, and he smiled, a little sadly. "I love you. Thank you." He placed a light kiss against her lips.

She regarded him warily. "What was that for?"

He grimaced. "Well, I needed one last…intimate encounter."

"Last?" Kit inquired, frowning suspiciously.

"I don't think you're going to be speaking to me much longer."

"Oh? Why?"

"Well, I'm going to threaten you again."

"Justin, you can't—"

"Can't, can't, can't. There you go again, Kit. I see it the other way. I can."

"Go on," she told him stonily. Why didn't she have the sense to argue with the man dressed? she wondered. They were still pressed together, all the heat of his body searing her own.

"Well, it's quite simple. You can get up and help me move your things over to the castle now, or…"

"Or?"

"I can have a long talk with Mike."

"You wouldn't do that!"

"Wouldn't I?"

"No. You wouldn't. I don't believe it. Not for a second."

He shrugged, the diabolical sparkle back in his eyes. "Well?" he asked.

She sighed softly, feeling her independence slip away. "All right. You win."

He stared at her for a long moment. "No, I haven't really won anything at all, have I, Kit?"

She bit her lower lip. "I love you, Justin."

"But you don't want to give that love a chance."

"I need…time."

He exhaled wearily, sitting up at last, gazing beyond the windows as he spoke. "I'll try to give you time, Kit. I'll try." Then he rose and headed toward the shower. Kit curled up on her pillow, wondering if she hadn't gone completely mad, after all. He was reaching out to her…and she wouldn't let herself take his hand. Maybe it wasn't so difficult to understand after all. It was going to be so hard to explain to Mike. To her parents and her friends, though they had always known that, no matter what his name was, her son was not her husband's child.

But did such difficulties really matter? she asked herself. Wasn't loving him worth so much more?

The shower stuttered off, but Kit, lethargic, didn't move until she felt a sharp slap on the curve of her derriere. Indignant, she rolled over, swearing.

"And they say the Irish have tempers!" he said cheerfully.

"They do. At least you do," she retorted.

"Up, love. We're moving. Now."

She leaped up from the bed—on the opposite side from where he stood—and saluted him briskly. "Yes, sir!"

"Now that's the spirit!"

Exasperated, she headed for the shower herself. He was in a hurry now, so she just relaxed, savoring the heat of the water as minute after minute ticked by.

"Stay in there much longer and I'll join you."

She bit her lip, thought about the possibility, then quickly turned off the water. She came out wrapped in a towel, then stopped in startled surprise when she saw that he was completely dressed and she was completely packed.

"I don't remember asking you to do that."

"Well, I don't sit idle very well."

"You've made one mistake."

"What's that?"

"I'd like to get dressed now, and the outfit that I *was* wearing is covered with leaves."

He gave her a smile and set her big suitcase on the bed.

"Thank you," she said sweetly.

He watched her, then turned around quickly. "Hurry down. I think that's Douglas Johnston dropping Mike off."

She nodded, quickly slipping into a soft beige leather skirt and a silky blouse. She had just stepped into her shoes when she heard her son's voice as he came scampering up the stairs. She tried to straighten the bed, but he didn't even notice it.

"Mom, Mom!" He pitched himself against her, then gave her a quick hug.

"What, what?" she asked, laughing and scooping him into her arms.

"I need a costume! It's Halloween in just a few days. All Hallows' Eve, they call it here. And all the kids go to a party, where they have a big bonfire and all kinds of food and candy. We're going, right?"

She tousled his hair. "Of course we're going."

Finally Mike stopped talking about the party long enough to ask her about the suitcase. He was, as she had expected, delighted that they would be staying in the castle.

Kit picked up the suitcase, heading toward the door. She would bring it down so Justin could put it in the car; then she'd come back for Mike's things and to straighten up the room. But she paused at the top of the stairway.

She could hear voices—angry voices. She frowned, unable to make out the words. Then she realized that Douglas and Justin were fighting, though not throwing punches, at least so far.

"Mike, stay here," she told him, racing down the stairs. To her surprise, she realized that they weren't even in the cottage; they were outside. "Justin? Douglas?"

The two men fell silent, and Douglas lifted a hand to her in greeting. "Good afternoon, Kit McHennessy."

"What's the matter?" she asked them.

They looked at each other, shrugged, then looked back to her, smiling.

"Nothing, Kit," Douglas said.

"But I heard you—"

"Were we that loud?" Justin laughed and laid a hand on Douglas's shoulder. "We were talking about a soccer match."

"Aye, that we were!" Douglas agreed. "I was rooting for the Italians, and Justin thought the Basques were a much finer team. Well, I've got to be goin' now. See you in the morning, Mike."

Kit turned around. Mike had followed her downstairs, and now he was smiling happily. "At the castle!" he told Douglas excitedly, adding a belated "Please, sir."

"At the castle, Mike. Justin already told me where to find you." He tipped his cap and went toward his car.

"I'll get my duffel bag, Mom," Mike told her as Douglas drove away.

As soon as he was gone, Kit seized her opportunity to ask Justin, "What was that all about?"

"What? Oh, you heard. Soccer." He seemed preoccupied.

"Justin, you're a liar."

"My business isn't always yours, Kit, and you don't really want it to be, do you?"

She spun around and walked back to the cottage. Mike was still upstairs, so when Justin followed her, she attacked again, turning on him and demanding an explanation.

"You know, Justin, when I first came here, Douglas asked me out to dinner. Then I saw you, and he never asked again."

He set his hands on his hips, returning her stare. "Well, it's not because I'm the O'Niall, or any other such crazy thing," he said flatly.

"Then?"

He laughed, catching the side of her face. "Katherine McHennessy, you're a beautiful minx, but trust me, that wasn't over you. If Douglas didn't ask you out again, maybe it's because he realizes just how closely you and I are tied."

And with that he turned and strode back outside, leaving her alone with her unsettling thoughts.

Chapter 11

Molly was delighted that Kit and Mike had come to stay.

"I was wonderin' just how long it would take ye ta find some good sense!" she told Kit chidingly.

Kit looked quickly to Justin, wondering if he had told Molly about the doll or her experience in the woods, but he only shrugged.

Molly usually left for home right after dinner, but this time she stayed to see to their rooms. Mike was given Justin's old room, where a wonderful big rocking horse still sat in the corner. Kit would be right next to him—in the same room where she had awakened all those years ago, after Michael had died and she had passed out in Justin's arms. As she walked around the room, she could still remember her awful feelings of loss and devastation—and disbelief. She and Michael had been so young; they hadn't really believed in death, not for them, yet it had come to Michael....

Right after dinner Justin had politely excused himself to work. Mike had homework, and now Kit decided that she might as well work, too. She hesitantly interrupted Justin to ask him if she could borrow his typewriter. He obliged her, quickly setting up one of the empty rooms as an office for her. When she thanked him, he told her coolly that she was welcome, and she surmised that a cold war had begun. Well, what did she expect? She had been coerced into coming here—even if she did feel safer.

At eight-thirty Kit went up to tell Mike that he had to go to bed. He was, as she should have expected, sitting on the big rocking horse, and he smiled at her shyly.

"Justin says that Devil is almost two hundred years old!" he told her proudly.

She touched the thinning yarn mane on the exquisitely carved creation. Devil. That figured. But she smiled at Mike. "New York is hundreds of years old, too, Michael. It was named for James II, when he was Duke of York."

Mike watched her politely, but he really wasn't very interested. "I love it here!" he told his mother fiercely. "Can we stay forever and ever?"

"'Nothing lasts forever but the earth and sky,'" Kit quoted, tweaking his nose.

"Can we stay here a long time, then?"

"I'm going to have to go on to other towns, Michael. I have a book to write, remember?"

"Oh, I know. But we'll still be in Ireland, so we can come back here."

She lifted her hands helplessly. "Don't you miss your friends at home?"

"Well, sure. But I have friends here, too, now. Petey McGovern, Harry Adair, Timothy—"

"Okay, okay!" Kit laughed. "You have new friends. But don't you get homesick?"

"Sometimes," Mike admitted. He smiled and threw himself from the horse to her, wrapping his arms around her neck. "Wherever you are, Mom, that's where I want to be," he told her. "But I do like it here."

"I like it here, too, Mike," Kit admitted. "But now, bedtime."

"Aw, Mom…"

"Bedtime. You want to go to school in the morning, don't you?"

Mike ran into the small bathroom to brush his teeth. Kit dug through his things—bless him, he'd already filled the drawers—until she found his pajamas. When he got back he grinned to show her the spot where he was missing a tooth and kissed her again. She sat on the bed and picked him up, cradling him against her.

"I'm glad we came here, Mom."

"Well, if you're glad, I'm glad."

Kit suddenly noticed a shadow at the open door. She glanced up to see Justin framed there, silent, brooding. He smiled for Mike, though, and walked into the room to tousle the boy's hair.

"You got everything you need, Michael?" His voice sounded husky and Kit was careful not to meet his eyes.

But Mike jumped away from her and hugged Justin, catching him by surprise and throwing him off balance. They both landed on Kit, and all three of them ended up tangled together. Kit burst out with a protest, but by then Mike and Justin were laughing. When Mike begged for a story, they all sat up, and then Justin told him one about leprechauns that was awfully similar to *Rumpelstiltskin*. She enjoyed it, though; he was a great storyteller. And, despite herself, she felt warmth steal through her at the sight of the two men in her life together.

Justin rose at last, kissed Mike on the forehead and watched while Kit tucked him into bed. Then he touched her chin lightly with his knuckles. "Good night," he told her softly.

After he left, Kit hesitated for a few seconds, then went back to her own room. She took a long shower and went right to bed, but sleep was a long time in coming.

Mike was already out of bed when Kit went to check on him the next morning. She hurried back to her own room and got dressed, then hurried down the stone stairway. She could hear Mike talking away a mile a minute. When she pushed open the heavy oak door to the kitchen, she found him sitting at the breakfast table, wolfing down oatmeal and applauding Molly's newest array of creations. Potato heads, squash and even some small, sad-looking pumpkins lined the countertop.

"More?" Kit asked her.

"All Hallows' Eve is just two nights away now," Molly said.

"So it is."

Kit helped herself to a cup of coffee and sat down at the table. "So tell me, exactly what happens?"

"It starts at eight—Justin must start it, being the O'Niall, you know. He lights the fire. Then the musicians play, and there are contests, dancing, singing—oh, and of course candy all around." She winked at Mike, then smiled at Kit again. "'Tis fabulous, love; you'll enjoy it. The dancing is spectacular, and some of it dates way, way back, which should help with that book of yours."

"I'm sure I will enjoy it very much."

Douglas Johnston's horn began to beep, and Mike jumped up from the table, gave Kit a quick kiss and raced out.

"Douglas is so kind," Kit said to Molly, who beamed with pride.

"Aye, that he is. Now, lassie, what'll you have for breakfast?"

Kit didn't often have the luxury of letting someone else make her breakfast. She demurred at first, out of politeness, but Molly persisted until she said she'd love some bacon and eggs. But even when she had finished eating, Justin still had not appeared.

"Where *is* 'the O'Niall'?" she asked Molly lightly. "Still sleeping?"

"Oh, heavens, no! He's not a sleeper, that man. Needs no more than five or six hours a night. He's in his den, working."

Kit nodded and thanked her. She should probably get back to work herself. For a serious author, she didn't seem to be very interested in her writing.

She didn't go upstairs, though; she went to the carved door of Justin's den and rapped on it. He told her to come in, then looked at her expectantly while she gave him an awkward smile and moved closer to his desk.

He was working on a blueprint of what appeared to be an old building, his T-square and a rack of sharpened pencils on his desk. It was all Greek to Kit, but she gazed down at the plans anyway.

"You're building this?"

He looked up at her smiling, then shook his head. "It's

an old cathedral in Dublin that needs some reconstructive surgery or else it will fall into rubble. I've been asked to shore her up, right and proper."

"Can you do it?"

"I think so." He finished drawing a line, then looked at her again. "Would you like to go to dinner this evening? And to the theatre?"

"I—"

"Don't say that you can't."

"What about Mike?"

"I've already asked Molly to stay." His eyes searched hers when he spoke again. "A double date, you might say. With Julie McNamara and her husband, William. You've met Julie, I heard."

"You really do seem to know everything."

He shrugged, looking down at his blueprint again. "Finding that out hardly called for James Bond." He was grinning when he gazed up at her again. "There's only one bookstore anyone from around here would suggest, and that's Julie's. And when I had occasion to talk to her, she mentioned how much she had liked you."

Kit considered his offer for only a second. "Fine—if you're sure Molly doesn't mind."

"Molly adores Mike. Kit…"

She stiffened automatically at his tone. "What?"

"I have to go to Dublin soon. I was thinking of leaving on All Souls' Day, and I want you to come. Now wait! I can't leave you here alone—"

"I'd be with Molly."

"Still, I'd rather that you were with me. And surely you need to go to Dublin. She's a big city, but in many ways the heart of our history lies there. The Viking invaders founded her, and then there was Cromwell, not to forget our quest for the dethroned James, and then—"

"I'll go."

"That simply?"

She nodded, lowering her eyes. "You're right—I need to go to Dublin. For one thing, I have the names of a few photographers there. For another..."

"Go on."

"I like the idea of dating. I...love you, Justin. I'm just afraid of the future."

He watched her for a while, then turned back to his work. "Tonight we need to leave about seven. We've reservations at an Italian restaurant—"

"An Italian restaurant in Shallywae?"

"In Cork. And Italian restaurants are found the world over. We're not backward, my love. Seven?"

"Seven."

He lowered his head, a frown of concentration instantly knitting his brow.

Kit hesitated, then asked, "Justin?"

"Aye?"

"Why were you really arguing with Douglas Johnston yesterday?"

A shield fell instantly over his eyes. "I told you—a soccer game."

"You're lying."

"Kit, I'm busy."

She didn't feel like accepting that particular rebuff. "I'll plague you until you tell me the truth," she told him, then walked out and closed his door with a bang.

The restaurant was very Italian, and Kit loved it. There were fountains and vines, and wine bottles dangling from wicker baskets along the walls. Justin ordered a vintage wine before dinner, and it went down smoothly. Before they even ordered, Kit was feeling lazy and very much at ease.

Julie's husband already knew Justin, and he seemed genuinely pleased to meet her. William was friendly and easygoing, and as eager as Julie to offer suggestions about her book. Seeing Julie again was nice, too, but the best part of the evening was Justin.

He was in a black three-piece suit, and he wore it with a negligent masculine flair that made her feel breathless even before she touched her wine. His after-shave smelled delicious, and his hair, still slightly damp from the shower, was like ink and continued to fall rakishly over his forehead. He was the most striking man she had ever seen, and he loved her....

Her heart began to pound. She would never be able to leave him, so why did she keep holding back?

For a moment she closed her eyes, dizzy. He'd never once suggested that they could spend time in the States. No, he was the O'Niall, and Ireland was his home. He'd never suggested that they go easy with Mike, that perhaps he could adopt him first, then explain. It was all such a mess.

"Is that all right with you, Kit?" Justin was staring at her from his side of the small table.

"Uh...fine," she murmured, unwilling to admit that she hadn't been paying the slightest attention.

It *was* fine, though. He ordered too many courses for her to deal comfortably with, but she tasted them all, and they were all delicious. The show they went on to see was a Shakespeare comedy, ably performed.

By the time they parted for the evening, promising to

do this again, Kit was completely relaxed. She smiled and closed her eyes as she sat next to Justin in the car. She felt his eyes on her, and she kept smiling, but she didn't look at him.

His fingers curled over hers and he carried her hand to his knee. She inched it higher on his thigh until he made a slight growling sound—and returned her hand to his knee.

"Sex, sex, sex. All you want is my body—and you won't even marry me," he complained teasingly.

"Justin—"

"Never mind. I don't want to hear it tonight." He turned to smile at her. "I have an idea. Let's go to the cottage tonight."

"We can't stay out that late."

"Molly is staying overnight."

"Where? I'm in the guest room."

He chuckled softly. "Kit, there are rooms in that place where I haven't been myself in months. Years, maybe. It's small as castles go, but it's still got a lot of space."

She leaned her head against his shoulder. "Justin, please tell me. What were you and Douglas arguing about?"

He stiffened. "Are you bribing me?"

"No, I just want to know!"

He hesitated, his eyes on the road. "I accused him of putting the doll on your front walk."

Kit gasped out loud and turned on him, almost causing him to drive off the road.

"Kit, for God's sake—"

"For God's sake is right, Justin! You think he might have done that but you didn't tell me, and I've let my son—"

"Kit, stop it! He's my son, too. If I thought there was any danger to him—"

"Any danger! You're telling me that Douglas Johnston might be a murderer, but there's no danger—"

"I didn't say that. And it isn't possible. Douglas wasn't even in town when Susan was killed. I thought he might have put the doll there to scare you away." He paused. "Just like I think Liam O'Grady was running around in that cloak and mask the other day."

"Oh, my God! You think that Liam—"

"No, I don't. I think he did it for the same reason: to frighten you away before anything bad could happen to you."

Kit stared at him for several seconds before exploding. "You had no right to hide such things from me! Don't you see? This is my whole point! You have no respect for my intelligence!"

"Because you haven't shown me a hell of a lot of it!" he shouted in return. "I told you, I've no proof—I've only suspicions. But you don't want to listen to reason."

The car ground to a halt. At first Kit thought he had merely parked on the side of the road so they could continue their argument, but he hadn't. They had come to the cottage.

He turned off the engine, and she stared at him in silence, then exploded again incredulously. "You've got to be kidding!"

"No. Passion is a better release for anger than many another I know."

Kit got out of the car, slammed the door and started walking back along the road. The moon was nearly full now and offered plenty of light for her trek back to the castle.

"Kit!"

He caught her arm, swinging her back to face him, and then two things happened. She knew that she would never walk that trail again; the terror was still too fresh in her mind. And she noticed such a ravaged look of concern and fear in Justin's eyes that she buried her face against his coat. She needed to be held. The scratchy material seemed inordinately sensual against her flesh, and she was acutely aware of his wonderfully clean scent.

Neither of them spoke as Kit led the way to the cottage and up the stairs to the bedroom. Yet it was good. She was held; she was loved. And that made her feel secure. If there hadn't been, somewhere inside her, the memory of her anger, she might have had the nerve to really talk. To explain that she was simply afraid to let go of everything that was her own in life.

But she couldn't bring herself to speak, so everything was done in silence: their rough and desperate lovemaking; their lying together in the aftermath; their rising to dress and straighten the room.

Justin didn't speak until they had pulled up in front of the castle. "I'm asking you to trust my judgment, Kit. Please. I'm not even sure of what I'm saying—I only know that Douglas Johnston would never hurt Michael, and I know that he didn't kill Susan."

"I don't know, Justin," she said wearily. "I just don't know."

"After Saturday, we'll be away. In Dublin. We'll have enough distance to be able to see things clearly."

She shook her head, got out of the car and closed the door. She had a key to the castle, and now she used it without looking back. She walked all the way up the stairs without a word to Justin and checked nervously on

Mike. He was fine, sleeping soundly. Molly must have been sleeping somewhere, too.

Kit kissed his forehead, then went into her own room, where she shed her coat and her silky blue dress, put on her nightgown and slipped into bed.

Seconds later, she heard a soft knocking on her door. "Kit?"

"What?"

"Nothing. I just wanted to make sure that you were all right."

She heard his footsteps moving away down the hall.

Breakfast was a painfully polite affair. When Douglas arrived Kit ran outside and asked him if she could come along. He must have wondered why, but he cheerfully told her that she was more than welcome to sit in on his class.

When Justin realized that Kit was going, he just as politely determined that he would come along, too, and they both sat silently through the entire school day.

When it was over, Kit realized that Mike still didn't have a costume, and that All Hallows' Eve was the next day. One of his friends—Petey—told Kit that they didn't dress up the same way as American children did; they all wore some type of historical costume.

Justin drove them into Cork, where Mike found a Viking costume that he adored. Kit made the purchase, and then they stopped for fish and chips. Neither Justin nor Kit had much to say. Thankfully, Mike kept the conversation going, never even noticing that his elders answered him, but didn't have anything to say to one another.

By the time they got home, it was fairly late. Molly had left them a note saying that hot chocolate was warming on the stove. Kit smiled at Mike and told him that she didn't really care for any, but Justin said he'd have a cup. Kit went up to her own room, wondering at the little tremor that passed through her heart. She should have stayed downstairs. She should have stayed with Mike, not left him alone with Justin. Shouldn't have left him alone with his father.

He was already so fond of Justin. She couldn't help it; she felt as if she was losing her son.

Kit tossed and turned, knowing that Mike had a right to know Justin—and that Justin had the same right to know Mike. She shouldn't envy them their time together. She should be glad of it. And she was. She was so proud of them both—she loved them both so much. If only Justin were a regular man, a broker on Wall Street, a truck driver, anything!

But would she have loved him so much if he hadn't been exactly who he was? If only she wasn't such a coward. If only she had a little more faith—not in him, but in herself.

"Mom! Come on! Justin has to be there on time!"

Kit turned away from the mirror as Mike came bolting into the room. She had to smile. He was so excited—and so cute in his Viking costume.

"I'm coming. Right now, I promise."

Kit quickly put her lipstick on and dropped the tube into her purse. She glanced at her watch; she was running late. A bit ridiculous, she admitted sheepishly, especially when she'd had all day to get ready. But Justin had reminded her that he meant to drive to Dublin in the morning, and though she had thought about telling him to make the trip alone, she had decided that she needed to get out of the area for a while. So she had spent the day packing, then making a few adjustments to Mike's costume. And then she'd spent too long in the shower. So now it was nearly eight, and she was still dressing.

"Ready?" Mike demanded.

"Ready," she promised him. She took his hand and led him out.

At the top of the stairway, she paused. For one giddy moment she was afraid to see Justin. This was dress-up. What if she went downstairs and found him wearing the cloak and mask? She would surely scream and slide into madness.

"Kit! Mike!"

He came into view. He was dressed very much as she was, in comfortable blue jeans and a V-neck sweater. Teal. Almost the color of his eyes.

Kit and Mike walked down the stairs. Justin let Mike walk ahead of them to the door and caught Kit's hand, pulling her back. "Don't leave me, Kit. Not for a second. Not tonight."

She lowered her head, then nodded. It was All Hallows' Eve…an eerie night—especially here. She had no intention of leaving his side.

Justin drove away from the castle and the cottage, toward the southeast. Kit tried to get her bearings. They were going behind the forest that lay south of the cliffs. Not very far away at all. In fact, they were only a short walk from the cottage.

"The land is cleared there," Justin told Mike, smiling at him via the rearview mirror.

"So the fire will be safe, right?"

"Right."

Their dimples were alike, Kit noticed. They both

smiled in the same way, with those wonderful dimples, with that hint of mischief in their eyes.

"Was your mother blond?" she suddenly heard herself ask. She felt suddenly shy, but very curious.

Justin glanced her way with a devilish smile. "Nearly platinum," he assured her.

And then they were there.

Cars were parked all along the rolling hills that led to a vast plateau. There were people everywhere, chatting, laughing. Kit could already hear the pipes, and delicious smells were coming from various food stands. Dancers in emerald-green gowns were performing on a stage at the rear, while a juggler dressed as a clown paused in front of Mike, delighting him with his expertise, then passing on.

Kit felt a little ashamed to think that she had once wondered whether this celebration wasn't some type of pagan rite involving the whole village. It was wonderful, it was very Irish—and it was normal.

"Come on, we've got to get to the bonfire," Justin told her.

She met the mayor then, standing alongside Liam O'Grady. She found it hard to look at Liam, though, without accusing him of trying to scare her.

A ceremony followed in which the mayor gave a short speech in Gaelic and Justin answered in kind. Then he took the torch and lit the fire, and it seemed as if the hills all across the land lit up like Christmas. Kit cheered along with the rest of them, but by then Mike was pulling at her arm. He wanted to go play the games that had been set up for the children.

"All right, all right, just a second—"

Justin was still talking to the mayor. Kit tried to tell him where she was going, but Mike escaped her grasp and went rushing through the crowd. Kit forgot about Justin and the promise she'd made to him and went chasing after Mike. She reached the first booth, where the children were fishing for toys, but she didn't see him and instantly began to panic. She turned and crashed straight into Molly.

"Kit! Are you enjoyin' it, then?"

"Oh, yes, it's wonderful, but I've lost Mike. I have to find him."

"I just saw the boy, Kit, so don't ye go frettin'. Have a sip of some of our fine Irish mead, and I'll take you to him."

Kit started to say that she didn't want anything until she found Mike, but Molly had already forced a cup into her hand, so she smiled and drank.

"It's wonderful," she said, surprised. It was sweet, with a slightly bitter aftertaste.

"It's made with honey."

"Molly, I want to find Mike. Please."

"This way, Kit McHennessy. This way."

She followed Molly through the crowd, frowning as she realized they were heading toward the forest that met the cliff top behind the cottage.

"Molly? Are you sure he went this way?"

The branches fell closed behind her, and Kit looked back, only to realize that she couldn't be seen anymore. And then her knees buckled under her. She fell, reaching out to Molly for support. Mist surrounded her, and the air was growing darker and darker.

She had been a fool. Justin had warned her not to leave his side. She had suspected Old Doug and Young Doug and Barney and Liam and even Justin, but she had never suspected Molly.

And now she couldn't speak or move. She could barely make out Molly's tender smile through the mist.

"Ah, lass!" She stroked Kit's hair. "I'm ever so glad you drank the mead. It had to be tonight, of course. It really had to be All Hallows' Eve. That's so very important to the gods."

Molly's face melted into the mist as Kit crashed to the ground.

And, not far away, the sounds of laughter and merry-making continued.

Chapter 12

Kit came to in flashes. She vaguely remembered being slid onto some type of woven mesh stretcher. She knew that she had been dragged over rocks and sticks, but she had felt very little pain. But all along she had been dimly aware that she was going to be killed, and that, no matter how hard she tried, she couldn't speak a single word.

Somewhere along the road she blacked out again. This time, when she awoke, it was to a sea of mist. She couldn't tell if it was real, or a hallucination of her fractured mind.

Then she felt the wind. It rushed over her, and it was cold, very cold. She could hear its cry, its banshee moan. Instinctively she tried to wrap her arms around herself, but she couldn't. She realized that she was bound to a slab of stone. And that she was so cold because she was naked. Just like the doll…

A scream came from her throat as she found her voice at last.

It was happening, just as it had happened in her dreams. She was lost and adrift in a field of mist, bound and powerless. And the goat-god was coming toward her, coming out of the mist.

It wasn't the goat-god, she told herself. She had to stay sane! She had to talk and stall and pray....

The figure fell to its knees beside her and raised its arm. Kit shrieked in horror again, thinking that it was a knife that rose. But it wasn't. It was a paintbrush, and Molly began to hum and paint little symbols on the flat plane of Kit's belly.

Kit screamed again, loudly, desperately, but Molly just kept humming.

"I'm sorry, love, that the drug wore off so quick," Molly said finally from behind the goat mask. "You go ahead and scream if it makes ye feel any better. But 'tis an honor I bestow upon you girl, don't ye ken?"

Kit didn't want to die. She wanted desperately to live. Everything that she had ever wanted was here: Justin; his love; a family. All she'd needed to do was talk to him, explain that she had to go home sometimes, that he had to consult her, that... But it was too late.

"This symbol is the mark of the land," Molly said slowly. "This is the mark of fertility. And this is the mark for blood."

Tears stung her eyes. I do want to marry you, Justin, she vowed silently. I want to marry you tomorrow. I want to sleep beside you every night of my life.

But her life was ending. Here, atop this windswept cliff, a madwoman was about to steal it from her.

She had to try to save herself. She had to talk, to stall for time, to pray.

"Did you paint Mary Browne?" She tried to keep her voice quiet, calm, conversational, but hysteria still edged her tone.

"Mary, Mary, aye, the poor, presumptuous whore! If only I'd waited. I should ha' known the O'Niall better. Poor Mary. Aye, she wore the marks upon her. They were washed away by the tide. She needn't have died; such a dreadful waste of hope and time!"

"Molly, what about Michael? Michael McHennessy."

Molly actually paused, setting the mask aside. She smiled down at Kit, frowning slightly. "He saw me, ye see? So I had to pretend I meant to cast myself into the sea. He tried to stop me." She chuckled, smug and pleased. "He went o'er so easy, that boy did. It was necessary. But then…" A frown furrowed her forehead. "That Mary Browne! Had she not been dishonest, I'd not have had to hurt the boy. But then I'd not have had you, Katherine, lass."

New chills rippled through Kit. "What do you mean, Molly?"

Molly was drawing a sun sign around her navel. "Ah, ye were so perfect, lass! Fresh and pure and beautiful, with that air of innocence. I knew ye were the one. And he was so drawn to ye. But him with his morals and ye with yer grief, were on opposite poles, even after all that time. I had to get you together."

"The tea," Kit breathed.

"Aye. Justin knew, but he knew, too, that I cared for you deeply."

"He thought that you were…trying to allow me to rest."

"The O'Niall. He's a fine man. His boy will be, too.

And now that the sacrifice is fully fulfilled, life will be good! The harvest will grow again. The men will find jobs."

"Molly, Molly, what about Susan?"

Molly stopped, rocking back on her heels. "Susan Accorn! That harlot! She wasn't worthy of the death she received. Justin didna want her. You hadna returned, and I had to rid him of her clinging arms, her demands. We had to have an heir, and a bride to feed the earth."

"Molly, you must let me go. You're wrong," Kit lied. "Mike is Michael McHennessy's son. You'll waste your time again; you'll—"

Molly shook her head with a secret smile, as if Kit was teasing her. "Go on with ye, lass! He's the very image of his father. I knew it the moment I saw him."

"No, Molly. Really!"

"Shh!" Molly brought her finger to her lips, then spread Kit's hair over the stone. "We must get to the rite now, Katherine, before they stumble upon us."

No...

Oh, Justin, I love you, Kit vowed silently. If I could only go back, I'd grab happiness. I wouldn't let anything stand in my way. I'd be strong, and I'd make you understand.

Molly was slipping the mask back on. Then she stood and began to sway in the night. Her voice rose in a chant, as shrill as the wind. "Kayla, kayla, kayla..."

"What?" Kit shrieked.

Molly paused, ripping the mask off again in annoyance. "Katherine McHennessy, I've sharpened and honed me knife to make it quick and easy. Now ye must shush!"

Tears stung Kit's eyes. There it was. The word that had haunted her for eight years. The word that Michael had whispered before dying. And now she was about to join him in death, the same word ringing in her mind.

"Kayla! Molly, what does it mean? It's not Gaelic."

Molly chuckled. "No, it is na Gaelic. 'Tis older even than that. It is the language of the ancients. Kayla. It means hosanna, hosanna to the great god, the goat-god, Bal, the god who gives us the harvest, who feeds and nurtures us, and must be fed in turn."

"Molly, you mustn't do this! What if Douglas finds out? I think he's suspicious of you already."

Molly's lips quivered. "I must do it for Douglas. Do ye not see? For all of them."

The mask went back into place, covering her face. The wind and mist swirled around them, and in the distance Kit could hear the waves crashing hard against the cliffs. They sounded angry, as if they, too, were waiting for her death.

In minutes Molly would slit her throat, and when her blood had drained into the earth, that mad old woman would cast her over the cliff and into those waves.

Kit began to scream again as Molly resumed her chanting and her swaying. She cast her paintbrush aside and reached beneath her cloak. She raised her arm, and this time she did have a knife. Huge, broad-bladed, and glittering in the moonlight.

When he had first discovered that Kit was no longer at his side, Justin had merely cursed and stridden off angrily to find her. But when he had come upon Mike playing a game at Douglas Johnston's booth, he had instantly panicked. He'd grabbed the boy roughly by the shoulders, frightening him, but not caring, because now he was frightened himself.

"Mike, where's your mother?" he had demanded.

The boy's eyes had widened. "With—with you."

"No, she's not."

Douglas had stepped closer. "Justin…?"

"She's gone."

"Kit?"

"Aye, damn it, Kit!"

"Wait, don't panic! She's probably watching the dancers, or listening to the music, or trying—"

"No, she's not! She's not with me. She's not anywhere!"

"What's wrong? What's wrong?" Mike demanded, close to tears.

Justin swallowed miserably, sorry that he had alarmed the boy. "Nothing, nothing. I just want to find your mother. Mike, you stay here with Douglas. Don't leave him. Do you understand me?"

Pale and ashen beneath his Viking horns, Mike nodded as Douglas set his hands on the boy's thin shoulders.

Justin quickly scanned the crowd. He saw Liam and Barney, drinking dark beer at a stall. He saw Old Doug, laughing happily and giving a small girl a piggyback ride while she giggled.

He saw most of his neighbors; he saw the mayor; he even saw Julie and William McNamara sampling lamb stew. He heard the laughter, and he felt the warmth of the bonfire. The flames were dancing and rising, flaring into the wind. And the wind was picking up, beginning to moan.

But he didn't see Kit. And, he realized suddenly, he didn't see Molly.

He turned on Douglas in a fury, grabbing his shoulders and throwing him up against the booth. "Your mother! Where's your mother?"

Douglas paled. "No, Justin, she wouldn't—"

"That's why you put the doll on her step. You knew! Damn you, you knew!"

Douglas shook his head. "All right, all right! I put the doll there. I wanted her to leave. I was afraid for her—because she was seeing you!"

"Stay with Mike," Justin said curtly. He was already running through the crowd, careless of the people in his way, heedless of the delicately built booths.

He knew where he was going. There was only one place that she could be: the cliffs.

Justin tore across the plateau to the trees, furiously berating himself. He should have brought her here in handcuffs, bound to him. No, he shouldn't have let her come here at all. He should have done something—*anything*—to make her leave. But instead he had fallen in love all over again when he had known that danger lurked…dear God! In his own home.

He didn't remember the forest being so deep and so dense. The moon lit his way, but branches seemed to reach out and tear at him, holding him back, as if they were the ghostly fingers of creatures whose voices became the howl of the wind.

He broke through to the grasslands beside the cliffs at last, and there he saw a figure clad in a black cloak, wearing the horned mask of the goat-god. Something glinted in the night. A knife, its edge reflecting the moonlight.

And there, lying on a slab of stone, a crude altar, was Kit. She was naked in the night, her pale skin beautiful in the light of the moon, her hair spilling in waves across the stone, her flesh eerily covered with strange designs.

The knife started to rise.

* * *

Kit couldn't take her eyes from the knife, from its glittering edge. She opened her mouth to scream again, but her tears choked off the sound.

Molly started to move, and the knife flashed downward.

But it never touched Kit's throat. She was aware of a blur of dark motion, aware that the scream that rent the air was Molly's, and then she heard the soft thud of bodies hitting the ground.

"Drop the knife, Molly. Drop it."

Kit wasn't sure what happened then. The air was still thick with mist, and she was blinded by her tears, but relief filled her. Justin was here. She recognized his voice. She would always know his voice.

"Kit, Kit…"

He was by her side, cupping her cheeks feverishly with his hands, studying her eyes, her face. She tried to touch him, but she couldn't move her hands, and he deftly cut the leather thongs that bound her. He moved to her feet and cut the ties on her ankles, then quickly stripped off his sweater and slipped it over her head. Finally he held her against his body, shaking.

"Kit…"

"Oh, Justin!" She pushed herself away from him, eager to feel the contours of his face, desperate to know that he was real. She held his face, then threw herself against him again. "Oh, Justin, I want to marry you. Today, tomorrow. Now. I nearly threw it all away, and I didn't know how desperately I wanted it until I nearly lost it all."

She stopped, startled by the sound of something behind them. Nearby, Molly was rising, panting, to a crouch.

"Sit still, Molly," Justin warned her softly. "Just be still and wait."

"Justin, Justin, my fine O'Niall," Molly murmured regretfully. "Ye've ruined it. Ye've ruined it all."

"Molly—"

Suddenly she was on her feet. And, just as suddenly, she was running—for the cliffs.

"Molly, no!"

Justin surged to catch her, but she was too fast. Too determined that the land and the sea should receive their due in human blood.

Justin stood on the precipice, holding the black cloak and nothing more. Molly screamed once, and then there was nothing but the sound of the surf crashing below.

Kit tried to rise, but the effort was too much, and she fell back to the earth.

She woke to find herself safe in Justin's arms. He was carrying her, and people were all around them. Liam and Barney, Douglas and Old Doug, Doc Conar, Meg from the pub. They looked so frightened, so concerned.

Kit reached out to Douglas. "I'm so sorry," she murmured.

"No," he told her. "*I'm* sorry." He squeezed her hand.

"I'll need her statement," Liam was saying to Justin.

"Tomorrow," Justin said softly.

Kit realized that they were at the car. She didn't see Mike, and, panicked, she sprang into full awareness.

"Mike! Where's Mike?"

"He's home. Julie and William are with him."

Justin set her in the passenger seat, and she realized that he had wrapped her in the black coat over his sweater. He closed the door, then got in on the driver's side.

"Can you make it home?" he asked her.

She nodded.

The others stepped back, waving to her. They were stunned, and they were sweetly grateful for her life, though they had lost one of their own, however demented she had become.

It felt so good to be alive and free, Kit thought.

The car pulled onto the road, and she hazarded a glance at Justin. His features were painfully tense. She slid nearer to him, reaching for his hand, curling her fingers into it.

He glanced her way quickly. "Oh, God, Kit..."

The torn sound of his voice reached down into her soul.

"Justin..."

"I brought this on you. You could have been killed. I should have made you leave."

"You couldn't have."

"I should—"

"Justin, *you couldn't have made me leave*. Pull over, please. Please, you're still shaking."

Strangely, she felt very calm herself. Calm—and strong.

He pulled the car onto the shoulder of the road, and Kit moved as close to him as she could, taking his face between her hands.

"Justin, I love you. I need you very much. I want to marry you. I came back here because I had to. And I'm alive, Justin. I *am alive*!"

"Kit, you don't need to be sayin' this. I'd not threaten Mike; if I tried to make you believe that, it was because I believed that I could protect you by saying such things to force you to stay with me."

She smiled. "You did protect me. You saved me. Justin, touch me. I'm alive! But I came so close to losing you and Mike. Justin, please, hold me!"

He did. His kisses fell against her forehead and her hair, over her cheeks and on her palms. He held her against his heart so tightly that it was nearly painful, yet she didn't utter a word of protest.

His lips trembled, and his hands shook, but the depth of his love was evident in his touch, filling her again with the joy of life—and the beauty of love.

He leaned back, just touching her cheek and studying the moon. "Do you mean it?"

"Yes."

"You want to be married?"

"Yes."

"I'm going to ask you again tomorrow."

"My answer will be the same."

"Where?"

"Pardon?"

"Where do you want to be married? Here or in the States?"

She looked at him and suddenly started to laugh. Once it had seemed so important, but now... "Wherever you are, that's where I'm happy."

He arched one brow.

"Mike said that to me once. And he's right. Oh, Justin, I don't care! Here is fine; New York is fine. No, here, because I want to get married as soon as possible."

"Mike has some beautiful thoughts—and so does his mother," he told her softly.

She smiled. "We'll tell him—"

"In time. When he's accepted me."

"Oh, Justin."

"Where shall we live?"

"I love you so much—I don't care!"

"Well, we'll work on the future later. Right now I'm going to take you home. I'm going to wash that horrible paint from your body, and I'm going to put you to bed and give you something warm to drink and make you better in body and soul."

He headed back to the castle, and Kit leaned back against the seat. There was going to be sorrow, for Molly, for the sickness that had plagued her, for the horrible things she had done because of it.

But the wind was a cleansing thing, just like the waves that crashed along the cliffs. She and Justin had lost something, but they had also gained each other.

"Body and soul," Kit mused.

"Aye."

"Can we start with the body?"

He smiled, and then he laughed, and then he drew her close.

They were going home.

Epilogue

There was a mist, light and soft and magical. And through it, he was coming to her. As he had always come to her in her dreams.

Dreams these days were sweet and good. No nightmare beasts haunted her sleep, for life itself was sweet and good, the stuff of dreams.

She smiled as he walked through the mist, naked and beautiful, with that slow, purposeful gait. He smiled, just slightly, his eyes alive with desire.

The mist cleared. It was only coming from the hot shower she was enjoying after their trip up Dunns River Falls.

Compromise, they had learned, was the spice of life. And so they had been married in Paris, with only Kit's parents in attendance.

Her mother had cried, of course.

And now they were on their honeymoon—in Jamaica—with Kit's mom and dad watching Mike back at the castle. They hadn't told them anything yet, but that time would come.

He reached her, then took her into his arms. His lips met hers, and she felt as if their bodies had fused together, he was holding her so close.

She could feel her heart racing like the river, and she could feel the sweetness sweeping through her.

He picked her up and carried her out of the steaming shower, grinning as he looked down into her eyes.

"A beast, huh?"

"Never," she promised him sweetly. "Just a temperamental Irishman."

"Temperamental?"

He laid her down on the bed, and she stretched out her arms to him, her smile self-satisfied and sultry, her eyes dazed with love and desire.

The beasts were all gone from her world. He had dispelled them. All that remained was beauty, richer because of all that she had almost lost.

"Come love me, Irishman," she invited him softly.

And, tenderly, he complied.

* * * * *

Books by Delores Fossen

Harlequin Intrigue

Longview Ridge Ranch

Safety Breach
A Threat to His Family

The Lawmen of McCall Canyon

Cowboy Above the Law
Finger on the Trigger
Lawman with a Cause
Under the Cowboy's Protection

HQN

A Wrangler's Creek Novel

Lone Star Cowboy (ebook novella)
Those Texas Nights
One Good Cowboy (ebook novella)
No Getting Over a Cowboy
Just Like a Cowboy (ebook novella)
Branded as Trouble
Cowboy Dreaming (ebook novella)
Texas-Sized Trouble
Cowboy Heartbreaker (ebook novella)
Lone Star Blues
Cowboy Blues (ebook novella)
The Last Rodeo

A Coldwater Texas Novel

Lone Star Christmas
Hot Texas Sunrise
Sweet Summer Sunset
A Coldwater Christmas

For a complete list of titles by Delores Fossen,
visit the Author Profile page at www.Harlequin.com.

CONFISCATED CONCEPTION

Delores Fossen

To my brother, Mike, and his wife, Ann Marie.

Chapter 1

Jared heard the footsteps a split second before the man aimed a semiautomatic at his head.

"Don't move," the officer ordered. He stepped around the side of the ranch house and approached Jared as if he were a cobra ready to strike. In a way, he was.

With the thick envelope still clutched in his hand, Jared lifted his arms in a show of surrender. "I'm Lieutenant Dillard, San Antonio PD. I believe you're expecting me?"

"It's all right, Smitty," a woman called out from inside the house. "He's Rachel's husband. I recognize him." The door opened, and Detective Miller, the dark-haired officer on the other side, motioned for Jared to enter.

"Lieutenant Dillard," she greeted. "I wish you were here under different circumstances."

The officer glanced at the envelope, and from the somber expression on her thin face it was clear that she thought it contained the divorce papers that Jared had mentioned on the phone.

It didn't.

But it would have been far better if it had.

Jared stepped inside and made a mental note of the weapons that were neatly arranged in a rack next to the door. Side arms and rifles for backup. Extra magazines of ammunition. Ditto for the two Texas Rangers posted at the checkpoint at the end of the road. They were armed to the hilt.

Maybe the four peace officers wouldn't try to use those weapons against him before this visit was over.

He glanced around the sparsely furnished place and spotted Rachel right away. She was in the adjoining room that had been converted to a gym of sorts. She was barefoot. Her shoulder-length dark blond hair was pulled into a sleek ponytail. She wore a pair of loose gray boxers and a red sleeveless T-shirt.

Oh, man.

She looked good. It'd been months since Jared had last seen her and well over a year since he'd had her in his bed. But even after all that time and after everything that had gone on between them, the thought of making love to Rachel still set his blood on fire.

He had too-vivid memories of her naked body slick with perspiration. The feel of her firm breasts beneath his hands. The scent of her arousal mixed with his. The heat of her mouth. The eagerness of her touch.

Which obviously wouldn't be so eager now.

Jared watched as she pounded her fists and then her forearms into the punching bag. The blows weren't random but part of a workout routine. Shaolin boxing. And from the looks of things, she wasn't a beginner.

"Hello, Jared. You're early. I didn't expect you for

another hour." Rachel spared him a cool glance with those intense jungle-green eyes before she peeled off her scarred boxing gloves. She picked up a bottle of water from a weight bench, took her time drinking it and then strolled to the window.

Ah, the ice princess act. Her favorite. He recognized it immediately. It probably fooled her bodyguards, but it sure as hell didn't fool him. She was riled by his visit.

Interesting.

"When did you take up Shaolin boxing?" he asked, walking toward her.

Rachel wiped the perspiration from her forehead with the back of her hand. "About a year ago."

Of course. It made sense. After all, there was a reason she was in protective custody. This was probably her way of dealing with the constant fear and stress from Clarence Esterman's death threats.

"You're good at it."

She shrugged. "Well, if I'm ever accosted by a punching bag in a dark alley, I'll be able to hold my own." The comment might have been lighthearted, but that lightheartedness didn't quite make it to her voice. She flexed her eyebrows, a mild indication that the chitchat was over. "Let me get a pen so I can sign those papers."

So much for breaking the ice. This obviously wasn't an ice-breaking sort of moment. Unfortunately, he had to proceed anyway.

Jared went to her, slipped his arm around her waist. Before she could protest their bodily contact—or use one of those Shaolin boxing moves on him—he upped the ante. He crushed his mouth to hers.

The kiss was, well, *interesting*, too. Even though it was supposed to be all for show, it sent a jolt of pure heat through him. Too bad he couldn't say the same for Rachel. If she felt any heat, it was likely from temper and not passion. She shoved her forearm against his abs and jerked away. Jared didn't let her get too far.

"Play along," he whispered against her ear. He slipped the thick envelope into the inside pocket of his jacket. "It's important."

No cool dismissive glance from her this time. Rachel's scalpel-sharp gaze sliced him, her eyes asking a lot of tough questions. Questions he couldn't begin to answer in front of the other officers.

Jared touched her arm with his fingers and rubbed softly. More of the pretense. It was a gesture meant to comfort and reassure.

It didn't work.

He felt her muscles tighten even more.

"Could you give us some time alone?" Jared asked the detectives. He didn't look back at Miller and Smith, nor did he take his attention off the obviously irritated woman in front of him. "Rachel's going in the Witness Protection Program after she testifies against Clarence Esterman this afternoon, so this is my last chance to be with her."

Detective Miller practically marched across the room and joined them. "Sorry, but I'm not allowed to let Rachel out of my sight. Especially not today."

Jared gave her his best wise-guy glare. "Then, you'd better brace yourself for one helluva peep show, Detective, because I intend to take my *wife* in the bedroom and do my best to *talk* her out of this divorce."

Rachel opened her mouth and then closed it just as quickly. She pulled her eyebrows together. Jared gave her arm a gentle squeeze, hoping it would buy him a little more cooperation. It bought him a scowl.

"I have orders from the captain—"

"I'm a cop," Jared reminded Miller. "Head of Special

Investigations and your superior officer. The captain's order is that Rachel be guarded at all times. She will be—by me—and it'll happen in the bedroom."

Jared didn't wait to see if Rachel or Miller would call his bluff. He latched onto Rachel and got her moving toward the back of the house.

"What's this all about?" Rachel demanded in an angry whisper.

Jared didn't answer. Not with the detectives right behind them in the hallway. He'd studied the floor plan of the house so he knew where her living quarters were. He maneuvered Rachel into the makeshift suite and slammed the door before Miller could invite herself in.

"I don't have time to explain everything," Jared informed her. "I have to get you out of here—*now*."

Surprise and then outrage raced through her eyes. It was an understandable reaction. He was feeling plenty of outrage himself.

Jared clamped his hand over her mouth before she could voice her emotions. "Just listen."

But she didn't. Rachel shoved his hand away. "I don't know what kind of game you're playing, but I want no part of it, understand? Just give me the divorce papers, damn it, and I'll sign them."

"There are no divorce papers."

Other than a somewhat shocked look, Rachel didn't have time to react to that news flash.

"Rachel?" Detective Miller called out. "Are you sure you're all right in there?"

Jared moved quickly when he heard the door open, and he cursed himself for not locking it. It was time to beef up the charade, since Miller obviously wasn't backing off.

He snapped Rachel to him and kissed her as if they hadn't been separated for the past fourteen months. In the same motion, he slid his hand beneath her T-shirt. With everything else going on, he sure as hell shouldn't have noticed that she was wearing only a tiny, silky swatch of a bra.

Lace, at that.

Miller cleared her throat. "If you need me, Rachel, just yell. I'll be right outside."

The moment Miller shut the door, Rachel pushed Jared away from her. "What the heck is wrong with you?"

"Plenty." Jared hurried to the door and locked it. "It's been a really bad night, and the morning hasn't gotten any better."

Not wasting any time, he went to the closet. It was in perfect order. As he'd known it would be. Rachel arranged and organized things when she was nervous. And when she was really nervous, she paced. He figured she'd be pacing and organizing a lot before this was over.

Jared grabbed a pair of running shoes and jeans from the closet and thrust them into her hands. "I don't have time to soothe your doubts or convince you that I'm doing the right thing. I have to get you out of here."

"I'm not going anywhere with you." Rachel dropped the shoes on the floor, but with incensed tugs and jerks, she did put on the jeans over her workout shorts. "In a little less than three hours, I'm leaving to testify against Clarence Esterman, and the officers outside will be the ones driving me. Not you."

"You can't testify," Jared said. "Not today, anyway."

"Judas Priest!" Rachel propped her hands on her hips and stared at him. "Are you saying there's been another trial delay? Because if there has been—"

She stopped, and just like that, the color drained from her face. She slowly sank onto the edge of the bed. "My God, did Esterman get to you? Did he send you here to try to talk me out of testifying?"

Jared cursed. Hell. She obviously thought he was lower than slime to have suggested something like that. It meant there was nothing he could say that would make her change her mind about leaving with him.

Instead, he'd have to show her.

Jared finished putting on her shoes, tied the laces with far more force than required and then reached inside his jacket. He yanked out the envelope.

"I told you earlier on the phone that I'd sign the divorce papers," she continued, her voice getting more indignant with each word. "There's no reason for us to go through this—whatever the heck *this* is. You can have the town house. The car. Everything. I'll need to start fresh anyway, once they give me a new identity."

Jared ignored her, opened the envelope and extracted the photo of the newborn baby. When she refused to take it, he dropped it on the bed next to her.

Rachel glanced at it and shrugged. "So? What does that have to do with our divorce or with me testifying against my former boss?"

He had to unclench his jaw so he could speak. "I've been told that the baby in that photo is my son."

Her head whipped up, her eyes narrowed and accusing. He could almost see her process that bit of startling information. She didn't process it well. With reason. Before they'd gone their separate ways, Rachel and he had spent two long years trying to conceive a child.

They'd failed.

And so had their marriage.

Rachel swallowed hard. "You have a son?"

Jared wasn't immune to the hurt he saw on her face. But that hurt was nothing compared to what he'd no doubt see when he told her the rest.

"It seems that way. He's six days old." Jared hadn't

meant his explanation to grind to a halt, but then, he hadn't counted on his mouth turning to dust either. Hell. He hated the people who'd set all of this in motion.

Rachel shook a head, a nervous shudder. Obviously she didn't understand. But how could she possibly understand this? He'd had hours to try to absorb it and still didn't understand.

She reached for the picture, but instead her fingers curled into a tight fist. "My God, you didn't waste any time. So, who's the baby's mother? Is she someone I know?"

Jared caught her shoulders. Their gazes locked. "You're the mother, Rachel. According to the DNA report, he's our son. *Ours.*"

The only thing that saved Rachel from losing it then and there was that Jared was obviously lying. He had to be. But what she couldn't figure out was why he was doing something so intentionally cruel.

"Why are you telling me this?" She got up from the bed, snatched up the photograph and shoved it back into the pocket of his black leather jacket. She didn't want even another glimpse of that image of the newborn. "You want to upset me? To get back at me for all the things that went on between us? Then, fine. You've upset me. Now, get out of here."

He caught her hand when she started to pace. "It's the truth, Rachel."

That stopped her in her tracks. There wasn't any hesitation in his voice. Not even a hint. And it was that sheer conviction that had Rachel studying him. What she saw in the depths of those whiskey-colored eyes sent her stomach plummeting to her knees.

"You're not lying?" she mumbled.

But how could that be? She hadn't been with Jared or

any other man in over a year. And she darn sure hadn't given birth. *That* she definitely would have remembered.

Jared released the grip he had on her and scrubbed his hands over his face. He groaned softly. "I don't have time to sugarcoat this, so here goes. According to the letter I received late last night, someone claims they stole a frozen fertilized embryo that we'd stored when you were trying to get pregnant. This person says they took it so they could use it to impregnate a surrogate."

It took her several tries just to gather enough breath to speak. "And?"

"And according to them, they succeeded."

Oh God.

Success in this case could mean only one thing. What was left of her composure went south in a hurry. Rachel had no choice but to sit back down on the bed, because her legs gave way.

"There's really a baby? Our baby?"

"According to the letter, yes. Of course, we'd stored several unfertilized eggs as well, so I'm guessing they could have gotten one of those, instead. I just don't know at this point. I've got the people at the fertility clinic checking to verify what's missing, but it doesn't look good. Apparently, frozen embryos aren't a high-theft item so security was pretty lax."

The information was coming at her way too fast. Rachel pressed her hands against her head and tried to concentrate, but it was impossible to absorb something that didn't make sense. "Do you believe it?"

Jared lifted a shoulder, but there was nothing casual about that gesture. And there wasn't a relaxed muscle in his body. "Whoever's behind this included a saliva swab so we could do an independent DNA test. I sent it to the lab before I drove out here, but it'll be a couple of days before we can get the results."

Days. She'd have to wait days to learn the truth. And even then, the test results might not be definitive. After all, someone sinister enough to come up with a plan like this wouldn't hesitate to doctor DNA results.

Still, it wasn't the possibility of doctored DNA results that'd put that strained look in Jared's eyes.

"You must think the child is ours, or you wouldn't be here," Rachel insisted.

He hitched his thumb to his chest. "I'm here because they gave me no choice. All I know at this point is there's *a* child, and Esterman's people have him."

"Yes." It sickened her to know that a man like Esterman held the fate of a baby in his hands. The man was a killer. "But why would he do something like this?"

The moment the question left her mouth, Rachel knew why. God. She knew. "It's because of my testimony, isn't it?"

Jared nodded. "They want you to lie this afternoon when you take the stand, to exonerate Esterman. If you don't, they say they'll kill the baby."

The adrenaline and the emotions slammed into her like a fist. She fought to keep her breath level. But lost that battle. Rachel tried to remind herself that it might not even be true. The photo and the DNA report could be fakes. It was possible this was all just a ploy to stop her from putting a killer away for the rest of his life.

But it didn't feel like a ploy.

It felt as if her child was in horrible danger.

"Now that you know, it's decision time, Rachel. I could force you to go with me, but in the end I'll need your co-operation."

Cooperation? She wasn't sure she could even move.

A dozen emotions assaulted her. None good. So many doubts. So much confusion.

A baby. God, *a baby*.

"Rachel, are you sure you're all right?" Detective Miller called out.

"Don't open the door," Jared whispered.

He extracted a small tool kit from his pocket, went to the window and proceeded to disarm the security system. That explained why he was wearing a jacket on a muggy spring day. He had to conceal heaven-knows-what to help them escape.

But the real question was—did she want to escape?

"Convince her to give us some time alone," Jared instructed. "Lots of time. We'll need it if you're leaving with me."

Rachel nodded, somehow. And somehow she managed to get off the bed. She made it to the door, praying her voice wouldn't break.

"I'm okay," she lied. "Jared will be staying until we leave for the courthouse."

The silence on the other side of the door didn't do much to settle Rachel's raw, tangled nerves. It was obvious Jared didn't want either of the other officers involved in this, and Rachel would go along with him on that.

For now.

But there were still too many questions that needed answers before she'd leave with him.

"Maybe I should call Captain Thornton?" Miller suggested. "I mean, just so she'll know Lieutenant Dillard is here visiting you."

Rachel understood the implications of that. And they weren't good implications. Miller wasn't a fool and she no doubt suspected something was wrong.

She looked over her shoulder at Jared. He merely shook his head and continued to work on the window.

"No need to call anyone." Rachel pulled in a long breath so she could finish. "I just want to, um, talk things out with Jared."

Another pause. Rachel pressed her forehead against the door and waited. She really didn't want to speculate what would happen if Detective Miller decided to make that call.

"Okay. Whatever you say, Rachel. But I'll stay put right out here in the hall. Just yell if you need me."

Oh, she would do that. Too bad it might become necessary. Because she didn't know if she could even trust Jared. Their last months together hadn't exactly fostered a trusting relationship. There'd been too many incidents where they'd frozen each other out. Along with that had come the bitter feelings and the accusations. He definitely wasn't the same person she'd vowed to love, honor and cherish five years ago.

But then, neither was she.

During their separation, they'd grown as far apart as two people could get. Heck, they hadn't even contacted each other the entire time she'd been at the ranch house. Yet here he was, right back in her life.

Jared put his tool kit away and eased open the window. The morning breeze stirred the curtains when he shoved out the screen. No alarms went off, which meant he'd successfully deactivated the system.

"If you're doing this, we have to leave now," Jared insisted.

But Rachel held her ground. "And then what?"

Obviously not pleased with her lack of cooperation, he mumbled some profanity under his breath. "I need to take you someplace safe so you won't have to testify. The courts will almost certainly ask for another trial delay while they try to locate you. In the meantime, we find this child and get him out of danger."

It was a simple plan. Also a vague one. And it had holes in it the size of the Alamo.

"You didn't turn this over to the police," Rachel pointed out. "Why?"

This was one of those times she wished she didn't know Jared so well. His mouth tightened. A muscle stirred in his firm jaw. And a sickening feeling crawled down her spine before he even answered.

"The person who wrote that letter said the baby would die if we told the cops, and I'm pretty sure there's a leak in the department. A big one from a person who can do lots of damage if he puts his mind to it. I'll give you the details once we're out of here."

Great. Just great. Her life had just been turned upside down and inside out. Somewhere out there, a child—maybe their child—was possibly in grave danger, and they couldn't even go to the police.

Rachel debated and wished like the devil that she had more time to figure out what to do. This could easily be construed as the point of no return. Once she went out that window, she would essentially be on the run. A fugitive. But if she stayed and told the truth to convict a killer, then a child might die.

Jared helped her decision along. "Every minute we waste here, we could be using to find the baby."

He was right, of course—about that particular argument, anyway. She couldn't be sure about anything else.

However, when Jared gripped her arm, Rachel didn't argue. Didn't take a step back. She climbed out into the yard with him. Then she prayed, hoping this wasn't the biggest mistake of her life.

Jared didn't give her time to dwell on her doubts. He kept low, his gaze darting all around. He led her to the side of the house, toward the detached garage.

"We're taking one of the detective's cars?" Rachel whispered.

"No. But I need a distraction."

Looping his arm around her waist, he ducked behind some thick shrubs. He paused a moment and checked out the yard before he continued to the side door of the garage. From the corner of her eye, Rachel saw him try to turn the knob.

It was locked.

Other than one single harsh word of profanity, he said nothing. Instead, he rammed his shoulder into it, but when that didn't budge it, he snatched the tiny tool kit from his pocket and got to work picking the lock.

Rachel's gaze whipped back to the open window where they'd escaped. No sign of the officers. Yet. But they'd come. After all, it was their job to get her to the courthouse. Once they realized she wasn't in the bedroom, the search would be on.

For months, she'd prepared herself for that testimony, and for its aftermath. A divorce. A new life. A new identity. Out with the old and in with the new. But instead of putting the undercover investigation and her past behind her, she was apparently about to leap headfirst back into it.

God.

Was she doing the right thing? Maybe there was some other way to save the child. Some way that didn't involve them going on the run.

Rachel heard the sound at the exact moment that Jared apparently did. Footsteps. Some movement along the driveway on the side of the house. He reacted quickly.

Jared shoved her behind him and pressed her against the wall of the garage.

She waited. And listened. Even over the thuds of her own heartbeat, Rachel clearly heard the footsteps on the cement. They were hardly more than whispers, but it wasn't difficult to tell where they were headed.

Right toward them.

It was probably Detective Smith doing a routine check of the grounds, but if he saw them, there'd be nothing routine about his reaction.

Jared turned, facing her, and he went back to picking the lock. She saw the intense focus in his eyes. Felt his breath brush against her cheek. Felt the heat of his body.

But she also felt his shoulder holster, and his weapon.

That didn't do much to steady her heart. Thank God he hadn't drawn it, but he probably would if that was the only way they could get out of there.

The footsteps suddenly stopped. She'd seen Smith do a check of grounds dozens of times and knew he was thorough. He'd no doubt be coming around the side of the garage very soon. Too soon. She and Jared needed to get inside, or Smith would certainly see them.

The lock finally gave way, and Jared pushed her inside and quickly followed. There were two cars parked in the dark, cramped space. He opened the door on the one nearest them and retrieved the remote for the garage.

"Come on," Jared whispered. But he didn't use the remote. He opened the side door again and peered out.

"Rachel?" she heard Detective Miller call out, the sound coming through the open window of her bedroom. But it wasn't the only sound. The officer soon began to pound on the door. "Open up. I want to make sure you're all right in there."

Jared glanced over his shoulder at her and put his finger to his mouth in a stay-quiet gesture. He led her out of the garage, staying behind the shrubs, and they made it to the side of the house. Only then did he lean back around the corner and press the button on the remote opener.

The noise started almost immediately as the metal door began to lift. Jared didn't waste any time. He tossed down the remote, latched onto her and got her moving toward the front of the house where he'd parked.

Smith shouted something to Miller, and a second later, Rachel heard the back door slam. The diversion had worked.

Well, maybe.

Once the officers verified that both of their vehicles were in the garage, they'd start looking elsewhere.

Jared opened the door on the driver side of his car and pushed her through to the passenger seat. He peeled off his jacket, tossing it on the seat. Probably so he'd have better access to his shoulder holster.

Not a comforting thought.

The key was already in the ignition, and he wasted no time starting it.

Rachel caught a glimpse of Miller and Smith as they raced around the side of the house toward them. Both had their weapons drawn and ready. That didn't deter Jared.

"Get down, Rachel," he ordered.

He gunned the engine and headed for the road.

Chapter 2

Jared shot past Miller and Smith and sped along the gravel road in front of the house. His best chance was to make it to the highway and try to outrun the two cops. And maybe, just maybe, those Texas Rangers at the checkpoint wouldn't shoot first and ask questions later.

Of course, escape from the safe house was just the first hurdle. He didn't want to speculate how many hurdles they had ahead of them after that.

Or what those hurdles might be.

Even some serious detective work and a fair amount of luck might not be enough to help them find the child—and stay ahead of danger.

"Are they following us?" Rachel asked.

Jared glanced in the side and rearview mirrors. "Not yet."

But he quickly had to amend that. The moment the

words left his mouth, he saw the dark gray car barrel out of the garage, coming right after them.

"They're behind us," he said. "Stay down. The tires are bullet resistant, but they might try to shoot them out anyway."

"Oh God." She mumbled another curse under her breath. "What have we gotten ourselves into?"

He was asking himself the same thing. Jared tried not to think beyond saving this child that *might* be theirs. But even if they managed to get the baby out of harm's way and put Esterman behind bars, there would be consequences.

Huge ones.

After all, he was essentially kidnapping his soon-to-be ex-wife so he could obstruct justice. The department certainly wasn't going to see that in a favorable light, no matter how good his intentions. When this was over, he'd have some serious explaining to do.

Jared kept his eyes on the zigzagging road and spotted the Rangers' checkpoint station just ahead. Both men were there. Waiting. The detectives must have alerted them, because the Rangers had angled their car to create a roadblock.

Without slowing down, Jared veered around them, using every inch of the grassy shoulder, and raced past the checkpoint. As he'd figured they would do, the Rangers jumped into their vehicle and followed in pursuit. They wouldn't just give up and let him leave the area with Rachel.

"What now?" she asked.

She lifted her head and looked out the side mirror. Jared pushed her right back down. If the officers tried to shoot out the tires and missed, he didn't want Rachel to become the victim of "friendly" fire.

Rachel didn't exactly cooperate. The minute his hand was off her shoulder, she slipped right back up in the seat and pinned her gaze to the mirror, and their pursuers. From her soft gasp, she obviously knew things weren't going well.

He took the next curve, and the other cars made the turn along with him. And worse. Jared saw the detectives drop back so the Rangers could overtake them. One of the Rangers leaned out of the window and aimed his weapon at the tires.

Hell.

Jared pushed Rachel down in the seat again. He definitely didn't want her to get a good look at that rifle. With her fear of firearms, she might have a panic attack. There wasn't time for that.

He didn't slow down. Jared kept the pressure on the accelerator and snaked over both lanes so the tires wouldn't be such easy targets. Unfortunately, that didn't protect them from a quick jab of Murphy's Law.

"Hang on," Jared warned.

At seemingly a snail's pace, an old beat-up truck hauling a flatbed of hay pulled out from a side road and directly into their path. He managed to swerve around it. Barely. The car jerked to the right when he clipped the ditch. Jared corrected and then corrected again so he wouldn't broadside a tree.

He heard the sound of metal scraping and buckling and saw the cause of that noise in his rearview mirror. The Rangers and detectives hadn't been so lucky in avoiding an accident.

They'd sideswiped each other to avoid the truck, and

the impact had sent both cars careering into a waist-high ditch. Everyone looked unharmed, but their vehicles were temporarily out of commission. It'd probably take a tow truck to get them back on the road.

Jared didn't waste any time. He stomped on the accelerator and got them out of there.

"We can't follow the highway," he said.

He sped toward the farm road that he'd already checked out. By his estimation, it would take five minutes to get there and another five minutes to start working their way through the maze of back roads that would eventually lead them to the cabin.

"They'll set up blocks to find us."

When she didn't respond, Jared glanced at her. Rachel was no longer sitting low in the seat. Nor did she have her attention focused on the accident behind them. Rather, she was looking at the envelope and the photograph that had fallen out of his jacket pocket.

"Who is she?" Rachel asked.

The picture lay between them. The gruesome image that he hadn't wanted Rachel to see.

Jared checked the mirror again to make sure they weren't being followed. They weren't, but it wouldn't stay that way for long. He hadn't intended to get into an explanation like this until they were someplace safe. Of course, he didn't have a clue when that would be.

He tried to put the picture of the dead woman back into the envelope, but Rachel pushed his hand away.

"Esterman's people sent this to you, didn't they." Rachel's voice was ragged, laced with nerves and adrenaline, but there was fire there as well.

Jared knew exactly how she felt. He'd had the same reaction the first time he saw it. It wasn't any easier the second time around. "Yeah. It was in the envelope with the letter and the photo of the baby."

He debated how much more he should tell her, but the debate didn't last long. This was a critical piece of information that he couldn't keep from Rachel. She'd risked as much as he had by leaving the safe house. Besides, he needed her cooperation, and this unfortunately might do it.

"I computer-matched that photo to the one in her police record," Jared explained. "Her name is Sasha Young. She did time for forgery, and she's—"

"The surrogate mother," Rachel finished. "The woman who supposedly gave birth to our child." She paused and moistened her lips. "They murdered her?"

Oh, man. This wasn't an easy thing to discuss with Rachel. If the people behind this would kill a young woman, they probably wouldn't hesitate to kill again. But then, Rachel must have come to that same conclusion. If she hadn't truly thought a child was in danger, she wouldn't have climbed out that window with him.

"It appears they murdered her," Jared admitted.

She narrowed her eyes. "*Appears?* That's twice you've used that word today, and it's starting to annoy me. Cut the doublespeak, Jared. Is she dead, or is this a doctored photo to scare us into doing what Esterman wants?"

If he hadn't been so concerned over what they were about to face, he might have smiled. Might have. Here, he'd expected the news to send Rachel into a near panic. And it no doubt had. But even so, she was holding herself together—for now, anyway. However, they weren't even close to finishing this.

"I don't know if she's really dead," he admitted. "I checked the morgue, and there's no Jane Doe fitting her description, but that doesn't mean anything. They could have taken that picture and then disposed of the body so that it wouldn't be found—ever."

"Yes." Rachel took a deep breath, and another, and rested her head against the seat.

"I know this isn't easy, and I'm sorry." That picture probably reminded her of her own murdered parents. It was the main reason Jared hadn't been eager to show it to her.

Her head whipped up. "My God, your mother and your sister. Esterman might go after them—"

"I've already taken care of it. I sent Karen and Mom on a little trip out of state this morning. With bodyguards. They'll be fine."

At least, Jared hoped they would be. He was thankful that his family had gone willingly into hiding. Of course, he hadn't given them much of a choice. Jared was sure the only reason Esterman hadn't thought to use them sooner was that Rachel and he had been separated. If Esterman had believed for one minute that he could get to Rachel through them, they would have become his first choice of targets.

"They must be terrified," Rachel concluded.

Yep. But Jared wasn't about to confirm it. It would only push their feelings of panic up a notch. "They know I'll defuse this situation with Esterman as fast as I can."

She glanced at him. Not exactly a vote of confidence. Rachel shook her head. "After the cops asked me to spy on Esterman, I learned the horrible things that he's capable of doing. Well, at least I thought I had. But this… God, this. I didn't know anyone could come up with something so sinister. And to think I used to work for this man. Heck, I used to believe we were friends."

Friends. Oh yeah. Jared had caught wind of some of that. When things had been at the worst in their marriage, Rachel had mentioned something about having a few long talks with her boss.

That still didn't set well with him.

Not just for the obvious personal reasons, either. It likely meant that Esterman knew some of the details of Rachel's and his breakup. If the man knew that, then he was also aware of how much Rachel desperately wanted a child. Esterman must have used that information when he put this plan together.

And he'd come after her with a vengeance.

"I don't regret spying on him," she continued several moments later. "And I don't regret turning over the information to police. Money laundering. Murder for hire. All under the guise of a respectable accounting firm." Rachel placed the photo in the envelope and neatly tucked it back into his jacket pocket. "But I do regret that the investigation brought things to this point."

So did he. And even after hours of thinking of little else, he just hadn't come up with a way to fight Esterman. But then, Esterman had had a year to come up with his plan to stop Rachel from testifying. Jared had had just hours, and precious few of those.

Jared turned onto the little-used farm road and checked his mirror again. Still no sign of any Rangers or cops, but they had almost certainly called for backup. By now, peace officers all over the area would be responding. His captain would have been alerted—and maybe even the city officials. It put a hard knot in his stomach to know that for the first time in his life he was on the other side of the law.

"How long do you think we have before they find us?" she asked.

Probably not long enough. But he kept that to himself. Best to dwell on the things they did have some control over.

"I don't know, but we start by getting out of sight," he explained. "Then, we find the baby so you can testify. Before I came to get you, I called the prison where Sasha Young was an inmate. The warden's administrative assistant told me that she had a frequent visitor, a man named Aaron Merkens. I've already located him and arranged a meeting for tonight."

"Tonight," she repeated on a heavy sigh.

Jared understood that sigh all too well. Tonight was still hours away, and a lot could happen between now and then. The two bodyguards were after them. The Rangers. Maybe even his own fellow officers. Added to that, there was a storm brewing. The thick sludge-colored cloud looked ready to burst wide open, and that would certainly put a damper on his driving like a bat out of hell.

But those things were only part of their problem. He and Rachel couldn't go far since they needed to be in San Antonio for that meeting with Aaron Merkens. As meetings went, that one was critical. Merkens might be able to tell them the location of the baby. The flip side was that he might lead them straight into a trap.

It was definitely a rock and a hard place kind of situation.

Yet, there was nothing Jared could do about it. He had to meet with the man. He had to figure out where to start looking. But first and foremost, he had to make sure that he and Rachel weren't captured.

As much as he hated to admit it even to himself, they and they alone were the baby's only chance for survival.

Clarence Esterman calmly leaned back in the stiff prison-gray chair and stared through the thick, dingy glass at his employee. Gerald Anderson was on a roll, his words fluid. His voice strong and steady. But Clarence looked past that news-at-five veneer and saw a man who was scared spitless of being the messenger for this particular communiqué.

"I'm listening," Clarence assured him when Gerald paused and gulped down some water.

But there was no reason for Clarence to listen too carefully. The oily beads of sweat over Gerald's ample upper lip said it all. Someone had screwed up badly enough that it had warranted a visit from his personal assistant and security specialist.

That did not please him.

There were only two things he hated more than receiving bad news: the stench of the jail and the woman responsible for putting him there. Make that three—he could add yet another thing to his hate list. Lieutenant Jared Dillard.

"Our friend was supposed to have been observed 24/7. No exceptions." Even though he whispered that little reminder, Clarence enunciated each word into the offensive-smelling phone that he was forced to use. He'd already bribed the guards to make sure the conversation wasn't being monitored, but he still chose his words carefully. "Please tell me why that didn't happen."

Gerald made a vague who-knows motion with his hand. "He managed to, uh, shake the observer. I guess he's better at that than we thought he'd be."

"He's very good at what he does," Clarence said calmly. "Lots of citations and plaques for his I-love-me wall. But everyone knew that before we ever made him our messenger boy. So, if I take that 'he's very good' information to the most obvious conclusion, then everyone, including you and the observer, should have anticipated that he'd try to stop us from keeping tabs on him."

No more news-at-five demeanor. The transformation he saw in Gerald was something immediate and akin to a deer crashing straight into the headlights of a fully loaded semi with its pedal to the metal.

"We'll find him" was Gerald's comeback after he'd guzzled down more water.

"Oh, I have no doubt of that, not with what I pay you. And when you do locate him, you'll remind him of the little package we have. That should help him get his priorities back on track. You'll also inform him that he's deeply pissed me off with this little evasion tactic."

Gerald nodded, as Clarence had known he would do. "Absolutely."

But that wasn't enough. Not when his freedom and his life were at stake.

"Shake things up a little," Clarence continued. He ignored the guard's impatient request for him to hurry his visit. "I want our mutual friend to realize how important it is that we have his cooperation."

Gerald leaned forward until his nose was practically against the glass. "You're not saying what I think you're saying…"

Clarence leaned forward as well, but unlike Gerald, he was absolutely certain there wasn't a trace of fear or concern in his baby blues.

"I merely want him…surprised," Clarence explained.

He wasn't totally opposed to killing a cop, but he wasn't giving up on getting Dillard's help in bringing in Rachel. "Have I mentioned that someone very close to him has a fear of guns? A childhood trauma. Something about witnessing her parents' murders. Use that."

Gerald shook his head. "How?"

Clarence slowly brought his teeth together, and it took a moment to unclench them. It was hard to maintain composure when dealing with a certifiable moron. Too bad he needed this particular moron.

For a little while longer, anyway.

"Educate her the hard way, Gerald. Send her running from her estranged husband, and she will run right where we want her."

"And if she doesn't?"

Clarence didn't bother answering that. He had no doubt whatsoever that Rachel would cooperate once the truth sank in about the baby. Simply put, the child was what mattered most to her. Not her super-cop estranged husband that she hadn't bothered to contact in over a year. Not her warped sense of devotion to be a do-gooder for the sake of society.

The baby was Rachel Dillard's Achilles' heel.

And he would use it to break her.

Clarence placed the phone back on the wall, knowing that Gerald would do what he had been told. Hopefully, this time he'd manage it without the mistakes. Of course, Clarence did have a margin for error.

All seven pounds and three ounces of him.

It would be interesting to watch Rachel beg for the child's life.

Chapter 3

Rachel looked out through the rain-streaked windshield and spotted the picturesque log cabin. It was nestled in a thick grove of moss-strewn oaks, making it difficult to see from the road.

Difficult, but certainly not impossible.

And that explained why Jared parked the car at the back of the cabin where it would be out of sight.

"This place belongs to a friend," Jared explained as they made a dash for the back porch. "We can use it as long as necessary."

Rachel wondered if the friend was a man or a woman, but she quickly pushed that question aside. His relationships, personal or otherwise, were no longer any of her business. After all, she and Jared had called it quits months ago. He was a healthy, red-blooded, thirty-two-year-old male, and it was likely—very likely—that he'd been seeing other women.

While the rain pelted them and the lightning slashed across the sky, Jared fished a key out of his pocket and unlocked the door. The place was musky but dry, and a lot larger than it looked from the outside.

Well, sort of.

The combined living and kitchen area was large enough to accommodate two people, but what Rachel didn't see was a separate bedroom. The double bed tucked away in the corner seemed to be the sum total of the sleeping quarters. Hopefully, they wouldn't have to spend the night.

"We'll be safe here until it's time to meet Aaron Merkens?" she asked.

"We should be." After Jared entered the code on the wall pad to disarm the security system, he grabbed a towel from the closet near the door and tossed it to her. "I figure you're the safest woman in America right now. Esterman will do just about anything to keep you alive. You're his get-out-jail-free card. Or so he thinks."

Yes. But her supposed safety came at a huge price. Esterman would only want her alive as long as she could be of service to him.

All bets were off after that.

"I asked if *we* would be safe," Rachel clarified. She watched as he lifted a laptop from the top shelf of the closet and set it on the pine table. "That plural pronoun included you."

With an almost amused look on his face, he brushed past her so he could plug the modem line into the phone jack on the wall. She caught his scent. The wet leather of his jacket. Faint traces of soap.

He still used the same shampoo.

It had always reminded her of the sea. And sex. But then a lot of things about Jared still reminded her of sex.

He was so unlike the other guys she'd dated in college. No comparison really. He was basically a grown-up bad boy who'd won his share of fights, some with his fists. The tiny scar on his chin and the other on the edge of his right eyebrow were evidence of that.

Like the rest of him, his hair was a bit untamed, a little too long—with a natural style that fit his personality to a tee. No glossy polish. No pretenses. Just a man who had a unique way of reminding her that she was very glad indeed to be a woman.

Even now, with all the uncertainty of the moment, she still had the same reaction to Jared that she usually did. Much to her disgust, he pretty much stole her breath. God knows how many times that had happened, so she couldn't blame it on the adrenaline. All he had to do was walk into a room and she melted into a puddle of…something.

Something that Rachel quickly pushed aside.

Those days of lust and great sex were over. They were on the brink of a divorce and their lives were in turmoil. This wasn't the time for the-way-we-were musings.

"I appreciate the plural pronoun, and the concern for my safety," Jared commented. "But I seriously doubt Esterman wants to tangle with me."

Rachel wasn't so sure. Tangling seemed to be something that didn't intimidate Clarence Esterman, and that was only one of the reasons why the thought of his going free chilled her to the bone.

She checked the time. It was nearly twelve-thirty. In a half an hour she was supposed to be on the stand to testify about all the incriminating documents and memos she'd observed her boss shredding. Since there were no other witnesses, she was essentially the prosecution's case. Yet, here she was, in a remote cabin at least thirty miles from the courthouse. The district attorney's office and dozens of other people were probably in an uproar by now.

"I can build a fire if you want to dry off," Jared offered.

"No thanks." Despite the rain, the room was muggy and warm, which wasn't unusual for a Texas spring afternoon. However, that combined with the spent adrenaline was making her feel woozy. She definitely needed a clear head for the things they were about to face. "I'd rather try to figure out how we're going to find the baby."

The sooner that happened, the sooner she could take the stand. And the sooner she'd know if *the* baby was actually *their* baby. Rachel didn't want to think beyond that. One step at a time was all she could handle right now.

He draped his jacket over the back of a chair, the drops of rain sliding off it and spattering onto the hardwood floor. "Like I told you in the car, I'm hoping Aaron Merkens can give us a starting point."

Yes. That would prevent them from having to take the needle-in-a-haystack approach, but it still wasn't very reassuring. After all, Sasha Young had been in prison, and Merkens was her friend.

"You think you can trust him?"

"No way in hell."

She almost wished Jared had hesitated. The fact that he hadn't meant the meeting that was supposed to take place in seven hours might just be a trap.

Maybe Esterman had known they'd find Merkens and try to get information from him. And if Esterman had known that, then he also could have arranged for the cops to be there to take her back into protective custody.

Talk about the ultimate irony. When it came to her testimony, Esterman and the cops were now on the same side. Both would do just about anything to get her to take the stand. One, however, wanted her to lie.

With his back to her, Jared peeled off his wet shirt and hung it over one of the other chairs to dry. "Remember Mason Tanner, the P.I. I've used for some of my cases?"

"Sure." When she and Jared were still together, Turner came to the house a couple of times. "What about him?"

"He's helping us out. A lot. I'm having him check out the park where we're meeting Merkens, and he'll try to make sure it's safe. I can't leave you here by yourself. You'll have to come with me."

Rachel hadn't considered staying behind to be an option, anyway. As difficult as it was to be around Jared, it would have been impossible to do this solo.

"What about this leak in the department you mentioned earlier?" she asked, trying not to look directly at him. It seemed a little too intimate to be so close to him while he was half naked. Instead, she straightened the stack of old magazines in the center of the table.

It didn't help.

Her body still knew he was half naked.

"A couple of weeks ago someone put a tap on my phone at work." He extracted the envelope from his jacket and tossed it next to the magazines. "Then I caught this officer over in homicide, Sergeant Colby Meredith, trying to access some security files. Files that would have told him the location of the safe house where you were staying."

"Sweet heaven." Rachel had never heard Esterman

mention this particular person, but he had a lot of people on his payroll. "You confronted Meredith?"

"Sure did. He only recently transferred in from Austin, so he covered for himself by saying he wasn't familiar with the files and accidentally typed in the wrong code. I didn't believe him for a minute, so I've been watching him. But I figure Esterman put Meredith in place to find you so he could have one of his hired goons personally deliver the news about the baby. When Meredith wasn't successful, Esterman had no choice but to use me as a middleman."

Of course. They probably hadn't wanted to involve Jared since he was a cop, but he was one of the few people who could get to her. That one little detail had embroiled him in all of this.

He turned to type something on the keyboard, and Rachel saw the scar. An angry slice across his chest, just below his heart. She actually took a step back, to put some distance between her and that brutal reminder of what had happened nearly eighteen months earlier.

"Pretty disgusting, huh?" she heard him say.

Only then did Rachel realize she'd been staring at his chest.

Unable to answer him, she merely shook her head. *Disgusting* wasn't the right word. More like *distressing*. The injury had nearly killed him. In fact, the doctors told her that his heart had stopped beating while he was in surgery.

Jared shrugged and went to the closet. He grabbed two T-shirts off hangers, slipped on one and handed the other one to her. "They tell me it'll fade with time."

The scar would, yes. The memory of it wouldn't. Nor would the rift it had caused between them.

In the end, the event that had caused that scar had also cost them their marriage. For Rachel, it had been easier to fall out of love with Jared than to risk another nightmare like that. She'd had enough nightmares to last a lifetime.

Rachel changed her shirt in the tiny bathroom and hung the other up to dry. She turned to leave, but first made the mistake of glancing in the mirror. No makeup. Her hair was soaking wet. She was much too pale. She looked even worse than she felt—something she hadn't thought possible.

"We're connected to the Internet," Jared called out. "Think you can try to find out some information about Sasha Young's last known address?"

"I'll try." Glad that she could do something to get her mind off their situation, Rachel went back into the room and took the seat in front of the computer.

Jared moved the envelope closer to her, and she noticed the address written on the outside. "I got that from Aaron Merkens," he explained. "It's supposedly a rental house on the south side of town, but it could be bogus. There was no phone listing for it. While you're doing that, I need to call Tanner."

Jared took out his cell phone and walked into the kitchen to make his call. Rachel didn't waste any time. She used some of her CPA knowledge and located the real estate tax records for the county. With any luck, the actual owner of the property would be listed.

While she waited for the file to load, she glanced at the envelope. She already knew it contained the photos of the dead woman and the baby, but she was almost afraid to find out what other surprises it held—especially since they were dealing with Esterman here.

Trying to ignore the envelope, Rachel quickly scanned

the tax information on the screen, but it wasn't good news. The owner of the rental property was a corporation. Probably a dummy company at that. If Esterman owned the house, he was too smart not to bury that information under layers of paperwork.

She fed in the next search to try to find out more information about the corporation, while toying with the flap on the envelope. Rachel tried to talk herself out of opening it, but even knowing that the contents could break her heart, she couldn't stop herself. The first thing she saw when she glanced inside was the photo of the baby.

It took her a moment just to find her breath and longer to steady it. As if it were fragile and might shatter in her hand, she lifted it out and placed it neatly on the table next to the computer. She hadn't really looked at the image when Jared tried to hand it to her in the bedroom at the safe house, but she studied it now.

The tiny round face was perfect. Beautiful. A delicate mouth. A spattering of bronze-colored hair on his head. The color of Jared's hair. Of course, that meant nothing. Lots of babies had brown hair.

He could be anyone's child. Anyone's. And Esterman could be using him the same way he'd used dozens of other people over the three years she'd worked for him. Still, Rachel couldn't seem to take her gaze off that precious little face.

His eyes were closed in what appeared to be a peaceful sleep. She prayed that it was indeed peaceful, and that he had no comprehension whatsoever of the danger he was in.

God.

He was in danger because Esterman had chosen to use him as a pawn in a very sick game.

But was this her baby?

Was this the child she'd desperately wanted but had given up hope of ever having?

The memories of her infertility blended together with the tormenting thoughts of the baby. Looking back on it, Jared had never seemed as committed to having a child as she had. He hadn't objected. Not really. But then, he hadn't poured his whole heart into it, either. He'd proven that when he refused to let her use the fertilized embryos immediately after they separated. He hadn't wanted to bring a child into a broken relationship.

Or so he said.

At the time, his steadfast refusal had felt like the ultimate slap in the face. It still did. If she hadn't gotten involved with the undercover investigation into Esterman's wrongdoings, she almost certainly would have pursued the issue in court. That was the only reason the embryos still had been in storage. So, in a way it was her fault that Esterman had been able to carry things through to this point.

She touched the photograph again, running her fingertips over the baby's mouth. His lips were pursed slightly as if he'd just had a bottle. That brought on another wave of fear and panic. Were they feeding him? Was there anyone to hold him when he cried?

Rachel wasn't even aware that she was crying until she felt a tear slide down her cheek. More followed, and though she tried to choke it back, the sound of her sob cut through the room.

Jared was suddenly there, next to her. He didn't reach out for her. Thank God—she didn't think she could handle that right now.

"I'm sorry," Rachel whispered, shaking her head. "I tried to hold it together."

"No apology necessary." He slid his hands into the pockets of his jeans and rocked back on his heels. "I know this isn't easy for you."

"Still, the tears won't help. They never do." She swiped the rest of them away. "You're the only man who's ever seen me cry. You know that?"

"Women tell me that all the time." Jared smiled. "I'm not sure it's a compliment."

It was the right thing to say. A lighthearted and typical Jared comeback to diffuse an otherwise tense moment. Rachel wanted to give in to it, to sit there and let him comfort her. But she couldn't. If she took that kind of comfort from him, it would be too easy to fall back into the same old patterns.

Jared was still a cop. A cop who put duty above anything else, including his own life.

And that would always be there between them.

Rachel stifled the rest of her tears and returned to the computer. But Jared didn't move. He stood there staring down at her. When she lifted her gaze to his, she saw that his immobility wasn't just because of her tearful reaction to the photo.

"Did you get through to Tanner?" she asked.

Jared nodded. "We couldn't talk long. He had to make another call."

"What's wrong?" Rachel held her breath and waited for an explanation.

"Tanner just told me that the cops found Sasha Young's body a couple of hours ago."

"Oh." It hit Rachel a lot harder than she would have thought it would, and the breath swooshed out of her.

Moments earlier, Sasha Young had been simply a possibility. A potential piece of a puzzle.

"She was murdered," Jared continued. "Strangled. Her body was dumped in the Guadalupe River, but some fisherman spotted it and called the cops."

As horrible as that was, Rachel knew he wasn't finished. There was more. "And?"

"Tanner knows the medical examiner, so he got the guy to give him a preliminary report. Miss Young recently had a C-section." Jared looked her straight in the eye. "He estimates the surgery was done about a week ago."

A week. The timing was perfect. The pieces were starting to come together—with one horrible, inevitable conclusion. Esterman's plan was real. Not some hoax meant to scare her into cooperating.

There was indeed a child.

Somewhere.

And he was in terrible danger.

Chapter 4

He listened while Mason Tanner fleshed out the news he'd just delivered, but Jared seriously doubted the fleshing out would make it any more palatable.

Basically, it sucked.

"Your captain wasn't pleased when I told her I didn't know where you were," Tanner continued. "I guess she figured we'd be in touch, and that I'd try to talk some sense into you. Well, consider yourself talked to, because I'm on your side all the way. I don't think you have a choice about what you're doing right now."

"Thanks," Jared mumbled. But he didn't need anyone, including his friend, to reiterate the fact that his options were slim and none. He was painfully aware of it.

"So Captain Thornton basically thinks I've kidnapped Rachel?" Jared asked Tanner.

That garnered Rachel's attention. Jared saw her fingers still on the keyboard, and she looked up from the screen. Her left eyebrow arched questioningly. She probably wanted to know how he felt about that.

In other words, a rhetorical question.

Jared decided it was a good time to stare out the window and finish his conversation.

"Have they made it official?" Jared asked, lowering his voice. "Is there an APB or anything else I should be aware of?"

"No. Not as of an hour ago, anyway—but the cops are *quietly* looking for you. The chief of police apparently isn't too eager to put out an APB on one of the department's most decorated officers. Face it, Jared, you're the Dudley Do-Right poster child for SAPD."

Jared shook his head and silently cursed Tanner's sarcasm. "And they think their poster child has gone skydiving off the deep end but that I'll soon come to my senses?"

"Something like that. A temporary insanity kind of thing brought on by the upcoming divorce and the ordeal that Rachel's been through."

The affirmation had his throat tightening. Hell. He'd known all along that it could come to this. His reputation would basically be trashed. Perhaps along with his career. A career he'd spent twelve long years building.

Esterman couldn't have planned it any better. In one swoop, the man had hit both him and Rachel where it hurt the most.

The baby and the badge.

Jared didn't even want to guess what else Esterman had in store for them. Round one sure wasn't going that well.

"What about the meeting with Merkens?" Jared asked, forcing his attention back to the matter at hand. He couldn't dwell on things he couldn't fix, and at the moment his reputation at headquarters was well out of the repairable mode. He had to solve this case before he could even start damage control. "Is that a go?"

"Sure, but you know there's no way I can guarantee that either the location or Merkens will be safe. Too many variables and too much open space."

"I know. I didn't pick the location, and I wasn't asking for miracles. I just don't want to be ambushed by Esterman's men before I step out of the car."

"I'll do my best. My advice—watch your back. And your front."

Oh, he would do that. But Jared wasn't certain that'd be enough.

Jared ended the call and slipped his phone back into his jacket pocket. "Good news," he told Rachel. Best to try to sound optimistic even if there wasn't squat to be optimistic about. "They delayed the trial to give the prosecution a chance to find you."

She didn't say anything for several moments. "The cops are after you?"

It really wasn't a good time for her to ask that. And maybe it was his imagination, or else the massive amount of baggage between them, but Jared heard the old disapproval in her tone. Not that he needed more, but it fueled his frustration and put him on the defensive.

"I still have my badge," he said quickly. "I'm still a cop."

She made a sound that could have meant anything, or nothing. Unfortunately, it felt like *something.*

"Look, I know you don't approve of what I do, Rachel, but if you don't mind, I'd rather skip the cold shoulder and lecture this afternoon. I've already got enough to deal with here without rehashing the past."

She issued a dismissive glance and calmly turned her

attention back to the computer screen. "Thanks for that reminder, Jared." He couldn't help but notice that she pressed the keys a little harder than required. "I was starting to have a few lustful thoughts about you, but I'm sure that'll fix the problem."

Jared had already geared up to move on to the next subject—the meeting with Merkens—but then her comment sank in.

"Lustful thoughts?" he repeated.

Rachel nodded. "You know, as in those thoughts dealing with lust?"

Nope. He hadn't misunderstood her. It was a very succinct and sarcastic answer. Now, the question was—how should he respond? *Should* he respond?

Rachel helped him along with his decision. Well, in a roundabout sort of way. She didn't even blink. But she did hike up her chin and pull the ice-princess act that he pretty much hated. And she knew it, too. He could tell by the almost smug glint in her eye.

"Believe me, that wasn't the clarification I was looking for," he insisted. "What I meant was…" Jared stopped and rethought the question that had been about to fly out of his mouth. There was a fine line between a request for information and an idiotic remark. Best to go for the direct approach. "What the hell are you saying, anyway?"

She shrugged. "I don't have Alzheimer's, Jared. I know how good we once were in bed."

So did he. And for some reason those memories had gotten a lot more vivid since he'd seen her at the safe house.

He could still remember the taste of her.

Damn it.

"But I also recall what sent us running in opposite

directions," she continued. Rachel moved the envelope, aligning it with the table edge. "You nearly getting killed. Me whining to you every few minutes about you nearly getting killed. Both of us resenting it. I'm sure neither of us wants to go back there again. Right?"

"Right. I guess."

Actually, *going back there* suddenly didn't seem like a bad idea. With his body humming and the sexual energy suddenly zapping back and forth between them, sex seemed like a good thing to consider. It wasn't, he reminded himself. It really wasn't.

"Anyway," she went on, after she adjusted the envelope again. "Forget what I said. I should have kept my thoughts to myself."

He might have had a darn good comeback for that if Rachel hadn't turned the laptop around, drawing his attention to the screen. "There's the information you asked me to get," she announced.

Well, her timing was lousy. She'd basically started a verbal sparring match—about sex, no less—and he couldn't continue. Not with everything else they had to do. Besides, within the next couple of minutes, they had to leave for their meeting with Merkens.

Trying to mimic her composed exterior, but knowing they were far from composed, Jared looked at the screen. The name practically jumped out at him—and put a huge damper on the fit of temper that he wanted to nourish and feed for a while.

"Lyle Brewer," he read. "Esterman's attorney?"

Rachel nodded. "And he's one of the owners of the company that manages the rental property for the place where Sasha Young was staying. It could be a coincidence, but I seriously doubt it."

So did he. Anyone on Esterman's payroll was suspect. "Maybe Brewer's the person who's been helping Esterman. Or maybe he can at least lead us in that direction." Jared checked his watch. "We need to get going. I have to swap cars with Tanner before we drive to the park."

She turned off the computer. "You never did say—how will we recognize Aaron Merkens?"

"Easy. He said he was an Elvis impersonator. I don't think we'll have any trouble spotting him, even if he's not in costume." A flamboyant image popped into his head. "God, I hope he's not in costume. I'd like to get through this without attracting an audience."

Jared reached for his keys, only to remember another important detail. "By the way, something else I didn't mention—Merkens demanded payment for this meeting."

Her eyes widened. "How much?"

"Only five hundred bucks. Don't worry, I have the money. I just thought you should know that his concern for Sasha isn't necessarily dictated by his heart. That'll tell you the kind of person we're dealing with here. In other words, I want you to be careful."

He didn't wait for her to respond. Jared tossed her a dark blue baseball cap that he'd taken from the closet. "Here, put this on. It's a sorry excuse for a disguise, but it might buy us a little safety."

"Safety," she repeated—and paused, obviously giving that some thought. "Maybe this is a good time to ask—what exactly are you anticipating might go wrong tonight?"

Jared put his hand on the small of her back and got her moving toward the door. "Anything and everything."

Chapter 5

Jared got back in the car, bringing the scent of the rain and the park in with him. He cursed under his breath, but it wasn't so soft that Rachel couldn't hear it. Obviously, his mini reconnaissance mission hadn't gone well.

What else was new?

Not much had gone their way so far.

The cops and God knows who else were after them, and they were meeting an Elvis impersonator in a public city park. The operative word being *public*. To say she didn't have a good feeling about this was putting it mildly.

"I guess there's no sign of Merkens?" Rachel asked. She put the rest of the burger and fries that Jared had picked up for them earlier at a fast food place away. It'd taken care of the hunger, but the meal hadn't made her stomach feel any better. Not that she'd expected it would. That was asking too much of mere food.

Jared shook his head and checked his watch again. "He's nearly a half hour late."

Yes. And she'd felt every single minute tick off in her head. "He might still show."

But that was wishful thinking. Rachel didn't know Aaron Merkens, but if he'd heard about the cops finding Sasha's body, then the promise of five hundred dollars might not be enough to stop him from going on the run.

And she didn't blame him.

If Jared had been able to piece together Merkens's association with Sasha, then Esterman would have been able to do the same. Esterman probably wouldn't care much for Merkens sharing information with them and might do whatever it took to stop the meeting.

In Esterman's case, *whatever it took* could mean just about anything. Including murder.

Rachel wiped the condensation off the window with a paper napkin from the sack of fast food. She had another look around. It was almost dusk, and because of the constant drizzle, the place was deserted.

Jared had parked beside some playground equipment. They were in sight and yet tucked away from the main park road—safe but definitely still out in the open. Of course, they hadn't had a choice about that. They needed Merkens to be able to see the car so he could find them.

"I should have pressed him for an earlier meeting," Jared grumbled. "Or maybe grilled him better when I got in touch with him this morning. I damn sure shouldn't have let him off the phone until I had some answers. Hell. This is costing us valuable time."

Rachel had a lot of doubts about what they were doing, but those doubts didn't include Jared's investigative skills. He'd almost certainly done his best to get whatever he could out of Merkens.

"Let's assume the worst—that he won't show. What's plan B?" she asked.

He gave her a flat look. "Believe me, there are worse things that can happen than Merkens being a no-show."

All right. She agreed with that, but it didn't help them now. They had to aim their energy in a positive direction. If there was indeed a positive one.

The phone rang, the sound cutting through the silence. "Thank God," she mumbled, hoping it was Merkens so he could explain why he wasn't there. Then, maybe Jared could browbeat him into hurrying.

Jared took the phone from his pocket and put it to his ear. "Tanner," he said several seconds later.

So she didn't get her wish, after all, but that didn't mean Merkens hadn't gotten in touch with Tanner. Unfortunately, she couldn't tell from Jared's monosyllabic responses if it was good or bad news.

Maybe Merkens had phoned to reschedule the meeting, but she prayed not. Rachel wanted to talk with him now, to get the information and then move on to the next step. Time suddenly felt like their enemy. The longer it took them to find the baby, the longer it would be before she could take the stand. Every minute was a gamble that the cops or Esterman's people would find them first.

"Tanner said he just got a call from Lyle Brewer, Esterman's attorney." Jared slipped his phone back into his pocket. "Brewer said it was important that he speak to us right away."

Lyle Brewer. Just great. First, the cops had contacted Tanner to try to get to them, and now Brewer. Maybe it wasn't a good idea for them to rely on a man who suddenly seemed too obvious a connection to them. Of course, the alternative wasn't much better. It was hard to set up security for a meeting while they were in hiding.

"Brewer says he has something important to tell us," Jared continued. "He won't say what it is until he sees us face-to-face."

Rachel's first instinct was to say no. An emphatic no. She didn't want anything to do with the man who might very well be Esterman's so-called silent partner. But the fact that Jared hadn't already vetoed the meeting meant he was at least considering it.

"You don't think Brewer would bring the baby to us, do you?" she asked. And hoped. But that would be a stupid move on his part. She knew for a fact that Esterman wasn't stupid, and doubted his attorney was, either.

"Brewer might be able to tell us more than we'll get from Merkens. If we even get anything from Merkens. I think we need all the help we can get."

Absolutely, but that information could cost them their lives. After all, Brewer owned the house where Sasha Young lived, and perhaps died.

Jared must have seen the movement at the same moment Rachel did, because his head snapped up and his gaze raced to the cluster of playground equipment near the passenger side of the car.

The man stepped around the slide and looked in their direction. He was tall. Dark hair. Wearing a tan raincoat. And he held a perky yellow umbrella over his head. Obviously, he wasn't that concerned with someone seeing him. Or maybe he simply wasn't aware of the danger.

"Stay put," Jared whispered to her as he reached for the door handle.

Staying put was certainly the safer option, but not necessarily the best one. Rachel grabbed his arm to stop him. "You're a cop through and through, Jared. I'm not. With everything that's happened, maybe Aaron Merkens will trust me more than he would you."

He didn't hesitate. Jared simply shook his head. "There's no reason for both of us to play sitting duck. Tonight, you do the sitting and I'll be the duck."

And with that decree, he must have considered the debate a done deal because he stepped out of the car and motioned for Merkens to come closer. Even that simple gesture had *cop* written all over it.

God, he was hardheaded.

Rachel held her breath and watched the encounter unfold in front of her. The two men paused as if sizing each other up, and Merkens finally started toward Jared. His long stride quickly ate up the distance between them.

Before he even reached Jared, Merkens aimed his index finger at her. "Who the hell is that? This was supposed to be a private meeting. You didn't say anything about bringing someone else along."

"Well, you didn't say anything about carrying a prissy umbrella that can be seen for miles. Trust me, that isn't a good thing. Get rid of it."

Since it seemed as if this could turn ugly, Rachel quickly stepped out of the car. Jared motioned for her to get back in, but she ignored him and extended her hand to Merkens. "Sorry to crash the meeting, but I didn't think one less duck would matter. I'm concerned about Sasha. That's why we're all here, right?"

"I guess," Merkens snarled, after apparently giving it some thought. He didn't shake her hand. Instead, he closed the umbrella and turned his attention back to Jared. "You have the money?"

"Yeah," Jared assured him. "But this is a buy now, pay later kind of deal. You give me the information about Sasha Young, and you'll get paid."

Merkens nodded, eventually, but the arrangement obviously didn't please him. He fidgeted with the plastic handle of the umbrella, and for the first time since he'd arrived, his gaze darted all around. Perhaps it was beginning to sink in that he might be in danger.

"I don't know how much more I can tell you," Merkens whispered. "Like I said, she disappeared about a week ago, and I haven't seen her since. I went by her house just this morning, but there's no sign of her. Even her clothes are gone."

He didn't know she'd been murdered. She hoped Jared wouldn't be the one to tell him. The mood among them certainly wasn't one of trust and cooperation. Hearing of Sasha's death probably wouldn't help that.

Jared kept his right hand near his shoulder holster and weapon. "You told me on the phone that she's pregnant. Is it your baby?"

"No. Of course not." Merkens looked at him as if he'd sprouted a third eye. "It's not like that between us. She's like a sister to me. And as far as the baby, I don't know whose it is. Sasha's a surrogate for some couple who couldn't have kids. They're paying her."

"Yeah. I know that's what you said, but I wanted to make sure it's the truth." Jared's hand snaked out, and he snagged Merkens by the coat and yanked him closer. The man protested rather loudly, but that didn't stop Jared from frisking him. "Is it the truth, Aaron? Because I'd really hate to think that you're lying to me."

"According to Sasha it's true. Now, get your freakin' hands off me." He jerked away, stepped back and indignantly readjusted his coat. "I'm not carrying a gun, and I've told you all I know—so give me my money."

Keeping eye-contact with Merkens, Jared extracted a roll of bills from his jacket pocket. But he didn't hand it over. He just continued with that intimidating stare. "First, I want you to think real hard, because that's what

I'm shelling out bucks for you to do. Has Sasha ever mentioned who asked her to be a surrogate?"

He immediately shook his head. "I can't help you there. That's one thing she always stays away from. The subject of the baby is a big no-no."

"Any theories about why she doesn't want to talk about it?" Rachel asked.

"No. And I don't ask. I figure, it's none of my business. Like a lot of other things." Merkens waggled his finger at the money. "I'll take that now."

But Jared didn't move. "You still have that phone number I gave you when we talked earlier? The one for a guy named Tanner?"

Merkens nodded. "Yeah. What about it?"

"If you remember anything about who hired Sasha to be a surrogate, then call Tanner and arrange for another meeting." He slapped the money into Merkens's palm. "I'll make it worth your time."

Merkens counted the money before returning his gaze to Jared. "I'll see what I can find out."

"Do that, but be smart about it. No more yellow umbrellas, metaphorical or otherwise. There might be people who'd object to you digging into this."

Merkens's eyes widened, then narrowed. He gave another nod before he turned and walked away.

"I don't think he's gotten the word yet that Sasha's dead, but he definitely knows more than he's saying," Jared concluded.

"How do you know that?"

"Easy. He didn't ask for an explanation when I mentioned that 'people who'd object' part. So he must at least suspect that there's more to this than me just asking a couple of questions about his friend."

She shook her head. "But why would Merkens withhold information? And why would he still want to meet with us if he suspected Esterman was after him?"

"He didn't keep this meeting for our benefit. He did it strictly for the money." Jared started back toward the car, and she followed him. "My guess is, he needs a fix, and soon. He'll sell his soul if necessary."

She wiped the rain off her face and slung it aside. "So this was a waste of time?"

"Maybe. Maybe not. We've planted the seeds. When he's desperate for more money, Merkens might just recall the very piece of information that we need to know."

Rachel was about to remind him that they might not be able to wait long enough for Merkens to come around, but a strange swishing sound stopped her. She turned her ear toward it, to try to figure out what it was, but Jared apparently already knew.

"Someone's shooting," he warned.

There was no time for Rachel to brace herself. No time to think.

Jared hooked his arm around her waist and pulled her to the ground. Panic gripped Rachel much faster than she could fight it off. As her heart pounded and her breath raced, the images immediately flooded her head. Her parents on the floor of their bedroom. The intruder's gun.

The smell of death.

Those images that had tormented her since she was seven years old and had witnessed their brutal murder. The memories roared through her with a vengeance.

"Try to hold it together," Jared murmured. "I'll get you out of here. I promise."

Rachel clung to the sound of his voice, clung to each comforting word. It didn't stop her physical reaction to the old demons, but she forced herself not to give in to the panic. She wouldn't let the fear cause them to get killed. Somehow, she'd get beyond this.

"The shots are coming from those trees," Jared said. He drew his own weapon. "And whoever's shooting, they're not aiming at us."

No. Not at the moment, anyway.

Rachel lifted her head a fraction and glanced at the thick oaks on the other side of the road. They were at least five hundred yards away and did a thorough job of concealing the shooter.

More shots followed. A few of them gashed into metal playground equipment and sent the creaky swing spinning. They came close. Too close. And the thought of them coming any closer sent Rachel's heart racing out of control.

She tried not to think of the baby in the photo. But her mind kept going back to that image. Unfortunately, it was spliced with the other memories racing through her head. Violent memories of her parents' murder. It was a painful reminder of the danger the child was in. Her heart ached at the thought of never learning the truth, of never seeing the baby that might be hers.

Jared levered himself up slightly and aimed his weapon. What he didn't do was fire. Thank God. She wasn't sure she could handle that with him so close to her. Instead, he paused. Waiting. Listening. Rachel listened as well, and the silence slid in around them.

Nothing.

For several excruciating moments.

Then, Rachel heard the faint sound of someone gunning a car engine. Followed by not-so-muffled gunfire.

Jared cursed. "We have company."

"Where?" Rachel looked out at the trees again but couldn't see anything.

"Two to one, the cops are here. That's why that second set of shots wasn't fired with a silencer."

Jared didn't finish the explanation. He didn't have to. If the cops were there, then they were very close to being captured.

"I doubt they want us dead," Jared continued a moment later. "But the bullets might not know that."

True. They could be killed simply because they were in the wrong place at the wrong time.

She leaped up when he did, but Jared grabbed her shoulder and pulled her right back on the ground. "Not yet."

He peered around the car door and waited for what seemed like endless minutes. By degrees, the sound of the gunfire slowly shifted in another direction. Moving away from them. Jared must have thought so as well, because he finally let her stand up, and he helped her into the car.

"We're getting out of here," he ordered. "Stay low in the seat so they can't see you."

Without turning on the headlights, Jared pulled onto the main park road and stomped on the accelerator.

"Hell," he spat out.

"What's wrong now?"

But she immediately saw what had caused Jared's reaction. When they passed a thick shrub, it was there. The body, facedown in a crumpled heap on the ground.

Rachel didn't need to see his face to know who it was. The tan trench coat. The dark hair. The yellow umbrella by his side.

It was Aaron Merkens.

And he was dead.

Chapter 6

Hell. Hell. Hell.

This was definitely a worst-case scenario coming true right before his eyes. The cops facing off against Esterman's hired assassins. This showdown could easily result in Rachel and him being captured.

Or worse.

Much, much worse.

Jared sped through the park, hoping he was moving away from both sets of shooters. He didn't have time to wait out the crossfire, and he damn sure didn't have time to stay behind and clear things up with the cops. He needed to rendezvous with Tanner in exactly a half hour, and that was one appointment he had to keep.

"They killed him," Rachel muttered under her breath. "They really killed him."

Jared added another *hell* to his mental rantings. Rachel had obviously seen the body, and that was something he'd wanted to avoid.

"Are you all right?" He didn't dare risk looking in her direction, but he did push her lower into the seat. Jared kept his attention on the road to make sure they weren't being followed.

She made a soft sound that couldn't hide her fear. "I've been better."

Yeah. A huge understatement. And the night wasn't over yet. He'd let her catch her breath first before he reminded her that this was just round one.

And they'd lost.

Merkens was dead. No doubt about that. Jared had seen the body and the blood. He didn't need a crystal ball to know who was responsible.

Clarence Esterman.

That meant Merkens had had some sensitive information that Esterman wanted to keep private. So sensitive and private that Esterman had been willing to kill to keep it secret. That also meant Jared had missed his chance to get the info—again. Hell. He should have beaten it out of the umbrella-carrying fool while he had the chance.

And while he was doling out should-have's and other insults, Jared decided he should have his own head examined for bringing Rachel into this. With her gun phobia, that shooting ordeal was probably a couple of hundred steps beyond terror. An incident like that could easily cause her to have a breakdown.

"I'll figure out a safe place for you to go as soon as I talk with Tanner," Jared promised. He made his way to an access road and then exited onto the interstate. "I won't make you go through something like this again. I swear, I'll do whatever it takes to keep you safe."

"Excuse me?"

Her tone caused him to take notice. It wasn't exactly a request for clarification. Even though her voice was trembling, it was snippy. And much too calm.

Never a good sign when it came to Rachel.

"Please don't tell me you're thinking about dumping me somewhere so you can try to find the baby all by yourself?" she asked. "You need help. *My* help. So spare me this Y-chromosome testosterone garbage."

He'd been right. Calmness in this case meant it'd take some fast talking to get Rachel to see his side. "I need you safe so I can concentrate on doing what has to be done." And to drive his point home, he added, "Do you have any idea how close you came to getting hurt tonight?"

"Some, yes. I got my first hint when that bullet whizzed past our heads and slammed into the swing just a couple of yards away."

Obviously she had a grasp on the situation. A smart-ass grasp. Jared had to unclench teeth before he could continue. "Then, you know I can't keep putting you in danger. What if you'd had a panic attack back there, huh?"

"I didn't—"

"But you could have."

"But I didn't!" She slapped her hand against the padded console. "God, I might as well find a wall to bang my head against. It'd be a better use of my time than trying to reason with you."

The sheer volume of her voice had him pausing, and it took Jared a moment to figure out why. It was the first time he ever remembered Rachel yelling at him. She wasn't the yelling type.

At least, she didn't use to be.

She obviously was now.

Rachel cursed. Not only was it loud as well, but it was also fairly creative. Had he not been the recipient of that profanity, it would have impressed him.

"Yes, I have panic attacks," she admitted, her voice still rather loud. "Yes, just the sight of a gun nearly causes me to hyperventilate. And yes, I was scared enough back there that I nearly wet my pants. But there is no way I'm going to sit on my butt and wait for you to rescue this child. Not when I can help. I'm in this as deep as you are, Jared, so learn to live with it."

With that ultimatum, she brushed him off with one of those icy looks and folded her arms over her chest. Both things, coupled with her stubbornness, riled him.

And pleased him.

Maybe Rachel hadn't been quite as close to a panic attack as he'd originally thought. Still, that didn't mean he wanted any more bullets flying in her direction.

His brow furrowed. "You are *so* stubborn."

"Yeah. Like you're not?"

This was a standoff. Unlike the yelling, it was very familiar ground. He tossed a glare at her. Rachel tossed one back, and he knew she had no intention of changing her mind. So, Jared tried a more logical approach.

"What is it exactly that you believe you can do to help me find this baby faster?" he asked. He took the exit to San Pedro Avenue where he was supposed to meet Tanner, and waited for her answer. An answer he was sure he could blast right out of the water.

"Well, for one thing, I can search hospital records on the computer to find out where Sasha had the C-section. When I have a doctor's name, we can question him and try to figure out who paid the bills. That might lead us to the person who helped Esterman put this plan together."

Jared had to scrutinize that response before he realized no blasting was required. As ideas went, it was a winner. It would take him hours to work his way through cyberspace, but Rachel had great hacker skills. Heck, she'd even helped him out on a few cases. She could probably figure out a way to get the information a lot faster than he could.

While he continued his mental debate about her participation, Jared parked near a bustling Mexican food restaurant. And waited.

With any luck it wouldn't take long for Tanner to show, and with even more luck, they'd be able to get lost in the crowded parking lot. Getting lost was about the safest thing they could do right now.

"Well?" she prompted. "Still thinking of a way to get rid of me?"

"It was never about me getting rid of you, Rachel. I just don't want you to have to face something that maybe you aren't ready to handle."

Rachel laughed, a short sarcastic burst of sound. "For three months I spied on Esterman. *Three months.* I suppose you think that was relaxing, huh?" She didn't wait for him to answer. She fired her words at him like gunshots. "And then he threatened to slit my throat when he heard I was going to testify. Definitely a day at the beach."

That wasn't an easy thing for him to hear. Christ! She'd done the right thing by agreeing to spy on Esterman. No one else had been in a position to bring down the man. Still, it put a knot in his gut to know that Rachel had gone through something like that.

"You know what?" she went on. "I didn't have a panic attack then, so quit treating me as if I'm a useless bimbo that you have to pawn off on someone else."

A little bewildered, he stared at her. "When did all of this happen, huh?"

"When did what happen?"

"This attitude."

"You mean me showing some backbone? It's always been there, Jared. I guess I just got out of the habit of showing it when we were together. You had enough backbone for both of us. Mine wasn't needed."

He geared up to disagree, to defend himself, but before he opened his mouth and risked inserting both of his size ten-and-a-half shoes, Jared gave it some thought. She might have a point. *Might.*

"Anyway, all of this is moot," she concluded. "We're in this together, whether you like it or not. Nod if you agree. If you don't, then please do us both a favor and keep it to yourself."

Whoa.

Jared took another mental step back to figure what he was going to do about it. From the steely look in Rachel's eyes, her participation in this little adventure was going to happen with or without his approval. And whether he liked it or not, he really needed her help.

Only because she didn't give him a choice, Jared nodded. Eventually. "Okay. No pawning you off on anyone. But you won't take any unnecessary chances, understand?"

"Deal," Rachel practically snarled. "And I'll expect you to do the same thing. You might be six feet tall and bear a striking resemblance to a certain superhero, but you're darn sure not bullet-proof."

Flattered and rather annoyed with her sarcasm, he forced himself not to smile. Or frown. This conversation had been an eye opener.

Who *was* this woman?

He wasn't sure, but he thought he really was beginning to like her. Of course, that same backbone could cause lots of problems for them down the road.

"Minus the superhero-resemblance part, that goes for your five-and-a-half-feet tall body, as well." He added a grouchy-sounding growl for good measure.

"This might be what some would call a memorable moment. We agree on something."

"And we argued." *Really* argued. Rachel hadn't run for cover at the first sign of conflict. During their marriage, she'd been much better at freezing him out or leaving the room than at dealing with direct confrontation.

Well, she obviously didn't have a problem with it now.

Jared just stared at her. They were parked beneath a neon sign, and a host of watery colors danced across her face. The bright hues didn't quite go with the scowl she aimed at him, but they did do some amazing things to her eyes.

Rachel was definitely something in the looks department, and Jared had never been more aware of that than he was at this moment. She wasn't drop-dead gorgeous; her face was much more interesting than gorgeous. It was an honest face. A face with character. A few tan freckles on her nose. Great mouth.

And suddenly she was staring as if she had no idea what to do with him.

Unfortunately, Jared had plenty of ideas.

Bad ideas.

Something hot and intense sizzled between them.

Her scowl faded. Their gazes met, and they exchanged a glance that only former lovers could have managed. A glance that conjured up the image of her naked beneath him. And her naked on top of him.

Hell, it just conjured up sexy images, period.

"And don't you dare say that outburst was a PMS thing," she added.

The corner of his mouth eased up, even though there sure was nothing to smile about. "I wouldn't think of it. If I did, you might use me for a punching bag."

The erotic images kicked up another notch. They were things he shouldn't be thinking about. Things that involved slow, wet kisses on just about every inch of her body.

The scent of her and the memory of Rachel's taste raced through him. Not good. He had too much to deal with tonight without having to fight another battle with his testosterone levels.

The timing sucked. Man, did it. She was coming down from a terrifying ordeal. For that matter, so was he. What he needed to do was step out of the car, to give her space. To give himself some space.

But Jared didn't do that.

Nope.

No space whatsoever.

Instead, he slid lower in the seat so they were eye to eye. And mouth to mouth. He eased his hand around the back of her neck and drew her closer. She didn't resist. And he didn't do a thing to encourage resistance.

She was trembling all over, and he held her, pressing his face against hers. He felt the rapid pump of her heart against his chest. Took in her rich feminine scent. Heard the slight arousing hitch of her breath that told him surrender of some sort was just around the corner. If he wanted her to surrender, that is.

He assured himself that he didn't.

He really didn't.

But even that assurance didn't stop the slow hunger that made its way through him. And he knew he was in trouble. Still, he didn't do a thing to stop it. In fact, he sped things along.

Cursing himself, Jared did something he figured he'd soon regret. He leaned in, gathered her close and captured Rachel's mouth as if it were his for the taking.

Chapter 7

It was instantaneous. Rachel heard the crash of thunder outside. Inside, there was a flash of heat between Jared and her.

He pulled her to him, his arms warm and welcome. The motion was seamless and surprisingly gentle. However, that was the only thing happening between them that was gentle. His mouth was suddenly on her.

That clever, hot mouth.

Maybe it was from bone-weary fatigue or just the fire that had always been there, but Rachel felt her willpower dissolve the moment he kissed her. Every wall that she'd built to distance herself from him came tumbling down.

He looked good. Smelled good. But, sweet mercy, he tasted even better.

He plunged her into a fire so hot that it nearly consumed her on the spot. The mating of their tongues. The intimate joining of their mouths. The heat of their bodies. The way they fit together, even now.

Jared was good. Beyond good. But then, she'd always known that. He could somehow turn a simple kiss into something almost as good as full-blown sex.

Almost.

Her body quickly reminded her that it was *almost* as good.

His tongue teased hers. His mouth pleasured. And it left her wanting more in the worst kind of way. A way Rachel knew she couldn't have.

Not now, at least.

After all, they were in a parking lot. Out in the open. Where anyone could see them.

Or kill them.

Jared's awareness of their situation must have kicked in at the exact moment as hers, because Rachel felt his sinewy arms tense just slightly. At first. Then, they tensed a lot more than slightly.

His mouth left hers, and he eased back a couple of inches. His breathing was uneven. His lips slightly parted. Their gazes came together again, and this time the heat was mixed with a fair amount of reality.

Reality wasn't especially welcome, since she still had the taste of him in her mouth.

"Guess that was one of those act now, think later kind of reactions," he mumbled.

"Yes."

There wasn't much else she could say. Without him feeding the fire in her blood, the kiss seemed, well, incredibly stupid. Here they were in the middle of a dangerous situation, having just witnessed a murder, and they couldn't keep their hormones in check.

Yes, definitely stupid.

"I was way out of line," he added. "And I'm sorry."

"Yeah. Me too."

But it was a lie. Rachel wasn't sorry that he'd kissed her; she was sorry that it had felt so good.

She wanted to try to explain away the whole incident, but she changed her mind when she heard the sound of an approaching vehicle. A sporty black truck. It drove past them. Slowly. The driver didn't park in the front of the main lot where they were but instead drove to the back.

The far back.

It was still within sight but barely. Rachel could see the vehicle in her side mirror.

"That's Tanner," Jared said. "And I'll bet Lyle Brewer won't be too far behind him. Make sure you stay low in the seat. The windows are tinted, but I don't want to take any chances."

What was left of that ember of passion evaporated on the spot. "Brewer, as in Esterman's attorney? What would he be doing here?"

"Meeting with Tanner. Remember, Brewer says he has something he needs to tell us."

Her mouth dropped open. Jared had already agreed to the meeting—and set it up—without even getting her opinion? So that's what the monosyllabic conversation with Tanner had been about.

"I thought I made it clear that I didn't want to be left out of the information loop," Rachel insisted.

"You won't be left out. Tanner stashed this in the car for us." Jared picked up a small receptor earpiece and ink-pen size communicator from the tray beneath the console. "We'll be able to hear everything Brewer says."

"That's not what I meant, and you know it. I should be

the one to meet with Brewer. Esterman wants me alive. He probably doesn't feel the same about Tanner. Or you."

"Brewer doesn't know you're here, all right." Jared made use of the receptor, holding it against his ear. "He thinks you're someplace miles away, and I want to keep it that way."

So did she, but not at the risk of endangering someone else. Still, there was little she could do about it now. Jared had already set things into motion.

Tanner got out of his vehicle, the wind and the drizzle spitting at him. Rachel recognized him immediately. Hard not to remember the desperado-dark hair that stopped just at the top of his shoulders. He always reminded her of a vampire who'd turned good but had a fifty-fifty chance of going back to his old biting ways. Still, Jared trusted him, so that had to count for something.

Just how much of something, Rachel didn't yet know.

After all, Tanner had obviously agreed with Jared to set up this meeting. She'd reserve judgment on whether that was a good thing.

Rachel leaned closer so she could share the receptor with Jared. He held it between them, but since the device was so small, she had to get closer. Very close. Until they were shoulder to shoulder and practically cheek to cheek.

Great.

The closeness wasn't an ideal arrangement so soon after they'd shared that kiss. But then, there was nothing about this situation that was ideal.

"Jared, Rachel," Tanner greeted, obviously speaking into some hidden communicator. He leaned against his truck and waited.

"Was this get-together your idea?" Rachel asked Tanner. Unfortunately, she had to lean against Jared to ask that. Her left breast pressed against his arm.

Jared noticed. He grunted softly. So did she.

Unaware of the touchy-feely session going on in the car, Tanner shrugged. "It was sort of a mutual decision. I think it's possible that Lyle Brewer knows a lot more about what's going on than he'll want to share with Jared or you."

She glanced at Jared. "I didn't need a meeting to tell me that. Has it occurred to you two that this might not be safe? A man was just killed, for heaven's sake. Brewer could be leading the gunmen or the cops right to us."

"Not tonight he's not," Tanner assured her. "We left the gunmen in the park." He pulled out a small bag of something from his pocket and started eating. Peanuts, she realized when she saw him throw the shells onto the ground. The man was certainly calm under pressure. Unlike her.

Rachel huffed. "And you think they'll just stay there because that's where you left them?"

"They'll need to clear up that mess they made with umbrella-boy. They won't want that kind of evidence left lying around for the cops to find." Tanner took his time munching on another peanut. "Plus, I arranged a little diversion for them when they're done with that. Esterman's men think you're at a hotel on the west side of town. They're likely providing that information to the cops as we speak."

That wasn't much of a reassurance. Diversions weren't necessarily a success just because they were diversions. Still, it was too late to do anything about it. They were here, ready to meet with Lyle Brewer. It was best to learn what they could from him, and then get the heck out of here.

Tanner tipped his head toward the front of the parking lot. "Speaking of the devil, there's Brewer. I do so admire a person who's on time for their appointments."

A sleek midnight-black car drove in and came to a stop just a couple of yards behind Tanner's truck.

"Stay down, Rachel," Jared warned.

From the side mirror she could see Lyle Brewer exit his car. She had no trouble recognizing him, as well. The perfectly styled salt-and-pepper hair. The polished demeanor. She'd seen him in Esterman's office numerous times. He was no doubt doing everything possible to get his client out of jail. Was he also in on the plan to hold a child hostage in exchange for her false testimony?

Rachel could certainly believe that. After all, Brewer worked for Esterman.

"For the sake of your suit, we'd better make this quick," Tanner insisted when he greeted Brewer. "I've heard overpriced Italian suits shrink when they get wet."

That didn't do a lot to improve Brewer's demeanor. Even at a distance, Rachel could see his shoulders stiffen.

"I spoke with my client's personal assistant this afternoon, and he asked me to get a message to Lieutenant Dillard."

"Oh, yeah?" Tanner tossed down another peanut shell. It landed on or near Brewer's shoes. "Does your client's personal assistant have a name?"

"He wishes to remain in the shadows, so to speak, but he assures me that he's acting on behalf of Mr. Esterman himself. Mr. Esterman is weary of the court proceedings and the trial delays, and he believes he'll be exonerated when the jury has all the evidence. So, he humbly requests that Rachel Dillard turn herself over to the proper authorities so she can testify."

"And if she doesn't?" Tanner challenged.

Brewer shrugged. "I'm not here to issue warnings or threats. I simply want a fair trial for my client."

Tanner chuckled. "In a pig's eye. You want him to walk."

Brewer nodded without hesitation. "That, too. No surprise there—he is, after all, my client. But I'm of no threat to the lieutenant or Rachel Dillard. I'm simply asking them to comply with the law. That shouldn't be a far stretch for the lieutenant, since he's a peace officer. I've heard rumblings that in a matter of hours, the chief of police will be demanding Dillard's badge."

Even though Jared didn't move or make a sound, Rachel was close enough to feel him tense. That was it. His only reaction to what had to be heartbreaking news. It was another of those weird ironies. Jared had done the right thing by stopping her testimony, but in doing so, he'd broken the law.

"Are you okay?" she whispered.

"Sure."

It was a lie. And even more than that, it was a taboo subject. During their marriage, they'd disagreed so many times over his devotion to his badge that just bringing it up now would make things worse.

Rachel turned her attention back to Brewer just as he slipped his hand into his jacket.

Before she could even blink, Tanner dropped the bag of peanuts, reached into his jacket and drew his weapon. So did Jared. He didn't stop there. He opened the car door a fraction.

With her heart pounding, she held her breath and waited. God, she'd known this could turn dangerous but she hadn't expected it to happen so quickly. If Jared was forced to fire to protect Tanner and if Esterman's people waited nearby, it would almost certainly lead to another gun battle.

"I'm not armed," Brewer assured him, his voice shaking now. "I just need to retrieve some correspondence from my pocket."

"No sudden moves, and use only two fingers," Tanner instructed.

Keeping his gaze locked with that of the man who had a gun aimed at him, Brewer extracted the envelope and stiffly extended it to Tanner. "From Mr. Esterman's personal assistant."

Tanner took it. What he didn't do was lower his weapon. "I'd love to do this the old-fashioned way and coax the information out of you, but I don't have time. So here goes—Where's the baby?"

Rachel moved to the edge of the seat and wished the rain and the darkness weren't between them so she could better see Brewer's expression. It was a long shot, but she might be able to figure out just how deep he was into this.

"I have no idea what you're talking about," Brewer insisted. "What baby?"

Tanner stood there for several moments, studying him. "Why don't you ask your boss? And while you're asking, tell him that he can contact me with the answer."

"I will. Not that I expect him to know, either. By the way, I'd like to offer some free advice. Personally, I'm not as anxious as my client to see Rachel Dillard on the stand, but it's my duty to advise you or her husband to take her to the nearest police station."

No long pause this time. Tanner's response was immediate. "Here's some free advice right back at you—go to hell and take your scumbag client with you."

If Brewer had a reaction to that, he didn't show it. He simply turned and walked back to his car.

Tanner waited until Brewer had driven away before he got back in his truck. Rachel could hear him opening the envelope.

"Well?" Jared asked. "What was so hell-fired important that Esterman had to tell us?"

"It's a blank page," Tanner relayed to them.

Rachel shook her head. "What does that mean?"

Jared started the car. "It means Esterman's people will be following Tanner so they can try to find us."

Of course they would. That's the reason they'd wanted this meeting in the first place. "And what will we be doing?"

"Following Brewer." He pulled out of the parking lot and onto the street. The car was just ahead, in the flow of traffic. "It's time we found out just how much he really knows about the baby."

Chapter 8

"**W**ell?" Rachel asked the moment Jared ended the call with the fertility clinic. She stared at him, tension showing all over her face. "What did they say?"

Not what Jared had wanted them to say, that was for sure.

He handed Rachel the cell phone so she could reconnect it to the modem for the laptop. "Both the fertilized embryos and unfertilized eggs were stolen."

"Great." She blew out a ragged breath. "So the baby…"

"Could be yours or ours," he supplied when she didn't finish.

"Or neither."

"Yeah. But then, we've known that was a possibility right from the start." Despite the seriousness of the conversation, Jared kept a close watch on Lyle Brewer's vehicle that was two cars ahead of him.

"So, where does that leave us?" Rachel asked.

"Not where I'd like us to be, but there's some good news. Well, potentially good news, anyway. Whoever stole the embryos left two unfertilized eggs, so the hospital can get a sample of your DNA from those and match it to the saliva swab that was in the envelope. They'll soon be able to figure out if the child is yours."

She obviously followed that to the next logical step. "And what about *your* DNA?"

"I donated blood just a couple of weeks ago, and thankfully the hospital still had it. We could know something as early as tomorrow morning."

She didn't say a word, but Jared knew what she was thinking. Tomorrow morning might be too late. It was anybody's guess as to when the cops or Esterman's men would find them and haul them in.

He finished off the rest of his cold cheeseburger and continued to follow Lyle Brewer. After they'd left the parking lot at the Mexican food restaurant, Brewer had dropped off his dry cleaning, used the ATM at the bank and picked up a prescription at a drive-through all-night pharmacy. In other words, routine stuff. He certainly didn't seem to be a man on the verge of revealing the location of the baby.

Rachel's fingers stilled on the computer keyboard for a few seconds when Brewer turned down another street. "He lives somewhere in this area. You think he's going home now?"

"I sure hope not."

But what Jared hoped for was a long shot. He wanted Brewer to lead them straight to the child. Tonight.

Talk about a tall order.

It was entirely possible that Brewer had no part in any

of this, but Jared had to make sure. Besides, now that Aaron Merkens was dead, Brewer was one of the few leads they had. God help them.

They followed the car for another mile before Brewer stopped for gas. Jared waited on the narrow side street next to the store and hoped that the attorney hadn't caught on to the fact that he'd been tailed for the better part of an hour. If so, then God knows how long Brewer would keep driving around in the hopes of losing them. Or boring them to death.

"I don't guess you've found anything in those hospital files?" Jared asked, glancing at the computer screen.

"No. But that could be important information in itself. If there's no hospital record, that means Esterman's people probably used a private facility to do the C-section. But even private facilities can leave paper trails."

Yeah. But it was another long shot. What they needed was a break—and soon.

Because it was too heart-wrenching to consider, Jared hadn't let himself dwell on the possibility that Esterman might not even keep the baby alive. According to the evidence Rachel had unearthed during her undercover surveillance, Esterman had killed before.

Plenty of times.

Jared pushed that to the back of his mind. If he started dealing in what-if's when it came to the baby's fate, he wouldn't be able to do his job. And he couldn't let that happen.

He eased back out into traffic to follow Brewer from the gas station. The rain kept up a slow steady drizzle. The wipers slashed across the windshield and blended with the sound of Rachel's keystrokes on the computer.

He heard her breathe and make that odd little sound she made when she was frustrated.

"Despite our differences about my Neanderthal approach to conflict resolution, I'm glad we're doing this together," he said.

Her fingers stilled. What she didn't do was look at him.

"Me, too."

The moment was oddly right, despite everything that was oddly wrong. He might have said more. He might even have apologized for everything that had gone on between them, but the moment was over when Jared had to make the next turn to follow Brewer.

Brewer drove into an upscale residential area, went several blocks and came to a stop in front of a large colonial-style home. Jared killed the headlights and stayed back, parking behind another car just up the street.

"The address is 623 Hanshaw Lane," Rachel provided. She grabbed her notes from the console and scanned them. "It's not Brewer's place, but he lives a few miles from here."

Jared craned his neck to get a better view of the front of the house. "There's no name on the mailbox. Think you can find out whose place this is?"

"Hopefully."

She got to work, her fingers dancing over the keyboard. Jared kept his attention on Brewer. With his briefcase clutched in his hand, the attorney exited his car and walked up the sidewalk to the front door. Jared barely got a glimpse of the man who answered.

White male. About six feet tall. Silver-gray hair.

"Got it. It's the residence of Donald Livingston." Rachel's gaze raced across the screen before her eyes widened. She turned to him. "He's the warden, Jared. The warden of the prison where Sasha Young was incarcerated."

"Bingo." And despite the fact that it still was a long shot, Jared smiled.

"Wait. I'm positive I recognize that name. Let me check something." Rachel typed in another search. "Yes, I was right. He's Clarence Esterman's former client."

Okay. Jared hadn't expected that, but it might fit nicely. "In what capacity?"

She entered more information, but shook her head when she got the results. "I don't know. Livingston's name is listed in the company's records, but it appears his files were among those that Esterman deleted."

"Even better. Esterman wouldn't have deleted them unless there was a reason. I think we just might have gotten our first big break."

"Yes." Rachel pulled in a long breath. "But what do we do with it?"

His smile faded. Good question. He had answers, but Jared wasn't sure how they fit with the questions.

"Keep digging for information on Warden Livingston," Jared told her. "It's too risky for us to sit here all night, but I'll have Tanner assign one of his detectives to watch the house. When the place is empty, we'll go inside and have a look around."

"Breaking and entering?" she asked.

Her tone was just slightly too self-satisfied for his liking. "You got a better idea?"

"No. I'm willing to do whatever it takes."

Good. Because it would take a lot. Jared was absolutely sure of that.

"You're supposed to be resting," Jared pointed out, glancing at her over his shoulder.

"So are you," Rachel countered.

She closed her eyes for a few seconds, but when she opened them, the words on the computer screen were still just as blurry as they had been for the past hour.

Cursing the fatigue, Rachel set the laptop aside, got up from the bed and went into the bathroom to splash some water on her face. Her head was pounding. Her mouth was like a wad of cotton. And every muscle in her body was knotted to the point of being painful.

Sometime in the four hours since she and Jared had checked into the low-budget hotel, the surge of adrenaline had caused her to crash and burn, leaving her with a bone-weary fatigue that a hot shower definitely hadn't cured. What she needed was a good night's sleep. Which she wouldn't get anytime soon.

She checked her clothes that she'd hung over the towel rack after her shower. Still too damp to put back on. The bed-sheet toga would have to do a while longer. Not good. Even though she was covered from shoulder to toes, it seemed a little risqué to walk around wearing just a sheet with her soon-to-be-ex in the room. And it wasn't her imagination that Jared had noticed the sheet, either.

He'd definitely noticed.

And *she'd* noticed that *he'd* noticed.

The attraction was still there between them, just as it had been from the first day Rachel had seen him waiting on the steps of the campus administration building.… It was winter. Her senior year in college. He stood there, an icy breeze stirring his long black coat. And his hair. When she caught his gaze, he smiled, causing a dimple to flash in his cheek. She was already half in love with him before she learned that he was a cop.

Odd that the physical attraction would survive and the love wouldn't.

"Are you okay?" Jared called out.

"Just taking a little break."

And going through her own version of hormone Hades. The adrenaline might have caused a crash and burn, but it didn't do a thing to dull her senses. At the moment, a good sense-dulling would have been a blessing.

Gathering up her toga so she wouldn't trip, Rachel walked back through the room and peeked out the window. The cars trickled past on the nearby highway, but on the other side of the six lanes, she could see the street that led to Livingston's neighborhood. They were still five miles away but could easily be there in less than ten minutes.

But first they had to get the go-ahead from Tanner.

It was approaching midnight, and they still hadn't received a call from the investigator that Tanner had placed near Livingston's house. Not that she'd expected that call before morning. However, Rachel had prayed that Livingston would leave so they could figure out if he had any information to link him to the baby.

Livingston was divorced, she'd learned from her computer search. No kids. And he lived alone. What Rachel couldn't be certain of was that he was truly *alone*. There could be someone else staying in the house. A lover. A relative. A housekeeper. Any one of them could pose a problem when she and Jared actually went inside the house. Still, it was their best bet for finding new information.

At the moment, their only bet.

She hadn't wanted to let herself hope, but were Esterman's people holding the baby there? It didn't seem logical that a man of Donald Livingston's reputation would risk something like that, but the child had to be somewhere. Besides, Livingston was one of the few connections they had to Sasha Young. Livingston and Lyle Brewer.

And in a bizarre circle, both of them were connected to Esterman.

"You should try to get some sleep," Jared reminded her. "God knows, you need it."

She made a sound of agreement. "This coming from a man who's put in more hours than I have. How long have you had that envelope, anyway?"

He didn't answer right away, which meant he knew where her comment was leading. "Since around eleven o'clock last night. A courier brought it to the town house."

"So that means you've been working twenty-four hours straight, but my guess is it's been even longer than that since you've had any sleep."

"You'd guess right." He looked at her over his shoulder. There was nothing especially incredible about that look except the fact that Jared was the one doing the looking.

From the moment he'd told her about the baby, Rachel had tried to prepare herself for all the challenges she might face. However, the challenge at the moment was all the feelings for him that still whispered inside her. Those whispers were rapidly turning into a roar.

Keeping her hands plastered to her side so she wouldn't be tempted to touch him, she walked closer. From over his shoulder she saw that he'd spread out the contents of the envelope on the desk. The letter, the DNA results and the two photographs. Jared was reading the letter, probably to see if there were any hidden clues. And as with her computer search for hospital records, it didn't appear that he'd been successful in finding anything else. Still, he was plugging away at it.

Devoted to duty. That was Jared, all right. Always on the job. But this time, he didn't have the support of his fellow officers and he couldn't use his badge. Despite all that, he hadn't given up. And that brought Rachel back to something she'd been mulling over all afternoon.

"I've decided to call your captain," she informed him. "I'll tell her that it was my decision to leave the safe house, that I forced you to come with me. It might get you out of hot water."

He turned around in the chair to face her. "Thanks for the offer, but I knew the consequences before I went to see you this morning."

"I know. And that probably made it a thousand times harder for you." She paused, keeping her gaze on the computer screen. "I'll make that call after we learn what we can from Livingston."

"No, you won't. I'd rather you focus on finding the paper trail for the medical facility that did Sasha Young's C-section. I'll settle up with the captain when this is over."

"But then it might be too late to save your badge."

He flexed his eyebrows and turned his attention back to the letter. "Are you having trouble figuring out if that's a good or a bad thing?"

A year ago, that would have sent her into one heck of sulking session, but Rachel was too tired to sulk. Besides, it was an honest question.

"I never wanted you to lose your badge, Jared."

"No?" He shrugged. "You just wanted me to give it up voluntarily."

That was the truth. But only because he'd come so

close to dying. Still, that admission was another sulking session in the making. In Jared's opinion, possible death was part of the job description.

"I don't want to go through this tonight." She rubbed her hand over her face. "Those old issues don't even matter anymore. We're practically divorced, and the only thing really left between us is to find this baby."

It wasn't exactly true. If they found the baby, there would certainly be tons of other issues to work out, but they seemed miles away.

"What about the lust you mentioned earlier?" he asked. Not calmly, either. There was an edge to his question. "That's certainly still between us. If you're keeping a tally, it has to go somewhere at the top of the list."

She had to hand it to him—Jared knew how to keep her on her toes. Or maybe that was designed to knock her off her toes a bit since they were breaching taboo waters. Rachel hoped her body didn't get any ideas from all this lust talk.

It wasn't an invitation.

"Okay, we'll put lust as number two on the list, right after finding the baby," Rachel said, and she took up where he left off. "And for three, we can add all this knight-to-the-rescue stuff that you dole out. That's still between us, as well. Even now."

"I beg your pardon?"

She leaned her hip against the table. "I've had a lot of time to think over the past year, and I believe you married me because you have a knight complex. It's a dominant part of your personality."

"You mean because I took care of my mom and kid sister after my dad ran out on us?"

Rachel nodded. "And you did that when most teenagers couldn't have handled it." She smiled when he scowled. "Don't look insulted—it was an honorable and selfless thing to do. You continued that selfless lifestyle by becoming a cop. Then I arrived on the scene, and, well, let's just say I was the ultimate damsel in distress to keep fueling all your knightly impulses."

"Because you have panic attacks." He spared her a considering glance. "And you believe these selfless knightly impulses of mine were the reason we got together?"

She didn't really care for the way he phrased that. "That was a large part of it, yes."

"You left out the lust again."

Great. He just wouldn't get off that subject, and it wasn't a safe one for them to dwell on. "I meant to leave it out. Because despite its prominent place on this theoretical list, it no longer applies to us—even if it feels like it does. It's a facade, an illusion, brought on by adrenaline, forced proximity...and this blasted toga."

He smiled, but like his comments, there was something a little off about it. Something hot and dangerous simmering just below the surface.

It sure felt like an invitation.

To something.

Rachel pushed herself away from the table and started to pace. Jared just sat there. Staring. "What, no opinions about that?" she asked.

"You tell me what I think," Jared challenged. This time she got more than a glance. And it was more than a considering one. He stood and raked his gaze over her.

Oh boy. The man certainly knew how to put some spin on a simple gaze.

"It doesn't matter now, anyway." She tried to sound dispassionate. And failed miserably.

"Wrong guess. That wasn't what I was thinking."

She scowled at his sarcasm. Or, at least, she tried to scowl. Since that wasn't working, it seemed a really good time for that nap, so Rachel turned to head for the bed.

Jared obviously had other ideas.

He snagged her wrist so fast that she didn't even see it coming. But then he stopped. Stared at her. And eased his grip slightly as if to give her the chance to retreat. When she didn't, when she met that challenging stare of his without backing down, he drew her closer and pressed her hand right against the front of his jeans.

He was aroused.

Mercy.

Fully aroused.

And so was she.

"I don't want you to do anything about this, got it?" he grumbled. "I just want you to know that our marriage might have failed, but the attraction didn't. So that lust part definitely still applies, without any qualifiers. Got it?"

Rachel expected to see some sort of battle going on in his golden-brown eyes. But there was no battle. No hesitation. And that sent a wild rush through her.

He moved his hand away.

She needed to do something, to say something to make this situation better. But nothing good came to mind. Unfortunately, something bad did.

She didn't move her hand.

"Rachel," he warned.

"You put it there." She'd meant to make it sound arrogant, but there was nothing arrogant about her tone, her touch. Or especially her mood.

And Jared reacted.

He leaned in, slowly, and touched his mouth to hers. She'd braced herself for a full assault like the one in the car, but this was an assault of a different kind. Just as potent. Just as arousing. Just as lethal. Her body suddenly felt as if it were about to burn from the inside out.

"We used to be good at this," he reminded her, his mouth moving like silk over hers.

It took her a moment to find her breath. "We apparently still are."

With that affirmation, he went back for seconds. His mouth was warm. Possessive. Thorough. And welcome. He went lower, nipping her bottom lip with his teeth. He went lower still and used that clever mouth on her throat. On her pulse. On that much-too-sensitive spot just below her ear.

Without stopping the kiss, he released his grip and slid his fingers along her arm. To her breast. He eased down the makeshift toga. A fraction.

But it was just enough.

She whimpered when his lips pressed against the swell of her right breast. She cried out when he circled her nipple with his tongue. By the time he had taken her into his mouth, Rachel had all but collapsed against him.

She begged for mercy.

She begged for more.

He gave her both.

Jared gave her other breast the same attention. The same tongue kiss. The same fire bath. Then, he repositioned the sheet to cover her and eased away. Not easily. And only after a couple of hard breaths and a throat clearing. But he eventually eased away from her.

"Nice toga," he managed to say. Again, not easily. But he finally got out the words. "Now, wasn't that more relaxing than pacing the floor or straightening a stack of magazines?"

She couldn't answer right away. "I'd say so."

"Liar."

The corner of his mouth eased up ever so slightly, but he didn't put that lethal, sexy grin to work—something that would have caused her to push things just to see how far they would go. Instead, he helped her into bed and tucked her in.

"Sleep tight, Rachel."

Not a chance. Not with her worries about the baby, Esterman and Livingston. Not with this renewed attraction she felt for Jared.

No, a restful night's sleep probably wasn't in the cards for her tonight. Still, Rachel snuggled deep into the covers and closed her eyes.

Chapter 9

All they had to do was literally walk in the place. No one was home because Donald Livingston had already left for work. Tanner's people had deactivated the security system, unlocked the doors, and had even done an infrared scan to make sure the house was empty.

It was.

So why didn't all those precautions make Jared feel even marginally better?

He stood behind a row of stately white pillars on the back porch, his hand on the door and Rachel by his side. He contemplated the uneasy feeling that had settled in his stomach. Maybe it was from lack of sleep, even though both Rachel and he had managed to get a couple of hours of much-needed rest. Maybe the uneasiness was simply because they were at the residence of the man who might have the child. Or maybe it was nothing at all.

"Is something wrong?" Rachel whispered.

Highly probable, but that wasn't what he said to her. "Everything's fine." And while Jared was doling out assurances, he tried to convince himself—again—that they were doing the right thing.

He wished that Rachel weren't with him for this one, but the alternative was leaving her in the hotel room with Tanner. That might help lessen the uneasy feeling, but it'd rile the hell out of her. With reason. She had as much right to do this as he did.

Even if it went against his gut feeling.

His instincts were to protect her, especially now, to shield her from the things that might hurt her. But Jared was quickly learning that Rachel no longer wanted that from him. It was possible she never had. Maybe it was something he'd assumed she wanted—and needed.

He was quickly learning that he'd been wrong about a lot of things when it came to her.

"Is this a good time to remind you to focus on what we're supposed to be doing?" Rachel grumbled, obviously impatient that they were still lurking around outside Livingston's house. "The sun's starting to rise, and I'd rather not wait out here much longer."

Jared pushed her impatience aside and listened one last time for something he didn't hear. No footsteps. No whispered sounds. No indication whatsoever that there was anyone else on the property.

Hoping the uneasy feeling was just a fluke, but not totally dismissing it, either, Jared opened the door and got them inside.

"I need to find Livingston's computer," Rachel reminded him.

He certainly hadn't forgotten that. It was the main reason they were here. If the warden had left any incriminating evidence, the computer was their best bet. But now, to find it. The house was sprawling, and it would take hours just to search the place.

Making their way through the kitchen, they meandered through a series of rooms before they located an office. Rachel didn't waste any time. She sat at the desk and got to work while Jared had a look around.

Nothing seemed out of the ordinary. The room was utilitarian with coffee-colored paneling and lots of filled bookshelves. There were plaques and framed awards neatly arranged on the mantel above a stone fireplace. One award from the mayor. Another, from the chief of police. From all appearances, Livingston was a model citizen.

But something about it didn't ring right.

He was almost *too* model.

There were two doors leading off the room. One led to a covered patio area and beyond that was a swimming pool. Jared eased open the other door to Livingston's bedroom. Like the rest of the house, it was large. And perfect. The four-poster bed was made with precision. The matching throw rugs were straight. No scattered clothing. The only sign that it wasn't a static display was the glass of water on the nightstand next to the bed.

Livingston was obviously a perfectionist. Not good. Attention to detail wasn't an asset that Jared wanted in a suspect. He'd take a sloppy opportunist any day.

"Stay put," he told Rachel. "I'll look around in the bedroom."

"Wait, I might have found something already."

Jared quickly crossed the room to the oversize desk. Rachel was searching through the "Sent Items" folder in Livingston's e-mail inbox.

"Livingston has his defaults set so that his computer automatically saves a copy of each message that he sends out. It's a break for us and an even bigger break that he hasn't deleted them."

She pointed out a pair of messages sent to a Dr. Randall Sheridan. But it wasn't just the word *Doctor* that garnered Jared's attention. It was the dates. Livingston had sent the messages exactly one week ago.

The date the baby was probably born.

Rachel opened the first message. It was short and sweet. "'Inform me when procedure is complete and the outcome,'" she read aloud. She clicked onto the next one. "'Payment for your services will arrive by courier.'"

"Payment," Jared repeated.

He glanced at the time difference between the messages. A little over two hours. That was most likely enough time for Dr. Sheridan to have completed the C-section and given Livingston the news. Of course, it was entirely possible that this message thread had nothing to do with Sasha Young or the baby.

But Jared's gut instincts said otherwise.

"Go ahead and have a look around the rest of the house," Rachel insisted. "I'll see if I can retrieve the messages that the doctor sent to Livingston."

It was a good idea, but Jared didn't intend to get too far away from Rachel. He left her to do her e-mail search and went back into the adjoining bedroom. If Livingston had left what might be critical information on his computer, he might have left it elsewhere, too.

Jared checked the drawer of the nightstand, but it was empty except for some generic-brand condoms. Even though he tried to stave off the thoughts, the condoms reminded him of sex.

And Rachel.

But, of course, he hadn't really needed the condoms to ignite any memories or lustful thoughts. In the past twenty-four hours, despite fatigue, danger and the harrowing search for the child, he'd thought about sex a lot.

And Rachel.

Once this was behind them, he really needed to sit down and figure out what they were going to do about, well, everything. Whatever they'd thought was over between them had certainly gotten a second wind. It had for him, anyway, and he was almost certain Rachel felt the same. Especially after that toga incident. But the real issue was—would either of them be willing to take the kind of risk necessary to jump into another relationship?

Again, he relied on his gut feeling. After those toga kisses, just about anything was possible.

Forcing his attention back to his search, Jared glanced into the small, color-coordinated trash can that was near the massive walk-in closet.

Nothing.

The closet itself didn't look promising either. Shoes, clothes and ties in such perfect arrangement that it made Jared shake his head. Still, he rifled through the shelves to make sure nothing had been tucked out of sight.

He had just pulled aside a stack of crisp white undershirts when he heard the sound.

A *click*.

Just a click.

And then Jared's worst fears came true. Because the *click* was the sound of a door opening.

Not in the bedroom.

But in the office where Rachel was still working on the computer.

Drawing his weapon, Jared quietly rushed to the door and peered into the bedroom. Empty. He hurried to the entrance to the office, and the second he made it there, the lights in that particular room flared on. He caught just a glimpse of the snow-haired man coming in through the patio.

Donald Livingston had apparently come home.

Hell.

"I just have to change my clothes," he said to someone. "I won't be long."

Silently cursing himself and their rotten luck, Jared frantically glanced around the office and finally spotted Rachel beneath the desk. She looked terrified but was unharmed. Thank God.

From Livingston's angle, he wouldn't be able to see her. Well, hopefully not. But that might not last. Besides, Jared knew *he* was in a highly visible spot if Livingston came into the bedroom.

Jared debated just latching onto Livingston and holding him at gunpoint so Rachel could escape, but he had no idea who was on the other side of that patio door. If it was a hired thug, Rachel would be in more danger than she was now.

He motioned for Rachel to stay quiet, and then scrambled beneath the bed so he could still see the corner of the desk in the office. God knows how long it would take the man to change his clothes, but Jared hoped Livingston would do it immediately and get the devil out of there.

Livingston strolled into the bedroom, his pricey leather shoes whispering over the thick platinum-colored rug. And then—damn it—he shut the door.

Jared choked back a wave of fear and concentrated on listening for Rachel. If the other visitor came into the office and spotted her, Jared would almost certainly hear her react. And then he'd get to her, no matter what that took.

Even if it meant going through Livingston first.

Jared pulled in his breath, kept his gun ready and braced himself for whatever was about to happen.

Oh God.

She'd barely made it under the desk in time. Another second, and Livingston would have seen her at his computer. She prayed he wouldn't look in the direction of the monitor, because he would notice that it had been turned on.

This was obviously one of those worst-case scenarios that Jared was always talking about. At least, that's what Rachel thought when Livingston slipped into his bedroom and shut the door.

She was so wrong.

The worst was yet to come.

Almost immediately she heard another sound. The rattle of a doorknob a split second before it opened, and it wasn't the one from the bedroom where Livingston had just entered. It was the one that led from the patio, and that sound sent Rachel's heart to her throat.

Someone strolled into the office. She'd known Livingston was talking to someone outside, but Rachel had prayed the other person wouldn't come in. But not only was this person in the house, but the sound of footsteps seemed to be coming straight for the desk.

Rachel squeezed herself as far back as she could go. Drawing her knees against her chest, she tried not to make a sound. She tried not to breathe, hoping Jared would stay put, as well. She didn't even want to speculate about what would happen if he came bursting out of that bedroom with a gun in his hand.

The footsteps stopped. Directly in front of her. And she saw the visitor's legs. It was a man wearing dress slacks, and he was so close she could have reached out and touched him.

She pressed her fingertips to her mouth. And waited. She didn't have to wait long. He moved quickly. Away from the front of the desk. Behind it.

Behind her.

"Mind telling me what you're doing down there?" the man snarled.

The sound that she'd choked back escaped as a small, barely audible gasp. A thousand thoughts went through her head. None good. But she forced herself not to panic. Maybe she could defuse this situation so Jared wouldn't have to use his gun.

Praying, Rachel crawled out from beneath the desk and looked up at him. Whoever he was, he was huge and towered over her. A wide face, hulking shoulders, and a thick head of cropped blond curls.

However, it wasn't just his physical appearance that sent her heart pounding. It was the shoulder holster and gun she saw beneath his open jacket. That coupled with his mere presence would have been enough to scare her, but it was only the beginning. Her gaze landed on his name tag.

Sergeant Colby Meredith.

This was the very person that Jared suspected of being a leak in the department, and he was also likely on Esterman's payroll.

Now, *this* was a worst-case scenario.

Rachel somehow got to her feet. How, she didn't know. Her whole body suddenly felt as sturdy as cotton balls, and there was a shiver going up her spine. If she'd been an animal in the wild, she'd have run for cover immediately because her every instinct was telling her that she was in danger.

"I'm Mr. Livingston's new cleaning lady," she managed to say. "It's my first day on the job."

"Oh. And what were you doing under the desk—looking for dust bunnies?" His voice was a throaty growl, and his icy gray eyes matched that tone.

Good question. Rachel said the first thing that came to mind. "I didn't think anyone was supposed to be here so I got scared when I heard you come in. I thought maybe you were a burglar."

God, could she possibly sound wimpier? She would never convince him to back off if she didn't put up a better front. Rachel hiked up her chin and tried to look as if she belonged there.

It didn't work.

The step that Meredith took toward her put a serious dent in what little fight she had managed to assemble. All she could think of was Jared and the baby. If Meredith was the one who killed Aaron Merkens, then he probably wouldn't show much mercy to Jared or a child.

Rachel caught the edge of the desk to steady herself. The last thing she wanted to do was faint, but by God she felt a dizzy spell coming on. Still, she didn't let that dizziness turn her to mush. She instinctively knew she had to show some backbone or things might quickly get out of hand.

"I'm leaving," Rachel said with authority that she certainly didn't feel. She fought all the old demons, the old fears from her parents' deaths. "I'll come back after Mr. Livingston is at work."

Meredith caught her arm.

Because she had nothing else to rely on, Rachel went on pure instinct. She shoved his hand away and again tried to go around him. She had nearly made it to the patio door before Meredith snagged her arm again. His fingers dug into her skin. It hurt, and she winced in pain.

That did it. Rachel gave up any pretense that this would end with placid requests. "You're asking for a knee in the groin, mister."

Inching his body closer, he trapped her against the door. "Don't you think I know what you're doing?"

As threatening as that sounded, she preferred that to his knowing *who* she was. She hoped he thought she was a thief. Now, the real question was how she could get away from him without Jared having to use his gun.

"It was stupid for you to come here," Meredith insisted. "Dillard didn't do a very good job of protecting his woman, did he? But his stupidity is my gain."

He knew.

God, he knew.

Meredith pushed harder, and Rachel felt the sting of his hand on her arm. She'd have bruises, but she prayed that was all she'd have. It didn't help that he loomed over her and outweighed her by a good seventy-five pounds.

She could feel the rage in him. And he was ready to unleash it all on her. Since this could easily turn into a fight for her life, Rachel lunged for a glass paperweight on the desk.

Meredith beat her to it, and knocked it out of reach.

Rachel tore herself away from him, but before she could put some distance between them, he latched onto a handful of her hair. With seemingly no effort Meredith shoved her face-first against the wall.

"You really shouldn't have done that," she said through clenched teeth.

She hadn't wanted to fight him, but she wouldn't stand there while he beat the heck out of her, either. Rachel pivoted, fully intending to send his reproductive organs right into his throat, but with a flash of motion, he drew his gun.

And aimed it right at her.

Her reaction was instant. Something she couldn't stop. Something beyond fear. Something raw, primal and totally beyond her control. Rachel felt every muscle in her body turn to iron. Her breath froze in her lungs.

Move, she ordered herself. *Do something.*

But she couldn't. Her feet wouldn't cooperate. Neither would the rest of her body. Only her mind seemed to be functioning at full capacity, and all she could do was stare at the gun.

That thin black chamber.

The glint of the morning sun on the metal.

Meredith's finger on the trigger.

He probably wouldn't kill her. Because he needed her alive to testify. But from that cold look in his eyes, she had no doubt that he would hurt her. Rachel fought a silent battle. She had to move. She had to save herself.

Meredith suddenly snapped backward. She heard the slam of muscle against muscle just a split second before she saw Jared. He rammed his fist into Meredith's face and sent the man sprawling.

Meredith cursed and put his hands on the floor, preparing to launch himself at Jared.

"I'd think twice about doing that if I were you," Jared warned. He kicked Meredith's pistol aside and aimed his gun at the man.

Meredith hesitated. He shook his head and slowly started to get to his feet.

"Are you all right, Rachel?" Jared asked without taking his attention off Meredith.

"Yes." She was afraid to say differently. Jared had a dangerous edge to his voice, and Rachel wasn't sure what he would do. "Where's Livingston?"

"Tied up in the bedroom."

So that left just Meredith for them to deal with. Of course, that was more than enough.

As if on cue, Meredith actually grinned at them. He seemed to be on the verge of saying something arrogant, or just plain stupid, but then he shut his mouth. But then, almost anything he said at this point would probably be incriminating.

"You'll regret this, Lieutenant Dillard," Meredith challenged.

"Not as much as you will. I've got nothing to lose, so listen carefully. Don't even think about going for your gun. Instead, do the smart thing and cooperate. Get facedown on the floor and do it now."

The moments seemed endless, but Meredith did as Jared requested. Jared worked fast. He took a roll of clear packaging tape from the desk and used it to truss Meredith's wrists to his feet. In less than a minute, he had Meredith restrained, and they were on their way out the door.

Jared had parked at the end of the street, but he slowed her to a walk when she tried to run. She realized that it would attract too much attention from the neighbors. Still, if anyone took a close look at her face, they'd know that all was not well. She'd just endured one of the most frightening incidents of her life—and what made it so bad was that it wasn't over.

"Are you really okay?" Jared asked after he'd gotten them in the car and sped out of the neighborhood.

"Yes."

He glanced at her. "Try that answer again, Rachel, but this time leave the B.S. out of it."

"All right. I'm still a little shaky." It was a huge lie. She was a lot shaky, but Rachel tried to keep the moment light, hoping it would soothe some of the anger she saw in Jared's eyes. She didn't want him to lose it, especially since she was already so close to the edge herself. "Meredith really gave me a scare when he pulled that psycho-without-a-cause routine."

"Yes." And he repeated it under his breath. "I don't think he knows how close he came to dying. When I came in that room and saw his hands on you, I wanted to kill him."

Because she knew it was the truth, Rachel touched his arm and rubbed lightly. She only hoped that he didn't notice that her fingers were trembling. That would certainly cast some doubt on her *I'm okay.* "You showed great restraint, considering."

"The day's not over yet. I'm still toying with the idea of going back after him."

"But you won't. It'll only cost us time that we can't afford to lose. Besides, we have to find this Dr. Randall Sheridan. He's the key, Jared. I just know it."

He nodded. "We need to talk to him. I'll call Tanner and get him started on this right away. It's probably not a good idea if we go searching for the doctor in broad daylight, but Tanner's people can locate Sheridan and set up a meeting."

"Yes." Rachel had to take several deep breaths before she could continue. "And Sheridan will lead us to the baby."

This time, Jared didn't nod. But she repeated the words to herself. For reassurance.

They would find the baby and get him to safety, away from people like Meredith. They had to.

Because the alternative was unthinkable.

Chapter 10

Jared tossed the car keys on the desk and swore liberally. "I never should have taken you to Livingston's house with me. *Never.* I had a bad feeling about the place the second we got there—but did I pull back? No. I let you walk in there and face Meredith."

With each mile that he'd driven to get them back to the hotel, reality had sunk in a little deeper. Just minutes earlier, Rachel had practically been killed, and—damn—it was all his fault.

"Hindsight is such a wonderful thing, isn't it?" she murmured.

Rachel looked the pillar of strength standing there. She had her arms folded over her chest and her eyes focused. She even had her mouth set in that stubborn line. The facade worked, temporarily.

Until Jared glanced at her arm.

"What the hell is this?" He caught her wrist, shoved up the loose sleeve of her T-shirt and examined the reddish marks on her forearm.

Rachel didn't answer. She didn't have to. Because Jared put it together immediately. And it turned his stomach.

"Meredith did this to you." The cursing reached a whole different level and intensity. "Hell, I can't even protect you while you're in the same house with me."

Rachel pulled her arm from his grip and slid her sleeve back in place to cover the marks. "It's not your job to protect me, Jared. As I recall, you were busy taking care of Livingston at the time. Besides, these are just bruises. They'll go away in a couple of days."

A spark of rage shot through him. "But the memory of that bastard putting them there won't."

"I know," she whispered. "I know."

She sank onto the edge of the bed and folded her hands in her lap. Only then did Jared realize she was trembling. But not just trembling. She was shaking. Hell, here he was ranting and venting, and he had forgotten all about what she might be going through.

He went to her immediately and wrapped his arm around her. While he was at it, he checked her eyes to make sure she wasn't going into shock. She wasn't. But Jared saw things in those green depths that made him want to tear Meredith limb from limb.

"It's over," Jared said softly, hoping his words would soothe her enough to stave off a panic attack. He brushed a kiss on her temple and felt her pulse hammer against his mouth.

"It's never over," Rachel countered. "Any idea how many hours of therapy I've had?" She didn't wait for him to answer. "Too many to count. Plus, the hypnosis and the various medications. You name it and I've tried it. Nothing's worked. I'm still too terrified of guns to protect myself. Talk about a genuine wuss."

"You're not a wuss. You have a phobia. Lots of people do. But that didn't stop you from standing up to Meredith today. I know how much it cost you to do that."

She waved him off. "I don't want your sympathy."

"Good, because this isn't sympathy. This is me telling you that we succeeded this morning. You managed to get the info about Dr. Sheridan, and we both made it out of there alive."

"Yeah, thanks to you. I froze, Jared. When I saw that gun, I was seven years old again. I was right back in that room with my parents' bodies, and I was just as ineffective today as I was then."

"You were a kid when that happened—you were supposed to be ineffective. If you'd tried to confront that burglar, he probably would have used that gun on you." The reminder didn't do much to settle the acid churning in his stomach. "And even with all that baggage from your past, you still didn't have a panic attack today."

She shrugged. Not a casual, dismissive gesture—every muscle in her body was still knotted. "I'll repeat what you said earlier about Meredith. The day's not over yet. I still might go medieval on you, so you might want to hold back on those compliments."

Because there was a slight touch of humor mixed in with all the other emotions, Jared smiled and pushed the hair away from her face. "No way. Because of you, we'll soon find the doctor. And the baby."

Of course, that last part was wishful thinking. He'd phoned Tanner with the information on the drive back to the hotel, and he had no doubt that Tanner would find Dr. Sheridan, in time. There was no guarantee that Sheridan would lead them to the baby, but then, there'd been no guarantees of anything right from the start.

Rachel lay her head on his shoulder and slid her arm around his chest so she was holding him. "Thank you for stopping Meredith and for getting me out of there."

"No problem." He went for a cocky, light tone, hoping it would help. "Consider it my knightly deed for the day."

Jared skimmed his fingers over her cheek. Rachel turned, moving into his touch. And he suddenly found his fingertips on her mouth.

They didn't stay there for long.

Just like that, she brushed his hand aside, and Jared saw her eyelids flutter down. That was the only warning he had before her mouth came to his. Not some gentle kiss of reassurance.

Not this.

This was hot and needy. Pure, uncut passion. Rachel wound her arms around him, pressed herself against him and made love to him with her mouth.

Jared took everything she offered. Everything. The silky heat of the kiss. The intimate contact of their bodies. The promise of more. Much more. But then, he felt her hand on his arm.

She was still trembling.

"Rachel," he warned. Somehow, he managed to untangle himself from her. "We shouldn't be doing this."

She stared at him, her breath coming out in short spurts. "Sorry. I thought...well, I just thought..." She shook her head. "Obviously, I thought wrong."

"No. You didn't." Jared started to explain, to tell her that he'd pulled away not because he'd wanted to but because she was responding to leftover adrenaline. But the words didn't come.

"You need to rest," he finally managed to say.

Because he was watching her so closely, he saw the emotions run through her eyes. Not hurt, exactly. Something deeper. Something that sent him reaching for her. Rachel stopped his hand before he could touch her.

They sat there. In silence. Their gazes connected. Jared could still hear her breathing even over the heartbeats that pounded in his head.

"There are rules about this sort of thing," he said. "I can't—"

Jared knew anything he was about to say would be a useless explanation. Rachel knew their situation as well as he did. She was scared—yes. And coming down from a terrible ordeal—definitely. Still, that didn't change what was going on between them now.

It wasn't just adrenaline he saw in her response. He saw heat. The same need that he felt racing through his body. Too bad their mutual needs were racing in the same general direction.

And it was really too bad that he wasn't going to do a thing to slow them down.

There would be hell to pay. No doubt about it. But Jared figured whatever the price, it'd be worth it. After all, this was Rachel.

Rachel waited for Jared to give her another get-some-rest snarl.

That didn't happen.

Instead of a snarl, Jared reached out and laced their fingers together. Gently.

"Jared?"

It wasn't even close to a warning, but he didn't let her finish, anyway. He pressed his fingers to her mouth and shook his head. "If you're planning to stop me, Rachel, do it now."

That warning wasn't much of a deterrent, and she certainly didn't stop him. Nor would she. Rachel had known that the moment she started this.

Jared settled things. He reached for her and kissed her. It was one of those hard, slow, long ones. One that fed the passion she already felt. The heat seeped from his mouth all the way to her toes.

"Well?" he asked.

"I'm not stopping anything."

Rachel braced herself for a frantic onslaught, for the fire and energy she'd felt during the toga kiss. But Jared surprised her when he gently took her by the shoulders and laid her on the bed. He didn't continue the kiss. Not on her mouth, anyway. Instead, he worked his magic on her neck, trailing a line of kisses to her breasts.

"Let's see if I can remember exactly how to do this," he teased.

Oh, he knew. He knew every inch of her body, and he seemed ready to prove it.

Jared planted her hands on the bed just above her head. He slid his fingers up her shirt, inch by inch. Because she was watching him so closely, she saw his eyes darken. "You're not wearing a bra."

"It's still drying in the bathroom."

"A convenient place for it." He slid up the T-shirt. "It saves me a step or two."

But it didn't seem as if saving time was a huge priority. Those slow, clever kisses continued at a very leisurely pace. He ran his tongue over her skin. And drove her mad.

When she reached for his shirt, Jared simply clamped onto her hands again. "That wasn't what I had in mind."

"Oh, yeah?" Her breath was thin and shallow now. Every inch of her was humming from anticipation. "So, what exactly are we doing?"

She should have known that he wouldn't skirt around a challenge like that. Jared unbuttoned her jeans and stripped them off her. Her panties soon followed. And then he showed her what he had in mind.

Jared placed one very wet kiss on the inside of her thigh. The upper, upper inside. A place where his hot breath was just as arousing as the kiss. Then, he latched onto her hips and put his mouth to work right on the feverish center of her body.

Rachel almost jumped off the bed.

"Come here," Jared murmured, his voice a gruff whisper. "Let's do something that doesn't have a thing to do with stopping."

Rachel quickly realized he planned to finish what he'd started. While the idea greatly appealed to her, she wanted more. "I prefer making love to be a mutual satisfaction kind of thing."

"Don't think for a minute that I won't be enjoying this. I will."

She tried to go after his zipper, but Jared stopped her by gripping her wrist. He kissed her, stealing her breath.

Rachel managed some profanity. Nothing that even she could understand. But then, words weren't needed. The way he used his mouth said it all, and her response let him know that. She slid her leg over his shoulder, pressed herself closer to his mouth and just took what he offered.

Jared was very good at offering.

He kissed. Nipped. Used his tongue until the pleasure closed around her. Rachel grabbed onto handfuls of the sheet, trying to anchor herself.

She felt the upward spiral start. The rise. The swirl of sensations so immense, so right that her body could hardly contain it.

Then, Jared somehow took her even higher.

He savored her, and let her know that this gave him as much pleasure as it did her, even though Rachel thought she could argue that case later. And when he was done with her, when she could take no more, he gave a clever flick of his tongue and sent her flying. In that last desperate second, she called out his name.

Jared gave her some pleasant aftershocks with a few more of those well-placed kisses. Still, Rachel forced herself to come back to earth as quickly as possible so that she could return the favor.

With her body still trembling and her breath racing, she held Jared's shoulder to get him moving in the right direction, but he stopped her again.

A groan escaped from deep within his chest. He took her hand, kissed it and moved off the bed. Out of her reach. He walked to the other side of the room, turned and looked at her.

"Get some rest, Rachel."

"Hold on." She didn't intend to let him get away that easily. "Are you saying that you're not going to join me on this bed?"

He nodded. Not easily. But it was a nod. "It's for the best."

"Says who?"

"Me," he clarified.

It was some clarification, all right. And it riled her. "I know what you're doing, Jared. You've given me some great sex, but what you haven't given me is yourself."

He stared at her. "What the hell does that mean?"

"I repeat, you gave me *great sex*. Still, you're holding back. You figure if you don't make love to me—really make love to me—if you only give instead of take, then you'll be able to stop yourself from getting too close to me again. It doesn't work that way."

He groaned again and pressed the back of his head against the wall. "I know what's happening between us, damn it, but I also know it's something that'll have to wait. We have too many things to work out first for us to get into a discussion about our future."

True enough. There were more obstacles than she cared to consider. But even the obstacles couldn't make her put aside what she felt for Jared.

No.

She was falling in love with him all over again, and that scared Rachel almost as much as the other obstacles they faced. But admitting that to herself didn't do a thing to help answer one huge question.

What was she going to do about it?

Chapter 11

Clarence Esterman ran his fingers over his slender gold ink pen and read through the letter that his attorney had just handed him.

"When did you receive this?" he asked Lyle Brewer.

"Less than an hour ago. Your assistant, Gerald Anderson, dropped it off at my office since you weren't allowed personal visitors today. I figured it was important so I brought it right over."

Oh, it was important. Critical, even. And it angered him to the point that Clarence's hand tightened. He snapped the expensive gold pen in half and cursed when the black ink oozed over his fingers.

Brewer quickly handed him a handkerchief, causing the guard on the other side of the glass doorway to take a step inside. "A problem?" the guard inquired.

Clarence gave him a sappy, sweet smile that no one

could have interpreted as sincere. "Not unless you consider shoddy manufacturing something that'd concern you. They don't make pens like they used to."

The guard cast uneasy glances at both men before he went back to his original position and shut the door between them. With that distraction out of the way, Clarence returned his attention to the letter.

So, Lieutenant Dillard had made the connection to Dr. Sheridan. It was a tough break.

Especially for the doctor.

Randall Sheridan had been prompt about repaying his debts, but he wasn't indispensable. Quite the contrary. He was a loose end in desperate need of elimination. Measures should have been taken days ago to do away with him. Soon, Clarence would personally find out why they hadn't been.

Clarence reached over and plucked the pen from his attorney's hand. Best to make this direct. And cryptic. After shredding all those incriminating documents, he certainly didn't want to give the prosecution anything they could use against him.

He jotted down a couple of key phrases at the bottom of the so-called report. Instructions that Gerald would have no trouble interpreting. By noon, the doctor would be dead, and Lieutenant Dillard would be receiving a rather nasty ultimatum.

Clarence refolded the single sheet of paper, inserted it into the envelope and sealed it. "It's best that you're not involved in this," he told Brewer, when his attorney cast him a questioning glance. Clarence handed him the envelope. "You'll take that to Gerald Anderson immediately. He'll know what to do with it."

Brewer nodded. "There was one other thing—"

He paused, his mouth thinning and his Adam's apple bobbing. Clarence knew the man well enough to know that something was bothering him.

"I spoke with the DA this morning, and he mentioned that you'd asked to have a private conference with him."

If Clarence had had another pen, he would have crushed it into a thousand pieces. Apparently, confidentiality meant nothing to the district attorney. It was a serious error in judgment on both his part and the D.A.'s.

"I wanted to discuss this latest trial delay," Clarence lied. He calmly handed Brewer the ink-soiled handkerchief. "I believe the expression that applies here is fish or cut bait. In other words, I'm entitled to a speedy trial and I want that trial to progress with or without Rachel Dillard and her so-called testimony."

The attorney shrugged. "We've been granted four delays during the past year. This is the first one for the prosecution. The DA will toss a request like that in your face."

"Perhaps. But it does no harm to ask." Or to offer. And by God, he had plenty to offer. But that was something he'd keep between the district attorney and himself.

Maybe it wasn't too late to save himself. Of course, that would mean throwing his partner—along with a few other insignificant employees—to the dogs.

No matter.

There were certain things that just couldn't be helped. Right now, he had to focus all his attention on the Dillards.

Jared stepped into the steamy shower and let the hot water pound against him. It didn't help ease the throbbing pain in his head and neck.

Nor did it ease anything else that was throbbing.

What it did do, however, was give him a little time to think. It didn't take him long to reach the conclusion that his judgment was sorely lacking in a couple of critical areas.

He was batting a thousand today in the stupidity department. First, he'd ignored all kinds of primitive warnings—warnings that had saved his butt on too many occasions to count. Yet, he'd pushed them aside this time, and it had gotten Rachel hurt at Livingston's house.

Then, as if that incident weren't enough to throw things into turmoil, he hadn't kept the latest comforting session at the cuddle-and-kiss level. Oh, no. Not him. He'd made love to her under the guise of helping her overcome her ordeal.

Yeah, right.

That'd been part of it, of course. A major part. However, somewhere around the time he'd gotten her on that bed and stripped off her clothes, the thought of helping her overcome her ordeal had gotten significantly overshadowed by the thought of some great oral sex.

He hoped that had relaxed her—even if it had done the exact opposite for him. Being with Rachel had caused a frenzy in his nether regions. So far, the shower wasn't helping. Nor would it. A shower couldn't cure that kind of discomfort.

Jared heard the bathroom door open, but before he could even turn off the water, the vinyl curtain slid back. Rachel stood there, the phone in her hand. She didn't avert her attention from his totally naked body. In fact, she slid her gaze down the length of him. It was a challenge. A sexual gauntlet.

That would have to wait.

She handed him the phone. "It's Tanner."

"Thanks." But he was talking to the air, because Rachel had already turned and walked away.

Even though he obviously had some unfinished business with Rachel, he welcomed the call. He hoped it was the news he had been waiting for. News that would ultimately lead to a showdown. Him against whoever the hell had the baby. His only regret was that Rachel would have to be there to witness it. He didn't want her in any more danger, but he couldn't see a way around it.

"You have something for me?" Jared asked. He wrapped a towel around his waist and stepped out of the tub.

"Yeah. I tried to call about fifteen minutes ago, but your line was busy."

"Busy…" He'd been in the shower for the past fifteen minutes. Jared shrugged it off. Rachel had probably had the cell phone tied up with the computer modem.

"I managed to get an address for Dr. Randall Sheridan," Tanner explained. "That's the good news, but the bad news is he's not there. I sent one of my people through the house. Just a cursory look. No signs of a baby or anything else."

Jared hadn't expected a smoking gun. However, he had expected to speak to the man, and soon. "What about his office?"

"Office*s*. He has two of them. We came up empty there, too. Sheridan has a private practice, but he mainly works at a downtown clinic that caters to the poor and uninsured. He didn't show up for work this morning, even though he was scheduled to come in nearly an hour ago. The staff is worried. They say it's not like him to miss work without calling."

"Hell." Had Esterman's people already gotten to the doctor—to silence him?

Tanner must have come to the same conclusion. "I've put every available man on this. If the doc is alive and in the area, we'll find him. And as soon as we locate him, I'll see what I can do about setting up a safe meeting. No repeats of what happened at Livingston's."

That was the critical part. He couldn't put Rachel through that again. "I really owe you for this."

"You bet you do. Don't worry, that pound of flesh won't hurt too much when I collect." Tanner paused. "There's more. I'll start with the simple stuff and work my way up. Dr. Sheridan is a parolee. A fairly recent one. He was in jail because of a DWI that resulted in some pretty serious injuries. He was supposed to serve three to five years, but he got out after fourteen months. Guess who helped him to secure an early release?"

"Esterman."

"You got it."

It wasn't much of a surprise, and it went a long way toward convincing Jared that Dr. Sheridan was the man they were looking for. Jared hoped the doctor was still alive, so he could help them.

"Maybe we should carry this parole thread a little further," Jared suggested. "I'll have Rachel do a computer search for someone that Esterman could have hired to take care of the child."

"You mean like a nurse?" Tanner asked.

"Yeah. Or maybe a nanny or a day-care worker. If Esterman got the doctor from prison, maybe he did the same thing with the caregiver."

"Then, that leads us back to Warden Livingston. You think he's Esterman's partner in all of this?"

"Could be. But that doesn't rule out Sergeant Meredith or the attorney, Lyle Brewer." Jared cradled the phone against his shoulder and dried his face with a towel. "Maybe all three are Esterman's silent partners."

"Did you get a feel for that when you spoke to Livingston at his house?"

"No. We didn't actually *speak*. When he walked into the closet to change, I put him in a chokehold, wrestled him to the floor and tied him up. I don't even think he got a good look at me."

Not that it mattered. While Jared was doing all of that, Meredith was assaulting Rachel in the other room. He should have just clubbed Livingston and gotten to her immediately. It would have saved her from going through that ordeal.

"I guess it's time to go another rung up that information ladder." Tanner blew out an audible breath. "I had the DNA tests walked through for you, and the lab just called me with the results."

That drew Jared right out of his thoughts about Livingston. With everything else going on, he'd almost forgotten about the DNA results. Yet, those results were critical for Rachel's and his future.

"Are you still there?" Tanner asked.

"Yeah." Jared cleared his throat and tried to brace himself. "Tell me what you have."

"What I have is a match for the kid, Jared. Sorry to just toss it out like this, but he's yours. Yours and Rachel's."

Chapter 12

Jared hadn't anticipated that the news would feel a whole lot like a punch to the gut.

But it did.

It felt like that and more.

The photograph flashed in his mind. The tiny innocent baby. *His* baby. A baby that was in the worst kind of danger.

A sickening feeling hit him so hard that Jared had to lean against the sink. It wasn't every day that a man learned he was the father of a child he'd never even seen. A child that he could easily lose.

"Are you okay?" he heard Tanner ask.

"Not really." He let go of the sink and leaned against the door. He didn't want Rachel to walk in and see him like this. He had to get control of himself. "Just how accurate is that test?"

"It's like that soap commercial—it's ninety-nine point nine percent."

Yeah. That's what Jared figured. Tanner wouldn't have told him the news, otherwise. "I have to go. Rachel needs to know this."

"Sure. I understand. I'll get back to you as soon as we locate the doctor."

Suddenly, that search took on an even greater urgency. And so did the tight fist that had hold of his heart. Hell, he couldn't protect Rachel or his child. Yet, he had to. Somehow, he had to keep them safe.

Jared dressed quickly. He certainly didn't want to deliver the bombshell to Rachel while he wore nothing but a damp towel. He'd barely gotten his jeans zipped, however, before she tapped on the door.

"What'd Tanner want?" she asked.

He told her the part about Dr. Sheridan while he put on his shirt. But there was no way he wanted that door between them when he told her about the baby.

Wishing for a double shot of whiskey, Jared took a deep breath instead and opened the door. Rachel was right there. Waiting. And she immediately studied his face.

"Something's wrong," she concluded.

"Sit down." He took her by the arm and led her to the bed.

She shook her head. "If it's bad news about the baby, then sitting won't help. Just tell me what Tanner found out."

"It's not bad." Well, not in the strictest sense of the word it wasn't. It just made everything a lot more personal. And more urgent. "Tanner got the DNA results."

"Already?" She stared at him for several moments,

obviously looking for clues as to what he knew. "I think I'd like to sit down now."

He nodded. Jared felt the same way. He sank onto the bed beside her, eyes fixed on the floor and tried to grasp the enormity of what they'd just learned.

He couldn't.

Best to say it fast because there was no easy lead-in for news like this. "The child is ours, Rachel. The tests are almost one-hundred percent accurate. We have a son."

A son.

Rachel slowly let that sink in. A baby she'd never carried inside her. Never held in her arms. Never even seen. And yet, he was already there in her heart.

Tears threatened, and she hurried to the chair where Jared had left his jacket to pull the photograph from the envelope. Despite her watery eyes, the image suddenly seemed so much clearer.

And more painful.

She had a child, and Esterman's people might hurt him before they could find him.

"I'd given up hope of ever having a baby," she admitted. She ran her fingers over the picture. "Especially when you refused to let me use the embryos after we separated."

"Yes."

That was it. The sum total of Jared's response. But Rachel didn't hold it against him. She wasn't sure how she was supposed to respond, either. Most couples had nine months to build up to a moment like this. Nine months of hoping, planning and dreaming.

Their dream was one big nightmare.

"We have to find him," Rachel mumbled. She stood

and went to the desk. There was nothing to arrange other than two pens and some paper. She settled for that. "We have to get him away from Esterman. We have to bring him…"

She almost said *home* before she realized she had no home. Not anymore. In a sense, Esterman had taken that from her, as well.

"Let's walk through this," Rachel insisted, trying not to panic. But she could feel the panic so close to the surface. "I need to know what we're going to do. I mean, I know we have to find our child. Then, the next step is, we'll go to the cops and explain why we've been on the run. You'll get to keep your badge, and I'll testify against Esterman." She turned around and faced Jared. "And then what?"

He shrugged. "Then, we find Esterman's partner and put him behind bars, as well."

Yes. But what Jared didn't say was that that might not happen. They might never find this other person. And that meant she'd never be safe.

Nor would their son.

So, they were back to square one, a place Rachel was very tired of being. With Esterman's partner on the loose, she and the baby would likely have to go into the Witness Protection Program. A new life and a new identity. But that left her with one huge question—

What about Jared?

"Just take it one step at a time," Rachel heard him say. "That's all we can do."

Sound advice. But it was also impossible to embrace. She might be a new mother, but her instincts were screaming for her to protect her child.

"Why don't you go back online and search for information on Dr. Sheridan?" Jared suggested. "You might find something that Tanner missed. Also, I think it's a good idea for you to look for recent parolees that Esterman could be using as a nanny."

She knew he was trying to distract her, to get her mind on something productive. And he was right. Worrying would accomplish nothing. Too bad it felt impossible to do what was sensible.

She plowed her hands through her hair and groaned. "He could be right under our noses, Jared, and we wouldn't even know it."

"I know, but I'll do whatever it takes to find him," he promised.

She believed him, but what worried her was that that might not be enough. Whatever they did might not be enough, and that was too painful to accept.

"We can't give up," Jared added, as if reading her mind. "If we do, Esterman wins."

Yes, and their son would lose. It was the right thing to say, to get her moving in a more constructive direction. She wouldn't let Esterman win this one. Not when her child's life was at stake.

Rachel took one last look at the photograph, put it back in the envelope and got to work.

Chapter 13

"Four names," Rachel murmured.

Sitting next to her, Jared read through the information on the computer screen. All four people were recent parolees. All were released with Clarence Esterman's assurance to the parole board that the four would have gainful employment through his company. Any one of the four could be the caregiver for the baby.

Or none of them.

In other words, nothing definitive yet. Maybe Dr. Sheridan could help them in that area. If he was still alive, that is. And if Tanner's people could actually find the man. It'd been nearly three hours since Jared had spoken to Tanner, so obviously they were having trouble locating Sheridan.

Not a good sign.

"That's it—just four names?" he asked. "I was worried there might be more."

"There might be. I went for the obvious so I could narrow down the search. They're all female, none over the age of seventy. None of them have any serious health problems. Two of them are nurses, one was a licensed child-care provider, and the other has some day-care experience. I think these are our best bets."

"Can you go ahead and get current addresses on all of them?"

Rachel nodded. "I already have them for the first three, but there isn't anything recent for this one." She tapped the last name on the list: Agnes McCullough. "I've checked property listings, employment records, Internet listings, you name it. She's just not there." Rachel paused. "But then, if Esterman's managed to get to Dr. Sheridan, maybe he's also gotten to anyone else who could incriminate him."

True. But Jared tried not to dwell on that depressing thought.

"Esterman isn't perfect," he reminded Rachel. While he was at it, it was a good reminder to himself, as well. "You were able to uncover his dirty dealings, proving not only that he's vulnerable but that he's capable of making mistakes."

And maybe Clarence Esterman would make yet one more mistake that would put him away for good and help them find their child.

Rachel groaned softly and rubbed the back of her neck. It wasn't an ordinary moan, either. It was laced with fatigue and frustration. Of course, she had been staring at that screen for hours while they waited for Tanner's call. Added to that, she'd been working too hard and eating too little. The takeout Chinese food that he'd picked up from across the street was still sitting there on the desk. Unopened.

Jared moved her hand away and took over the neck massage. "You're worrying and thinking too much. Believe me, it doesn't help."

"I know, but I can't seem to make it stop. All these crazy thoughts keep going through my head. I swear, I'll need a padded cell before this is over."

Jared knew the feeling and decided they both could use a little levity. He went for the obvious. "Well, I would distract you with some carnal suggestions, but I figure Tanner will call any minute. I hate getting interrupted while in the throes of passion, don't you?"

It worked. She made a small sound of amusement. Not quite a laugh, but it wasn't one of those frustrated groans. It didn't last, though. A moment later her eyelids floated down, and she shook her head.

"Distract me with something," she whispered, her voice strained. "Please."

It was the *please* that got him right where it hurt. God, he hated to see her like this.

"All right. Here goes." Jared went for the not-so-obvious this time, but it was something that he'd been dwelling on a lot lately. "Remember the first time I kissed you? It was your senior year at the university. We were sitting in my car, just outside your dorm. I reached for you. You reached back. At the end of all that reaching, you were in my arms. Right where I'd wanted to get you all night." He paused a heartbeat. "We fogged up the windows."

Rachel glanced over her shoulder at him. She bunched up her forehead. "Are you trying to distract me or get me hot and bothered?"

Jared smiled, and after the nightmare they'd been through, it felt good to share a light moment with her. "Hell, if you have to ask, I've failed already."

She stared at him and studied him before her face relaxed slightly. "I definitely remember our first kiss. You treated me like…glass. Well, for a second or two, anyway. Then we sort of devoured each other. It was French and fantastic."

Jared suppressed a groan. Her memory was way too good for this distraction game. "Well, that's what hellions like me do to innocent college girls like you." He continued the massage, working his fingers across the tight muscles. "We corrupt them with French kisses, all the while trying to cop a feel or two."

Rachel managed a short-lived smile. "I still dream about it."

So did he. It was pretty darn memorable if after six years he could still remember the exact taste of her. That wasn't all. He could also remember every last detail about how her breasts felt when he closed his fingers around her.

The distraction was working. Well, for Rachel it apparently was. It was giving Jared a whole new kind of distraction to deal with. There was suddenly a three-ring circus going on in his boxer shorts.

"And then the second time you kissed me," she continued, "we were at the lake. You'd taken me out on your friend's boat. It was more than just one kiss, though. More like twenty. It qualified as making out."

"And then some." He'd taken a long, cold shower after he dropped her off at the dorm.

It hadn't helped.

And neither was this conversation. It was probably best if this stopped while he could still walk.

"Come on. Let's try some other way to burn off this excess energy." He stood and braced his hands, palms out, in front of his chest. "Without inflicting any permanent damage, show me what you can do. Give me your best shot."

She stood. Slowly. "My what?"

Another wince. "Okay, bad choice of words. I meant, give me your best boxing move, and I'll see if I can block it. Remember that part about no permanent damage, though. And no aiming at any part of my body that contains vital organs. Let's go."

Rachel continued to stare at him. "You're sure?"

"You bet." Well, not really, but this had to be a better way to lighten her spirits than talking about French kissing sessions. "Let's get the juices flowing with a little one-on-one."

Even though she still looked uncertain, there was nothing tentative about her maneuver. Rachel gave him a warning signal just a second before she slammed her fists into his palms. First one and then the other. Then she pivoted and thrust her elbow against his hand.

Jared grunted at the force, and he managed a grin.

Barely.

"Classic Shaolin attack. The soles of your feet were aligned with your palms. The move wasn't too high to give me an opening," he complimented. "And if I hadn't blocked it, it would have hurt like hell. Okay, let me see if I can stop you. Come at me."

She did so with no hesitation, her right hand aimed at his face. Jared executed a defensive move of his own, deflecting the blow with his forearm. He pivoted, trapping her hand under his arm and then grabbing her wrist.

Rachel looked up at him, scowled. She came back at him immediately with a sidekick aimed at his midsection. Jared was thankful that she pulled back before impact, or she could have done some serious damage. He deflected the kick with his hand.

"A Bruce Lee move?" he asked, surprised.

She shrugged. "Whatever works. The trainer taught me a variety of techniques for defending myself. I think she did a good job with her instruction."

Obviously. And Rachel had done a good job learning. "This is a little more dangerous than I thought it'd be. Either we'd better try a different distraction technique, or we might have to consider sex, after all. This is starting to feel a little like rough foreplay."

He'd meant it as a joke. A really bad joke. But there was no humor in Rachel's eyes. There was, however, a fire. A scorching heat that had him inching toward her.

Just as the phone rang.

"Tanner always did have lousy timing," he mumbled. Then, "This better be good news," Jared said into the phone.

"I guess it'd qualify as good. For us, anyway. Esterman might not feel the same way."

He went completely still, and any aggravation he felt over the interruption was long gone by the time Tanner made it to the end of his sentence. Jared was almost afraid to voice the conclusion he drew, for fear it would vanish before they could do anything about it.

"You found Dr. Sheridan?" Jared asked.

"Yep. He's not only alive and well, he's with me. Ready to come over here and meet him?"

"You bet." He grabbed the notepad and jotted down the address that Tanner gave him. "I'll see you in about ten minutes."

Rachel quickly grabbed her shoes. "Tanner has Dr. Sheridan?"

Jared nodded but didn't waste any time. He took Rachel's arm and hurried out the door.

Chapter 14

The idea of any kind of foreplay went straight out the window. In its place, Rachel felt another huge surge of adrenaline. Another wave of panic. And some hope. They raced out of the room and to the car.

"Where did Tanner set up this meeting?" Rachel asked as Jared drove away from the hotel. She pressed her foot against the dash so she could tie her shoelaces.

"At Sheridan's private office downtown. It's closed today, so we'll get a chance to talk to him without any-one interrupting us." He paused. "Well, hopefully there won't be any interruptions."

Yes. The memory of the fiasco at Livingston's house hadn't dimmed much. Nor had the nauseating reaction she still had to Sergeant Meredith's attack.

"There won't be a repeat performance like the one at

Livingston's," he assured her. "Tanner's going to stand guard while we're inside."

That was something, at least. Maybe that meant they could find some answers and get away from there before Esterman's people arrived. And maybe those answers would lead them straight to the baby before another day went by.

And then what?

She settled back against the seat and contemplated that. It was a question that had come to mind at least a dozen times in the past twenty-four hours, but since learning the child was theirs, it'd taken on a new urgency along with new complications. What did the future hold for them?

Through all of this, through the search and the steamy kissing sessions, he hadn't said a word about wanting to be part of their baby's life.

Or hers.

However, Rachel doubted he'd just let her walk away with their child. Besides, her leaving would mean the obvious—that their baby wouldn't be with his father, and *she* wouldn't be near Jared, either.

An ache made its way across her chest and sank right into her heart. Was that too much to hope for, that he would ever want her back in his life?

Maybe.

God, maybe it was.

Rachel saw her reflection in the vanity mirror over the visor. She watched the cold, hard realization take hold of her face. Jared might never risk loving her again.

Never.

This could possibly be as good as it ever got between them. And if so, she might have to accept the fact that the most she'd ever have of him was his child. A child that they couldn't even raise together.

"You're quiet over there," he murmured. "Are you thinking too much again?"

She tied her other shoelace. "No. Now, I'm obsessing. Seems like a good time for it."

As if it were the most natural thing in the world, he took her hand, brought it to his mouth and brushed a kiss over her knuckles. The gesture was obviously meant to comfort her, but all it did was remind her that there was more at stake here than just their child.

"Have you thought beyond this?" she asked. The question was too vague to make sense, but Rachel thought that maybe Jared would understand.

He didn't answer right away. He concentrated on driving. "It's hard not to think about it."

Okay. That didn't tell her much. She pressed for more. "If I'm in witness protection, what do we do about the baby? I mean, about you seeing him."

She had to choke back a groan. She hadn't intended to be so forthcoming, but skirting around issues definitely wasn't her forte.

"I know what you're asking," Jared volunteered. "And I don't know what to say. It's hard to think beyond now, beyond this visit."

Rachel quietly agreed. But it was also hard *not* to think beyond it—

"This is it," she heard Jared say.

Rachel checked her watch. Barely twelve minutes since they'd left the hotel. She hoped, Tanner had had time to set up security.

Jared stopped the car in the back parking lot of the one-story vanilla-colored brick building. There were only two vehicles in the lot. Tanner's black truck and a white car that must belong to Sheridan. It certainly appeared that they'd have privacy.

The place wasn't in the best part of town, and it was modest by anyone's standards. Either being on Esterman's payroll hadn't been lucrative for the doctor, or else Sheridan was a master of deception. Not good. Rachel was praying that he'd be willing to skip the pretenses and spill his guts.

Tanner was at the back entrance, looking much like the guardian of the gate. He held open the door, motioned for them to hurry inside, and then followed right behind them.

"How did you get Sheridan to agree to this meeting?" Rachel asked.

Tanner shrugged. "Let's just say I made him an offer he couldn't refuse."

And with that ominous response, Tanner directed them into a private office. Sheridan was there, seated behind a desk littered with manila folders and other assorted papers. He had a cup of coffee in one hand and a cigarette in the other.

He wasn't quite what Rachel had expected. He was thin, almost wiry. Stress and worry lines were all over his face. And even though he was probably only in his mid-thirties, his auburn hair had streaks of gray.

Tanner immediately turned to leave. "I'll leave the three of you alone."

The moment Tanner closed the door, Jared walked behind the desk, bracketed his hands on each side of the chair and got right in the doctor's face. "Let's make this quick. Do you have any idea who we are?"

Sheridan nodded.

Rachel released the breath she didn't even know she'd been holding. It wasn't a tell-all confession, by any means, but at least he wasn't going to try to stonewall them.

"And you know why we're here, don't you?" Jared again. But instead of a question, it sounded like a threat.

"I know what you want." Dr. Sheridan turned his hazy blue eyes in Rachel's direction. He crushed the cigarette in an ash tray and slowly blew out the leftover stream of smoke. "I'm sorry, but I can't help you. They'll kill me. You must realize that."

"Do I?" she countered. She walked closer. "Or are you the one who put this plan together?"

"No. Never. It was Esterman."

Jared pulled up a chair, parking it right in front of the doctor. "I need names and information. And I need it now. Where's my son?"

"I don't know," Sheridan answered immediately. "I swear I don't."

"Then, you'd better start telling me what you do know, because Esterman isn't the only one you should be afraid of. As far as I'm concerned, my child is in danger because of you, so that makes your life worth next to nothing." Jared paused just long enough to move a fraction closer. "Convince me otherwise, and you might just get out of here alive."

Normally, the threat of violence would have sent her heart pounding, but it was pounding for a different reason now. Jared was a good cop. She knew that for a fact. If anyone could get answers from Sheridan, it was Jared.

With his hand shaking so much that the coffee nearly sloshed out, Sheridan took a drink before he responded.

"I'm sorry for what you're going through. I'm even sorrier that I wasn't able to stop this."

"You can stop it now," Jared pointed out.

"But Esterman—"

"You can go into protective custody. Hell, you should have done that already. Because if we can find you, then Esterman won't bother to keep you around much longer. You're a huge liability to him now, and you're living in a dreamworld if you think otherwise."

That must have sunk in, finally. The doctor glanced at both of them and took a deep breath. "You really believe you can arrange protective custody so I'll be out of Esterman's reach?"

Jared nodded. "Not me personally, but I'll put you in touch with someone who can."

If Sheridan believed that, it didn't show on his face. He gave a heavy sigh as if surrendering to the inevitable. The inevitable in this case being not protective custody but something much worse.

"Esterman's assistant came to me in prison a little over a year ago," Sheridan began. He sat his coffee cup aside and rubbed his hand over his face. "He said he could get me out early if I'd do a surgical procedure. He didn't explain beyond that. He just said that I'd have to keep it a secret, and that it might not be legal."

No surprise there. Many things that Esterman did were illegal. "But you agreed, anyway?" Rachel asked.

"Yes." Sheridan stared down at his hands and repeated it. "Because I would have died if I'd stayed in that prison. I swear, I would have died. I was being threatened by this…thug who had this intense hatred for anyone in the medical profession. He'd already gotten to me twice, and each time I ended up in the infirmary. I knew if I stayed there, he'd kill me."

Even though there were tears in the doctor's eyes, Rachel could feel no sympathy for him. He'd known that he was agreeing to do something illegal before he ever left prison, and in this case, the illegal activity had put others in danger.

"So Esterman got you out early," Jared finished. "And you did the in vitro procedure on Sasha Young—"

"Were there others?" Rachel interrupted. It was something that had bothered her from the beginning. After all, several embryos were stolen from the clinic. "Or was Miss Young the only surrogate?"

Sheridan shook his head. "She was the only one as far as I know, and I think Esterman would have told me if there had been others. I did the surgery here in the office. Not ideal conditions, I can assure you. But it was successful."

Yes. Very. And because of that success, she, Jared and their son were facing this horrible ordeal.

"That's a great start, but keep talking," Jared insisted when Sheridan paused.

"I did the prenatal checkups on Miss Young at her house. Nothing much more than cursory exams. Then, last week Esterman called me to do the C-section. It was a little sooner than I would have liked, but he insisted."

Rachel latched onto that right away. God, she couldn't believe she hadn't asked about that earlier. "The baby was healthy when you delivered him?"

"He was fine. Good Apgar." Sheridan glanced in her direction again. "That's the test we give newborns to evaluate their heart rate, muscle tone and other physiological indicators."

So her baby was alive and well.

At least, he had been about a week ago.

"Esterman had a backup plan," Sheridan continued. "If for some reason the child didn't survive, he wouldn't have told you. He intended to use the infant's DNA to prove the infant was yours, and he thought that would be enough to get you to cooperate."

Rachel held onto the desk. That wasn't an easy thing to hear. She'd hated her former boss before this, but after listening to Sheridan spell out Esterman's intentions, her hatred reached a whole new level. If all Esterman had wanted from the child was a DNA sample, then maybe…

But Rachel couldn't even finish the thought. She couldn't let her mind go beyond the moment. She was thankful that Jared was able to continue the questioning.

"After you delivered the baby, did you murder Sasha Young?" he demanded.

"No!" Sheridan's face bleached out to a sickly color. "It was that man, Gerald-something. The one who calls himself Esterman's personal assistant, the one who visited me in prison to tell me about this arrangement. He's really a hired killer, that's what he is. He strangled Sasha before she even came out of anesthesia. You have to believe me, I had no idea that Esterman had planned something like that."

"I'll bet Sasha Young didn't, either," Jared tossed back at him.

"Yes. You're right. She was the innocent one in all of this. She just wanted a way to make some money. She wanted a new life. And instead, she was killed."

Yes, and they had to stop him before he killed again.

"Where's the baby?" Rachel managed to ask.

Sheridan shook his head again. "I honestly don't know.

Gerald took him just minutes after the delivery, and I haven't seen either of them since."

"Then, give an educated guess as to where you think Gerald took him," Jared ordered.

The man touched his fingers to his temple and mumbled something as if going through some old information. "I can't say for sure, but once when I heard Gerald talking to Esterman on the phone, I heard him mention a woman's name. Agnes, or maybe Alice. I think she could possibly be the one who's taking care of the child."

"Agnes," Jared repeated. "You have a last name for her?"

"No. I only heard him mention her that one time."

Rachel moved closer so she could whisper to Jared. "I know who she is. It's Agnes McCullough. That's one of the names on the list of parolees. She's an RN, but there wasn't an address for her."

Jared stood, reached into his wallet and extracted a business card. He tossed it on Sheridan's desk amid all the paper clutter. "Call that number immediately after we leave and ask to speak to Captain Elizabeth Thornton."

Sheridan didn't take the card, but he stared at it. "Who is she?"

"My boss. Tell her that you have information about Esterman and that you need to be placed in protective custody. She'll work out the arrangements."

"I'm really sorry about all of this." Sheridan sank his fingers into his hair and squeezed his eyes shut. "I had no idea anyone would get hurt."

"Yeah, right" was Jared's comeback. "You helped a monster put a sinister plan into action, and you figured no one would be hurt? At least with that kind of reasoning, you shouldn't have any trouble rationalizing away the fact you put innocent people in danger—including a child. Guess that Hippocratic oath you took of 'do no harm' didn't mean much when the bottom line was saving your own hide."

While Jared continued to talk with Sheridan, Rachel opened the door to find Tanner waiting on the other side. "We need to find a woman named Agnes McCullough," she relayed. "She's the one who might have the baby."

Tanner immediately took out his cell phone, punched in some numbers and repeated the woman's name to whoever had answered. She hoped it was someone with better contacts than she had. She'd had no luck finding out anything on the computer.

"I did a pretty thorough database search back at the hotel," she told Tanner when he finished the call. "But I wasn't able to come up with an address."

"Then, we'll have to do some hands-on searching. My advice is for Jared and you to lay low until you hear from me. Once Esterman figures out that we've found the doctor, he'll be gunning not just for Sheridan, but for Jared, as well."

Tanner was right, of course. There was no reason for Esterman to want Jared alive. However, there were some serious reasons why Esterman would want him dead.

"Esterman might do anything to keep you alive, but that courtesy doesn't apply to anyone else in the middle of this." Tanner kept his voice low. Almost a whisper. "In his sick mind, Esterman probably figures if he takes Jared out, you'll surrender. Remember that, when and if all of this comes to a showdown."

Rachel tried to grasp the reality of that. It wasn't easy. She'd known that Jared was in danger, but it sent her heart pounding to hear that threat spelled out.

"Did you hear what he said?" Jared asked, walking up behind her.

It took her a moment to realize that he was speaking to Tanner and not her. Rachel heard the two discuss their options for finding Agnes McCullough, but it was white noise. Background that she had to push aside so she could think.

Remember that, when and if all of this comes to a showdown.

Oh, she would remember, all right.

Rachel was sure of that.

Finding Agnes and the baby was critical. But so was keeping Jared safe. Staying alive so she could testify against Esterman would mean nothing if she lost Jared and the baby. Nothing.

Chapter 15

Jared stood just inside the back entrance to Sheridan's office and watched Tanner drive away. With luck, Tanner's P.I. staff would be able to find Agnes McCullough pronto. And with even more luck, maybe she'd have the baby with her.

"What now?" Rachel asked.

Well, it certainly wasn't what Jared wanted to do. He wanted to get his hands on Agnes *now*. He wanted the baby *now*. But apparently, that wasn't going to happen.

"I guess we go back to the hotel and wait." He stepped out and checked the area to make sure it was safe. Only then did he motion for her to follow him to the car.

Even with everything else going on, he couldn't help but notice that Rachel had been awfully quiet since their conversation with Sheridan. Too quiet. Maybe all of this was starting to get to her. But if so, Jared prayed she could hold it together a little longer. He didn't want to tell her that the worst was probably yet to come.

They had barely made it halfway across the parking lot when he heard the sound. It registered immediately.

A shot.

Just one.

But it was more than enough to make Jared draw his own weapon, and to send them running for cover. It was too far to make it back to the office and too far to the car. So, he gripped Rachel's arm and pulled her to the ground next to Sheridan's vehicle.

She moved closer so she could whisper in his ear. "Was that what I think it was?"

"Afraid so."

She groaned softly, and he pushed her behind him. They waited. In silence. Even though he could hear Rachel's breathing coming out in short spurts.

"Do you see anyone?" she asked.

Jared shook his head. The sound had come from behind them. Not good. Because behind them was the office. Right where they'd just left Sheridan.

"It was a handgun," Jared said, more to himself than to Rachel. "Or else a rifle chambered for a handgun."

"That makes a difference?"

All the difference in the world, and that difference wasn't good. "If it's a rifle, it means someone probably shot into the building."

"As opposed to someone who was already inside," Rachel finished.

Yes. Either way, Jared damn sure didn't want a rifle-toting assassin to fire shots at Rachel. Or Sheridan. It was possible the doctor could still help them find Agnes McCullough.

While keeping a vigilant watch around them, Jared pressed in Tanner's number. It was a risk. A big one. If the gunman heard the phone ring, he might turn the gun on Tanner. Still, Jared had enough faith in his friend. Tanner had probably already taken cover and was waiting for Jared's situation report.

"I heard the shot," Tanner said the moment he answered. "Are you all right?"

"For now. Did you see anything?"

"No. I'm at the front of the office. Some cars have passed, but no one's stopped."

"Same here. I don't have a visual on anyone. Could the gunman have gotten inside the place when Rachel and I were going out the back?"

"Negative. I had men posted at the front door and the side. They left less than a minute ago."

Less than a minute ago was just about the time that he'd heard the shot. Jared checked the area again and was about to tell Rachel they'd have to make a dash for the car. But something stopped him. The dull heat in the back of his head. A tightness in his stomach.

Something beyond the obvious was wrong.

Levering himself up just slightly, Jared looked on the roofs of the surrounding two-story buildings. It was just a glimpse. A glint of reflected sunlight.

A rifle.

Hell.

Jared didn't waste any time getting that information to Tanner. "The shooter's on the roof of the brownstone. I need a distraction so I can get Rachel out of here."

Tanner didn't answer for several moments. "I see him." He mumbled a curse. "He's got a scope. If he's after you, the second you try to drive out of here, he'll have you in his range and pinned down. The windows on the car aren't bullet resistant."

That meant going back into the building. It wasn't exactly Jared's first choice of escape plan. He needed to get Rachel the hell away from there. If someone nearby had heard the shot, they might already have called the police. Not good. Still, he couldn't risk some stray bullet going through the car window and hitting her.

"We can't stay around here long. Think you can manage to have our shooter off that roof in under ten minutes?" Jared asked Tanner.

"I'll try. Get Rachel in the office and stay down until I give you an all-clear."

He handed Rachel the phone so he could keep his hands free. "Come on. We have to go back in." Jared positioned her between the gunman and him, hoping that was enough. "If something goes wrong, get inside. No matter what."

"Excuse me?" She pulled him back when he started to move. "I should be the one protecting you. They don't want me dead."

No way would that happen. "We don't know that for sure. They're making up the rules as they go along. Just like we are."

"Then, why do you have to be the one in the line of fire?" she asked.

"Because I'm bigger." It was a weak answer, but he didn't want to waste any more time arguing a point that wasn't open for debate. "Let's go."

He didn't give her a choice. Jared looped an arm around her waist and got her moving back toward the office. His heart pounded harder with each step. No more shooting. Thank God. He didn't know if that was because

Tanner had managed to distract the gunman or because the guy was just waiting until he had a better shot.

Jared opened the thick metal door and pulled Rachel inside with him. "I swear this will make a praying man out of me yet," he mumbled.

Rachel started to back into the hallway that led to Sheridan's office, but Jared caught her again and repositioned them so he was in front. If by some chance Tanner was wrong and a gunman had managed to get inside, he didn't want Rachel coming face-to-face with him.

Jared kept his footsteps light so he could hear any movement in the other room. But it was silent.

"Dr. Sheridan?" he called out.

Nothing.

This wasn't good. The man knew the sound of his voice and should have responded. If he was capable of responding, that is.

Jared had already anticipated what he might see long before he got to the doorway.

And he was right.

Dr. Randall Sheridan was slumped over his desk. Facedown. His lifeless eyes staring at the wall.

There was blood. Plenty of it. But that wasn't what captured Jared's attention. It was the gun still cradled in Sheridan's limp right hand.

The doctor had found a way to avoid Esterman's wrath, after all.

Rachel gasped when she saw the body and quickly turned her head away. She wasn't quick enough. In that glimpse, she saw what remained of Dr. Sheridan. She clamped her teeth over her bottom lip to stop herself from screaming.

Jared motioned for her to stay put, but he walked closer and checked for a pulse in Sheridan's wrist. "I guess he decided against protective custody…"

When he didn't finish, Rachel followed his gaze. Sheridan's phone. It was off the hook, lying on the desk. Jared put his ear closer, listened and then cursed.

"Captain Thornton?" Jared said. "Sheridan called you?"

Rachel couldn't hear the captain's response, but it couldn't have been pleasant. Nor was it short. The woman seemed to be explaining something. Or rather, ordering Jared to do something. Jared's eyes narrowed, and he aimed that narrowed glare at her.

Oh God. Not this. Not now. Rachel definitely wanted to put off this particular confrontation, but from Jared's glare, she could see that wasn't possible.

Jared didn't pick up the phone, but instead he used the end of his key to press the speaker button—perhaps so he wouldn't mar any possible evidence; this was now essentially a crime scene. Still cursing under his breath, he went to the window, lifted the blinds a fraction and peered out.

"Well?" the woman on the phone asked. That one word hung in air for a while. "Cat got your tongue, or are you just wasting my time?"

Rachel recognized the voice. It was definitely Captain Elizabeth Thornton. Jared's boss.

"Sheridan said he was about to kill himself," the captain continued when Jared didn't respond. "He made it clear that Rachel and you weren't responsible. Now, while I'm relieved about that, I'm not pleased with the rest of your actions, Lieutenant Dillard."

"I know. And I don't have time to explain things. A baby's life is at stake—"

"So the doctor mentioned. Drive to headquarters, and we'll discuss it in detail. By the way, in case you missed the subtle nuance in my tone, that was an order."

Rachel braced herself. An order. This was no doubt why Jared hadn't wanted to speak to his boss. He knew he would have to disobey her.

"I can't go to headquarters," Jared answered. Rachel didn't miss the nuance there. The words were strained. His voice, tight. It matched his expression. "Not until this is finished." And with that, he reached over and clicked off the phone.

Even though Jared didn't say it aloud, there was a bottom line to all of this, and it could cost him his badge.

"Wanta save some time?" Jared asked.

Since Rachel was pretty sure where this was leading, she stalled. "That depends."

"That comment's not my idea of saving time, Rachel." He tossed her one quick, icy glare before he turned his attention back to the window. "Why did you call the captain this morning and tell her that it was your idea to escape? Jesus H. Christ!" It took him a moment to regain his composure. "You told her that you held me at gunpoint and forced me to go with you."

"Oh, that." Rachel quickly ran through her options, only to realize she didn't have any. Jared wasn't about to let go of something like this. His pit bull instincts had already kicked in. "Okay, but I warn you, this is like the proverbial Pandora's box. Once opened, you might not like what you find inside."

"Try me."

She tried him, all right. Rachel didn't pull any punches.

"I didn't want you to lose your badge. Not because of this. I know you're doing this for me."

"I'm doing it for *us*. For our son. And I don't need you to defend my reputation or whatever the hell you thought you were doing, got that? You could have accidentally said something to Thornton to give us away. She could have found us through that phone call."

"But she didn't." Rachel had already geared up to add more, much more, but Jared put his finger to his lips in a be-quiet gesture.

"Hell. It's Sergeant Meredith," Jared grumbled. "Just what we don't need right now."

She froze. Which was a good thing. It saved her from panicking. "Where is he?"

"I see him on the roof. He's got a rifle."

Forcing herself to move, Rachel made her way past the doctor's body and across the room, but Jared kept her back when she tried to look out the window.

"Are we trapped?" she asked, frightened of the answer. It wasn't just because of Meredith. This was costing them valuable time.

"I'm not sure. Let's give Tanner a couple of minutes to lead Meredith away from here, and then we'll try to get out."

Good. She didn't want to stand around in a room with a dead body any longer than necessary. She was so close to a panic attack that she could taste it.

"Why don't you think of our first kiss?" Jared said, his voice anything but romantic. A moment later, she knew why. "Or else you can think about how I'm going to yell at you for calling the captain."

Well, that was a sure-fire way to stave off a panic attack. Rachel decided to wait to panic, or defend herself.

Jared lifted his head slightly and turned back toward the window. "Listen," he whispered.

But she didn't have to listen hard. She heard the sound immediately. A siren. It wasn't close, but she was positive it was headed their way.

"Captain Thornton must have sent out a unit," Jared explained.

Yet more bad news. It might scare off Meredith, but it put them in danger of being found.

"Let's go," he said.

Together they sprinted down the hallway. He didn't stop when they got to the door. Jared shoved it open, scanned the parking lot and gave her the go-ahead.

"I'll walk out first," he instructed. "If all goes well, follow me. Pay particular attention to that 'if all goes well' part, Rachel. Don't go out there if anyone, including me, is shooting. Got that?"

She nodded and braced herself for the run to the car. Tanner might have distracted Meredith so they could escape, but that didn't mean Meredith hadn't doubled back to come after them. Fortunately, she didn't get a chance to dwell on that theory because the phone rang.

"Answer it," Jared insisted. "It'll be Tanner."

Yes. And perhaps with news that he'd lost Meredith. But it wasn't Tanner.

"A mutual acquaintance got this number for me," she heard the man say. "No easy accomplishment, I can tell you. The lieutenant obviously values his privacy."

The voice made her blood turn to ice.

"Esterman." Just saying his name took the breath out of her. Rachel had to pause a second. Beside her, she heard Jared ask for the phone, but she ignored him.

She covered the mouthpiece. "Concentrate on getting us out of here," she whispered to Jared. "I'll take care of this."

Jared objected. As she knew he would. But Rachel disregarded him.

"What do you want?" she asked Esterman.

"Let's see—what do I want?" he repeated, his tone cold. "I want you to do as you've been told."

Rachel didn't back down. "And I want my son."

"Yes. I can only imagine. Your own flesh and blood, and yet you've never even seen the little fellow. He has good healthy lungs, from what I understand."

God, he would use something like that—the suggestion that her son was crying. It tore at her heart—just as Esterman had known that it would. It didn't break her, though. Too much was at stake for her to let him do that.

"I want to see him." Rachel silently applauded herself. Her voice sounded calm and steady. Beneath all that calmness, however, her entire body was one raw nerve. "Where is he?"

"In due time. You should be thanking me, you know. After all, this was my plan. I'm the one who's responsible for that child being born. Without me, you wouldn't have your son. The son you've always wanted."

"A son you've threatened to kill," she reminded him.

"Only if you don't cooperate. The choice has been yours all along. But what have you done with that choice? You allowed your ex to sway you in a seriously bad direction. How many more people must die before you do what's necessary? You are responsible for this."

"Wrong. You're responsible."

"Each second you waste is putting your child in greater danger. So far, I've shown compassion. Don't expect that compassion to continue."

And with that, he hung up.

"What did he say?" Jared asked immediately.

She took a moment to gather her breath. "Nothing that we didn't already know. Our son is in danger, and Esterman is the one responsible."

"That really was Esterman on the phone?"

Rachel nodded. Just nodded. It seemed the best response while she kept hold of the emotions that threatened to break free.

"What the hell did he want?" Jared demanded.

"The impossible." Rachel closed her eyes for a second and fought to hold herself steady. "Now, let's get out of here and find our son."

Chapter 16

Rachel paced across the hotel room while Jared finished his conversation with Tanner. A conversation that had been going on since their return from Sheridan's office.

From Jared's reaction, it seemed things weren't going as well as they'd hoped. Apparently, Tanner's people were having trouble coming up with an address for Agnes Mc-Cullough. Not that Rachel had expected it to be easy. If Agnes did indeed have the child with her, Esterman had no doubt made certain that she was hidden away.

So Rachel kept on pacing. It didn't help. There was so much explosive energy inside her that she was about to scream. No amount of pacing—or organizing—would help that. She'd already organized any and everything in the tiny hotel room.

With both the doctor and Aaron Merkens dead, Esterman seemed to be a little farther out of her reach. And yet in some ways, that mattered less than it probably should have. All Rachel could think about was finding Agnes and the baby. Only then would she be able to concentrate on Esterman getting what he deserved.

"They're still looking," Jared informed her when he got off the phone. "So is the patrol unit that Captain Thornton sent to the doctor's office. We have to lie low until Tanner can arrange for us to see Agnes McCullough."

"Yes. Lie low. Wait." She drummed her fingers against her crossed arms. "Since you didn't mention screaming, I guess that's out?"

He smiled, but the smile quickly faded. "Unless you can manage to scream without attracting attention. We already have enough attention as it is." He propped his hands on his hips. "But you could use this time to explain why you called Captain Thornton and lied about kidnapping me."

Rachel rolled her eyes. "Sheesh. Of all the subjects we could disagree about, you would pick that one? There are bigger and meaner fish to fry, Jared."

But that wasn't entirely true. Just lately, she and Jared hadn't disagreed about much. In fact, that particular phone call to the captain and his me-Tarzan approach to her safety were the only subjects that had put them at odds.

Interesting.

In the past day and a half, they'd gone through hell together and had somehow mended a few rifts along the way. Here, they'd been separated for over a year, and she'd miraculously found the secret to putting her marriage back together. Too bad it'd taken a crisis of huge proportions to do it. And too bad it might be too late for anything, short of a miracle.

Since Jared still seemed to be waiting for an answer about Captain Thornton, Rachel stopped pacing and faced him. "All right. Here goes. I lied when I said that I called her only to save your badge. That was part of it, but it was just the tip of the iceberg. I did it because I still care about you, and I didn't want you hurt. Especially since you were doing the right thing when you got me out of that safe house."

He paused a moment. "That's admirable, but you risked getting yourself hurt. Kidnapping is a felony, Rachel. Add to that, I'm a cop—it's a wonder that Thornton didn't call in the FBI to come after you."

She shrugged. When she'd started all of this, she hadn't expected to pour out her heart to him. Still, it didn't make sense to hold back now. Somehow, they'd manage to sift through everything and had reached ground zero. "Well, that just goes to show you the depths of my feelings, huh?"

He just stood there and stared at her. Rachel did the same thing. Not necessarily a good idea. With him that close, she had no problem seeing every emotion on his troubled face.

His ruggedly handsome face.

Which reminded her of lots of other things.

Even with that reminder, she didn't move. She didn't back away. The idea that drifted through her mind took hold, and suddenly it was the only thing that made sense.

"I could probably talk myself out of doing this," she warned. "But I figure I'll explode. You'll make a good substitute for a scream."

It was more than that, of course. Much more. Part

of her wanted to say that to him, to bare her soul even more than she already had. Best not to complicate things, though. This might be a hard sell to Jared as it was. After all, he was trying to keep some distance between them.

Rachel latched onto the front of his shirt, pulled him to her and kissed him. She kept it short and sweet, but it sure as heck wasn't some lustless peck. And then she let go of him. Satisfied that she'd convinced him she didn't want to argue, or scream, or even bare her soul, she backed up so he could have a chance to escape.

She made it a step.

Just one.

Before he grabbed her wrist and stopped her.

Rachel turned toward him, her shoulder brushing his. He looked into her eyes. She didn't need to ask his intentions. She could see it. And feel it. She might have been the one to start this, but Jared was more than willing to finish it.

"I don't want to be a substitute for anything," he said.

Rachel nodded. "Believe me, you're not."

That was it—all it took to complete the mutual invitation. He nodded in return and dragged her closer, pulling her into a searing kiss.

His mouth pleasured and coaxed. Teased. Ignited the spark into a full flame. Rachel felt her heartbeat race. Her body grew warm and golden, and she found herself wrapping her arms around him so she could have more.

"Yes," she whispered against his mouth. "Now, this is what I need."

Jared moved her hair out of the way so he could go after her neck. He took that clever mouth to the sensitive little spot just below her ear. "It's the adrenaline that's got you so wired."

"You think so?" She touched her mouth to his jaw and had the pleasure of feeling a muscle jump there. "If you use that line on every woman you kiss, I'll bet it puts a real damper on foreplay."

He didn't stop the assault on her neck. Or her ear. But he made himself crystal clear. "I wouldn't know. You're the only woman I've been foreplaying with for years."

She pulled back and looked at him. "Is that true?" But Rachel immediately shook her head. "Never mind. I don't want to hear the answer to that."

"Sure you do." He met her gaze head-on. "Go for it, Rachel. Ask. You might be surprised at what I have in my version of Pandora's box."

Maybe. But she didn't want to risk it. There were a lot of things she could handle, but hearing about Jared's sexual escapades wasn't one of them. Rachel went after his zipper, instead.

"Boxes aside," she insisted. Now, it was her turn to kiss his neck. "I think I'd rather just pleasure you. You know, the way you did me."

Jared pressed his hand over hers to stop her. "As wonderful as that sounds—and, believe me, it does—what I have in mind is good old-fashioned sex. Something mindless and mutually satisfying. We'll see how far we get before Tanner calls. But first, I want you to ask the question that's obviously been on your mind."

She studied his eyes, and his expression. Nope, he wasn't about to back down on this, either. If she wanted things to progress beyond the zipper-lowering stage, she had to ask what she really didn't want to know.

"All right. Have you been with anyone else?"

"No."

No hesitation. No doubt. That was it. Just that one firmly spoken denial.

It was, well, touching. And a little confusing. Fourteen months was a long time, especially for a man who hadn't been able to keep his hands off her when they were married.

His answer might have soothed her ego if Jared had given it a chance.

He didn't.

What he did was take the first step to fulfilling his promise of something mindless and mutually satisfying. Just as on that night outside her college dorm, she reached for him. Jared was faster. He hauled her against him and kissed her.

This would not be a long leisurely afternoon of lovemaking, but Jared was sure neither of them cared about that.

Those were about the only totally coherent thoughts that made it into Jared's head. This wasn't the time for coherency, anyway. This was about Rachel, and him, and about how much they needed each other.

She fought with his shirt and won. Rachel managed to get it over his head and send it sailing across the room.

"Take me now," she insisted.

To prove she was serious, Rachel went after his zipper again. She wasn't careful about what she touched along the way. She slid her hand down the length of him.

And repeated the move.

Several agonizing times.

Her nimble fingers took him from the primed stage to being fully aroused. Not that he'd needed much for that to happen. That *take me now* comment was like water to a man dying of thirst. Jared very much wanted to oblige her.

He managed to peel off her shoes and jeans. Not easy. Not with her working at the same time to free him from his boxers. They both succeeded, somehow, and he backed her against the wall.

He took her mouth again while she wrapped her legs around his waist. Her mouth was as hot and wet as the rest of her. He touched her, because it was what they both needed, and he saw exactly what his touch did to her.

"This won't be safe sex." Jared positioned her, and she wrapped her legs around his waist.

Rachel hissed out a breath when they made intimate contact. "I don't remember asking for safe."

If she hadn't kissed him and thrust the midsection of her body against his erection, he might have considered the double meaning of that remark. But that brief contact made him remember his priorities.

Jared held her in place with his body. Her naked body against his. Her bare breasts against his chest. And he watched her eyes as he took her. Jared slid into that hot, slick heat and gave them both exactly what they needed.

He stilled just a moment. To savor. But the savoring and stilling came to a halt when Rachel started to move against him, and with him.

It didn't take much. The intensity between them didn't allow more, even though Jared wished that it could last a lifetime.

"Fly for me, Rachel."

She did. At the sound of his words, he felt her body close around him. Felt her soar until she reached a shattering climax. Jared was right there to catch her.

Rachel returned the favor.

With the hot primal need driving him, she took and gave her all in that same moment that he surrendered. He saw her face. Just her.

And that was all Jared needed.

Because he had no choice in the matter, Jared slid to the floor, taking Rachel right along with him. They were both damp with sweat, and little wisps of her hair were clinging to her neck and forehead. She looked amazing in the afterglow of good, non-safe sex.

"Don't you dare say that you'll regret this," Rachel mumbled.

"I'm feeling a lot of things, but regret's damn sure not one of them."

And to prove it, Jared gave her a kiss that neither of them would forget. He left them both breathless and wanting more.

There was no turning back now. What had happened couldn't ever be dismissed as just plain sex, even if it had occurred in a heated rush against the wall. He and Rachel had made love. And that left him with one troubling question.

What now?

Now that his head was starting to clear, Jared knew this was just the beginning. They had so many issues.

"You've got that look of obsessing on your face. What are you thinking?" she asked.

Jared didn't want to dive right back into what could easily be a depressing conversation. So he went in another direction. "I'm thinking you didn't scream. I'm thinking with just a little encouragement, I might be able to make that happen."

She smiled. Nothing sarcastic. Nothing meant to minimize the moment. It was real. Just like Rachel. Just like what they felt for each other.

"You're bragging," she whispered. She began to nibble on his mouth.

"Am I, now?"

He was fully prepared to back up that claim, but the ringing phone put a stop to it. Without releasing his grip on Rachel, Jared reached up and grabbed his cell phone from the desk. He cleared his throat in case it was Esterman. But it wasn't. It was Tanner.

"We found Agnes," Tanner informed him.

"She's alive?" And Jared held his breath waiting for the answer.

"She was as of this morning. We found her through a credit card purchase, but she's not in San Antonio. She's got a rental house out on an island near Corpus Christi. It'll be about a two-hour drive for you to get there."

Jared was already reaching for his shirt. "We'll leave in a couple of minutes."

"Here's a warning, though—you might have a few problems with accessibility," Tanner continued. "There's a private road and bridge that leads out to the place, but the initial reports are that it's guarded. *Heavily* guarded. So your best bet is to go via boat. I'll arrange for one."

"Good. Any indication that Agnes has the baby with her?"

"Yeah. I'm working on getting us an infrared, but how's this for an indication—one of my people just got off the phone with the clerk at the general store on the mainland near Agnes's house. They delivered some disposable diapers and some formula there just this morning. Oh, and those diapers apparently come in all kinds of sizes, but the ones that Agnes requested were for a newborn."

"Let's go," Jared told Rachel. He jotted down directions while she dressed.

Two hours. That was it. Such a short amount of time considering all they'd been through already. Still, they couldn't just go barging into the place. It wouldn't be safe for Rachel, or the baby.

"You'll check out the place before we get there?" Jared asked Tanner.

"I'll do my best, but I can't guarantee security on this one. Hard to guard the Gulf of Mexico. Esterman might have patrols out on that water."

True. But that wouldn't stop him. Nothing would. "We'll deal with that when we come to it. See you in two hours."

Chapter 17

Rachel studied the place through the binoculars, while Jared spoke on the phone with someone from a security company. A light went on in the west side of the house, but there was no sign of anyone.

No guards, no Agnes McCullough.

And definitely no sign of the baby.

The house was two-story, white, with massive marble columns fronting a wraparound porch. It was perched in the center of a lush, finger-shaped island. Pretty upmarket for the residence of a parolee with no recent record of employment. Agnes had done well for herself.

It had taken Rachel much of the two-hour drive to verify it, but she now knew that the same corporation that owned Sasha Young's rental house owned this property, as well. In other words, it was connected to Lyle Brewer, who in turn was connected to Clarence Esterman.

They were no longer at the starting point. This house, Rachel knew, was the finish line.

Luck was with them as far as the weather was concerned. There were only a few milky clouds scattered in the sky. The breeze was mild. The waves moved in a gentle slosh around her feet.

The conditions were ideal.

Still, every muscle and every nerve in her body was on full alert. Even *ideal* wasn't much of a guarantee with her child's life at stake.

Once the sun had set—which was only a few minutes away—they'd be able to approach the house via boat under cover of darkness. It was their best bet, Jared had said.

After that, however, all bets were off.

Once they reached the grounds, they would be too far away for Tanner to help them, and well out of reach of any local law enforcement. Which might be a good thing. If Esterman had managed to buy off a cop in the SAPD, perhaps he owned the locals, too.

"It's not too late to change your mind about this," she heard Jared say. He walked up behind her and brushed his fingers over her arm. "You can always stay here with Tanner to make sure no one follows me out to the island."

"I'm going with you," she insisted, still looking for any sign of movement in the house.

Jared didn't argue, maybe because he knew it was an argument he stood no chance of winning. Her child was in that house, and she was going in after him.

Tanner's phone rang, and he stepped away from the boat to take the call.

"Did you learn anything from the security specialist?" she asked Jared.

"Some. He tracked down the person who did the original system for the house nearly ten years ago. It's pretty basic. Not too many bells or whistles. I should be able to get through it without too much of a problem."

Rachel didn't miss the key bit of information that he left out of his explanation. "Ten years is a long time. What if someone made modifications to the system after it was installed?"

"Then, I'll figure out a way to get through them, as well." Jared took in a long breath. "By the way, if something goes wrong—"

Rachel quickly pressed her fingers against his mouth so that he couldn't finish. "We both know what we have to do. Let's not spell it out."

Jared kissed her fingertips and gently moved them aside. "No doom and gloom predictions. I just don't want you to take any unnecessary chances."

She nodded. "The same goes for you."

Tossing her a you're-stubborn half snarl, Jared took the binoculars from her and had a look at the house. "I think our best bet will be to hide the boat when we reach the island and try to go in through the back. Hopefully, it won't be as well lit as the front."

"What about the infrared read that Tanner's been trying to get?" she asked.

He paused.

"There appear to be four adults," he finally answered. "And either a baby or maybe a small pet. The infrared wasn't conclusive."

She made a sound of acceptance and stared at the house. It was no pet. Rachel knew that with every fiber of her being. It was her son.

"Anyway, we'll go in through the back," Jared continued a moment later. "And we'll try to avoid the guards or whoever else is in there. If the baby's in the house, he's on the second floor. Or, at least, that's what the infrared indicated when it was taken an hour ago."

"Then we'll get the baby, sneak out and hurry back here," she finished. No need to dwell on the dozens of things that could go wrong between now and then.

"Yeah. And by then, Captain Thornton should have arrived. I called her about twenty minutes ago."

Rachel's head whipped up. "Thornton? Why would you call her?"

"To help wrap up things around here. I couldn't bring her in on this officially. Not with us breaking into the house."

She got that part. "That's the real reason we're not bringing Tanner with us?"

"Right. Even though he wanted to come, I need him here. But Thornton, well, that's a different matter. She never would have agreed to anything illegal. By the time she got the search warrants and assembled a team, it'd probably be too late. But I want her here to go in once we've gotten the baby out. I don't want anyone associated with this plan to walk. Thornton can help us with that."

Rachel carried that through to its logical conclusion. Thornton would arrange the arrests of the people in the house, but Jared's boss would take her in, as well. To testify and to answer any questions about the illegal things she and Jared had been doing to find the baby. Heck, Thornton might even arrest Jared.

So, this was essentially their D-Day. They had one shot to come out of there with the baby. Just one.

It had to count.

Jared curved his arm around her waist. "There'll be

no turning back once we're on that boat. I really wish you'd stay here with Tanner—"

"I don't want to turn back. And I don't want to stay. I just want this to be over."

The sun dipped even lower, until only a sliver of light was visible on the horizon. She held Jared's hand and led him toward the boat.

"Hold up one minute." Tanner slipped his phone back in his pocket and hurried to them. "I could go with you."

"I'd rather you watch that bridge and the shore to make sure no one follows us." He reached in his pocket and pulled out his badge. "By the way, when Captain Thornton gets here, make sure she gets that."

Tanner reached for it, but Rachel latched onto Jared's wrist. "Wait a minute. Why are you doing this?"

"Because it'll save Thornton the trouble of asking for it, that's why."

She shook her head. "You don't know that. I can't believe you'd just hand…"

Jared stared at her when she hesitated. Even in the filmy light, she saw his eyebrow lift a fraction.

"Questions?" he challenged.

"No." But she certainly had some answers. Answers that she'd been asking herself for years. She knew how much it cost him to hand over that badge. Being a cop was one of the most important things in the world to him.

But obviously not the *most* important.

It broke her heart. And made her feel like a genuine fool for ever doubting him. Later, when this was over, she'd tell him that.

While she was at it, she'd also let him know that she'd fallen in love with him all over again.

Tanner took the badge, glanced at it and slipped it into his pocket. "You need any extra weapons?"

Jared shook his head. "I wasn't planning to do a lot of shooting. A quick in and out. If all goes well, we should be back in under an hour."

It was an overly optimistic guess, but Rachel didn't correct him. She said goodbye to Tanner and thanked him when he wished them luck.

Jared started the outboard motor and got them moving. Of course, they'd have to turn off the engine when they got close to the house and paddle the rest of the way, but at least this initial boost of speed would save them some time. Perhaps very valuable time.

Without the sunlight, the water was eerily dark; she couldn't see even an inch below the surface. And the night closed in around them. She hoped that Esterman hadn't put guards on the shoreline. Or worse, on the water itself. The only things she and Jared had going for them were the element of surprise and their determination.

"Let's name the baby," she whispered when he turned off the engine. Rachel knew that sounded absurd at a time like this, but it suddenly seemed important. "He's a week old and he doesn't even have a name."

"We used to have that list, remember? I seem to recall that Michael was your favorite."

"Yes." She took one of the oars in the boat, and they started to row toward the shore. "But let's pick something different. Something *we* decide right here, right now. It'll be more meaningful that way."

He shrugged. "All right. How about we name him after your father, Benjamin? Or would that cause too many bad memories for you?"

She gave it some thought. "No bad memories, but I'd

like your name in there, too. How about Benjamin Jared? And we can call him—"

"Ben," they finished together.

Rachel managed a smile. "Maybe that's a good sign that we agree on the name?"

"Damn straight."

But if Jared indeed felt that way, the feelings didn't make it to his voice. Rachel heard the concern. The doubt. And even the fear. They mirrored what was going on inside her.

They quietly got off the boat and pulled it onto the shore, hiding it in a thick clump of shrubs. Jared paused a moment and looked around them.

"There doesn't seem to be any perimeter security," he mumbled.

At least, none that created an audible alarm. In fact, the place was quiet. The only sound was that of the surf and the cry of an occasional seagull.

Rachel followed him across the sandy beach to the back of the house. Jared had been right—it wasn't well lit. Just some spotlights on the patio. No guards in sight, either. That didn't put her at ease. In fact, it did just the opposite. Maybe Esterman had used Agnes McCullough, and this house, as a trap. But Rachel prayed she was wrong.

Keeping close to the wall, they walked slowly around the house. Jared tested the first window they came to. It was locked, and they moved on. He repeated that process three more times before he finally stopped and took out the tiny tool kit from his jacket.

Rachel stood on her tiptoes and peered inside. It was a dining room. Dark. Shadowy. And not a soul around. It also appeared to have easy access to a hallway. Beyond that, she could see the stairs.

"Keep a close watch on the yard while I'm doing this," Jared whispered.

Rachel turned so that she'd have a better view of the massive yard. The scarcity of lighting made it more secure for them, but it didn't help her with her surveillance. The grounds were littered with trees, shrubs and outbuildings. Any one of them could provide a hiding place for Esterman's hired guns or for some well-placed cameras that could be monitoring their every move.

Jared used a tiny glass-cutter to take out a fist-size section of the window, and then he reached in and disarmed the security wires. It likely wouldn't disarm the other windows, but it'd at least give them access to this one.

Taking out his weapon, he held it by his side so she wouldn't easily see it and panic. Rachel appreciated that, but he couldn't do that for long. If they encountered a guard, Jared would almost certainly have to use his gun. She prayed that she could deal with that when the time came.

He climbed in first and had a look around before he helped her through. Unlike the night air, the air in the house was cool, a trio of fans whirling overhead. The place smelled of furniture polish and disinfectant.

Jared went to the doorway. Paused. Looked around. And then motioned for Rachel to follow him. He turned off the light as they made their way down the hall to the set of stairs.

Then Rachel heard the footsteps.

Jared didn't waste any time. He jerked open the door to the storage area beneath the stairs and pulled her inside. It was dark and musky, an indication that it didn't get much use. The last thing they needed was for one of Esterman's people to find them before they even had a chance to search for the baby.

Someone opened a door. Not the one to the closet, thank God. Rachel heard the *click* of a knob in the hallway. Next to her, she felt Jared's arm flex. Nothing more than the readjustment of a few muscles, but he was obviously preparing himself for a fight.

Rachel's body made its own preparations. Her heart pounded. Her breath became rapid. She refused to let the fear paralyze her, but it definitely had her by the throat. Instead, she tried to channel her energy to her fists in case it turned physical. All that Shaolin training might come in handy, after all.

"I don't see the suitcase," someone called out. A man.

But she didn't recognize the voice. It definitely wasn't Brewer or Meredith.

"Don't worry about it right now. We can look for it later." A woman that time.

Rachel had no doubt that it was Agnes McCullough.

There was a sudden shuffle on the stairs overhead. Followed by more footsteps down the hall. Nothing frantic. Just two people going about some routine business. The footsteps trailed off to silence.

The seconds crawled by.

Jared eased open the door. Paused for a moment. Listened. Apparently satisfied, he motioned for her to follow him. They made it halfway up the steps before she heard the sound. It was soft. So soft. And yet Rachel knew exactly what it was.

A baby crying.

Her breath stalled in her throat, and she froze. Jared

didn't, thank God. He seized her arm and got them moving. They made it to the landing.

Another sound.

Faint but definitely a cry.

Even over the pounding of her own heartbeat, Rachel managed to follow Jared and that sound to a room at the end of the long hall.

The door was open several inches. Like a beacon, pale yellow light seeped out and bled onto the carpet. Jared flattened his back against the wall and inched toward the light.

When they were closer, he braced his right wrist and held the gun in front of him in case he had to fire. Crouching low, he pivoted so he could peek around the doorjamb. Rachel had a look, as well.

No one was there.

Cautiously, they went inside. Jared eased the door shut behind them and locked it. Immediately, he began to search the closet and beneath the bed to make sure they were alone. Rachel didn't help him. She spotted the white wicker bassinet in the corner and raced toward it.

She saw the movement of the blanket. Tiny squirms and kicks against the pale blue fabric. And then she saw his face. He was sucking on his fist and apparently not very happy that it wasn't a bottle.

"Jared," she somehow managed to whisper. "He's here. He's really here."

Too many emotions went through her to try to sort them all out. Besides, it didn't matter. The weight of the world just seemed to melt away.

With her hands trembling and her heart in her throat, Rachel carefully lifted him up, and for the first time held her son in her arms.

Chapter 18

Okay.

Jared took several deep breaths and he watched the miracle unfold in front of him. He'd had a lot of expectations about this moment, but not once had he prepared himself for his mouth going dry and his stomach landing on the floor.

The transformation in Rachel was equally startling. The smile. The look in her eyes. The light in her face. The way she brushed her mouth over the tiny forehead. The simple gesture must have been comforting, because their son stopped crying immediately.

Their son.

This child was their son.

Unsure of what he should do, Jared reached out and gently ran his fingers over the thin mat of brown hair. There was an instant connection. Unconditional love so strong that it nearly brought him to his knees, and it was all aimed at that little bundle who was suddenly studying them with inquisitive gray-blue eyes.

"Welcome to the world, Ben," Rachel whispered. "We're your parents, and we're very happy to meet you."

It was a moment too precious to cut short, and yet Jared had to push what he was feeling aside and get them the heck out of there.

"Let's go," he insisted.

Rachel seemed to be in a daze, so he wrapped his arm around her waist and urged her toward the door. The baby whimpered, the sound loud in the otherwise silent room. Before Jared could worry if the noise would alert Agnes, Rachel put the tip of her thumb into their son's mouth. It soothed him instantly.

"Good idea," he told her. Thank God for maternal instincts. So far, his paternal impulses were only focused on one area: escape.

They made it all the way to the stairs before Jared heard something he definitely didn't want to hear. Footsteps and voices. Since they already sounded too close for comfort, he pulled Rachel and the baby into the nearest room and locked the door. The lock wasn't much, but if necessary it might buy them a couple of extra seconds.

Unfortunately, those extra seconds could soon become necessary.

When his eyes adjusted to the darkness, he could see that it was some kind of large storage room, stuffed with old furniture and such. He hid Rachel and the baby behind a stack of boxes, reholstered his gun and went to the window to disarm the security wires.

"Hell," he mumbled, looking out.

There was only a thin lip of roof and then a twenty-foot plunge to the ground below. If that was their only escape route, they were in trouble.

Trouble came a lot sooner than he'd anticipated.

"He's gone!" someone yelled. A woman. Agnes, probably. It hadn't taken her long enough to figure out that the baby was missing.

They didn't have much time now. She'd no doubt alert the guards and God knows who else.

There was sudden movement in the hallway. Footsteps. Harried whispers. Then nothing. Jared continued to work on the window, which was no easy feat. Unlike the one in the dining room, this one had double sensor points on each side, which he had to work his way through.

Several seconds passed, before someone touched the doorknob. Just a touch. Followed by another frantic female whisper. Jared heard the baby fret. A sound so quiet that no one would have heard it unless they were listening closely.

Which someone apparently was.

The knob twisted. A fraction. Then, another. The lock held under the gentle pressure, but it wouldn't hold long.

He managed to cut the last wire of the security system and throw open the window. Not wasting any time, he drew his gun and motioned for Rachel to hurry toward him. She did.

But it was too late.

The door suddenly flew open, bits of wood pelting them. Rachel automatically sheltered the baby by turning her back toward the debris. Jared ignored the splinter that slashed across his cheek and tried to shove Rachel behind him.

"I wouldn't do that if I were you," a man called out. Jared saw him out of the corner of his eye. It was Sergeant Colby Meredith. Agnes was right by his side, and she was armed, as well.

"Drop your gun, Dillard," Meredith ordered. "And put your hands in the air so I can see them."

Rachel gasped and buried her face against the baby's blanket, terrified at the sight of the guns aimed at her. Jared could feel her tremble. He hoped she could stave off a panic attack until they were out of there. Now, the real question was—how *were* they going to get out of there?

"Take deep breaths," Jared whispered to her. "And focus. I really need you to focus."

Staring at Meredith, Jared quickly ran through his options. Rachel might have a chance if he could somehow push her out onto the roof while he fired at Meredith. But it was a huge risk—she could easily fall. Neither she nor the baby would survive something like that.

"Drop the gun," Meredith repeated, and he aimed his weapon. Not at Jared. Not even at Rachel. But at the ultimate bargaining tool—the baby.

Jared tossed down his gun immediately. "Play along," he whispered to Rachel. "We'll get out of this. I promise."

This was a plan B kind of moment. Evade and escape. He would have to wait until he was close enough to Meredith and Agnes, and then he'd try to overpower them.

All without getting Rachel or the baby hurt.

Of course, he had to make sure that Meredith didn't kill him first. His fellow officer was probably more than willing to pull the trigger and permanently take Jared out of this equation.

Without taking his attention from them, Meredith reached behind himself and turned on the lights. "Agnes, go put on some tea or something."

That simple order was all it took—the woman quickly scampered out of the room.

However, Meredith obviously wasn't done. He looked at Jared and then Rachel. "Come on. Let's all go back downstairs and have a little talk."

A man in charge. Or maybe that was just what Meredith wanted them to think. Either way, Jared had to wonder if he was finally looking at Esterman's accomplice.

Rachel spoke up. "It's me you want. Let Jared take the baby and leave. You can take me back to San Antonio, and I'll make sure my testimony exonerates your boss."

Jared tried to push her behind him, but she wouldn't let him. She thrust the child into his arms, lifted her hands in the air and started to walk toward Meredith. He also noticed that she closed her eyes. It was probably the only way she could approach the man while he was armed.

The baby whimpered and squirmed against his chest. Jared didn't let it distract him. "Rachel, I don't want you to do this."

Her eyes fluttered open and she glanced at him over her shoulder. And what Jared saw in the depths of those eyes wasn't exactly a look of surrender.

Hell! She was going after Meredith herself.

"Rachel!" he tried again. Jared stooped to lay the baby on the floor. He couldn't let Rachel take on Meredith. It would be suicide.

"You should hold your son a little longer," he heard someone say. "It might be the last time you have a chance to do that."

Jared's gaze flew to the door. It was Donald Livingston. Smiling.

And armed.

He wasn't alone. There were two other guards with

him. Since the infrared had indicated only three adults in the building, these were probably hired guns that had been guarding the bridge. However, it didn't matter where they came from. There were too many of them to fight head-on.

The warden shouldered Meredith aside and strolled into the room. Meredith didn't protest. Sentry-like, he took his position near the door, no doubt to await further orders. Livingston wouldn't have to kill anyone, not when he had Meredith around to do the job.

"Rachel, come and get the baby," Jared insisted.

She did. She must have realized that there was no way she'd get past Livingston, Meredith and the guards. When she finally picked up the baby, Jared eased her behind him. If bullets started flying, he didn't want her in their path.

"How are you this evening, Lieutenant Dillard?" Livingston calmly asked. He motioned toward Jared's weapon on the floor, and Meredith hurried to retrieve it.

Livingston walked closer. Just a few steps. And from that arrogant swagger, Jared knew he was facing the real boss. Meredith was simply a henchman.

"We figured we'd find either you or Lyle Brewer here," Jared said.

"Brewer? Not likely." Livingston made a dismissive gesture with his hand. "He's a peon, even though he has been invaluable at passing me vital information from Clarence. Of course, Brewer wasn't really aware of that. He's one of those Boy Scouts like you, Dillard."

Jared ignored the comparison. Maybe if Livingston came closer, or if Jared could distract him, he could grab him and use him as a human shield so he and Rachel could get past Meredith.

"So, all of this was your plan?" Jared asked.

"You mean the whole stolen embryo thing? No. Definitely not my idea. Too messy for me. I prefer a simpler approach, but Clarence put all of this into motion before I could stop him. He's a very determined man when he sinks his teeth into something. He got, well, obsessive about getting back at Rachel. When he couldn't find her to have her killed, he figured the baby was the way to do it."

It wasn't an easy thing to hear. His baby and his wife were merely pawns in one very sick game. "Let Rachel and the baby go."

"Touching, but not possible," Livingston said quickly. "I need her alive." He snapped his fingers at Agnes when she came back into the room and motioned for her to take the baby.

Rachel stepped back, but both Meredith and Livingston aimed their guns at the baby. She looked at Jared, fear and worry in her eyes. He nodded for her to hand the child over. This wasn't the time for a fight.

But soon.

Definitely soon.

Agnes walked closer, cautiously, and took the baby. Rachel didn't make a sound, but Jared heard the rough intake of breath and saw her hands clench into fists.

"Don't hurt him," Rachel said softly. "I'll cooperate. I'll do whatever you say."

Livingston placed his hand over his heart. "Definitely touching. But kill him? No. Well, not at this moment, anyway. Later, perhaps. I doubt any of this will surprise you, but you, my dear, are going to go to the courthouse and exonerate my good friend and partner, Clarence Esterman. You will clear him of any and all charges. I want no doubt in the jury's mind that nothing illegal ever went on. And you'll do it convincingly, or else your baby will pay the price. The child might not have been in my original plan, but now I intend to make good use of him."

The warden came closer but stayed just out of Jared's reach. Jared prayed for him to take one more step, and he might be able to get to him.

"And you, Lieutenant," Livingston continued. "I have a mission for you, as well. After Rachel's finished giving her award-winning performance on the witness stand, and after Clarence walks out of the jail as a free man, you'll be right there to meet him."

Jared shrugged. "Okay, I'll bite. Why would I want to do that?"

Livingston smiled. "So you can kill him, of course."

Chapter 19

Rachel barely heard what Livingston said. She kept her attention on her child. On Agnes. The woman hovered in the doorway, the baby clutched in her arms. Agnes was obviously waiting for her boss to tell her what to do.

"Why would you want me to kill Esterman?" she heard Jared ask.

Only then did Livingston's comment sink in. She glanced at Livingston and saw that he was serious. He really wanted Esterman dead.

"Let's just say that he has the potential to become a liability. He's been chatting with the DA about possibly cutting a deal. I don't approve, and I'd rather not sully my own hands in ridding the world of Clarence Esterman—after your wife has cleared him, naturally. I don't want anyone digging in my direction because of Clarence." He checked his watch. "And without further *ado,* I'll send you two on your way. When your mission is done, your son will be returned to you. You have my word on that."

That gave Rachel no hope whatsoever. His word was worthless.

It was as if an iron fist took hold of her heart when Agnes turned to leave the room with Ben. She couldn't lose her baby.

Rachel started after them, but Jared stopped her. "Not now," he whispered.

And just like that, the baby was gone.

Other than choking back some tears, Rachel didn't have time to react. Livingston moved quickly. He gave the nod to two guards, and one of them ordered her and Jared out of the room. They got behind her with those guns so she didn't have to look at them, but it was paltry consolation. No panic attack, but her heart was breaking.

God, what was Livingston going to do with her baby?

They went down the stairs. Quickly, thanks to the guards shoving them in that direction. No sign of Agnes. She'd probably taken their son back to the makeshift nursery. Maybe Livingston wouldn't try to take him off the island.

"What do we do?" Rachel whispered to Jared.

He didn't answer until they were outside and headed toward a boathouse. "On the count of three, drop down. If you can, grab some sand and throw it in their faces. I'll take it from there and try to overpower them."

Rachel nodded and fought to keep control of her breath. It wasn't much of a plan. A lot of things could easily go wrong. Still, it was a chance, and she'd take it.

"Quit yapping," the guard snarled.

Jared ignored him. He did, however, give her a reassuring look when they were only a couple of yards from the boathouse. "One. Two…"

With the roaring in her head, Rachel didn't even hear Jared say the final number, but she saw the critical word form on his mouth.

Rachel fell to the ground, landing on her knees, and scooped up handfuls of sand. The guard on the left shouted something, and she saw him take aim just as she launched the sand into his face.

He cried out. Dropped the gun. And clutched at his eyes. She didn't stop. Rachel just kept tossing as much sand at him as she could.

Jared used the distraction to go after the other guard. He delivered a judo kick to the man's chest. His rifle went flying, and Jared retrieved it. He turned, and in the blink of an eye, had both men covered.

It had worked. The plan had worked!

"Get in the boathouse," he said to the guards. Jared kicked the other man's fallen weapon aside.

Rachel didn't have time to ask Jared what to do next. When the four of them were inside the boathouse, he ordered the guards to get facedown on the narrow deck next to a boat. The boat that was to take them back to shore so the guards could do Livingston's dirty work.

"Move and you're dead," Jared warned them.

And from the tone of his voice, he meant it.

"Rachel, see if you can find some rope so we can tie them up."

She looked around the area, but the best she could do was some fishing twine that she took from a tackle box on the deck. While Jared held the rifle on the men, she trussed their hands to their feet. When she finished, Jared stuffed some rags into their mouths, tested the twine, and then tossed them into the boat.

Then he took her arm and started back toward the house.

They hadn't made it far when she heard the sound. Not gunfire, but something much more frightening.

A helicopter.

And it was about to land on the roof of the house.

"The baby," Rachel managed to say. "Livingston's going to take the baby."

Rachel started to race toward the house but only made it a couple of steps. With her attention on the approaching helicopter, she didn't even hear Meredith step out from a cluster of shrubs.

Jared aimed his gun.

But it was too late.

Meredith latched onto her, hauled her in front of him and put the gun to her head.

Jared's heart jumped to his throat. The bastard had Rachel. He had her.

Hell, how had this happened?

Jared met her gaze. For only a second. But he couldn't believe the look he saw in her eyes. Not fear. Not even a hint of it. And he knew it cost more to hide the fear than to show it.

"Let her go," Jared bargained. "There's no reason for you to do Livingston's bidding. With your connections, God knows how low you can plea down this case. Turn state's evidence, and you could be a free man."

It was another lie—there would be no plea bargaining for a hired killer—but Jared was willing to do whatever it took to save Rachel.

"I'd rather not call my lawyer right now, if you don't mind."

Meredith's voice was calm. Too calm. Either he was a certifiable lunatic or else he killed as easily as he breathed. Jared didn't want to guess which.

Meredith glanced at the rifle that Jared held. "Put that down. Now." And to emphasize his request, Meredith shoved his gun even harder against Rachel's temple. She winced in pain. "And, Jared, if there's anyone else waiting in the wings to try to help out, remind them that I can do lots of damage to her before they can even get a shot off. I'm not as committed to keeping Rachel alive as Livingston is. If necessary, I can kill her and Esterman myself, and that way cut out the middle men. By the way, you and Rachel are the middlemen, in case you haven't figured that out already."

He was right. But not for long. One way or another, Jared would eliminate the threat. Then, he had to make sure Rachel was all right. In the grand scheme of things, Meredith was the disposable one.

"Just go after the baby, Jared," Rachel managed to say. "Save him."

Meredith tightened the chokehold on her neck. "Bad advice. Real bad. If you turn to run, I shoot you. It might be quick and relatively painless, but I can promise you, it won't be nearly as nice and neat for Rachel."

That was enough. It was too big a risk to take. Jared reluctantly placed the rifle on the ground. From the corner of his eye, he saw the helicopter approach. It was definitely going to land on the roof. Once that happened, Livingston could be out of there before they had a chance to stop him.

"Now, step back," Meredith ordered. "I'm going to

take Rachel here for a little drive straight to the court-house. If all goes well, and if she cooperates, I'll release her unharmed. I'll let you find your own way to take care of Clarence."

"Why don't you take *me* on that trip instead?" Jared suggested. "I make one hell of a hostage."

Meredith smiled. "Yeah. I'll bet you would, but I prefer Rachel. She's half your size and a lot less trouble."

And much easier to hurt.

But Jared didn't get a chance to voice that.

Rachel shouted, the sound of rage and fear. Using one of those Shaolin moves, she rammed her elbow into the man's stomach, pivoted and went after him with her fists. Even though Meredith managed to turn, he wasn't as successful at turning his gun toward her.

Jared caught Rachel and shoved her aside. That didn't deter Meredith. He spun toward Jared.

His gun aimed.

Ready to fire.

Jared had only a split second to react.

He dove for Meredith's feet. Rachel went after him again, as well. Together they knocked Meredith to the ground, and Jared grabbed the gun from his hand.

Jared didn't have time to go back for the fishing line so he could tie up the man. But what now? He didn't want to take Meredith back inside, not where he could continue to be a threat.

With such limited choices, Jared rummaged through Meredith's pocket and found what he was looking for—a pair of thin plastic cuffs. Standard cop issue. But just one pair. Still, it would have to do. Jared clamped one side onto Meredith's wrist, and hauled him to one of the thick shrubs and handcuffed him in place.

When Jared was sure Meredith was sufficiently re-strained, he turned to Rachel. "Let's go," he shouted over the noise of the helicopter. "We need to get to the roof."

They sprinted to the house. Jared didn't want them to be out in the open any longer than necessary. Besides, every second counted. If Livingston left with the baby, they might never find him.

Trying to keep watch around them, they hurried up the stairs. Both flights. And came to a narrow door that led to the roof.

The noise from the helicopter stopped. Maybe the pilot had turned off the engine so they could get the baby in-side. Or maybe the baby wasn't up there at all.

God knows what he would face on the other side, but since he didn't have a choice, Jared moved Rachel behind him. He took a deep breath and kicked open the door.

He got a glimpse, just a glimpse of Agnes holding the baby. And of Livingston.

Before the bullet slammed into Jared's right shoulder.

Rachel screamed and tried to catch Jared so he wouldn't fall.

She wasn't successful.

Livingston was there. Right there. He grabbed her and slung her out of the way. Rachel landed against the wall, and Jared fell just inside the door. So did his gun. Livingston kicked it across the floor.

Rachel came up fighting. For all the good it did her. Livingston merely smiled and aimed the gun at the baby. Both the gun and his murderous expression stopped her in her tracks. She would risk her life without thinking twice, but she couldn't risk the baby's.

"Jared, are you all right?" she asked. She held her breath.

"I'm fine."

But he wasn't. There was a bright red stain making its way across his shirt. She prayed the bullet hadn't hit an artery or a major organ. If so, she didn't stand much of a chance of getting him to the hospital in time. She could lose him. Dear God, she could lose him.

The pilot stepped from the helicopter and aimed an accusing finger at Livingston. "You said no one would get hurt—"

Livingston was quick. He turned and fired two shots—both hit the man in the chest. Then he calmly aimed the gun back at the baby.

Rachel glanced at the pilot. If he was still alive, he wouldn't be for long. She wanted to beg Livingston to call an ambulance for Jared and the other man, but it wouldn't do any good. She could see it in his eyes. If Jared died, Livingston would just make other arrangements to deal with his partner.

In his mind, Jared was expendable.

So was the baby.

So Rachel tried a different approach. There was no icy sneer on Agnes's face. She was scared, volleying wide-eyed glances between Livingston and the pilot. Maybe that fear was a weakness Rachel could exploit.

"Agnes, you can't let Livingston get away with this. It isn't right. That's my son you're holding. Do something to stop all of this."

The woman frantically shook her head and backed up a step. "I can't. I can't stop anything."

Jared moved. Just a fraction. Still clutching his shoulder, he leaned closer to Livingston.

Rachel almost called out for him to stop. But she knew in her heart that Jared felt the same way she did. They had to do whatever it took to save their child.

In this case, that meant a distraction, whatever the risk.

"I'll go with you now," Rachel told Livingston.

It was a lie. But it worked. Well, at least it got his attention.

Livingston eased the gun away from the baby. And smiled. The smile quickly faded, however, when Jared grabbed his leg. He managed to knock Livingston off balance, sending the man to the floor.

Jared didn't stop there. Despite his injuries, he dove at him. There was a clash of bodies. Muscle slamming against muscle. Livingston somehow managed to hold on to his weapon and do some other damage. Jared grunted in pain when Livingston landed a punch to his wounded shoulder.

Rachel lurched toward them to help Jared. However, she wasn't fast enough. Livingston threw Jared off him and against the doorjamb.

"No!" Rachel yelled.

Jared groaned in pain but went after the man again. He wouldn't stop. Not until one of them was dead.

Rachel heard a sound and snapped her head toward it. Agnes had kicked Jared's gun her way, and it skittered across the floor and stopped at her feet. The woman had decided to help them, after all.

All Rachel had to do was pick it up.

She sank to her knees and forced her hand to move toward it. But the pitch-black tunnel that her mind created closed around her, narrowing her vision so that all she could see was the gun.

Not Livingston's gun. But the one that had killed her parents.

Livingston shoved Jared aside, slamming him full force into the helicopter. There was no way Jared could get to him in time if Livingston decided to shoot him again.

And Rachel was sure Livingston would do just that.

If she didn't act now, he'd kill Jared.

"You can't do it, can you," Livingston taunted. While he held the gun on Jared, he chuckled. "Clarence told me all about your little problem. Too bad."

She clamped her teeth over her bottom lip to stop it from trembling. Nothing could stop the feeling of terror. Absolute terror. After everything she'd done to keep it away, the nightmare had returned.

And here she was, right in the middle of it.

Focus, she heard Jared say. But he hadn't spoken. Rachel heard the reminder from deep within her heart. *Focus.* Yes, that's exactly what she had to do.

Livingston got up from the floor. Not easily. Obviously the blows from Jared had shaken him. But not enough. He still had his weapon, and, dismissing her, he turned toward Jared.

"Don't you dare shoot him," Rachel warned, her voice a whisper.

Livingston tossed her a carefree smile. "What—do you plan to stop me?"

She nodded.

Just nodded.

Livingston stared at her. A challenge. While he took aim at Jared.

Something slammed through her. Not fear. Nor the turmoil of childhood trauma. Rachel had never felt more in control in her life. She reached down. Her fingers closed around the gun.

She lifted the weapon and turned it on Livingston.

He laughed. And she heard in that laughter what he planned to do—kill Jared.

"You won't stop me," he assured her.

Rachel shook her head. "You are *so* wrong."

Without taking her gaze from his, she aimed low. Curved her finger around the trigger. And squeezed.

The blast was instantaneous. Deafening. The bullet slammed into Livingston's leg. He howled in pain, but even that didn't stop him. He turned the gun toward her.

Just as Jared dove at him.

The men collided and went sprawling. Rachel heard herself scream. They were right at the edge of the roof. The left side of Jared's body was dangling in the air.

"Jared, be careful!" she shouted.

Livingston levered himself up and brought back his arm so he could fire at Jared. It was a mistake. A huge one. The maneuver off-balanced him. Livingston reached for Jared to try to stop himself from falling.

He dropped the gun.

His hand grasped at the air.

And he plunged over the side.

It took Rachel a second to understand what had happened. Moving back out of harm's way, Jared looked down and shook his head.

"It's over. Livingston's dead."

"Over," she repeated. It was really over.

Still on her knees, Rachel tossed the gun aside and went to Jared as fast as she could.

At the same time, Jared scrambled across the floor. They met halfway, and he hauled her into his arms.

"What you did was stupid. God almighty! You never should have gone at Livingston like that. He was armed, and he's a killer. You could have died."

Rachel pulled back and pressed her hand to his mouth. "I'm all right. You hear that? *All right.* You're the one who's hurt. And it wasn't stupid. You would have done the same thing in my place."

She could also tell that Jared wasn't prepared to hear the truth. Maybe later he'd listen to reason. For now, Rachel settled for a quick kiss and helped him to his feet.

"Come on. Let's take the baby and get you to the hospital."

She made eye contact with Agnes and said a quick prayer that the woman would cooperate. Rachel didn't want to fight any more battles right now, but if necessary, she would.

"I'm sorry," Agnes muttered. "I'm sorry for everything."

Agnes's hands were shaking when she walked to them. She held out the baby and put him in the crook of Rachel's arm. Without releasing her grip on Jared, Rachel took her son, pulled him to her and held on tight to both of them.

Chapter 20

It was a scene as close to perfect as Jared figured he'd ever see. Rachel and his son napping peacefully on the bed next to him.

He sat up a little, wincing at the tug of the stitches in his shoulder, and just watched them. Unable to resist, he touched his finger to his son's cheek. Ben opened his eyes for a second and then nestled back into his mother's arms.

Jared smiled. Only a new father would consider that tiny event to be a miracle.

The doorbell rang, but he was so happy, it was hard to get riled even by an interruption.

"It's Captain Thornton," Tanner called out a moment later. "Should I let her in?"

Okay. So Jared had been wrong. He could get riled. He'd been out of the hospital only a couple of hours and he didn't want to share his homecoming with anyone, including but not limited to, his ex-boss. In fact, he'd planned on thanking Tanner and sending him on his way as soon as Rachel woke from her much-needed nap.

"This won't take long," he heard Thornton say.

In other words, she was trying to barge her way past Tanner. While it might have been fun to hear Tanner try to stonewall her, this was a meeting he probably should get out of the way.

"Let her in," Jared answered.

As he'd known it would, the sound of his voice woke Rachel. Her eyes were still ripe with sleep when she lifted her head and looked in his direction. The sleep, however, soon cleared, and she smiled at him.

Another miracle.

Jared managed to plant a kiss on her mouth before the captain appeared in the doorway. She stood there a moment and studied them.

"Well, well, Dillard. You've gone all domestic on me. Looks good on you. Both of you," she added, nodding a greeting at Rachel.

"I didn't expect you today," Jared said quickly.

"Yeah. But it couldn't wait."

Dressed in a dull gray pantsuit and wearing her usual sensible shoes, she propped a shoulder against the doorjamb. There were a lot of compliments he could pay the captain. Good cop. Hard worker. Loyal. But fashion sense wasn't something that readily came to mind. And she wouldn't have considered that an insult.

"The chief's pressing me for an update on your condition. I'm supposed to check your boo-boos and give him a report."

Jared eased back the side of his shirt so she could see

the bandage. "The boo-boo should be healed in a couple of days."

"Weeks," Rachel corrected. "The doctor said *weeks*."

She raised herself to a sitting position. As if it were the most natural thing in the world, she leaned over and put the baby in his arms.

"I'll give you and the captain some time alone."

Before Jared could tell her that he didn't want her out of his sight, Rachel brushed a kiss on his cheek and the baby's before she disappeared into the adjoining bathroom.

"Cute kid," Thornton said, walking closer. She peered into the blanket. "I heard the doctor gave him an a-okay. And he doesn't seem to be any worse for wear. He's sleeping like a baby."

"Are you just going to stand there and toss around bad clichés?" Jared asked.

"Nope. Guess it's time to toss something else at you." She sat on the foot of the bed, reached into her pocket and pulled out his badge. She dropped it next to him.

Jared looked at it and then her.

"What?" she barked. "Did you expect me to polish it or something before I gave it back to you?"

"No. But I did expect you to give me some grief about what I did to find my son."

"No grief. Livingston and Esterman put Rachel and you through more than anyone should have had to go through. Still, you owe me. I'm talking about working patrol on New Year's Eve with all those drunks barfing all over your shoes."

He pretended to look very unhappy about that, but it was a small price to pay for what he'd gotten in return. "Thanks."

"Yeah, yeah. What can I say—I'm a sap for a guy holding a cute kid. Brings out all my maternal instincts." She stood and ran her fingers over the baby's toes, which were peeking out of the blanket. "You fed him a bottle and burped him yet? I hear they like to spit up all over the place during that little maneuver."

He tipped his head toward his wounded shoulder. "Hard to do much of anything with this."

"Wuss," she grumbled. But she did it with a wink and a smile. Thornton went to the bathroom door and tapped on it. "By the way, Rachel, you should hear this next part."

Rachel came out. She'd changed her clothes and was wearing one of those thin floaty dresses that went to mid-calf and skimmed along her body. Jared smiled to let her know that he liked her choice of fashion—and that later, he'd enjoy getting her out of it.

"The jury's back on Esterman," Thornton explained. "Thanks to your testimony, Rachel, he's a goner. Life in prison without the possibility of parole. And after browsing through Livingston's computer records, we've managed to round up all their little henchmen. And the final blow—Agnes McCullough will turn state's evidence so she can spill her guts about anything and everything else. That should put a cap on this Esterman-Livingston fiasco."

"And what about Sergeant Meredith?" Rachel asked.

"Ah, the scum sucker. Well, he's behind bars, where he'll stay because Agnes can pin Merkens's murder on him. I hate dirty cops. Hope he gets a cellmate who feels the same way and isn't afraid to show it." Captain Thornton waved goodbye. "Enjoy your new family. You two deserve it," she added before she closed the door.

"We do deserve it," Rachel agreed. She walked closer and glanced down at the badge. "Did you two work out everything?"

Jared nodded. "How do you feel about that?"

"I'm pleased." She lifted the baby from his arms and gently placed him in the bassinet next to the bed. "I know the danger will always be there. It's part of who you are. I still don't like it, but I'll accept it because I love you. And because I know that badge will never mean more to you than what we have right here."

His response wasn't automatic, not some rote words to accommodate the moment. Jared pulled her to him and looked into her eyes. "You are...everything to me. *Everything.* My hope. My happiness. My future. I love you, Rachel."

The tears came immediately. Smiling, she tried to blink them away. "Just my luck. I wait years to hear you say those words just the way you said them, and I start crying."

"Let's see what we can do about drying these tears."

He ran his fingers over the tiny buttons on the front of her dress. "Considering my injuries, I think sex against the wall is out. Let's try for something equally satisfying but a lot less dangerous. And we might want to do it soon, before Ben wakes up for a bottle."

"But what about Tanner?"

Jared looped his good arm around her and pulled her onto his lap. "He'll have the good sense not to come anywhere near this bedroom with that door shut."

"You're sure?" She smiled. Kissed him. And helped him with the buttons.

"Absolutely. Now, hush and have your way with me."

She did.

* * * * *

We hope you enjoyed reading

Sinister Intentions

by *New York Times* bestselling author

HEATHER GRAHAM

and

Confiscated Conception

by *USA TODAY* bestselling author

DELORES FOSSEN

Both were originally Harlequin® series stories!

From passionate, suspenseful and dramatic
love stories to inspirational or historical,
Harlequin offers different lines to
satisfy every romance reader.

New books in each line are available every month.

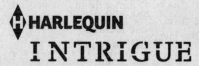

**SEEK THRILLS. SOLVE CRIMES.
JUSTICE SERVED.**

Harlequin.com

Uh-oh.

That was McCall's first thought. For just the flash of
a second, she knew this wasn't a smart thing for Austin
and her to be doing. But the flash became a wonderful
scorching heat that zinged through her.

His mouth was incredible. So much more than when
they'd been kids. Of course, her woman's body could feel
a whole lot more, too, and Austin was making sure she
got a full dose of those feelings.

McCall felt herself moving and realized she was
getting off the seat and going straight into Austin's arms.
That gave them some chest-to-chest contact, but the tutu
became sort of a chastity belt. Probably a good thing.
Because McCall figured she was going to need all the

chastity help she could get to stop this from going further than a make out session.

Austin made the most of the kiss, deepening it so that she got the jolt of his taste. There was the hint of the wine, but the rest was all man. A reminder she didn't need because McCall could feel the muscles stirring in his well-toned chest. Of course, her breasts were doing some stirring, too, and she knew it wouldn't be long before both her breasts and she wanted a whole lot more.

She eased back to give herself a moment to catch her breath, but she kept her mouth hovering next to his.

"Too fast?" he asked. "Too slow?"

"Too right," she answered honestly. And that was McCall's cue to step back even more.

She immediately saw those sizzler blue eyes. A color so wild and rich that it seemed as if she could dive right into them.

"Too right sounds…promising," he drawled.

"Yes," she admitted, and she was about to tell him that, for both their sakes, they had to go slower, but she was saved by the bell. Or rather by the ding to indicate she had a text. She'd intended to turn off her phone, but maybe it was a good thing she hadn't.

Don't miss
Chasing Trouble in Texas *by Delores Fossen,*
available June 2020
wherever HQN Books and ebooks are sold.

HQNBooks.com

PHDFEXP0620R

HARLEQUIN
INTRIGUE

SEEK THRILLS. SOLVE CRIMES.
JUSTICE SERVED.

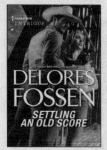

Save $1.00

on the purchase of ANY Harlequin Intrigue book!

Available wherever books are sold, including most bookstores, supermarkets, drugstores and discount stores.

Save $1.00

on the purchase of ANY Harlequin Intrigue book.

Coupon valid until July 31, 2020.
Redeemable at participating outlets in the U.S. and Canada only.
Not redeemable at Barnes & Noble stores. Limit one coupon per customer.

52616714

Canadian Retailers: Harlequin Enterprises ULC will pay the face value of this coupon plus 10.25¢ if submitted by customer for this product only. Any other use constitutes fraud. Coupon is nonassignable. Void if taxed, prohibited or restricted by law. Consumer must pay any government taxes. Void if copied. Inmar Promotional Services ("IPS") customers submit coupons and proof of sales to Harlequin Enterprises ULC, P.O. Box 31000, Scarborough, ON M1R 0E7, Canada. Non-IPS retailer—for reimbursement submit coupons and proof of sales directly to Harlequin Enterprises ULC, Retail Marketing Department, Bay Adelaide Centre, East Tower, 22 Adelaide Street West, 40th Floor, Toronto, Ontario M5H 4E3, Canada.

5 65373 00076 2 (8100)0 12457

U.S. Retailers: Harlequin Enterprises ULC will pay the face value of this coupon plus 8¢ if submitted by customer for this product only. Any other use constitutes fraud. Coupon is nonassignable. Void if taxed, prohibited or restricted by law. Consumer must pay any government taxes. Void if copied. For reimbursement submit coupons and proof of sales directly to Harlequin Enterprises ULC 482, NCH Marketing Services, P.O. Box 880001, El Paso, TX 88588-0001, U.S.A. Cash value 1/100 cents.

® and ™ are trademarks owned by Harlequin Enterprises ULC.

© 2020 Harlequin Enterprises ULC

BACCOUP14663

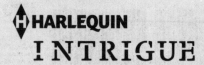